MIDSUMMER

MIDSUMMER

MARCELLE CLEMENTS

Harcourt, Inc.

Orlando   Austin   New York   San Diego   Toronto   London

www.HarcourtBooks.com

The author wishes to express her gratitude
to the Corporation of Yaddo.

Library of Congress Cataloging-in-Publication Data
Clements, Marcelle.
Midsummer/Marcelle Clements.
p.   cm.
ISBN 0-15-100836-1
1. Hudson River Valley (N.Y. and N.J.)—Fiction.
2. Parent and adult child—Fiction. 3. Women—Fiction.
4. Country homes—Fiction. 5. Friendship—Fiction. I. Title.
PS3553.L397 M53 2003
813'.54—dc21   2002153525

Text set in Bodoni
Designed by Cathy Riggs

Printed in the United States of America

First edition
A C E G I K J H F D B

CONTENTS

MIDSUMMER

TUTTI

FOURTH OF JULY WEEKEND

Thursday

The rose garden needed watering. By midday the ground was parched and the fullest, heaviest blooms seemed to be waiting for the wind to rise and scatter all their petals. Impossibly open, already a little seared on their edges, they yielded the last of their beauty to the sun. To be beautiful a few hours more or less, what does it matter to a rose?

As if they had noted the lack of shadow on the old sundial, the birds and the butterflies had all left for their naps. Only one inebriated bee, on his way to the hive, still zigzagged greedily from flower to flower. Then, all was still, save for the perpetual trickling of a fountain: For the last hundred years the trio of bare-breasted naiads had been about to dive into the alabaster pool below, forever ready to frolic, forever unreasonably young and desirable (taunting thirsty roses for all eternity).

And the truth is the fountain really should have been drained and cleaned, but never mind that for now. From the mansion's big parlor casement windows, Dodie glanced down toward the rose garden again and made yet another mental note—she never wrote anything down and it must have been the thirtieth time she reminded herself—to call the landscape guy, remind him the summer people were arriving tomorrow. Dodie sighed. Her husband was supposed to do the watering, but who knew where he was.

The house was ready. She had checked and double-checked the upstairs. There were ten bedrooms. Ten! Although there would only be five tenants, or maybe six if the son came, all the rooms needed to be ready, just in case. All week, during daylight hours, the rooms had been aired, doors and windows wedged open, breezes vigorously communicating, lifting a white piqué curtain here or the corner of a dotted-swiss bedspread there, caressing the *matelassé* coverlets spread over two chair backs, while on the beds, mattresses and pillows brazenly sprawled, stripped down to their striped ticking. Now each room was done, its door primly closed.

Well, if you weren't super-rich, that's probably what it took, was five of you to rent this place, thought Dodie. *I don't know, maybe ten of you.* They may have gotten a discount because one of them, Susie Diamond, was a friend of Mr. Durrell's. Or Bennett, as he seemed to think Dodie should call him, though she never would if she could help it. The only thing she knew about Susie Diamond was that she was a costume designer in the theater. Mr. Durrell had been living in Italy for the last ten years, and when he came to New York it was usually to go on a talk show, so he stayed in Manhattan at the Carlyle and never came upstate at all. When they had established their arrangement, a decade ago, Mr. Durrell had explained that he wanted the house kept just so and that he might be back at any time. But he never returned. Dodie thought it was perhaps because the young man who had lived here with him had died, early in the AIDS epidemic, but of course that's not something Mr. Durrell ever mentioned.

One spring, in the course of their quarterly transatlantic phone call, when Mr. Durrell confirmed decisions about upkeep and repairs, Dodie had pointed out that it was difficult for the house to be in really good shape if there was never anyone in it. "Ah," he had said. "Yes."

"Are you going to sell it?" she had asked, baldly. She'd been worried about it and just wanted to get the conversation over with.

"Sell it?" he asked, as if bewildered. "No, of course not. I don't know. Would you like to live there as a caretaker?"

"No," said Dodie. She had already worked this out. It would be too far to get the kids to school and she couldn't trust Joe here, anyway, was the truth. Who knew when he'd go on a bender and trash the place. "No, but thank you very much, Mr. Durrell," she said.

"Please, call me Bennett," he said.

"Thank you, Bennett," she dutifully responded.

"Maybe we'll rent it for the summer," he had said.

"Good idea," said Dodie.

She had assumed nothing would come of the conversation, but, on the contrary, two weeks later Mr. Durrell had called and said a family would be arriving on Memorial Day weekend. Could the house be ready by then?

Two young girls from town had come to help Dodie. She'd had the same ones for three years running now. At the beginning they were real cutie pies, who took instructions well. This year one of them had purple-and-orange hair and the other one was pregnant and Dodie's proportion of the work had risen. They weren't all that interested anyway since, as a rule, the summer tenants had small children, which was a windfall for the girls, who took turns baby-sitting. This year, if Dodie understood correctly, it wasn't a regular family; it was five single people.

Usually it was a mother and one or two or three children. They arrived promptly on Memorial Day to stay for the summer and the husband would come on weekends, bringing guests. This year, for one thing, they'd be coming late, not until the Fourth of July. For another, it was three women and two men, who were all friends but none of them was married, Susie Diamond had told her.

"On some weekends my son may also be there," Susie Diamond had said.

"Will you need baby-sitting?" Dodie had asked.

Susie laughed. She had a very good laugh. Dodie laughed too. "No," Susie said. "My son will be twenty-three in July."

"Oh!" said Dodie. "You don't sound old enough to have such a grown-up child."

Susie laughed again. "Thank you," she said. "What about you? Do you have children?"

"Yes," said Dodie. "Three boys. Eight, six, and four."

"Goodness!" exclaimed Susie.

"But don't worry. They'll be with my mother."

Their deal was that Dodie would come every afternoon on the weekends, to prepare dinner and tidy up. The teenagers would be by during the week—*Supposedly!* thought Dodie—to help with the heavy cleaning. "Everything will be ready for you," Dodie said. She paused, and then added, "You'll have a wonderful summer." That sort of thing didn't come easily to her, but she felt it was necessary.

Susie laughed again. "Really?" she said. "Yes, you're right, I'm sure we will."

Friday

They were more than halfway there. Susie was driving. All three of them had been in excellent moods, summer-is-starting kind of moods, even Kay, but when Susie announced they had just driven past the halfway mark, Kay sighed. Billy noticed and smiled at her. She smiled back.

"What?" said Susie.

"I'm getting hungry," said Billy.

"We just ate," said Susie. At the sound of Susie's voice, the dog barked and unsteadily rose on Kay's lap to stare at Susie.

"Hi, poochie. Hi, sweetheart," said Susie. She stretched her neck toward him, and the dog immediately began to lick her mouth and chin.

"Watch it," said Billy. "You're drifting."

The entire back of the car was so loaded with their summer things that the rear mirror was useless. Though he knew them well,

Billy had been flabbergasted by how much the two women had brought with them.

The dog hobbled over across the emergency brake to Susie's lap. He settled down in a more or less perfect circle and Susie set to driving with one hand, so she could pat and caress him with the other.

"The kids get a puppy!" announced Susie, who had this spring developed a strain of humor that consisted of proclaiming topic sentences which might have served as captions for illustrations of nineteenth-century children's books.

Susie had bought the dog, a couple of months ago, on impulse. On her way uptown, striding by a pet shop window on her way to a meeting with a director—she was ambivalent about whether she wanted the job and she was already late—she had happened to have made eye contact with a very young husky. Her meeting over—she had taken the job—she had returned to purchase him. She had immediately named him Otto. When she had gotten home, the puppy had bounded onto the couch where Billy was lying, smoking a cigarette with his eyes closed.

"Whoa!" Billy had called out. "Well, and who are you?" The puppy was already vigorously licking his face.

"I'm calling him Otto," Susie had said. "He looks like an Otto, doesn't he?" she had asked Billy.

"Yeah, right," Billy had said. They hadn't had a dog since he'd gone away to college. His very first week away, their ancient spaniel had contracted some rare form of canine leukemia—*As if he couldn't tolerate Billy's absence?* they had both secretly wondered—and within thirty-six hours, in a taxi on the way to the vet, had expired in Susie's arms. "Now I'm really alone," Susie had told the taxi driver, and then had to endure a lengthy conversation, stuck in traffic during the ride back to her place after they'd dropped the corpse off at the vet's. Despite Billy's emphatic recommendation, Susie had refused to get another dog, saying it didn't go with her life anymore.

Nearly five years later, when introduced to Otto, Billy prudently refrained from expressing any direct verbal approval for his mother's action. She was so oppositional that he often feared supporting any sound point of view, unsure that it wouldn't send her off on some peculiar circumvention. But he had gotten down on the floor and rubbed his forehead against the puppy's, who, on cue, wagged his tail. "I don't know about whether he looks like an Otto, but he looks like a winner."

"By the way, why are you smoking?" Susie had said.

"I'm stopping tomorrow," Billy had said.

Indeed, Billy hadn't had a single cigarette all day, and it was difficult not to constantly be thinking about smoking.

It was July 3, Billy's twenty-third birthday. Susie had given him a Gibson electric bass at the end of the school year, but he knew— because he'd been looking for something else in her bedroom and had come upon his presents, waiting to be wrapped—that he would soon be in possession of the new Proust translation and a fine sweater in an exquisite *encre de Chine* color, so close to black he would actually wear it.

In the car the three of them had eaten turkey sandwiches out of wax paper and shared two bottles of beer, intending to celebrate more elaborately once they got to the house. A rubber band secured a plastic bag around the neck of a bottle of Moët & Chandon.

There was very little traffic, there was no wind, and they had a boom box and a shoe box full of cassettes, including every album Roy Orbison had ever made. They had decided to be on a Roy Orbison kick.

In Susie's old Saab, Otto had at last come to rest. The Taconic had narrowed. There were more and bigger trees, more green, more sky. All three drifted into a reverie until Otto licked Kay's ear and she gasped, startling Susie and Billy.

"Otto!" said Kay. "You rascal."

"This dog's a thief of hearts," said Susie.

"Even Kay's," Billy pointed out, "Kay's solemn heart."

"You're becoming pretty solemn yourself, Billy," said Kay.

"He's beginning to resemble you more than me," said Susie.

"That's because no one can compete with you, Susie," said Kay, more or less by way of a joke.

"Maybe he's growing up faster than I am," said Susie.

"No doubt about that," said Billy.

"Well, there's some doubt," said Kay. "There are different ways of growing old. Susie, I think, will be eternally young."

"I'm getting more and more stupid, you mean," said Susie. "And more and more guilty of the sort of triviality that passes for the lightheartedness of youth."

"I don't think you're ever trivial," said Kay.

"You're not trivial, you're zoned," said Billy.

"That's what makes you seem so incredibly youthful," said Kay.

"Phew," said Susie, her eyes on the road. "I guess that if I've made it this far and I can still create that illusion, I must be in good shape. Or does it mean I'm in terrible shape?"

"And what about you, Kay?" Billy asked. "How young are you?"

"Terribly old." Kay laughed. "Terribly, terribly old."

"Not true," said Susie. "You're much younger now than a couple of years ago. You just need to be tricked into being your younger self."

Kay had had one of those catastrophic breakups, four years ago, complete with public infidelity with an obnoxious tart, betrayal, deceit, and humiliation. Several weeks later Kay miscarried while, at the restaurants and at dinner parties she now carefully avoided, the obnoxious tart was constantly sighted, conspicuously and radiantly pregnant, in the company of Kay's ex-boyfriend. The numerous friends who encountered the new couple here and there around town and who turned out to be meticulous reporters of such matters informed Kate that the ex-boyfriend seemed very peppy.

"What are you going to do about it?" Susie had asked Kay.

"Do?" Kay had said. "What is there to do?"

Susie had tried to talk Kay into starting out on some new, energizing project, but instead she had gotten a call from Kay the next day to say that their conversation had led her to realize that she had to leave New York as soon as possible and that she had decided to take advantage of an offer she'd rejected some time back to write a book that would require a good deal of research at the Library of Congress.

"Washington!" Susie had exclaimed.

"What's the difference?" Kay had said.

Kay's friends wondered to one another how long it was going to take to recover and lately had begun to consider what was going to happen if she didn't. Four years. Did people's lives get ruined, just like that, because some lowlife wanted to get laid? Maybe. The truth is that Kay seemed totaled, erotically.

Susie, for her part, had recently broken up her own long-standing relationship and, for the first time in her life, had no plan to replace it. She didn't even know why, exactly. It wasn't a policy decision, but she suddenly realized that she felt comfortable alone.

"Isn't this odd?" she'd say to Kay in the course of one of their frequent New York–D.C. phone visits.

"Yes," Kay would say.

Susie balked at spending a lot of time in Washington, but she had managed to convince Kay to come into New York at least a weekend a month and, one evening this spring, on impulse, had persuaded both Kay and herself that it would be a splendid idea to get a few friends together and rent a place in the country for the summer and, as she put it, "maybe have fun." Susie and Kay alike were still somewhat in a state of disbelief that Susie had actually seen the plan through, gathered the friends, found the house, and here they were, on their way up, more than halfway there.

Kay was apprehensive. She had sublet her place in Washington and, unlike the others who would be commuting from Manhattan on weekends, she planned to stay out at the house for the summer. It had seemed like a good idea at the time she made the plans. Perhaps she'd do some writing, she thought. She had imagined herself, with great relief, in peaceful rustic solitude. However, in the last couple of days she had begun to feel extremely anxious about the idea of spending the weeks alone in a remote place where she knew no one. But Susie had said she hoped she could stay out part of August. "And I've no plans for the summer, or for the rest of my life," Billy had pointed out—he himself was hoping for an invitation beyond this weekend which, thus far, had not been forthcoming from Susie, Kay noted with amusement. In the car with Susie and Billy she had cheered up and, of course, the puppy made it almost impossible to stay worried and somber.

Both Susie and Billy were extremely gratified by the fact that the puppy's charms had been irresistible even to Kay, whose dignity was, in their view, pleasantly compromised by Otto's frantically affectionate bonding maneuvers. When she turned her face away, he licked her jawline with tremendous intensity for a few moments and then settled down droopily on her lap again.

"Yes," she said, "I have to admit it, he's adorable."

"Almost as adorable as Billy," said Susie. Both women looked at him, smiling.

Susie turned her eyes back to the road. "Isn't he beautiful?" she asked.

"Yes," said Kay.

"Oh, Jesus," said Billy.

"Though he's so young it's possible that he may truly feel his beauty is an inconvenience," said Kay.

"You're so excessive in your compliments," said Billy to Susie. "Don't you know it screws up my sense of self?"

"I'm entitled to some excess as a mother," said Susie.

"No, you're not," said Billy.

They all three laughed. They were in very good moods. "Yes, she is," Kay said.

Roy Orbison was growing on Kay. There was one funky old cassette that had a ridiculous amount of hiss on it, but Susie played it over and over again, and by the time they had heard it five or six times, they could sing along with it.

"Well, I've been traveling night and day..."

Susie said to Kay: "Do you remember my dream?"

"Yes," said Kay.

"What dream?" said Billy.

"I told you," said Susie. "The melody-in-the-forest dream."

"I had a horrible dream last night," said Billy.

"What?" asked Susie and Kay together.

"I don't remember," said Billy.

"Those are bad," said Kay.

Billy dimly tried to recall his dream. Along the highway the trees were growing still taller and darker green, the sky cerulean. Billy tried to let his mind ease enough to recapture even a single image of the dream, but the landscape was overpowering. There were fewer, simpler shapes now, a little enchanted seeming in this light. Finally he gave up. Maybe it was just as well not to remember.

When they pulled up to the house, Kay opened the door on the passenger side and Otto gingerly alighted, then stood his ground next to the car, barking passionately at the house. Finally he galloped away, in all-out pursuit of something small and furry.

"Should I hold him?" Kay asked, too late, distracted by the very grand facade. "Oh," she exclaimed. "This is unbelievable."

The house was quite as spectacular as Susie had described it. An Italianate limestone edifice whose impressive structure couldn't be divined from the driveway, it was framed by weeping willows and blue pines. The Hudson lay beyond, opulent, shimmering blue satin.

"It's all right," said Susie. "He won't go far. Yes, oh my goodness, this house!"

"Shouldn't he be on a leash?" asked Billy.

"Yes," said Kay.

Otto gamboled back toward where all three still sat in the car, contemplating the house. "Wow," said Billy, forgetting for once not to show he was impressed. "Unreal."

"It's summertime!" Susie announced the latest caption.

Otto ran in a squiggly circle as they got out of the Saab. He ardently dashed back in their direction as they climbed the tall stone stairs, and when Billy pushed the rather large, creaky door open, Otto was the first one into the house.

They walked, all together, through the mansion—the vast hall, studded with paintings of someone's ancestors, a formal dining room, a drawing room that could easily accommodate thirty for tea, a small, paneled library, a huge white turn-of-the-century kitchen into which new appliances had been inserted, an enclosed patio at the back of the house that looked out on the lawn sloping to the river. To the left was the pool. To the right were the gardens.

Susie had been right, Kay was thinking as they reached the patio from which they could see the path that led toward the rose garden. The patio was a semi-octagonal room, wainscoted in green, with its own dormered ceiling. The walls were mostly glass.

"This is where we'll have our drinks," said Susie.

"This is unbelievable," Kay said.

"Yes, it'll do," said Billy.

"Every day we'll have cocktails as the sun sets and we'll talk about love," said Susie.

"Oh, please," Kay said.

"I have nothing to say about love," said Billy.

"That's because you don't know enough about it yet," said Susie. "You'll learn from us."

"That's what you think," said Billy.

"Why, do you think you have nothing to learn from us?" Kay said.

"No," said Billy. "I mean that's what you think that I don't know anything."

"Look, we've started already," said Susie. "But without drinks. Let's go upstairs and see the rest and then come back down and have our drinks."

"And celebrate Billy's birthday," Kay said.

"And celebrrrrate," sang Susie. It was a Purcell ode she and Kay had learned in school. "This glo-o-o-rious day."

Otto galloped in. "Hello, sweetie. Hello, handsome," crooned Susie as she swept the dog up in her arms.

"There's one certainty about this summer," said Billy, "which is that this dog is going to get spoiled."

Upstairs, bedrooms, dressing rooms and bathrooms, absurdly ample linen closets, weird crannies and niches succeeded one another according to an indecipherable plan. When one looked down any hall, up any staircase, there was a zany prospect. Each ceiling was of a different height. Each room was of an unpredictable shape. Suddenly there'd be the hollow of a gable or the unexpected wall of a chimney, all in seeming disarray or disposed according to some vastly complex design that could not be inferred on a first visit. Indeed, the loony Gothic inside of the house bore no relationship to the gracious Palladian exterior with its stately columns, its elegant fenestration, its insistently noble proportions. The place had been gutted late in the nineteenth century by moneyed aesthetes who found the Greek revival style old hat and were willing to indulge their preference for the Victorian without any reservation. Agitated ornament, wooden bas-reliefs, coffered ceilings, mosaics, torches, bronze, gilt, brass, and velvet abounded. It all made the classical exterior of the mansion seem like a joke on those who had entered it.

"Wow," said Susie when they ended their tour by examining the two dozen—Billy counted—pen-and-ink ruins hanging in proud incongruity on the red-and-black raised leaf-pattern wallpaper of the landing. Kay, face upturned to the ornate *boiserie* of the ceiling, said, "Really . . ." Billy shook his head.

They each picked a bedroom. Kay's and Susie's looked out over the patio, toward the rose garden and the river. Billy's was a small corner room, which faced both the gardens and the lawn. He opened the window and leaned out for a moment. The light was sultry and carried the odor of phlox, jasmine, pine, grass especially, but also an ineffably lovely, unidentifiable aroma composed of innumerable plants' final exhalation of the day.

In her room—chosen because the wallpaper featured fat mandarins in pink pajamas—Susie lay down and closed her eyes for a moment. She breathed deeply. She felt immense relief.

In Kay's room there were white piqué curtains on the window. The room was papered with large blue roses; there was a bureau, a dressing table, an armchair adorned with antimacassars that someone had darned here and there with a meticulously small stitch, a lovely faded Persian on the floor, a sleigh bed covered with a white piqué spread that matched the curtains. She stood in the middle of her room, her arms crossed, gaze lost in the Persian's pattern.

In his room Billy turned away from the window. It was almost too intoxicating. There was a print on the wall and he drew nearer to look at it. It was an engraving of the abduction of Helen of Troy.

"But if Helen was that thick waisted and bulbous breasted, it's hard to see what the fuss had been about," Billy said to Susie and Kay when they gathered on the patio again, drinking their champagne at last and recounting their impressions.

"I don't know anything about Helen," said Susie.

Kay squinted at the light.

"But then there used to be a different idea of beauty?" Billy suggested.

"Of course," Susie and Kay said at the same time.

Each of the women mused for a moment.

"It's so exhausting to think of beauty," said Kay.

"Really? I find it restful," said Susie.

The sun dropped below the clouds. Kay looked at Susie and Billy. Mother and son looked beautiful in the falling golden light. Kay shivered.

"What's the matter?" said Susie.

"Nothing," said Kay. "I don't know."

"A ghost," said Susie.

"Yes," said Kay.

"Helen didn't have to be so beautiful," said Billy. "It isn't beauty that makes men crazy."

"But it helps," said Susie. "What is it that makes men crazy?"

"Desire, of course," said Billy. "But beauty doesn't provoke it, it only reminds you of it."

"Is that true?" said Susie to Kay.

"I don't know," said Kay.

"Well," said Susie. "Theoretically, that might be true."

"Structurally," said Billy.

"Psychoanalytically," said Kay.

"Well, I don't know," said Susie. "Some people say the love of beauty is a defense."

"Idiots," said Billy.

That night they ate some cold chicken Susie had brought from New York—not realizing that Dodie would have stocked the fridge—while Otto begged, whined, and attempted to climb on the dining-room table. In lieu of a birthday cake they finished with an apricot tart. Here in this place, the fruit seemed almost intolerably delicious. The crust was flaky and delicate; the apricot very slightly stinging, soft on the tongue; the cream just sweet enough. *Mmm,* they kept saying, or *yum.* They each had two pieces. They finished the champagne. Billy became melancholy, but no more than was appropriate. Susie drank exactly the right amount of champagne, she declared, and felt perfect. In fact, she did have a moment, immediately after she said that, of actually feeling perfect.

Kay went in and out of feeling connected, but the others didn't expect much more. Susie and Billy were discreetly solicitous, that most soothing act of friendship, not imposing any consolation on her. But Susie thought Kay didn't seem as heavyhearted as she had been all spring.

Billy must have had one glass of champagne too many because as the conversation swung back to the subject of the summer, he suddenly pleaded: "Oh please let me stay here with you this summer!"

"You're welcome to come any weekend you want," said Susie, surprised.

"No, no," said Billy. "I want to come every weekend, all summer, with you. Don't worry, I won't be in the way."

Both women laughed. "Never in the way," said Kay.

"In the way!" Susie said. "Why, you'll be the belle of the ball."

"Well, no, thanks," said Billy. "I'll have the last of the apricot."

"You're embarrassing him with the gender confusion," Kay said to Susie. "He's too young to be relaxed about that."

"That's what you think," said Billy. "You're projecting because you're stuck in your fifties inhibitions."

"Sixties," said Susie.

"That's what you think," said Billy. "You think it's sixties but it's fifties. You just happened to have spent the decade of your adolescence trying to obliterate the lessons of your authentically formative years."

Susie laughed. "Whoa," she said. "That's a hefty retaliation for the belle-of-the-ball remark."

Kay felt sympathy for Billy. She'd always wondered whether, for all of Susie's charm, it might not be difficult sometimes to have her as a mother. If so, Billy never had let on, at least not to her.

"It'll be wonderful to have you here," she said with precision. "It's been a long time since we were in a summer place together."

"Eight years," he said, with precision. "Belle Isle."

"Is that true?" Susie said to Kay. "Was it really eight years ago that we had that house?"

"It's amazing," said Kay. "I can't believe it. It feels like, say, three years or five years. Or else, I don't know, twenty years."

"I don't believe how fast time goes," said Susie. "It's terrifying. Terrifying."

"You had a red-and-white striped bikini," Billy said to Kay, "that summer."

Susie and Kay laughed. "You're blushing," Susie said to Kay. "Isn't he cute?"

Billy looked up to the ceiling. Kay laughed. "I'm not blushing," she said. "I just can't believe I ever wore a bikini."

"It was five minutes ago," said Susie.

"Yeah, right," said Kay.

"So who are these people?" said Billy. "Why do we have to have them?"

"Well, you remember Dodge," said Susie.

"All too well," said Billy. "Even in the glorious pantheon of your old boyfriends, he stands out as one of the most annoying."

"The most talented," said Susie. "The best painter, anyway."

"I remember him as very talented at seduction," said Kay.

"Perhaps he's mended his ways," said Susie. "Though I doubt it—so at least he'll still be fun to have around."

"Didn't Dodge get married?"

"Yes," said Susie. "He was married a long time. And had a daughter."

"How old is she?" asked Billy. Kay looked at Billy and smiled.

"I don't know," said Susie. "Six, or seven, maybe. I've never met her. He just sees her on weekends or something. And then there's his friend, Ron Reiser. I am a little fuzzy if he is a comedian, or a comedy writer, or a lawyer who wants to be a comedy writer. Something like that."

"Oh god," said Billy.

"And Elise Dubrovsky is a sculptor," said Susie, "but lately she makes sort of falling-apart constructions."

"Oh god, oh god," said Billy.

"She's a little younger than we are," said Susie.

"But just a tad plump," said Kay.

"Why, Kay!" said Susie and Billy simultaneously.

"I can't believe I said that," said Kay.

Susie said, "This is going to be great. You'll see. Dodge is such an entertaining character. And Elise..."

"I'm a little worried about her," said Kay. "I recall her as rather wobbly. But I barely remember her."

"You're always worried," said Susie.

"I fear the worst about this summer," said Kay.

"It could be anything," said Billy.

"Well, whatever," said Kay. "I wish there were more apricot tart."

"Oh no!" said Billy, with loud operatic remorse.

Otto, who had been napping, picked his head up and howled, and they all laughed.

Looking back, let's be easy markers and say these three were happy.

Saturday

Early on July 4, Ron Reiser was downstairs in front of his building at the appointed time and then waited a good half hour for Dodge Moriarty to arrive. The day was overcast, the air heavy, the garbage not picked up. Ron, for reasons he could no longer remember, had worn his bathing suit under his clothes and quickly began to perspire. "What a mistake this was," he was saying to the stoop, the window boxes, and the fire escape just as Dodge finally materialized, astride a Harley 1200.

"You came on your bike!" Ron exploded. "You expect me to ride all the way up to that hellhole on the back of *that*?"

"Get on, Reiser," said Dodge. "Let's spare ourselves this part of the argument."

Thirty blocks south, down on Mott Street, Elise Dubrovsky was in a taxi, checking her wallet to make sure she had enough cash to pay her fare and a round-trip on the train. She didn't.

"Stop here!" she called out to the driver when she spotted a Citibank ATM. The driver, who wore a turban, seemed not to hear. "Stop!" She knocked on the Plexiglas partition. "No money! I can't pay!" she yelled. The car immediately veered to the curb and jerked to a stop.

The driver pushed the partition open and surveyed Elise. "You have husband?" he asked.

Up at the house, while the sun and the clouds played a slow and ambiguous game, Susie was awakened by the energetic Otto, whom she then took for a walk in the morning mist. Soon the sky cleared and the dew dried on the grass.

"Isn't this wonderful, Otto?" Susie kept saying to the dog.

The birds peeped with abandon. The sun was shining sweetly but softly, the air was fresh, and there was a caressing, slightly moist breeze. On the horizon Susie, who had good eyes, could just make out the mountains. Closer there were hills and plains and valleys that, in this light, seemed right out of the fairy tales and nineteenth-century children's stories she'd been thinking about so much lately. Perhaps she should consider illustrating a children's book.

Otto barked with pleasure and excitement when she talked to him. She felt so enamored of the puppy that she stopped and picked him up and hugged him. "I am crazy," she said to him, "to have fallen in love with you. What if it's not requited?" As if to prove her point, when she put him down, he clumsily rambled in a great big figure eight around her, as if he were only using her as a point he might refer to now and then in his circuitous exploration of the world.

"I must sound like an incredible jerk," she said to no one in particular, thinking of how she must look, in the clearing all by herself, talking to the dog. She lay down and stared at the clouds for a while. Otto rolled on the grass or galloped after imaginary rabbits.

Billy heard them come in and looked at his watch at around noon, then went back to sleep.

At one o'clock Kay heard the rumbling of a motorcycle. She'd been lying in her bed, sifting through memories. Today, perhaps because this new environment generated new permutations of painful associations, she'd been wading among some particularly miserable recollections. She reminded herself of someone addicted to playing solitaire. It was no longer fun, and she felt as if she knew all the odds by heart, but she still kept turning the cards over.

It was warm. Earlier the variety of bird sounds had been cacophonous, but now there was only the rich, plump quiet of a summer afternoon. A fat fly intermittently bumped against the screen. Subtle shadows played on the ceiling.

She didn't feel as bad as usual, yet she'd gotten up and put on her bathing suit, then gone back to bed, not quite ready to face breakfast. She kept telling herself that it was late, but she couldn't get herself to sit up. *The champagne,* she thought, as if a reason were needed.

It hadn't been so bad, though, as her mornings went, to wake up in that solemnly pretty bedroom, the sun filtering through the piqué curtains. To match that room's lack of irony, she had to go back to the Somerset Maugham–slept-here rooms of Singapore and Hong Kong—canopied beds under ceiling fans—of colonial hotels in their final phase in the Asian cities she'd wandered through as a young reporter. All of the various homes she had made, in several cities, had been equipped with self-referring signifiers that indicated she didn't really take their decor seriously. In decor, anyway, sincerity was restful, it turned out.

She got out of bed and put on a long white T-shirt over a pair of white shorts and headed out of the room and down the hall. The floor creaked. The smell was woody, slightly moldy, though extremely pleasant. There was a round window across the way, and she went over and opened it and looked down. She saw a motorcycle, a big Harley, the only metal interruption in the careful patterns of green and gravel and limestone. The two side compartments had been neatly secured with rope, as if they would have bulged otherwise. She assumed the bike was Dodge Moriarty's and that the side compartments contained what he had decided to bring by way of luggage. The symmetrical disposition of the rope indicated a conciseness that interested her.

They were all in the kitchen, except Billy. Susie was actually making pancakes. "There's a sight I never thought I'd see," said Kay.

The two men leaned against the counters.

"Hi," said Kay to Dodge and Ron.

"Hi," they answered together. Looking at Dodge in his black jeans and black T-shirt, Kay noticed how slim and dense his body seemed. He looked like a painter. Ron Reiser, muscled and tense, already had a tan. He wore khaki pants, a white T-shirt. *Jewish Ivy League,* Kay automatically registered. Ron grinned at Kay, while Dodge only looked at her, unsmiling but interested looking. Dodge Moriarty was, Kay thought, really amazingly handsome, almost dangerous looking. He had cut his hair very short since the days when she would run into him now and again at a dinner. It must have been about ten years ago. Eight? Twelve? He seemed more alert, too, than she had remembered. He made eye contact for an instant, and she looked back into his light gray eyes with what she hoped was friendly neutrality. There was a moment of silence.

Susie was feeling panicked. *Why are these people in the kitchen?* They all seemed to be depending on her for something.

Kay was most aware of Dodge. Yes, he definitely emitted that breathtaking bit of intensity that truly seductive men manage to convey even when they're not really trying.

Dodge registered that Kay was attractive but was surprised at how WASPy looking she had become. You could tell even in those shorts and T-shirt. Or perhaps especially. Strong shoulders, slim torso. And those legs. All those sinews. The perfect triangle of the kneecap, on which light fell so as to make the patella seem particularly prominent. Kay had great legs, he decided, and exquisite feet.

Why is he looking at me like he's assessing me? Kay was thinking. She couldn't tell what part of her body he was looking at. She felt a small frisson of response and was very surprised. It had been a long time since she had even noticed that erotic communication in a man's glance. She turned her attention back to Ron Reiser. She didn't know what to think of Ron Reiser.

"How marvelous to meet you," he said in a fake British accent as he shook her hand.

"Charmed," said Kay.

"Excuse me," said Billy. He was staggering into the kitchen, dressed only in a pair of very short shorts. "I didn't mean to interrupt anything so civilized in the morning, but I just need to get

some coffee." Despite the fact that he had thought he was prepared, Billy found the arrival of the two men extremely unpleasant.

"You remember my son," said Susie.

"Hi, Bill," said Ron.

Bill? What an asshole, thought Billy.

"Hi, Billy," said Dodge. Dodge was amazed that Susie's son
was now an adult. The image of Dodge's own little daughter, Emma,
glimmered in his mind for a moment.

"Hi," said Billy to Dodge. "How're you doing?" *Still slinking
around Susie?* he was thinking.

Susie was glad to see Kay smiling. It would be good for her. She
wished Billy were more gracious. True, he was sleepy. When he
was a small child, she would dress him entirely in the morning,
while he still slept. She thought the worst was over. "Let's have
breakfast. Billy's right. Let's eat. You can't banter before breakfast.
What will you have left to say by dinnertime?"

"I hate to think," Kay said, leaning against a counter. She suddenly felt drained. Social exchange required a tremendous effort.

"Don't think, Kay, leave everything to me," said Ron. He
grasped her shoulder. He knew he should hold back. He knew it
was exactly the wrong tack to take with someone like Kay, but he
couldn't stop himself.

"Thanks," said Kay, moving away.

"Oh my god," exclaimed Dodge in a mock-mewling sort of
whine that totally robbed him of the dark dignity he usually worked
so hard to convey.

Kay laughed and suddenly thought to herself, *Oh, lighten up.*
"High school," she said.

"I miss high school terribly," said Dodge.

"I'll bet," said Ron. Which somehow conveyed such a clear
put-down of Dodge's putative maturity that the others laughed, all
together. *I guess it really is his timing,* thought Susie. Interesting to
spend a summer with a comedy writer. What a relief from visual
artists.

Kay was thinking that she only now completely realized that she had in fact been very worried about what the men would be like. In her imagination they'd grown menacing. But they now seemed rather harmless to her. Maybe the summer would be, just as Susie had promised, fun after all.

Dodge had blanked. He busied himself examining the kitchen wainscoting. He vaguely noticed that Ron had gone into a kind of instinctive male competitiveness at the sight of Susie and Kay, which he found silly yet not amusing.

Ron was now looking at Kay and thinking, *I'd like to fuck her,* which was precisely what he'd been thinking about Susie just before Kay arrived.

Billy was concentrating on his coffee. The cup had pretty little flowers on it. The porcelain was very thin. He didn't like it. The pattern was, to his taste, too Germanic. Berlin. Should he go to Berlin?

"Where's Otto?" said Susie. "Otto, sweetie!" she called.

"Who's Otto?" asked Dodge.

The puppy bounded in. "Here he is," said Susie. She patted Otto as he whimpered with enjoyment and wriggled about, attempting to offer the choicest spots on his abdomen to Susie's ministrations. "Yes," she intoned. "Yes, baby, yes, my darling Otto. Yes, poochie, poochie, sweetie."

"'*Poochie, poochie, sweetie* . . .'?" Dodge repeated with mock incredulity. "'Poochie, poochie, sweetie'?"

"What are we having for breakfast?" asked Ron.

"What have you got against this dog?" said Susie, straightening up.

"I'm just jealous," said Dodge.

"Whatever's for breakfast, I'm ready," said Ron. "Maybe I'll eat the dog."

Dodge felt as if Ron was competing with him even about hating the dog. Though he wondered if he did really hate the dog. In any event, he now saw that Ron might get on his nerves in a heavy way. *No good deed goes unpunished,* he reminded himself. Why had he brought Ron here, for god's sake.

"Yeah, I'm ready," said Billy, increasingly grumpy. He wished he had a cigarette.

With much ado and preparation, they finally ate pancakes and bacon on a painted iron table outside, a few feet away from the kitchen door.

At some point during the meal, they fell momentarily silent, as if they were old friends. There was a shift—they all sensed—and they began to feel a kind of communion, maybe just from the shared freshness of the air, the sunlight, and the slight anxiety about the rest of the summer together. They all felt unexpectedly frivolous, as if the morning air and the unaccustomed matinal badinage had loosened the joints of their minds somehow.

I feel loonier than usual, Susie told herself.

Susie is really out of it, Billy was thinking. *And Kay?* He couldn't read Kay, except for that obvious twinge of sadness in her eyes. He looked at Kay, her head tilted in the sunlight. *She's really beautiful,* he thought. He remembered the conversation they'd had about beauty. No, it was a thing like goodness, he decided. You just knew it when you felt it. There was no reason for it not to be subjective, but something was definitely radiated by the object. There was no doubt that Kay was beautiful.

I'm eating too much, Kay was thinking.

I wish I were in a bed with both these women, Dodge was thinking.

What a Lothario, Ron was thinking about Dodge, his half-closed eyes, his body easy and loose. The black of his jeans, the green of the chairs.

I don't like him, Billy was thinking about Ron.

He's weird, I kind of like him, Susie was thinking about Ron. *Even if Billy doesn't.*

I don't like the way he looks, Kay was thinking about Ron. *I'm suddenly tired.*

Of course, Susie and Kay like him, Billy was thinking.

I wonder if I could just get up and go back to bed, Kay was thinking. *No, I guess not.*

They chatted. Ron quipped. Dodge managed to look incredibly cool even in the afternoon sunshine. Kay laughed so hard at one point that Billy looked at her with surprise.

The table was poised at the edge of the great lawn. The grass looked strangely green and soft, so that one wanted to slip off one's chair and roll around. A couple of hundred feet away, the woods began where blue spruce posed regally against a perfectly blue sky. Birds sang, more melodious and less frantic than they had been in the early morning. When the humans' talk lapsed, the birds seemed to echo them, but more gently. When the birds' talk lapsed, the air seemed so sweet as to be inebriating.

"Oh, a ladybug!" said Kay, following the progress of the small orange creature across her empty plate.

"Aha!" said Ron. "The insect population makes its entrance."

"First of many, I'll bet," said Dodge.

"I wonder if there are any mosquitoes," said Susie.

"Well, my guess is this is Mosquito Central for the East Coast," said Ron.

"How many spots does the ladybug have?" Susie asked Kay.

"Who can count?" said Kay. "It moves."

"Put your finger down, it'll climb," said Dodge.

"Just concentrate," said Susie.

"Make it up. What difference does it make?" said Ron.

"I'm trying to count," said Kay, laughing. The insect was already dawdling away toward the edge of the table. "I'm not used to concentrating on anything so small anymore."

"You only look at big things?" said Susie.

"No," Kay said. The ladybug went over the edge and Kay looked up. She put her hands around her glass, as if she needed to hold on to something. "It's just so hard to concentrate on anything anymore, I've lost the habit."

"It's not concentration, it's focus," said Dodge. "It's getting yourself to focus on any one thing."

"I haven't focused on anything since around 1973," said Ron.

"I don't believe you," said Susie.

"It's a joke," said Ron.

"Even work isn't a form of focus," said Dodge. "It's a way of directing your attention and then allowing yourself to lose focus."

"Bliss," said Kay.

"I thought we weren't going to talk about work," said Susie. She sipped the last of her coffee, ran her hands through her hair. They all looked at her.

"That was serious?" said Ron. "But it's all we ever talk about."

"Exactly," said Susie.

"Can you do it?" said Billy. "I'd be amazed."

"I'm sick of work," said Kay.

"I'm not sick of work, but I'm certainly sick of the business of work," said Dodge.

"Well, there's one part work and a hundred parts business," said Ron.

"There you go," said Susie. "You're talking about work."

Billy scraped the last of the syrup off his plate, licked his fork, wiped his mouth with the napkin. He got up and stretched. Kay, Ron, and Dodge looked at him. A bathing suit shouldn't have been improper attire in such proximity to a pool, but he was nearly naked, and his golden boy-man's body was almost embarrassing.

"After we've been here a week, will we look like Billy too?" asked Ron.

They laughed. Billy stared at his empty plate, picked up his napkin, and wiped his mouth again and then threw down the napkin. "I'm going to the pool," he called out as he strode off. Kay smiled at Susie in acknowledgment of Billy's petulance, but Susie was too accustomed to it to have registered the message of disapproval.

Otto, who'd been hovering around the table waiting for hand-outs, trotted away in Billy's direction, then turned around and came back to Susie. Finally he stood halfway between the table and the house, barking fervently.

Susie laughed. "Poor Otto, poor lovely poochie," she said. "Torn in your loyalties. Go ahead. Go with Billy."

As if he understood, the dog turned and trotted away. "Amazing," Kay said, in all seriousness.

"Yeah, unbelievable," said Dodge, sarcastically.

"Why, Dodge, I believe you truly have some hostility toward that dog," said Susie.

"He can't stand the competition," said Ron.

"The dog's all right," said Dodge, somewhat sheepishly.

Ron imitated Susie. "Yes, Dodgie darling, Yes, Dodgie poochie, come here and lick me and let me thrill your soul," he mocked in a high-pitched voice.

They all laughed.

"Speak for yourself," said Dodge. There was something about his delivery that made clichés seem witty and they laughed again.

"Isn't it time to go to the pool?" said Susie tactfully. She knew Dodge well enough to see he was genuinely irritated.

"Yes," Kay said.

"Oh, we have all weekend," said Ron. "We're just revving up for the real tastelessness that will follow."

"Oh my god," said Susie.

"Correction," said Dodge. "We have all summer."

They made a program for the day, consisting of a stint at the pool, coming back and changing, which entailed a complicated system of staggered showers, eating dinner, and then going into town for the Fourth of July fireworks. They went back to the house to change while Kay walked directly to the pool.

She was glad for the time to be alone with Billy. The others did seem like a lot of effort. *Billy,* she reflected, *is always easy. Either easy or fun. More and more fun as he gets older.* The pool was on the side of the house, on a promontory. The lawn then rolled down to the river. The opposite shore was perhaps a mile away, graced by a line of trees that had been groomed, it would seem, to ornament the view. It was one of those resplendent vistas that the Hudson River Valley is so rich in, overwhelming in its generosity and beauty.

Billy had disdained the chaise longues and was lying on a towel on the concrete edge of the pool. The towel was red. The concrete was intensely white in the sun, the pool implacably turquoise. Billy's knees were bent and he was tapping the ground with one foot to a tune he was humming ("Blue Moon," more or less in the Cowboy Junkies' version). Otto was closely observing and sniffing the grounds around the pool.

When Kay approached, Billy opened his eyes and waved. He watched her walk carefully on the concrete walkway. Some déjà vu effluvium floated about in his psyche. He had always noticed her skin was pale and gorgeous in sunlight.

"How's it going, Kay?" he said.

"Not too bad," she said, pleased that he was making an exception from the laconic treatment he seemed to have settled on as a mode of interaction with the rest of the group. "How are you doing?"

"That guy Dodge is really an asshole," said Billy.

"Do you mean Dodge or Ron?" Kay asked.

"Both of them," said Billy. "But Dodge is really the brains behind the outfit."

Kay laughed. "I'm actually not so sure about that," Kay said. She pulled off her T-shirt and settled into a chaise longue not far from him. She wore a red bathing suit made of very thin fabric, now slightly frayed at the seams. It was an old suit but she had once known it was flattering.

"I am," he said. "That's the kind of guy that's always hovering around Susie," he said. "These real cool dudes who are total assholes." The description was uttered in an objective tone, as if to convey an observation rather than an opinion.

"What a luxury to be so young and categorical," Kay said.

"Why? Do you wish you were younger?" asked Billy.

"No," said Kay. She smiled at him and he smiled back.

"Or more categorical?" asked Billy.

"God, no," said Kay.

"You talk about your age a lot."

"No," she said quickly. Then she thought a little. "No," she said again, having really considered it. "But I do wish I could be more categorical. One of the problems of getting older is that you see the contradictions of everything, so that you're much more ambivalent all the time."

"Really," said Billy, sarcastically but affectionately.

"Dodge is a great painter," said Kay.

"Dodge is an asshole," said Billy.

She smiled at him again. He was on his stomach, leaning on his elbow, looking up at her and squinting. She restrained the urge to touch his shoulder with her toe. He restrained the urge to slide his hand up her leg.

"What?" said Billy, as if he responding to an imaginary movement.

"Nothing," Kay said.

The others arrived with considerable brouhaha and settled in. Susie dived into the pool. Otto was capering along the pool and yapping ecstatically, so she finally picked him up, called out "Okay!" and brought him into the water. He struggled a little and then became touchingly subdued, resting in her arms like a wet baby. She held him with one arm diagonally across his chest and abdomen in a Red Cross lifesaving hold and swam a very slow one-arm backstroke. *It's weird,* thought Susie, *how much you can love another creature when it depends on you. That's what's great about love—it's so stupid. It's so incredibly stupid.*

Dodge settled into his chair with a murder mystery, then looked up. "Can't he swim?" he asked.

"I guess not," said Susie without opening her eyes. She reached the end of the pool, pushed off, and headed back for a return lap.

There was silence for a few moments.

Ahh, thought Kay. *Finally.* She closed her eyes.

"What!?" hollered Ron. "No talking? This is what I get from coming to the country with gentiles. You're all going lie here like this and leave me alone. Am I the only highly verbal person here?"

"No," Susie called out. "You're the only one with the energy, though."

"I don't believe this," said Ron, addressing the sun. "Do you?"

"Ron," called Susie from the pool.

"Yes," said Ron.

"If you want, come in here and talk."

"No," he said. "I'm not ready yet to have my consciousness so radically altered."

Susie climbed out of the pool and walked gingerly toward her towel. Otto followed her, pausing a couple of times to do that thing that dogs do to shake wetness off, which of course showered the whole lot of them with chlorine. Everyone looked at Susie. She had on an old blue tank suit, the kind you could really swim in. Her body was lean and she had that kind of bright flesh that looks good even before it's tanned. Her wet hair seemed like a kid's, and you could see how well cut it was. She rubbed her head with a towel and then settled into her chaise longue, closed her eyes.

"Oh no!" said Ron. "Now she's assuming the position too. Is there no one here who'll talk to me? You!" he suddenly yelled. "You, you'll talk to me, right?"

"Sure," called out Elise. They all looked up. Elise was standing about twenty feet away, wearing a very fancy and low-cut black suit, dark stockings, and very high heels.

"My god, what happened to you, Elise?" said Susie.

"I guess my driver came in the back way. Maybe he thought I was the housekeeper or something."

"Hi," Kay called out to Elise.

"Hi," she said.

Susie said, "You remember Dodge and Ron."

"Yes," they all said simultaneously.

"You're here in the nick of time," said Ron. "Thank god, now I can talk."

The unarticulated observation flitted through Elise's mind that it was always the less desirable of two men who was the most sexually aggressive. *What about the other one?* she thought. She'd forgotten how attractive she had found Dodge, even though that had been one of the main incentives for scrounging up the money for her share of the house. She'd seen a piece on him in *ARTnews* with a not very good photograph and self-consciously cryptic quotes, and she had wondered if she had been totally out of her mind that night at Susie's. *No, he's very tempting.* She noticed Susie and Kay looking at her, with smiles. *Are they friendly or are they checking me out?* Elise took off her jacket. "I can't believe I made it!" she fairly yelled. "Summer is finally here."

She pulled her little white sweater up over her head, slipped out of her skirt, unhooked her bra and threw it in the grass, tossed away her shoes, stepped out of her panties, stood, naked and pretty for a moment. No woman who didn't have a very pretty body would have done this, and both Susie and Kay had time to reflect ungenerously that she bore her few extra pounds very well, so far.

She cannonballed into the water, and the others all stared for a bit at the frothing display that followed.

Dodge and Ron exchanged an amused and condescending glance that was observed by Billy.

"Jeez," Billy said, and exchanged an amused and condescending glance with Dodge, which Ron pretended not to see.

"Well done!" Susie called out to the concentric circles of bubbles.

Otto, who had been, like the rest of them, watching, dashed back to the pool and dived in without hesitation. They all laughed.

Elise bobbed up to the surface. She wore a big smile. Otto doggy-paddled madly.

"Well," said Ron.

"That's what I say," said Susie.

Susie set a towel on the side of the pool for Elise. Elise swam for a while and the others settled back into their chaises. Elise came out of the pool and wrapped herself in the towel and then walked on her toes to a chaise, where she lay down, opened the towel, and set herself to sunbathing with method, as if on a rotisserie, swiveling every fifteen minutes. They traded wisecracks for a while but then eased into quiet. Finally they all slipped into dreamy somnolence. Dodge actually fell asleep and dreamed he was on an island, motoring about in an old car, lost.

They had drinks on the patio as the sun set. As the season wore on, there were many tableaux from that first weekend that were collectively remembered. But the moment that remained in all their memories was that of the first dusk on the patio. They had liked it so much, sitting and lounging about together at sunset, that they repeated it often throughout the next two months (just as Susie had predicted). That was probably the snapshot of the summer, if only someone had taken it. Setting a precedent, they'd taken a long time to get ready and the sun was just setting. In the last of the light, the view was ridiculously gorgeous; the sky was ignited with crimson; the lawn glowed dark and majestic. It was precisely that minute of the day when, after their hour of being exquisitely vivid, colors begin to melt into one another and the dimming gold light. Inside the patio, the floors, the wall, the couches and chairs were softly golden.

They were in good moods. They half sat, half reclined on the wicker couches and armchairs that seemed to have been arranged for their pleasure and conversation in a large circle in the center of this attractive room. Yes, it was a room for pleasure. They were a little tanned from the hour they had spent out at the pool, all but Ron, who had stayed out longer and was rather on the red side. They poured margaritas from a pitcher and, despite Susie's protestations, Ron let Otto lap quite a bit from his glass.

"Otto, darling, come back here," called out Susie. Susie's hair was still wet. She was dressed in a white T-shirt and jeans and looked amazingly healthy.

"Otto, darling...," repeated Dodge in a bemused tone.

"There you go again, jealous of a dog," said Ron.

"Poochie," sang Susie in a high voice. Otto glanced back at Susie but continued to hover around Ron, from whom he clearly expected more margarita handouts.

"I'm jealous of the dog too," said Elise. "I wish I had his life."

"I know what you mean. They're wrong about a dog's life—it's a great thing," said Susie. "But that's exactly what summer's for. You can have a dog's life."

"Not really," said Elise. Elise wore a headband in her hair and a pink angora sweater she'd found in a thrift shop that left her midriff bare, and black pedal pushers. She sprawled on her chair like a teenager. "I mean, I could have the same activities as Otto, but there isn't anyone who'd take care of me the way you take care of him."

"Perhaps I could oblige," said Ron, turning toward Elise, whose midriff clearly fascinated him. He put his elbows on his knees and rested his face on his fists so that he was closer to her. "As long as you're willing to wear a leash. A red leash, I think."

"No," said Elise, who didn't move except to swing her leg a little. "If someone is going to treat me like a dog, I'd rather it weren't you."

"It could be a long leash," said Ron.

"No, thank you," said Elise.

"There'd be many biscuits," said Ron.

"Well," said Elise. "I'll consider it."

"I'm starving," said Billy. "Do we eat soon?" He was annoyed neither Susie nor Kay had commented on the fact that he wasn't smoking.

"I'm starving too," Kay said. She noticed she was really hungry, a sensation she hadn't had in quite some time. She wanted to stretch but she didn't know these people well enough yet. She was amazingly relaxed though. Considering.

"I'm going to go out for just a moment, to smell the roses and so forth," said Susie, "and then we'll eat."

"I'll come," said Elise.

Billy went out with them. The other three watched them walk down the lawn together, Susie's and Billy's blond heads glimmering in the last of the sunset. Even Elise's dark head seemed fair in that light. They headed toward the rose garden, Otto bounding about them.

"Poochie, poochie, darling," sang Dodge, in a fair but cruel imitation of Susie's calls.

"Do you like animals, Dodge?" Kay asked.

"No," he said. He poured himself another drink.

"Really? How can you not like a dog?" asked Ron. "Especially a puppy."

"Childhood traumas," said Dodge.

"Let's hear it," said Ron.

"No, I don't think so," said Dodge.

"You could make one up," Kay suggested.

"What?" said Dodge.

"A childhood trauma. Make one up."

"Okay. I was bitten by a dog the day my mother died."

Ron and Kay were silent for a moment. Dodge had spoken with such aplomb that they wondered if he was telling the truth. Dodge smiled at their expressions. Ron raised his eyes heavenward.

"You're a far-out cat, you know that?" said Ron, while pretending to be studying the delicately faded gilding outlining the vaulted ceiling. It was already too gloomy to see much of anything.

They all got a bit loaded that night at dinner, Dodie noted without disapproval. She served them meat loaf and mashed potatoes, which they greeted with cheers and applause.

They ate and drank and talked.

"Love eating scenes," said Susie.

"What?" said Elise.

"Everyone complains that French movies have too many eating scenes but I love them."

"Rohmer movies," said Dodge.

"Renoir," said Kay.

"*Rules of the Game* is my favorite movie," said Susie.

"Great displacement," said Ron.

"Great displacement?" said Elise.

"What, is there an echo in here?" said Ron.

"What movies have you seen lately?" Dodge said to Susie.

"Oh no," said Ron. "We're not going to talk about movies, are we? Or else we might as well all stay in Manhattan."

"We can talk about movies sometimes," said Kay.

"Just for a switch," said Susie.

"What's better than talking about movies?" asked Dodge.

"I like neutral conversations," said Ron.

"What do you mean, 'displacement'?" said Elise.

"Could I have more meat loaf?" asked Billy.

"I love conversations about movies," said Susie.

"I can read everyone's unconscious," said Ron.

"Oh no," said Dodge.

"Tell us," said Susie. "I have a feeling it's something we need to know."

"Do you remember the eating scene in *Tom Jones*?" Elise suddenly said. Ron laughed raucously.

"What?" said Elise. "What? What?"

"Does anyone want more meat loaf?" asked Susie.

"No, thanks," said Kay.

"No, thanks," said Elise.

"Oh no!" yelled Susie.

"What!?!" several of them said.

There was the slight sound of detonations, in the distance.

"We missed the fireworks. We missed the Fourth of July."

Sunday

The next morning Otto was missing. Susie had spent the first part of the morning in the house, looking for him in every possible hiding place. "How could he have gotten out?" she asked herself out loud.

Only Elise and Kay had made it down to breakfast and then both had gone back to their rooms. Kay went straight to bed. Elise did some exercises and then went back to sleep. At around ten-thirty, it began to drizzle. The house was damp and dark. Ron came down and spent the morning on the patio, mostly reading Friday's paper, sometimes nodding off. As the morning wore on, everyone idled in and out of the room at one point or another except Billy, who had already established a habit of sleeping all morning.

Shortly before noon Kay joined Ron on the patio, reading whenever she felt particularly aware of him or when there was anyone else in the room. It was *The House of Mirth*. She had decided to read all of Edith Wharton this summer. When she was alone, she often found herself daydreaming, the book on her lap. The rain stopped. The sky was low and hazy. The light on the patio was milky. Outside, the lawns and the trees gleamed.

Billy had an erotic dream and spent a long time, when he finally woke up, staring at the ceiling, but he couldn't remember the dream.

By noon Susie was very upset. She questioned the others, one by one, about who had last seen the dog. "Isn't he outside?" each of them said.

"I bet he made friends with a couple of other dogs from the neighborhood," Ron suggested to Kay sotto voce, but she didn't think it was funny. Dodge had joined Kay and Ron on the patio and picked up a part of the now rumpled Friday paper. Every once in a while, those on the patio could hear Susie calling, "Otto! Otto!" Her audible anxiety began to make them feel very tense.

Dodge slammed down his newspaper and Kay looked up, startled. "Otto!" he mocked in that mean voice. "Poochie! Poochie! Poochie, darling!"

"My goodness, you certainly have a problem with that dog," Ron said. Kay was actually frightened: there was something disturbing about his tenacious mockery.

"Yes," said Dodge. "I do. What is the matter with Susie, anyway? Why is she spending the whole morning looking for that dog? He's just a dog. He's probably out in the back trying to fuck a squirrel or something."

Dodge looked so intense, neither Kay nor Ron knew whether he was joking or not. Kay smiled nervously. They talked of other things.

Dodie arrived and headed into the kitchen, letting the screen door slam. She shook her head as Susie described the puppy. Susie went back outside and the others could hear her calling, "Otto!" Now they only looked at one another, silently.

At lunchtime the others persuaded Susie to give up for a while. Susie submitted but it was clear that she couldn't get her mind off the puppy. The conversation was desultory. Billy came down, looking as if he were sleepwalking, just as they were starting their tomato salad. About halfway through the cold chicken, he said, "Where's Otto?" And Susie began to cry.

"Have you called the police?" asked Elise.

"Yes," said Susie. "Twice."

"Okay," said Kay. "I think that after lunch we should form a search party."

"Let's have a strategy," said Ron.

Dodge stayed in the house. The rest of them spread out. It was Billy who found Otto, laid down neatly alongside one of the two boulders that flanked the gate, presumably by the driver of the car that had hit him because, tucked under his body, there was a plastic wrapper from a Kleenex pack into which someone had placed a folded ten-dollar bill and a piece of paper torn from a notebook on which there was written the word "Sorry" in carefully nondescript letters. Carefully, he lifted the puppy and carried him back in and laid him next to the patio wall.

Susie bounded out of the house and followed the rest.

"Car," said Billy, looking at Susie.

Susie crouched next to the puppy. The others looked at them. Billy went back to the kitchen and returned with Dodie, who was carrying a cardboard box and newspaper.

"God," said Dodie. She set down the box not too far from Susie and the puppy. "Well," she said. "He had a good life." She went back in, letting the screen door slam.

Billy placed the box next to the puppy's corpse. He couldn't bear to pick him up again.

"Where should we bury him?" Billy asked Susie.

Susie was silent. They all stood around the box.

"Maybe out by the rose garden," Kay said. "In the pine grove behind the rose garden."

"That's ridiculous," said Susie. She picked up the dog and lifted him—he was obviously a little heavier dead than he had been alive because at the last moment he slipped from her hands into the box and Billy gasped.

Susie turned away, then turned back. "There's no reason to be so sentimental," she said. She looked at the dog in the box and then rearranged one paw. He looked so cute in the box, like a dog valentine.

"Well," said Dodie, coming back out with a plastic bag. "I guess you have to bury him somewhere." There was a pause, during which Dodie took a crumpled-up paper towel out of her pocket and dusted a patch of the screen.

"Yes," said Susie. "That's true. Let's go."

Billy picked up the box and Susie took the plastic bag from Dodie. The others were all standing there, Elise and Ron and Kay. Dodge sat on the steps.

"Please, you don't have to come along," said Susie. "This is not an Alan Alda movie."

"No, we want to," said Elise.

"I'd rather you didn't," said Susie. "It's ridiculous. I know I'm ridiculous."

"We don't think you're ridiculous," Kay said.

"Only Dodge," said Ron. "And he's fucked up. The rest of us love Alan Alda movies."

In the end, they let them go on their own, Susie and Billy. They watched mother and son walk away toward the rose garden.

"Fucking dog," said Dodge.

"Jesus, Dodge," said Elise. "What's the matter with you?"

"Nothing," said Dodge.

"I need a drink," said Ron.

"Out-of-towners," said Dodie. By which she meant whoever had been driving the car that killed Otto.

Ron, Dodge, and Elise drove into town, but Kay decided to stick around, in case Susie wanted to talk. But Susie didn't want to talk. When they came back from the pine grove, she said she was going to go to her room and rest, and she spent the balance of the afternoon there.

She didn't show up on the patio at sunset time, and the cocktail hour was lugubrious. The others had the feeling they were waiting for her. Dodge looked increasingly sullen. Ron put on an Elvis Presley CD, and the others stared at the speakers. The tune seemed to ring hollow in the large damp space, until he finally took it off. Then they only heard, intermittently, Dodie clanking about in the kitchen and occasionally yelling "Shit!"

Billy asked Kay if she wanted to play gin, and when she said yes, he went and fetched a deck of cards he had previously scoped out from the drawer of a rickety game table. She didn't pay much attention to the game and lost several times in a row. She was looking at the tips of his fingers, narrow and delicate. Every once in a while, he would look up and smile. Then he would resume staring very earnestly at his cards. It started to rain again.

When Susie finally peered in, she had put on makeup and was wearing a short skirt and high heels and looked great. "Dinnertime!" she called out in a kind of singsong voice.

At dinner Susie assumed a brittle and forced gaiety that Kay found painful. Billy was unusually silent. Elise drank too much. Dodge and Ron were uncomfortable.

Everyone tried to help, but the atmosphere was almost unbearably despondent. The room itself seemed to reflect their gloom. The only light was from tall candelabras, and huge shadows played on the Empire wallpaper. The table was long, too long for them, and set with fine though patched linen.

"I feel like the owners' ancestors are going to come down and eat with us," said Elise.

"Maybe we should get some paper plates," said Ron.

"Why ever would we do that?" said Susie, sharply.

"Who are the owners?" said Elise.

"The scion of an old Dutch family, a gay novelist," said Susie.

"That explains it," said Ron.

"What?" said Elise.

"I don't know," said Ron. "I'm just filling time."

"It's too bad. I would have liked to have married him and lived in this house forever," said Susie.

"You could marry a homosexual," said Dodge. "It's done all the time."

"Or it used to be," said Kay.

"I've always liked the idea of a *mariage blanc*," said Susie. "I've always romanticized it."

"It always makes me sad," said Elise.

"Why?" said Susie.

"Why?" said Ron. "You don't think it's sad that two people should go to all the trouble of spending their lives together and then they don't fuck?"

"No, that's not the point," said Elise. "I think that what used to happen is that they wouldn't have sex together, but then the husband would have sex outside the marriage and the woman wouldn't."

"That sounds logical," said Ron.

"Well, but no one stopped the woman except herself," said Dodge.

"Dodge, darling," said Susie, edgily. "Don't tell me you're sexist too . . ."

"What do you mean 'too'?" said Dodge. He was smiling a little.

"In addition to being cruel and heartless," said Susie. She had another sip of white wine.

"It's true. Dodge is cruel and heartless," said Elise. "That's his charm."

"It's so retro," said Susie.

"Not really," said Elise.

"I'm a pussycat," said Dodge.

The reference to a cat reminded them all of Otto and they fell silent.

"Excuse me," said Billy. He stopped to kiss Susie on his way out. "I'm going to my room for a while."

"Anyway, women had affairs all the time," said Susie. "For all we know, they had more affairs than men did. They just were discreet."

After Billy left, Kay didn't pay all that much attention to the conversation, a fact that she noted with a start at dessert time. *What is this?* she actually asked herself for the first time. *Why this sudden flare of attraction for Billy?* Maybe not all that much analysis was necessary. Billy certainly had appeal. She hadn't seen him in a long time. She felt kind of startled by him. And disturbed. Maybe her loneliness was getting to her.

Elise was looking at Dodge. *What cheekbones,* she thought. *And what a prick he is. Trouble. Certainly trouble.*

I just can't bear feeling like this, Susie was thinking. *I just can't bear it. I don't know how to get through this dinner.*

Poor Susie, Kay was thinking. She turned her attention to Dodge. The candlelight flickered on his face. Dodge was listening to Susie, Ron, and Elise. He looked a little sullen, body half turned away from the table. He had beautiful hands, elegant fingers. *There's something sexy about painters' hands. I don't know why,* thought Kay.

Why does Kay keep looking at Dodge? Billy, in his bedroom, was wondering and feeling a strange stinging in his chest.

Ron was riffing on Fourth of Julys past. *Something always went wrong. Fucking dog,* he was thinking. *Had to die right at the beginning of the summer.*

Susie felt a ripping pain in her chest. She figured if she kept drinking she could dull it. She hated everyone.

Kay was watching Dodge look at Susie and then look at Elise and then at Susie again. He looked up and caught her eye. They both smiled.

Ron interrupted himself. "What?" he said.

"What?" said Elise.

"What happened?" said Ron. He was addressing Kay.

"Nothing!" she said. "Why?"

"Why the meaningful glance?"

"It wasn't about anything you said, Ron," Kay protested. She was laughing but could feel he was actually upset. There was something behind his eyes, some intensity. *Wow, this guy must be a world-class neurotic.* She felt something powerful emanate from him. That was usually someone's craziness, that feeling.

"It wasn't about you," said Dodge. "We were having a private moment."

"What was the nature of your private moment?" said Susie.

"Oh my goodness," Kay said, standing up and putting her salad plate on top of her dinner plate and heading for the kitchen. "What a bunch of paranoids."

When she came out of the kitchen and surveyed the group, she decided the dining room was too oppressive. "I'm going to rest," she said.

"I'm going out for a walk," Elise said, pushing back her chair. "If anybody wants to come."

As she was heading out the main gate, Ron caught up with her. Elise almost turned back when she saw they'd be alone, but it would have been too awkward. She decided he had surely calmed down by now. They strolled for a while, through the grounds. It was now a clear night, a nearly full moon. Ron didn't refer to the strange fit he'd had at dinner. He was embarrassed but he lodged the embarrassment somewhere in his mind, for later, like a squirrel would stash a walnut in its cheek. They talked of this or that person they both knew in New York and finally fell silent except to remark now and then on a line of moonlight on the lawn, a brushing in the leaves, the smell of the damp pines.

They walked back to the house in better spirits and into the empty kitchen, poured themselves glasses of club soda.

"Do you want to have a nightcap?" asked Ron.

"I'm pretty tired, I guess," said Elise. She was pleased with herself for being good. *Finally, I'm learning...*

So they headed upstairs. Elise was planning to be firm if Ron tried to follow her to her room. Probably.

"Look at this," said Ron.

They had taken the back staircase. In this part of the house, the walls of the halls were lined with bookshelves. The small library downstairs contained what was left of the former owners' good editions. Up here was literary bric-a-brac, British nineteenth-century travel literature, French tales, a bit of Hudson River Valley memorabilia. But what Ron had spotted, Elise saw as she came closer, was a doorknob among the books.

"What good eyes you've got," she said.

"My analyst says my hyperacuity corresponds to my unwillingness to notice anything in my immediate surroundings." Ron grabbed the handle and the door opened. Beyond was darkness.

They each groped on the wall on either side of the door for the light switch. "It feels like more books," Elise said. "Maybe we should come back in the morning."

"Wait a minute," said Ron. He grasped her wrist and led her back out. "Stay there for a minute, okay? Just stand guard for a moment."

He left at a run. She waited. It seemed like an amusing discovery. Elise sighed. She was glad to be distracted for a moment from the gloomy dinner. She wondered if the summer would be spoiled by Otto's death. She didn't know Susie well enough to predict.

Downstairs Ron looked for a flashlight and thought he'd like to go to bed with Elise. It was too soon. She might freak out if he even intimated it. He couldn't cope with a rejection this early in the summer and having to spend the next two months' worth of weekends in the house with her. On the other hand, it might be very easy. But also, in a way, he didn't give a shit. And that depressed him.

Or is this maturity? he asked himself. *Yes,* he answered. Maturity is knowing how much rejection you can handle and still keep your appetite. Or maybe it was realizing that you don't actually care, except for the wrong reasons. Or some combination. Now he remembered a letter he had left unfinished on his desk. "Goddamn it," he said out loud, alone in the hall in the dark. Then he realized he'd forgotten what he'd come downstairs for.

Elise squinted when the beam of the flashlight greeted her ahead of Ron.

"Okay," he said. "I'll be Indiana Jones; you be Abu. Then we'll switch."

"Why Abu?" said Elise as they entered the room.

As it turned out, the shelves in this room were lined with erotica. It was a small, weirdly shaped space, wood paneled. There was a red velvet divan, a frayed rug, a very old windup Victrola on a table, a stack of records, a kerosene lamp.

"This is like a secret room," Elise said.

"*My Lady Rules,*" read Ron off a book spine.

"*A Thousand and One Nights in the Bordello,*" she read off another.

"Holy shit," said Ron. "What is this, the master's secret room?"

"What do you mean?"

"Well, maybe he came here to jerk off, or to screw the maid or something."

"Or the mistress's," she said. "Where she came to jerk off or to screw the gardener."

By unspoken covenant, they'd been whispering. Now they heard a moan. Elise gasped and started. "What?!" said Ron.

They heard a moan again. Elise laughed nervously. "Is this place haunted?" said Ron. He struck the wall the voice seemed to come from and the sound stopped for a bit.

"Poochie, poochie, darling," said the voice. "Say 'poochie, darling' to me."

It was Dodge's voice. Ron and Elise now looked at each other.

"Say it," said Dodge's voice.

"Poochie, poochie, poochie, poochie, poochie," said Susie's voice.

Now Ron began to laugh. "Fucking Moriarty," he said.

Elise put her hands over her ears. "Let's go," she said.

"This is pretty funny," said Ron.

"Let's go," she said.

"Poochie, poochie, poochie," said Susie's voice, as if either in the final stage of an erotic encounter or engaging in some strange grieving rite.

"Let's go," Elise said again, and led the way. When Ron came out into the hall, she shut the door behind him.

"This is too weird for me," she said.

"Well, this'll make good breakfast copy," said Ron.

"I think we shouldn't talk about it," said Elise.

"Not talk about it! Are you kidding?" said Ron. "How can you not talk about a thing like this?"

"I don't know," she said. "It upsets me."

"You're not going to talk about it out of discretion or good taste?" asked Ron. "But think of the power it gives you over other human beings to have a secret like that about them. You don't want to have that kind of secret power?"

"I don't know. It's upsetting. I think it would upset Susie."

"I'm actually kidding," said Ron, thinking, *She's having an episode?*

"I don't know," said Elise. "How did that sound get to us, anyway?"

"I don't know," said Ron. "We'll have to check it out in the morning."

"Let's not," said Elise. "Let's just forget this happened."

Ron laughed. He looked at her, into her wide-open eyes, in the slightly pink light of the sconces. "You really are upset," he said. "What are you upset about? It's just two people fucking."

"No, it's the dog thing," said Elise.

"People say weird things in bed," he said. "Haven't you ever said anything weird in bed?"

"I don't think they were fucking, anyway," she said.

"Are you scared of Susie?" Ron asked.

"No," she lied.

Before she went to sleep that night, she lay in bed thinking about it and remembered the voices and tried to adopt Ron's attitude. But something about the scene had seemed too grotesque to her.

While he was brushing his teeth, Ron paused and said again to the mirror, "Fucking Moriarty."

Kay slipped in and out of sleep.

Billy lay undressed on the bed and stared at the ceiling again, in the dark now.

In Susie's room both Dodge and Susie were fully dressed. Now Susie was pressing her face into Dodge's chest and crying, almost noiselessly. A bigger and bigger patch of his sweater was becoming more and more soggy, she noticed, the observation side by side with an atrocious pain crouching in the middle of her mind like a fury.

"I don't know why," Susie managed to spurt, "anything you lose becomes everything you've lost."

"It'll go away," whispered Dodge. He knew there was no way Susie would be interested in sex tonight. He thought of the painting he was working on. The canvas was almost all gray, a rich dark gray with only glimpses of violent deep bloodred purples.

KAY

Friday

It was late afternoon. In her room with the door closed, she listened to the sounds of the house, the erratic clanking; the squeaking, creaking, settling of beams and jousts; and also to the commotion of the others entering and exiting, slamming screen doors, running water into noisy pipes, calling to one another across landings. The sound of summer.

Kay had spent the week alone in the house. The day after the others had left, while taking a walk in the rose garden, she had stopped midpath and mulled over the possibility that Susie's starting premise might have been wrong: maybe there really wasn't much fun to be had anymore. Last weekend had not been fun. It had almost been fun. It had reminded her of fun. To be fair, it was more fun than those evenings in Manhattan when she just waited for dinner to be over so she could leave.

The week by herself in the country (which would once have seemed to her like the fulfillment of an idyllic fantasy) had been pretty spooky. She had felt uneasy, had difficulty reading, was too preoccupied to spend much time at the pool, too anxious to luxuriate in the dormant solemnity of the lovely, pompous rooms, the frivolity of the patio, the peaceful old kitchen, though she wandered from room to room several times a day, now and then picking up a book and leafing through it. She had spent much of one evening on the second-floor landing, walking from one framed print to the next, reading the descriptive text at the bottom of each one. She had weathered the mood swings, the long blank afternoons, the several rainy days in a row. When Dodie and the teenagers came to clean, Kay retreated to her room. From behind her closed door, she could hear the teenagers chatting once Dodie had left them on their own to do the second floor. One of the teenagers, Kay had noticed with a jolt of misery, was extremely pregnant.

The week had passed quickly but was totally lacking the relief of solitude she had believed she longed for. Yet, even though she had been lonely, she had anticipated the others' return with anxiety.

The dead dog. Susie was careless.

She thought of her miscarriage. She turned the thought away. This had been Kay's habitual two-step process for four years now. The thought and the pushing away of the thought were so frequent and automatic and she took them so much for granted as part of herself that she would have been surprised to hear that she had long ago moved beyond the frame of what is known as normal grief.

The dead dog. It was disturbing to see Susie so upset. Kay had always been grateful for Susie's ability to make fun of everything. Why did the dog have to die?

Since the catastrophic breakup, Kay no longer believed in the significance of coincidence; she now dismissed it as a form of magical thinking. (Everything considered magical exasperated her.) There was occasional synchronicity, but so what? It was interesting, but only as a curiosity. Coincidence was one of the waste products of life. On the other hand, that train of thought tended to lead one to morose lack of interest in one's fate. It shouldn't have. But it did.

It seemed to her, as a matter of fact, that one of the things she hardly felt anymore was surprise. She missed it, in a way more than she missed, say, romance. Surprise turned out to be an accoutrement of hope, something she was short on, of late. Thinking about the future was so painful that it seemed to Kay like a bad habit she needed to break—which closely resembled her reaction to thinking about the past. She had stopped making plans.

Susie would suggest going out with this or that person, or exercising, or meditation, or some such thing—all of which were about as useful against despair as someone telling you to deal with anger by punching your pillow.

"Hmm," Kay would say, to end the conversation.

And about the miscarriage, and all that, Susie had been as dense as everyone else.

"Why don't you adopt?" Susie had more than once said to Kay.

"It's not the same thing," Kay would say.

"It doesn't have to be," Susie would say.

"I know," Kay would reply.

It annoyed Kay that Susie persisted even though she had let Susie see that she had to steel herself each time against the invasiveness of the conversation.

"Why don't you just adopt?" Susie would say, again.

"Because," Kay finally said one day, "because then there's the obligation to stay alive."

To that, Kay was relieved to see that Susie didn't know what to say. Kay knew Susie hadn't quite realized it was that bad. She felt guilty to sound so earnest and self-pitying, but in the end, Susie's optimism was an attack on her. It had nothing to do with her life or what she faced.

"You have to be able to at least do that . . . ," Kay had said, smiling, to make it easier for Susie. "It's not fair to the child otherwise."

"I guess you're not ready for this conversation," Susie had said to Kay.

It was a joke: they'd agreed long ago that not being ready was one of the great constructs of the end of the century. It implied that there was a possibility that all would come in its time. Whereas one knew very well, if one honestly evaluated one's circumstances, that there was very little one would ever be ready for. The idea that one would eventually be readier someday was one of the ways their generation could continue its addiction to the notion of potential.

Alone in the garden a few days ago, she had felt a wave of anxiety rush through her when she realized she had been standing immobilized and unaware of her surroundings for quite a while. She had sat down on a bench, near a rose bed she had come to think of as her favorite. It was planted with what were probably the oldest blooms, the most modest and discreetly alluring roses. She did love this garden. She closed her eyes for a moment, breathed. The air was heavy with sunshine and the smell of the earth. She had stared at a rose, the white petals delicately powdered with an unexpected coral hue. Well, there was an example of surprise. Nature's little surprises. No, that was depressing too. Nature was depressing. In the final tally, she was not grateful to nature.

She'd gotten up to inspect the ground around the rosebush. The earth was rich and moist and pungent with slightly damp rotted leaf mold. She had straightened and raised her face and closed her eyes and breathed in the early summer fragrance of the garden. And something sweet. What was it? Did the rose have a fragrance? She had opened her eyes and leaned down over the flower again. No. But since she had stopped smoking, her sense of smell was impaired, she thought. Maybe she could smell the soil and the trees, but not the rose. No, let's not get carried away. The rose had no smell, really. Yet another exasperating odorless rose.

She had ambled back to the house, forgetting to look around her.

She was always a little afraid someone was watching her, an urban habit hard to lose in this vast place. The closest neighbors were acres away. She'd seen them, over the hedge on the west side of the property. The mother, who wore sweatpants, the two straw-haired children in bathing suits all day, the pretty au pair, the smell of barbecue when the father came home on weekends. *No.* In the end, she was still glad she hadn't gone that route.

The ambiguity of her professional situation didn't help. She was either at a crossroads or stuck, and not knowing which it was didn't help. She felt at loose ends now that the Library of Congress research was finished. The fact was, she had told herself, she had to move back to New York. Washington had been a good delaying tactic, but she had to face it all now. Or in September, anyway.

She had turned down one project after another.

Asia? Asia beckoned. Maybe. But maybe she should do something American, stay put. What was going to happen here? She could not understand her country, could no longer envision a future for it. Whatever was foreign was easier to understand, lately, than America. History had scrambled all the signals, or what was left of them. Analysis seemed futile, and even ridiculous. But she couldn't quite resign herself to nothing more than membership in the aging semi-boho upper middle class that seemed to offer nothing but challenges that didn't interest her. Would this be it? Was she in for the duration? Lately she had begun to feel a cold and ugly fear.

Perhaps that was part of the reason the house had seemed so spooky. Though the house, of course, was truly scary, as she kept telling herself, with its fake external serenity and the insanity of the inside, all the sounds of night, the sudden bursts of noise, the lights left on when she was sure she'd turned them off, the slamming shut of a window she had never opened. One night she woke up thinking she had heard a violin. Just a few notes. She lay in bed with her heart beating hard, for quite a while. Then she'd gotten up, put on a robe, and walked through the house, holding a flashlight, calling out: "Hello?" There was an attic and a basement, but she had decided not even to look. She'd gone back to bed without taking off her robe and went to sleep with the lights and the radio on, waking up now and then to static until the dawn brought the birds back.

She should go downstairs. But she'd become so accustomed to her solitude that she felt a powerful reluctance, even when she heard the distinctive half-tempo rumble of Susie's Saab. When, a few minutes later, Susie knocked twice and then poked her head in, Kay, lying on the bed in her underpants and bra, started and gasped.

"Sorry!" said Susie.

"You scared me," said Kay, her hand on her chest. "I'm so stupid."

"I'm sorry," said Susie. "Next time I'll knock and wait."

"No, it's all right. I was daydreaming, I guess," said Kay. "But I'm glad you're here."

"I'll see you downstairs," said Susie. "I brought some shrimp."

"Great," said Kay. "How're you doing?"

"Not too bad," said Susie. "Better. See you later."

"Okay," said Kay.

The door closed behind Susie, and Kay lay back down again. At the beginning of the week, Kay and Susie had spoken on the phone several times a day. Now Susie was at the point where she no longer wanted to talk about Otto's death, a development Kay understood all too well.

Her gaze returned to the window. She was becoming addicted to the vista. Beyond the gabled roof of the patio, there was the symmetrical allée of the rose garden and then a wooded area that, she knew, hid the river from view. In the winter, she imagined, the river could be seen from this window. For a moment she had a fantasy of living up here year-round, dropping all this problematic life in New York. All this difficulty. All this perplexity. But it must be hard here, in the winter. Perhaps harder than the city, and hard in a different way she wasn't accustomed to. There would be snow and bare trees. Bare ruin'd choirs. Black and white and gray. Black trees, white ground, gray skies.

No, she couldn't stand the monotony. She was becoming more and more sensitive to tedium, even in New York, though in New York it was the tedium of ambition and endless conflict. And futility. Always, as she considered what she thought of as these dilemmas, she was struck by the notion of futility. *You might as well feel futile in New York, though,* she told herself. *Less boring.*

Through it all, besides, she liked New Yorkers. They were kinder than out-of-towners understood. Kay had been born in Manhattan, on the Upper East Side, which her fashionable friends now called "plastic." But she had known the Upper East Side as a much more dramatic and heterogeneous community than anything these people who lived in lofts in TriBeCa could imagine, a kind of sociocultural wind tunnel in which struggling working-class families on their way up and about to move out of the old railroad flats mingled with an erstwhile upper-middle-class population that was vertiginously downwardly mobile (though the expression hadn't been invented yet), in any event increasingly irrelevant. The latter still inhabited the ponderous between-the-war buildings in two-bedroom apartments where chintz slipcovers had miraculously become fashionable again and where lamb chops were still served with little paper bonnets.

At some point in her childhood, Kay had developed a theory that the reason there were little paper bonnets on the lamb chops was that everyone had had so many martinis before dinner that they couldn't have found the lamb chops without them. She had mentioned the theory out loud at dinner one night, and both her parents had paused for a moment, stupefied by her sarcasm. In fact it wasn't sarcasm—it was mere observation—but Kay concluded that it would have made things worse if they understood that.

Kay's parents had long ago retired to Maryland, to the old house where her mother's father had been born and died. They could no longer afford the place on Sixty-eighth Street off Park. Kay passed by there sometimes and, as she neared the familiar awning with its corny typeface—"The Latham"—was always surprised to find that it was no longer drowsily guarded by ancient Johnny D., the day man when she was growing up. There was no reason why the new man should recognize her, yet she felt something stinging wash across her chest each time.

Unresolved, she said to herself as she thought of it. *Unresolved sorrows.* And that, of course, reminded her of "the accident." She thought of her miscarriage and she pushed the thought away. She swung her legs over the edge of the bed and decided to get dressed.

What should she wear? There had been a leaning last weekend, on the part of the women, toward getting dressed for dinner, and Kay wanted to hold up the side. Susie would look great, of course. And Elise—who wasn't truly pretty—when she wanted to, could look quite stunning. *Though I couldn't bear to be her for a single moment.*

Kay reminded herself, when she noticed what she would have characterized as her own pettiness, that Elise's performance at the pool last weekend had put her off perhaps more than was strictly necessary, if the criteria were merely aesthetic. *Jealous,* Kay reproved herself. *Well, and why not?*

For some reason a girlfriend of Billy's she had met a few months ago popped into consciousness. Nina, her name was. Wearing a tiny miniskirt, with long thin legs, very big hair, full lips, unbelievably seductive. Kay hadn't realized until she got home that day that she'd felt devastated. She'd phoned Susie. "That used to be us!" she had exclaimed.

"I know," Susie had said. "The good old outré days . . ."

"Really," Kay had said. "Looking at her I felt so . . . dowdy!"

"Imagine how I feel!" Susie'd said. "Now what I've got to look forward to is being a grandmother . . ."

And Kay had laughed, because Susie as a grandmother was so outlandish. "You're never dowdy," she had told Susie. "You couldn't be dowdy to save your life."

"Well, neither are you," Susie had said. But Kay hadn't believed her.

Kay had always had a rather patrician look, which she used to try to play down. Now that it had stopped mattering quite so much, she wore her light chestnut hair up, which accentuated the classicism of her profile. Compared to, say, Susie, she truly believed that she looked "boring"—a euphemism indicating a reverse class problem she had never thought to question—and was continually surprised when she was cornered into acknowledging other people's considerably more enthusiastic view of her attractiveness. She wore no makeup but she had unusually clear skin, with the kind of luminosity that is peddled in women's magazines by young, expensive models in ads for fancy foundation. Lately she'd started wearing lipstick. Her mouth, it seemed to her, had become too pale. She noticed that many women her age who used to wear no makeup at all had taken to wearing lipstick. So much of aging for women seemed to have some connection to dissimulation, as opposed to fashions of one's youth, which were all designed to expose. She would look at her lips in the mirror to see if her mouth had changed. No. Not yet. But she didn't like looking at her mouth too long. The associations with sex, with being looked at or kissed, were too disturbing, especially early in the morning.

Kay always wore well-cut clothes in subtly handsome colors. She shopped at Bergdorf's and Banana Republic and occasionally, almost guiltily, sneaked into Talbots, as if returning to some of the comfort of her youth. Actually, her youth hadn't been all that comfortable. But perhaps that was the point of Talbots.

Susie and Billy were much more flamboyant. Susie wore expensive and very original clothes, short skirts in shiny fifties fabrics, weird shoes, shirts in gorgeous textures—silk, organza, suede—that she found way downtown somewhere and had made for her. Billy dressed, of course, all in black. So did Dodge. *Oh god,* thought Kay, *don't let Billy grow up into Dodge.*

What would Billy's father have been like? Susie was Kay's oldest friend, but Kay had never met Billy's father; neither had anyone else in New York, including Billy. All Kay knew was that Susie had run into him while cruising through Malaysia for the summer, and that she had flown back to the United States pregnant when the guy was picked up on a drug charge. When Billy was a baby, Susie had married some financial person—there had been a real wedding, with Kay as a bridesmaid. That marriage fizzled out with stunning rapidity, though Susie had somehow come out of it with her loft. Then there had been a gentleman-poet type—just a civil ceremony—who had lasted perhaps as much as three years. It seemed so long ago that it was almost fully faded in Kay's memory and, she assumed, in Susie's too.

It was true, it occurred to her, that Billy had more than reached childbearing age. A scalpel tore through her chest. That would

have to be lived through too, no doubt. She sighed audibly. "Well,"
she said out loud. "Well."

Kay reached into the top drawer of her dresser and extracted
pearl studs, which she inserted—without looking—into her ear-
lobes, then sprayed some agnès b. in the air and said, "The hell
with it," and left the room and went downstairs.

On her way to the dining room (though she could have taken
another route), Kay walked by Billy's room, and she saw him sitting
at the desk with his back to the door, with his head on his hands.
She paused for a moment, wondered whether she should speak to
him. But then decided not to. He seemed so unhappy, or did she
imagine it? Perhaps it was merely adolescent histrionics and
should be ignored.

Downstairs the others were assembled in the library, and she
heard their voices long before she reached the room. Susie's voice,
laughing. *Why doesn't she worry about her fucking son?* Kay caught
herself thinking, and then she pushed the thought away. Every
once in a while she was struck with resentment toward Susie, and
since it didn't seem to follow any external logic she could decipher,
she had come to reflexively ignore herself.

They were laughing as she walked in, and Kay noted that the
men seemed a little more animated than usual. She said, "How
long have you been drinking? Have I missed several rounds?"

"No, we just got here," said Susie. "But we had an afternoon
drink in town."

"An afternoon drink!" said Kay, striding toward the Bloody Mary
pitcher. "Without me?" But she only poured herself two inches of the
mixed Bloody Mary, which she knew would be quite powerful.

"We looked for you," said Ron. "Where were you?"

Kay settled in what had become her usual spot, a wicker love
seat perpendicular to the empty fireplace. Dodge stood up in his
utterly contained way and stealthily loped to the Bloody Mary
pitcher. Next to the pitcher there was an oval plate containing deviled eggs. Dodge picked up an egg, brought it to eye level, examined it, and then put it back down. *What's his problem?* Kay

thought. But then she remembered Dodge often had a way of staring at objects for reasons she assumed had to do with his over-developed visual relationship to the world, so she revised her diagnosis to *Probably a little drunk.*

"I guess I was out on a walk," said Kay.

"No," said Susie. "You were taking a bath. I heard you and I figured you wouldn't want to be disturbed. It was later I came and knocked."

"I thought of knocking on the door to say hello," said Elise, "but then I had a fantasy that you were having a wonderful fantasy and I didn't want to interrupt you."

"And did you?" Dodge asked Kay. She was so startled he'd addressed her, she stared at him for a moment.

"Did I what?" she asked.

"Did you have a wonderful fantasy?"

"I never have wonderful fantasies in the bath," said Ron. "I only get ideas for jokes that I then forget because I can't write them down."

"Why don't you take a pad into the bathroom?" said Kay. "That's what I do."

"Because the pad gets wet," said Ron.

"You write down jokes in the bathtub?" Elise asked Kay, puzzled.

"No," said Kay, amused that Elise seemed to know her well enough already to have caught the incongruity. "But I often get ideas, so I bring a pad and make notes."

"Kay!" said Susie. Susie drained her Bloody Mary before she spoke, her pretty throat momentarily exposed to the dying afternoon sun.

"Yes," said Kay.

"Did you have a wonderful fantasy?"

Kay laughed and sipped the last of her Bloody Mary. She was already a little tipsy despite the stingy dose she had poured. "Why should I tell you? Do you think I'm going to tell you?"

"Of course you're going to tell us," said Ron. "If you don't tell us now, you'll tell us later. If you don't tell us later, you'll tell us some other day. You're going to tell us everything, Kay, everything you never wanted to tell. We've got all of July, all of August."

"And into September through Labor Day weekend," said Elise.

Kay said to Elise: "Whose side are you on!"

"Yours," said Elise. "But it's true I'm curious about you too, but in a nice way, not like that concupiscent Ron."

"Concupiscent!" yelled Ron.

Kay looked at Dodge, who smiled at her. It was the sort of smile that seemed to convey a message. *What?*

Billy walked into the room.

"There he is," said Dodge.

"Hi, sweetie," said Susie.

"How're you doing?" said Billy. He went to the Bloody Mary table.

"Be careful with that," said Susie. "It's very strong tonight."

"Zowie," said Ron, pulling his lips back over his teeth in an eloquent rictus. "Zowie, zowie."

Billy carefully brought a deviled egg to his mouth and popped it in whole, then poured himself a glass and began to squeeze pieces of lemon into it. "Are you all getting drunk?" he asked, his back to them. He squeezed yet another piece of lemon into his drink.

"No," said Kay.

"God, these kids are puritanical," said Ron.

"Easy with the lemon," said Susie, addressing Billy. His sigh was visible in his back. Susie shook her head and shrugged, for Kay's benefit, and leaned back on the cushions, closing her eyes.

Billy was wearing a black T-shirt and perfect jeans. Kay noticed how great his body looked and then realized that Dodge, wearing almost the same thing, only looked great when he didn't have a twenty-three-year-old standing nearby. Billy squeezed another piece of lemon, perhaps the fourth or fifth, into his drink.

"He's making lemonade," said Kay.

"What?" said Elise.

Kay didn't notice Elise was addressing her.

When he finally turned around, he looked straight at Kay and she smiled at him. He came over and sat next to her. "I like your sweater," he said to Kay.

"Oh, thanks," said Kay.

"It's true," said Dodge. "It's a great purple."

"Oh," said Kay. "Thanks."

"Manganese violet," said Dodge.

"What were you talking about?" asked Billy.

"The color of Kay's sweater," said Dodge.

"Nice breasts too," said Ron, then clapped his hand over his mouth. "Oops," he added.

"You're disgusting," said Elise to Ron.

"Speak for yourself," said Ron. "Kay didn't object."

"You are disgusting," said Kay. "And drunk." She said it lightly, but in fact she thought he was fairly unpleasant.

"I'm sorry," said Ron. "I shouldn't have said that. I keep feeling it's my job to tell the truth here."

"Why?" said Susie. "You don't think we're capable of it without you?"

"We're much more honest than you are," said Elise.

"What does that mean?" asked Ron.

"You've got more to hide," said Dodge.

"Hey, you're ganging up on me," said Ron.

Kay felt Billy tense next to her. She turned toward him, and he raised his eyebrows and shook his head slightly, then got up and went back to the Bloody Mary tray.

"Why did you say that to Kay?" asked Susie.

"Because she does have nice breasts," said Ron.

"No," said Susie. "It's because she has the most natural dignity."

"Jesus," said Kay.

"And you wanted to destroy something," said Susie.

"It's true," said Elise.

"Well, of course, that's what makes it sexy," said Dodge.

"If you have terrible taste in sexiness," said Elise to Dodge. "Or if you're a sadist."

"It has nothing to do with sex," said Susie. "Only with having something ugly on the outside that matches something ugly on the inside."

"Isn't that sex?" said Elise.

"I take it back! I take it back! I take it back!" yelled Ron. "It was just boyish high spirits. I apologize." He stood and walked toward Kay, but she extended her arm, palm forward, to stop him.

"Fine," she said. "No problem."

With a flourish, he turned and retreated toward his armchair. The seat of his khakis was baggy.

"No, before I came in. What were you talking about before I came in?" said Billy, determined to bypass Ron. "Kay had a strange expression when I walked in."

They were all quiet for a moment. Billy squeezed another piece of lemon into his glass, and Susie expelled her breath. Billy walked back to Kay's bench and squeezed lemon into Kay's glass.

"Thank you. They're too drunk to remember," said Kay, eager to get away from the other parlay. She was acutely conscious of Billy standing next to her. She imagined she could feel the warmth from his body.

"Never mind," said Susie.

"Kay was about to tell us her most intimate thoughts," said Ron. "And we certainly were looking forward to hearing them."

Kay felt herself actually blushing and smiled nervously. "Why are you all picking on me tonight?" she asked.

"Ron," said Susie, "how many drinks have you had?"

"Oh, shit," said Dodge.

"What's the matter?" Susie and Elise asked simultaneously.

"No, I just remembered something," he said.

"I hate that," said Elise.

But they never got to what Dodge had forgotten. The conversation meandered away again, to Kay's great irritation. *Why am I so irritated?* she wondered.

She wished Billy would sit back down next to her.

"I'm hungry!" announced Billy, as he sat down next to Kay.

They all looked at the closed door leading to the pantry, through which they could hear, now and then, Dodie's clattering preparations.

Eventually they returned to the subject of aggressive truth-telling.

"I think it's hostile," said Susie.

"What do you mean?" said Ron. "It's useful. It's spiritually necessary. Every once in a while, you've got to lift the rock and look underneath. I'm just a guy who likes to lift that goddamn rock."

"I don't know," said Billy. "Once you lift the rock, you've got to stare at the maggots."

"Maggots are kind of interesting," said Elise.

"You're very tolerant," said Dodge to Elise.

"I have to be," said Elise.

"But then," said Ron, "the maggots slither away and bury themselves in the sand. That's the whole point of lifting the rock, then it winds up being clean underneath."

"I don't know," said Kay. "I mean, how do you know the metaphor applies to the subject of truth?"

"Well, you don't know," said Susie. "You hope."

"Maybe it's just an expression of optimism rather than an exercise in deduction."

"Well, if we don't believe in metaphors, what do we believe in?" said Dodge.

"Optimism," said Billy.

"Ah, youth," said Ron.

"Give me a break," said Billy. "That's not the way I meant it, anyway."

"How did you mean it?" asked Susie in all seriousness.

"It just seems a useful thing to believe in, as a modus operandi."

Kay opened her mouth to reply and then decided not to.

"What were you going to say?" said Billy.

"Nothing," said Kay.

"When do we eat?" said Ron.

At dinner Kay resolved not to drink any more that night. She never would have gone for this summer idea if she'd known how much these people were going to drink. They had already drunk more in this house than people did in a year in New York. Lately. Or maybe it was just Friday night and everyone was nervous and they'd calm down tomorrow.

By the time they finished the cucumber soup, the effect of the few sips of Bloody Mary had dissipated and her mind was very clear. She noticed she was the only one who ate her soup as she had been taught was the only correct way to eat soup, spoon against the side of the bowl.

She spent a long moment watching the others: not hearing their words, only watching their eyes and their mouths moving, and their gazes roving among the faces. Susie, she saw, still had some of that brittle gaiety from last Sunday and was obviously not recovered yet from Otto's death, the pain of which the return to the house must have rekindled. Elise, dressed in a predictably audacious halter top, was talking to Susie and Ron, but in fact her upper body was twisted toward Dodge. Dodge was staring up at the molding, though when she looked at him for a while he looked down and back at her and smiled, and then looked back at the molding again and then at Ron, who was talking to them, Kay noticed when she tuned in for a moment, about a problem connected with a club performance. Notwithstanding the initial agreement not to discuss work, whenever Ron's mind was at rest, it seemed to go to his problems with clubs, bookings, agents.

Ron was already exasperating her, and the summer was only starting. How would it be by August? Then she looked at Billy, who was looking at Ron as well, and she saw on his face an expression that matched the way she felt when she looked at someone without listening and realized that's how he must spend a lot of his time. She must have been within his peripheral vision, for he then shifted his gaze away a few degrees and looked fully into her eyes for the first time since they had sat down to dinner. She smiled at him and he smiled back.

Billy looked great in this light. But then Billy always looked great.

They drank a young Burgundy, which Ron had assured them with confidence would be better than the Bordeaux they'd had last week. Despite a good deal of discussion, no consensus was reached regarding this matter.

After dinner they all took their wineglasses back to the library except for Kay, who brought her coffee cup, and Billy, who was empty-handed. Susie, Elise, and Ron sat down with their glasses. Dodge stood with his wineglass over by the windows. Billy paced for a while, and then walked over to the windows, not the same ones as Dodge, Kay noticed, and stared out, hands in his pocket.

"It's crazy to stay inside when it's so lovely outside," Susie said.

"But it's buggy," said Ron.

"Should we go to the patio?" said Susie.

"Maybe we should go into town," said Elise.

"Well, that's a radical idea," said Ron.

"Maybe we should go to the patio and discuss it," said Susie.

"Yeah," said Dodge. "Let's go to the patio."

"I think I'll go for a walk," said Billy. He turned to Kay. "Want to come?"

"Okay," she said. "Anyone else?" But the others headed for the patio.

When Billy and Kay walked out alone together, she immediately felt a slight euphoria rising in her. "It's just unbelievably balmy," she said. "Isn't it?"

"Yeah," said Billy. "It's amazing out. I knew it would be great outside."

When they were about halfway down the lawn they heard a clanking sound and Kay felt a lurching fear that someone would follow them. She looked back toward the house. Susie was opening the patio windows, closing the screens. She waved. Kay waved back. Then she noticed Dodge was at another window. He waved. She waved back.

"I always feel as if I'm being observed around here," she said, in a low voice.

"It's a house full of voyeurs," said Billy.

She laughed.

It didn't seem necessary to say any more. The sky was still blue, a dusky blue so dense it was ravishing—Kay felt the beauty of it as a kind of pain—and the sun didn't seem in a hurry to set yet, but it was quite low and had dimmed enough to be looked at. Sure enough, glimmering very slightly over the lawn, there was a pale half-moon. The light was imperceptibly evolving from yellow to golden red. A solitary bee buzzed. There was no wind. The trees did not stir.

"It's like everything is waiting," said Billy.

"It's true," said Kay. "It's exactly like that. I wonder why."

They decided to walk toward the rose garden. "I feel giddy," said Billy.

"Me too," said Kay.

"I'm so glad that we're out here," said Billy.

"They should have buses to cart New Yorkers back and forth, don't you think?"

"Because they can use this, you mean?" said Billy.

"Yes," said Kay. Then she thought about all the places she'd been where summer heat only meant suffering. She tried to remember what it felt like then to end a summer day. Relief.

She tried to stay with that thought, but something about this moment, this light, this place, this feeling was too pleasurable to be denied. *I've gone a little crazy,* she thought. *A little crazy, but it's nice.*

She wondered if the others were still looking. She thought she could feel their gazes on her back. She wanted to turn around but didn't allow herself. Finally she glanced back and realized it was too distant for her to see if anyone was looking through the screen. *Who cares, anyway,* she thought. *Let them look if they want to.*

But all the while she thought this, what she really thought about was Billy. She kept trying to cast a larger portion of her mind—the part that included him—elsewhere, to the others, to work, to the visual, real world, to abstract patterns, but her mind wouldn't let go.

She was both herself and part of them, back at the house, looking at herself and Billy. How did they look, she and Billy, walking toward the rose garden? What were they saying, on the patio?

Since this started . . .

What is this? It was *this* attraction she felt. She couldn't figure out exactly when it had begun. Last weekend? No. She now realized it must have started some time in the spring. But last weekend it had burst into her consciousness with potent forward motion. At the beginning, on the ride up last Friday, for example, she kept noticing how young he was, and she now realized that a lot of the reason she had been doing that was in order not to think of him sexually.

Well, of course. I can't start to think of him sexually. It's out of the question, Kay told herself. But she already did. She tried again to put herself inside the heads of the people still at the house. *All right, it's dusk and they see these two people walking. They are very graceful together, though they don't know they are. His blondness and charm, and she has that willowy thing, doesn't she?*

Kay suddenly felt she wasn't willowy at all. It was an old compliment, something someone had told her when she was eighteen. More than twenty years ago. She remembered the saucy little nymphet, the friend of Billy's—what was her name? Nina—who had made her feel so dowdy a few months back.

Just then Billy bent toward her and she leaned a little way away from him. *What?* He straightened up and they kept walking. She wanted to ask him what he was going to say, but she made herself keep quiet.

She thought of the time she had spent in the garden alone this week, when the others were gone, how attached she had become to it, familiar with its eccentric layout. She'd studied the names of the roses on the little labels, staring at the brown earth, padded down by the gardener's fingers around the roses, or dark brown and wet when the plants had been watered or when it had rained. She remembered the moment on the bench, when she had smelled the moldy leaves around the white rosebush. She thought of herself alone, reading, or trying to read, on the stone bench, looking up now and then and becoming lost in her thoughts among the rosebushes. She had come to love the rose garden, but then she pitied herself in the rose garden. *Stop it, stop it, stop it,* she told herself. *Okay,* she thought. *Okay.*

"Look," she said. "Here is a Jack Kennedy rose."

Now she showed Billy this and that rosebush, pointed out this and that tree. It amused her to see he was not all that interested, but that he was making believe he was. Kay herself was now almost unbearably distracted by the sultry night and the strange pull between them, so she could imagine his confusion, but she could also see Billy really had no interest in roses. He was looking at her mouth. But did she accurately imagine what he felt? Maybe not. Maybe she was alone here, in the weird little bubble.

She said, "You don't have to be polite just because I'm your mother's friend."

He said, "I hope you are my friend too," echoing her formality.

She was surprised that he was able to be so direct. She said, "Yes, yes, yes, of course I'm your friend. I would be really happy to be your friend."

Then he looked at her and they smiled at each other, and it was clear that the whole thing was a lie because all they were thinking of then was something else and it didn't have to do with friendship. *Or maybe it does,* Kay told herself.

Suddenly she panicked. *What am I doing?* she thought. She walked on for a while. Had it been a long time since he'd said anything? This was too strange. She shouldn't be here. He knew it and that was why he said nothing. He didn't know what to say. He was too young to know how to handle this.

"Let's go back," she said.

"Back?" he repeated. He looked so aghast that she felt a quick jolt of pleasurable relief because he, clearly, had wanted to be with her.

"Yes," she said. "They must be waiting for us. Maybe they're going to go into town and they're waiting for us."

Billy didn't miss another beat. "Okay," he said, his expression back to normal.

But the others were still on the patio when they got back. Kay sat down. Her heart was beating. She didn't look at him. But Billy didn't sit down. He paused just inside the room and surveyed the group and said, "See you all," and went upstairs. His face was turned away slightly and Kay couldn't read him. She looked at his retreating back. Was he upset? Maybe he hadn't wanted to go back after all. When she went upstairs later she paused in front of his door. There was no light coming from underneath but she faintly heard music playing. She managed not to knock. She went to her room and got undressed and turned out the light and got into bed and lay, stiff and straight, between the sheets, like a corpse.

Saturday

She didn't make it down to breakfast, just stayed in bed and drifted back to sleep. At around eleven she got up and got dressed. She was sitting at the dressing table, very still, having slipped again into a daydream, when there was a knock at the door. She started. As a matter of fact, she had been recollecting walking up the hill, back to the house, with Billy. "Come in," she called.

It was Billy. He stuck his head in, looked at her, smiled, looked around the room. She smiled back. Would he come in?

"I have to go into the city," he said.

"Oh," she said.

"Just thought I'd say good-bye. I'll be back tonight."

"Okay," she said, with all the casualness she could muster.

"See you later," he said.

"Okay," she said.

The day seemed useless without him there. It was so hot. Too hot. What madness to get a house with no air-conditioning. In the afternoon Kay went into town with Susie to do some shopping, feeling heartsick. It was a great struggle to talk to Susie. She kept looking at Susie's face and searching for Billy's features. All her energy went toward not letting Susie know there was anything particularly wrong.

"Are you all right?" said Susie.

"Yes," said Kay. "Having a bad day today, but it's getting better."

They pulled up in front of Bruno's, the dingy grocery store they favored over the ferociously bright supermarket.

They each took a basket. "Napkins, toothpaste, watermelon," said Susie to Kay, reading from a list written inside the back cover of an old British mystery. "I'll get the ice cream."

Kay was trying to choose between luncheon and dinner-sized napkins when she saw the woman carrying a baby. It always happened when she was feeling vulnerable. Well, of course. There were babies everywhere. Everywhere. Everywhere. That was one of the absolute certitudes Kay had acquired when she began trying to get pregnant ten years ago—the worse one felt, the more likely it was that one would run into babies. Kay had innumerable opportunities to notice that this spring and early summer had produced a momentous abundance of pregnancies and babies. It was no comfort at all to know that this impression was no mere spectral dramatization of her own unrelenting and lugubrious bitterness, but a real-life statistical trend that was then endlessly reported, analyzed, and commented on in the paper and the newsweeklies.

Kay moved to the produce section, turning her head, but the woman passed by several times. She didn't have a stroller or any kind of a carrying device; she just held the baby. It was tiny. Maybe only a few weeks old. The intimacy of the woman holding the baby was wrong in the grocery store, where people were supposed to make all the little gestures of distance that make it possible for them to be comfortable in close proximity. The woman's holding the baby made Kay furious. At one point the woman stopped very near Kay. *As if to torture me, this is to torture me,* thought Kay, and tried to make herself look away but finally couldn't and brought her gaze straight up toward the baby. He was sleeping. The skin on his eyelids was so thin that all the veins glowed. Underneath, his eyes moved as if he was dreaming.

I'll just have to wait until this goes away, she said to herself, and headed out of the store, leaving her purchases in a pile on the counter. She got in the car and just sat for a long time, waiting for Susie to come out. The pain hadn't subsided so she had ridden home with it.

After they got home, Kay managed to dispel the worst of the feeling a little bit at a time, listening to the radio, showering, cutting vegetables in the kitchen with Susie and Dodie.

Billy. Billy was a sweeter thought than any she'd had in a long time. Now she understood how consoling the image of Billy was. She kept waiting for him to get back. She kept slicing another vegetable thinking, *This time he'll walk in,* but he didn't. She went upstairs and took another shower and thought, *By the time I turn the water off, he'll be here.* But she got out of the shower, dried herself, combed out her hair, dressed, went downstairs, fully expecting to find him, but he wasn't there.

She couldn't quite face the patio yet, so she went for a walk and, wanting to avoid the rose garden, headed for the pool. But there was Claudine, the little French au pair from next door. Susie had told her she could use the pool, and she now was to be found there at odd times, wearing an outrageously tiny bikini, tanning herself studiedly, to the purported amusement of everyone in the house. She was the age Kay and Susie had been when they met— that is, five years younger than Billy. At the slight noise Kay made Claudine looked up, waved a charming little wave. Kay smiled and waved back and then turned around to head back for the house. She didn't have the energy for an encounter with Claudine.

In fact, she realized on her way back to the house, she was exhausted.

Back on the patio the others talked and she said nothing. Every time she was addressed, she had to be reminded what they had been talking about.

"Where's Billy?" Dodge finally asked.

Kay nearly gasped.

"He thought he had a ride back but it fell through," said Susie. "So he'll be here tomorrow. Said to say hello."

Said to say hello? thought Kay. *To whom?*

But she said nothing. Drank a club soda, got through dinner, said, "I'm awfully tired; I don't know why," and went to bed.

At about midnight there was a knock. "Yes!" Kay called out.

It was Susie. "We're taking our lives in our hands and going to this dive, the Lickety Split," she said. "To go dancing."

"No, thanks," said Kay.

"Really?" said Susie.

"No, thanks, really, I don't know why, but I'm exhausted," said Kay. "I'm just about asleep."

Though she was still awake, several hours later, when they came back, teasing and jostling and shushing one another.

Sunday

She woke up thinking about the woman at Bruno's yesterday and the baby and the searing feeling came back. Now, though, if she thought of Billy, she could make the feeling that had to do with Billy take the place of the other. It was an interesting trick. As if the searing was there and the objects were interchangeable.

I'm thinking about him too much. Got to stop.

She lifted her head suddenly, then stood and walked to the kitchen. "Tea," she said out loud. She poured water into the kettle. And the weird yearning devil seemed to recede. But back in her room, she found herself just lying down on her bed again.

She sat up and put her feet on the floor. She sat on the side of her bed and made herself breathe deeply and kept saying to herself, *I've gone crazy.* It was clear why this was happening to her, she thought, the loneliness, the regression of the summer situation, the whole thing. It was a form of madness. Maybe she should leave. She felt a tremendous responsibility to Billy. She thought she must be a substitute for his mother, and that even what had happened between them thus far would irreparably damage him psychically. She wondered if she should leave. But going back to New York now was out of the question. She should have spent this time in Maryland with her parents, anyway. Writing another book. Mountain climbing. Studying the arts and crafts of Guatemala. Anything. What had she done? What had she done? What had she done?

She couldn't even begin to think of not thinking about this, though the only form it could take now was rage at her own stupidity. Why hadn't she seen it coming? It's because she had thought it couldn't happen to her anymore. Why hadn't she stopped it? Because she had thought she could control it. And him. Why hadn't she protected him?

She told herself, *You just have to wait until this subsides. It's like a tide coming in, this craving to make love with him, and it'll retreat. This is a much bigger wave than usual, but you don't have to drown in it. Just float around, as best you can, and if you go under every once in a while, wait until you bob back up. Just float until the tide recedes and flows away. It's just a natural phenomenon, like any other. It doesn't mean anything except the meanings you bring to it. Just let it go. Let it go.*

But she didn't want to let it go.

And, anyway, she couldn't. It's too big, this wave. It carries you.

No, not a wave. It's like a virus. It's like getting a cold from someone. Falling in love is a by-product of immunological vicissitudes.

But this pain. What about this pain? The pain is what one always gets back to. That place. Hell, really. Falling in love is the river that takes you there, back to the place of pain. The person you fall in love with is merely Charon—Charon in the glad rags of seduction, tenderness, promise, lust, rowing you across the Styx. You have to cross the Styx to get back to the pain that is the place you know. Falling in love is life's best opportunity for pain.

She lay down on the bed and breathed. She closed her eyes.

She opened them again: as soon as she closed her eyes, she saw him again, eerily present, blue eyed, smiling a little, looking cruel now, as indeed he was tormenting her. *No, I'm tormenting myself,* she thought. *I'm using him to torment myself. This is all in me. I can't possibly be attracted to this twenty-three-year-old in any kind of a meaningful way. This is ridiculous.*

She closed her eyes again and tried to count her breaths. Years ago, she had been to a zendo to learn a zazen technique and every once in a while she tried it. She kept bringing herself back to the counting, just counting from one to ten with each breath, counting each number once with the in breath and once with the out breath. It was amazing how many thoughts one can have even while count-ing. One with the in breath and she thought he was just standing in her mind like a toy figure in a toy theater, dressed in black, the the-ater in color, like the toy theater she had when she was a child maybe. One with the out breath, is he smiling, yes, he is smiling the smile she has given him lately, elusive, unreadable. Two with the in breath, and all she can see is Billy in her bed. She sees her-self in her bed with Billy. It is a little like one of those ads that has a picture inside of it of itself and a picture inside of that of itself. She sees herself with Billy and in her mind herself with Billy and in the mind of that one is herself with Billy. Two breathing out. She can imagine his mouth, if she lets herself go, and she can almost make herself feel her own mouth on his body and what it would be like to lie down with him naked, what his naked skin would feel like against hers, what the weight of him would feel like on her, what his mouth would be like on her neck and the shivers she would feel if he breathed near her ear and his smell. Three breath-ing in. No, just think of the number, three, three, three. Kay gives herself a graphics explosion. Three in every conceivable typeface. Three, the holy number. Three, the eternal triangle. Three, buckle my shoe. No, that was two. Three, three, three.

Kay dressed for dinner in a white dress she knew she looked good in, now that she had something of a tan, with white straps that crossed her back, but long after she heard the car doors slam downstairs and figured Billy had arrived and that they had all already gathered in the patio, she lay on her bed, fully dressed. When she heard footsteps on the stairs, she got up, went to the mirror, and looked at herself. She looked at herself for so long she forgot what she was doing. There was a knock on the door.

"Yah!" Kay called out.

The door opened. "Hi," said Billy. He was smiling.

She smiled back. "Hi," she said.

Susie's head appeared over Billy's shoulder. "Hungry?" said Susie.

"Yes," said Kay. "I'll be right there."

He closed the door again. She heard their steps as they traversed the landing and clattered downstairs.

She felt crazy but better. Her heart was beating hard.

At dinner, seeing Billy a few feet away from her at the table seemed to have chased away the small Billy figure inside her mind.

"What are those figures called that you have inside your mind of people you've internalized?" she asked.

"Like an imago?" Ron said. "Introjects."

"Oh, I get those," said Billy.

"Really?" said Susie.

"I think that's a symptom," said Ron.

"I get them when I'm in love," said Billy.

The others burst out laughing, all except Kay.

"And are you in love often?" said Elise.

"No," said Billy earnestly, neatly puncturing her coquettishness, Kay thought.

"What an interesting boy you are," said Elise.

"Hey," said Ron. "Be careful with the lad."

"I am careful," said Elise. "I only like to pick on those my own size."

The others went on talking, and the banter swirled away from Billy. They all sipped their wine. Susie was very merry tonight, and Kay was relieved that it had not been more difficult to hide her own discomfort. She scanned the table casually and when her glance fell across Billy, she saw that he was looking at her, brazenly, with a strange smile on his lips. Her heart leaped at the same time as a great wave of sensation between her legs.

I've gone crazy, she thought, looking at him and feeling her heart beat and her face burn. *I've just gone completely crazy.*

He kept looking at her, as if he were a bit crazy too. *Someone will see us,* she kept thinking. Finally, with the greatest possible effort, she diverted her glance.

All she could think of was touching him, when he wasn't looking at her. When he was looking at her, all she could think of was hiding that she wanted him to touch her, as if she was afraid she was going to say something out loud, right now in front of all the others.

She made a great effort to follow the conversation, to add a word or two, so she wouldn't be missed, but from sentence to sentence she would forget what they were talking about. They were all in black and white, and Billy was in color. They were two dimensional, and Billy was flesh and muscle. How golden his skin looked already. His hair was lighter. She knew he had just gone swimming and had slipped on his clothes just before dinner. He must smell faintly of chlorine, and maybe a little bit of suntan lotion. She could almost smell him. She could almost imagine what it would be like to be lying next to him in a bed, how he would feel, naked, what it would feel like to have her lips on his cheek, his neck, his shoulder.

It didn't take long after dinner. While the others chatted, Billy proposed checking out the rose garden at just the right moment in the right tone; Kay assented.

Silently, they walked to the rose garden. She had stopped thinking of making love because being near him now was so exciting that she didn't even have enough concentration left for her fantasies. Instead, her mind fragmented, and she felt as if she herself were dispersed into the summer air.

Though the light had begun dying, it was insistent. The lawn was an extravagant dark green satin. The breeze was laden with scents of blooms. There was very little noise, only the clickety-clickety of a frog somewhere, and one lone bird nearby whose song was a triple chirp and a glissando, repeated at odd intervals. But it all seemed magnified and eerily present, not separate from her.

She thought about how expertly he had managed their exit from the house. The observation of this aspect of his character actually caused her to forget, at last, about the age difference. He was at least as clever as she. Perhaps she'd been patronizing, she suddenly realized. She thought, *How calculated he is.* He was much more so-phisticated than she'd imagined. Maybe it was he all along who had been in control, who was manipulating her. No. Well, maybe. No.

She thought of the last conversation they'd had in the rose garden.

"You know, I meant that," she now told him. She felt like an imbecile, listening to herself trying to sound reasonable. She couldn't make contact with the right words. She felt like a musician who had lost her place in the score and knows she can vamp only a measure or two longer. "You don't have to be my friend. We've known each other all your life and..." She stopped. She'd forgotten what she was going to say.

He said nothing for a moment. Then he said, "Kay."

"What?" she said, and turned toward him.

"Don't be coy."

She laughed. "My god," she said. "How precocious you are."

They were almost at the bottom of the lawn. She had put a mint in her mouth just as they had walked out of the house, a big bon-bon that took a long time to melt if you didn't bite into it, and presently she felt giddy again, with the taste of mint and the light and the smell of the grass and the way the sky looked.

Now, music wafted down toward them. They both stopped at the same time and then looked at each other and laughed. It was too perfect. Billy turned back to the house for a moment, as if to hear better.

"Debussy," he said. "It's one of Susie's CDs."

"It's like a sound track for this movie," said Kay.

"It's often like that, isn't it?" said Billy.

"Yes," said Kay. "The patio seems a million miles away, doesn't it?" *Why am I uttering such platitudes?* she wondered.

"It's the psychological distance," said Billy.

"I know what you mean," said Kay.

She was aware of the others watching them, just like the other night, but this time she suspected he was aware of them too. She felt much more self-conscious than she had the other evening. She was afraid of looking at him, but she saw him in her peripheral vision. *How graceful he is.* She liked his arms, his neck, his eyelids. She wished she could touch him.

Then, abruptly, everything around them seemed ordinary. Everything was just what it was, not all that interesting, flat, the deep green lawn, the deep blue sky, and she found herself wishing it would all explode.

She suddenly knew he would be disappointed by the rose garden, had hid his disappointment last time and really had no interest at all, was just being nice to this friend of his mother's, but was bored, eager to get away, even mocking perhaps. Yes, of course he thought the rose garden pathetic and her admiration of it just a little amusing, pitiable maybe.

The rose garden was always better in memory. In reality it was just a hokey and badly tended garden, an idea that was not well realized, generated by an outmoded aesthetic.

"I don't know about this rose garden, actually," she said to Billy, as they entered through the trimmed barberry bush gate. "It's a little mangy."

"Well, yes and no," said Billy.

"But more no than yes," said Kay. *There, I knew it,* she thought. *He really didn't think much of it.* She felt more and more upset. The rose garden she knew was too powerful a metaphor, too obvious, sentimental. *Well, then, but why don't I go back up to the house?* But she knew very well that was impossible for her. They set to walking up and down the garden's neat alleys.

"Do you know about aerobic deficit?" Billy asked.

"No," she said, relieved that some other subject had been introduced. She hoped he would just keep going. "What's that?"

"Well, there are certain exercises, like say, climbing stairs, that make your heart go faster, but not while you're doing them. Like you're climbing and climbing, and you don't feel anything different, but then after you stop your heart beats like crazy."

Kay waited.

"It's sort of like this rose garden," said Billy. "While you're here it can seem kind of flat as an experience. And then it's only later that you realize that it's actually very strange."

"That's true," said Kay, feeling suddenly better. "It's funny, that's what it's like when you're in a place where there's a war too."

"What do you mean?" said Billy.

"Well, say you're taking a drive on a road on which you know that mines have been set. You're not thinking about it. You're thinking about where you're going and if you have enough gas to get there and how hot it is and what the driver is telling you about his wife and children, and you feel completely normal and maybe even bored with how long the drive takes. It's not until you get to your destination that you feel this incredible retroactive fear, and this exhilaration that you made it."

"Summer is sort of like that," said Billy. "It's one of those things that you don't really know is happening until it's over. As if it were a strange form of locomotion."

"Yes," said Kay. "Summer is like a cruise."

"Summer," said Billy in a mock-declamatory voice he sometimes used for humor, "is like nature letting her breath out."

Kay laughed. "That's a very funny metaphor," she said.

"Thanks," he said.

"Do you think in metaphors a lot?" she asked.

"What is this, fourth grade?" he asked.

She laughed again. "No, I'm sorry if I sound patronizing."

"Well," he said. "What do you mean, 'think in metaphors'?"

"Well, I don't know," she said. "I mean, I think in metaphors a lot. For instance, I get a lot of animal metaphors. Like yesterday my mind was a jungle with all the animals vigorous and ready to spring on each other, and by last night it was a pride of lions, scruffy and tired, and I just couldn't get them up. They were sleepy and just kept stretching and so forth but then lying back down, even when I threw them a carcass."

Billy laughed. "That's like Susie," he said. "Susie does that."

"Yes," said Kay. *Susie?* She tried to decide whether to be upset or not. *Well, this is so crazy . . .* Who knew whether to be upset anymore, and what to be upset by.

"Autumn is a leaf screaming," said Billy.

"Autumn is a daydream," said Kay.

"Autumn is a baseball game," said Billy.

"Spring is when the moon faints with pleasure," said Kay.

"Spring is a guitar solo," said Billy.

"What do you see when you talk?" said Kay.

"I don't know," said Billy. "What do you see?"

"Words and pictures," said Kay.

"I don't know. I guess I just see colors. I always know I'm okay if I see a field of blue."

They had nearly completed their tour of the garden's allées. In this patch where the ground was perhaps richer, the roses were particularly gorgeous.

"Aren't they heartbreaking?" Kay said.

"Why?" said Billy.

Doesn't he know? Maybe he's toying with me. "Oh, because they're just past their bloom," Kay said. The earth was darker around the roses. There were red ones and white ones. When she walked to the garden by herself, she always came to this spot. Each morning the soil around these roses was raked and groomed with, she thought, special care, so that every evening you could actually see which petals had fallen that very afternoon.

"Isn't this ridiculous?" said Kay.

"Why?" said Billy.

"Well, talk about metaphors," said Kay. "How can you be here and not think about the death of beauty?"

"I hadn't thought of it," said Billy.

"No, well, you don't have to," said Kay.

"Why do you have to?" said Billy.

"I don't have a choice," said Kay.

Billy leaned over a very full white rose. "It smells wonderful," he said.

"I don't think they smell," said Kay. "I've tried smelling a hundred of them. It's upsetting because I'm pretty sure roses used to smell."

He pushes aside the prickly barberry bush. She bent down and smelled a rose.

"No, nothing," she said. "Some perverse gardener planted only roses with no smell. It's just like this garden—everything about it is disappointing, close-up. The statues are trite when you examine them closely. All that vulgar marble with the picturesque moss growing out of the cracks. That absurd fountain with the dopey peeing naiads."

"They're not naiads, I don't think," said Billy mildly. "Aren't they mermaids or something? No, they have legs. Sea nymphs."

Kay laughed.

Billy crouched by the roses, put his face into first the one she smelled a moment ago, a very red rose, and then the white one he had smelled earlier.

"Here, Kay, try this one," he said. "You'd picked the wrong one. Try this white one here."

She approached the white rose and, like him, put her face in it, felt the petals against her cheeks. It did have a faint odor, she now thought, maybe, a faint wonderful odor. She rubbed her face just a little against the petals. She straightened up. They resumed walking.

"Oh, I think of it as ridiculous," said Billy.

"What?" said Kay.

"The garden," said Billy. "And the house too. To say nothing of the whole crew here. And Susie's hostess thing. It's ridiculous, this whole summer, this house, everything."

She felt crestfallen, as if by implication—just as she had expected—he was really telling her he found her ridiculous too. But Billy smiled at her. She smiled back. They both stood silently for a moment, as if they'd both forgotten what he had been saying.

"Ridiculous," he said, but still smiling, in that way he had of smiling at her. "Especially this garden. But instead of thinking of it as a bad version of something great, I think of it as a perfect version of something ridiculous."

Kay struggled for thoughts and words. What had they been talking about? "Well, but there's such a thing as real beauty too," she said. She meant to say something about their first night here, and Helen of Troy, grappled to verbalize her recollection, but failed.

She had now completely forgotten their age difference, which had so obsessed her all week. If she had thought of it, she would have said it was the least important thing here, anyway. Their bodies were the densest entities in the garden, where all was perfumed summer air and evaporating trees and bushes and petals.

"Let's go sit down," said Billy, pointing to a stone seat.

"Okay," said Kay.

"It reminds me of some other garden," said Billy as they settled into the semicircular limestone bench.

"Well, that's the thing about gardens is that they always remind you of another garden."

He got a pack of Camels out of his back pocket. She restrained the urge to say anything. (Really? Now he was smoking Camels?) She noticed he smoked holding the cigarette between the thumb and the index finger, and she was touched by the naive imitation of the gesture of movie hipsters.

"It's just not the right time," he said, "for me to stop smoking."

"Ah," she said. She tried to think what she should say to him about his smoking but couldn't figure it out.

"Why did you go to Panama?" he asked. "Originally? I mean, we used to see you all the time and then you disappeared."

"I had an article to do there once and I . . ."

"Yeah, but why Panama?"

"Actually, it was just to leave town," said Kay.

"Really, why?" asked Billy.

Kay laughed. "I don't believe this," she said.

"I thought you said you wanted to be friends," said Billy.

"Let's walk some more," she said.

They got up, began to stroll back toward the gate. "I may tell you," she said, "when we know each other much better. It's a long story. We'd have to go out for drinks, we'd have to know each other better. I'd have to tell it to you in parts."

"Maybe we could save a lot of time," said Billy. "Just give me a hint, okay?"

Kay laughed again. "No," she said. "Absolutely not. God, I haven't laughed this much in a very long time."

"You used to laugh more," said Billy.

"What about you?" she said. "I see you looking rather sullen around the house. I never know what that means."

"Sullen?" he said.

"Well, expressionless," she said. "I never know what you notice or what you're feeling."

"Oh, I notice everything," he said. "Everything."

She laughed again.

"You're so charming and glamorous. Susie is always trying to gather these people around her who are charming, but you're the real thing."

Kay laughed again. "I don't know," she said. "I think maybe I'm not that charming, but I'm tremendously attracted to charming people and to charming situations." *Am I laughing too much?* she wondered.

"That's interesting," said Billy.

"I'm sure that's one of the reasons why Susie and I became friends and stayed friends all these years," said Kay, "is because I've always been really receptive to her charm. And, you know, if you're interested in charm and in what constitutes receptivity to charm, Susie is a world-class specimen." *Why am I telling him this? Am I trying to kill it? Maybe, yes.* "Though Susie collects charming people and I prefer charming moments," she told him. "Charming moments. That's what I love the most."

"Like this one?" said Billy.

"Yes," said Kay, feeling herself blush. "Like this one."

"You're just using me for the charming moments I might provide," said Billy laughing.

Kay laughed. "Yes," she said. "Exactly." What really preoccupied her was trying not to touch him. The light had waned. She could no longer see the color of his skin, but she knew it was golden. She wanted to touch him. She wanted to so much that her mind was hurled into nature again. She was suddenly suffused with the feeling of the light, this dim luminosity in which he seemed to gleam. Was it with the feeling of the light? *Yes, that must be what it is,* she thought. Something filled her. Perhaps only adrenaline. And then she felt sad again. The light. The dusk. The dying light, the dying roses, the dying everything. The dying sky. "I'm assailed by metaphors," she said.

"It's really beautiful," he said.

"Let's go back," she said. "I'm sick of gorgeous sunsets."

"I know what you mean," said Billy.

They walked out through the gate again.

"There," she said. "That's better."

"Why did you go to Panama?" he said.

"Because I was pregnant and my baby died," she said.

He said nothing. They walked on. He closed the stone gate after them; they started walking up the hill of the lawn. *Why does he say nothing?* she wondered.

"I shouldn't have told you that," she said.

He was silent, still. Then he said, "And what about Frederic?" It was her former lover. Neither Susie nor Billy, both of whom had met Frederic a number a times, ever mentioned him anymore.

"What about Frederic?" said Kay.

Billy asked, "Did you still love him?"

Kay said, "I hated him."

Kay felt the black fluid of anxiety fill her. The last of the mint melted on her tongue. The mint had been in her mouth the whole time, and whenever she thought about this evening later, there would be the taste of mint.

"Let's go back," he said.

"Okay," said Kay.

They walked into the house together, but Kay went straight to the bathroom, without saying anything to him.

When she got to the patio they were all gone. The Bloody Mary pitcher was empty. She found them—all but Billy—sitting on the lawn that sloped down to the river. Facing west, the clouds' edges were still outlined in deep pink above a reddened horizon. After a bit the sky so brightened she wondered the others didn't gasp and turn in surprise. There emerged luminous bands of gold, orange, scarlet. Invisible birds were momentarily loud. Then a pale violet erased everything by minute increments, became more dense, melted into the remaining clouds, until the sky was uniformly dusky. When had the birds quieted? Frogs and crickets had been waiting for their cue.

The others still talked and laughed while heading back to the house. They didn't turn a light on as if they hadn't noticed that night had fallen. Kay was grateful for the darkness. She turned away from the disappearing garden and poured a vodka and soda, standing by an old print that she pretended to examine, though she couldn't possibly have made it out. Then she sat down with the others but found herself unable to concentrate on the conversation. She was thinking that Billy was full of the desire for power. He had wrenched her secret from her and then had taken control of the relationship.

She poured another vodka and went back upstairs to her room. She lay down on the bed and put the vodka on the night table, decided not to drink it.

Then she became filled with darkness. Darkness and, of course, roses. She thought it wasn't just because of the death of beauty; it was also because even this young boy could make her feel awful, and it was obvious that in all this time she had learned nothing.

She thought back to the rose garden and she felt a terrible pain, a terrible sadness for herself, because she would never be without a past again, without this terrible past, too womanly, that killed the girl she was. All this time she spent in foreign places fleeing and working and transforming herself into someone who is obstinately in forward motion, and she had to come back here to this rose garden to be violated by this young boy in the course of some banal flirtation. The sting of the humiliation mixed with her lost baby, her lost baby, her lost baby. She took several sips of the vodka. Got up. Went to the bathroom and washed up. Looked at herself in the mirror only briefly when she cleaned her skin with a cotton pad.

She lay down again and picked up a book of essays that had been on the floor next to the bed, but could not read. Finally her eyes closed and she glided. A moment later something in a dream startled her into enough wakefulness to realize she had been falling asleep. She turned off the light.

She woke up again two hours later. She remembered herself sitting on the stone bench, throwing back her head and laughing, and she became filled again with the darkness of humiliation and sadness for herself. Not because she was unhappy now but because she'd been merry then, for a moment. All in the desire to be desired. Why had she allowed herself to be so vulnerable? How powerful it is, how much it binds you to life, the desire to be desired.

She thought of the rose garden again and, actually, that seemed even worse than thinking about "the accident." Definitely worse. She saw the woman and the young man. She knew in a way it was a beautiful scene. Very charming. She had this terrible feeling, too much sweetness, too many roses, too much beauty, too much melancholy, the weight of years and flesh and of a lifetime of using charm to cheat despair of its due. The uselessness of it.

DODGE

Friday

Late Friday night Dodge was so exhausted on the drive up that he kept worrying he would fall asleep at the wheel. He had crashed into a stone post in precisely that way, once, in his twenties and had woken up with just the right number of seconds to spare to swerve the wheel a few inches, avoiding meeting the post with his own skull. He had gotten away with only some broken ribs. For a few years he had become a more cautious driver, but then the recollection began fading. Well, at least he was used to functioning while extremely tired and recognized that very small interstice between wakefulness and sleep when you can still catch yourself. It was a place in his mind he liked, in a way, except for then having to wrench himself back to wakefulness.

It was raining and cold for July. He'd left the bike in the country and was driving the van. The truth is that he had thought Ron could take the wheel if he really needed to sleep, but Ron had called at the last moment and said he had some problems in town and would see him at the house in the morning.

"But you're coming, right?" Dodge had asked.

"You bet, pal," Ron had answered. "I wouldn't dream of leaving you alone with those babes for an entire weekend. Fox and the hen-house and so forth."

"Yeah, some fox," Dodge had said. "The fox has been getting gum surgery. The fox would choke on the feathers."

"Well," Ron had said, "but what a way for a fox to go, choking on feathers. Sounds good to me."

In the car now he felt a dim discomfort that, if he had had those powers of analysis, he would have known corresponded to missing Ron's company on the ride up to the house. But it was even more of a struggle than usual to get any clear space in his thinking: he was preoccupied by the pain in his mouth. He'd had a curettage this morning and was rinsing with warm salt water every few hours and could taste the salt on his tongue still. Thinking of his mouth re-minded him that he wanted a cigarette, but he hadn't smoked in over a year. There were wads of plastic molded around his gums, over where the stitches were. Three thousand five hundred dollars is what the procedure had cost. Three thousand five hundred dol-lars! Incredible.

He was preparing for a show, and he didn't know whether it was the work or the business work, talking to his dealers, that was so draining. He was thinking he shouldn't have agreed to do the in-terview for *Art in America,* which was turning out to take so much time. But the truth was he had been insane, absolutely insane, to agree to come up on weekends. He'd even said that when Susie had called. "I'd be insane," he had told Susie, "with this show opening in September."

"Oh, come on," Susie had said. And that's all it had taken. He'd always had an impulse problem.

Talking Susie into agreeing to have Ron Reiser there, however, was worse than insane. But never mind, never mind, never mind.

Oh, really, Ron wasn't so bad. He felt easy in Ron's company. Somehow their differences had solidified their friendship, as if it was their differences, preventing any real risk of intimacy, that made them compatible.

They'd been friends since they were in primary school together in the West Village. Dodge's father had been out of a job most of the time, his mother a graphic artist, when she could get the work, while Ron's father was a dentist and his mother the sort of art lover who went to happenings and collected Warhols and Rosenquists and Stellas. Ron had three older brothers who were jocks, and that was a little hard because all three picked on Ron. In the sixties both Ron and Dodge fancied themselves guitar players, but they would usually have to go to Dodge's house to play, away from the sneers and gross jokes. At Dodge's house, though, the refrigerator's contents were on the sparse side.

Ron dropped the guitar after a couple of years. (Dodge still played sometimes, usually when he was in bed with someone new.) Also, Dodge had started painting and Ron had started drinking. They became more and more different from one another when Ron's family moved to Westchester. Ron played basketball, got taller and stronger fast, and eventually filled out ectomorphically. Dodge was lanky and cool. Girls liked him.

When they graduated, Ron often came along with Dodge and his friends, to the bars and the parties and the very late-night dinners. For Dodge, it was interesting to have Ron there, sort of like a spy from another subculture—except that he wasn't really incognito, since he stuck out like a sore thumb. But when he and Dodge were alone together, Ron would always have a very accurate take on what had been going on and would comment at length, quite instructively, about the narcissistic self-indulgence that Dodge took for granted, the destructive drug use, the hypocrisy of hip, and the crassness of the manipulation inherent in all the seduction that went on. Dodge thought it kept him honest, in a way, to have Ron as a friend. He tended not to frequent Ron's friends, who were usually go-for-the-jugular attorneys and business types. Then Ron got married to someone he had met in college. Eleanor. Dodge would go there for dinner and find himself with his hand inside Eleanor's thigh under the table. He didn't even know how it happened. How had it started?

After Ron and Eleanor broke up, Dodge continued to see Eleanor for a while, which was odd because then when he'd see

Ron, he'd have to hear from Ron about what a bitch, a horrible bitch, Eleanor was, or what a total sweetheart Eleanor was and what a total idiot Ron had been, depending on Ron's mood. None of what Ron said matched the Eleanor he knew, who just wanted to fuck all the time.

Eleanor had moved to somewhere. Sweden? Iceland? Something like that. Or maybe Minnesota.

At some point not too long after that whole thing, Ron had dropped out of law school and decided to become a stand-up comic, to the horror of his family until he began making real money.

In the late seventies Ron's rich friends had begun to collect art, and Ron did them the favor of bringing them around to Dodge's studio. There were times in the early days when Dodge had so little money that he had to borrow ten dollars from a neighbor to buy lightbulbs for the loft when Ron's friends came to visit. He had been making do with a tensor light by the bed and lighting only the canvas he was working on. During the obligatory dinners that surrounded a transaction (which were as important an investment for Ron's friends as the art they would bring home), Dodge not only got well fed but discovered that the rich men were often interesting to talk to, as long as they were on their own territory.

Dodge had almost no other close friends of his own, though there was a crowd in which he circulated. Over the years he had intense albeit dishonest relationships with numerous women. At any one time there were usually several of them (though, amazingly, they each seemed totally vivid to him). His sentimental life and extraordinary sexual activity left him exhausted and with little time for male friendships, except for Ron, who refused to stay away. Dodge's relationships with women (there seemed to be an endless supply of them) continued through his first marriage, but ended with the divorce, six months later. It wasn't that the supply dried up; it's that he realized he had become too tired to work. It hadn't helped his second marriage that he had been faithful, almost totally, for the eight years it lasted.

Sometimes he wondered why work had become so much more interesting than sex. But about the latter, it had become increasingly obvious that it was too easy. There was a time when Dodge was amazed at every conquest. Later, the more notorious he became, the more the assumption of success came to seem natural and came to justify, for him, the ease of the seduction. And also the more impossible it came to seem that any of these willing, lovely or unlovely creatures would understand him enough to be able to draw out of him what he couldn't articulate about himself. He'd given up and was now relying solely on the paintings for mirrors. The final result was that there was no more authentic conquest in a seduction. On the contrary, each time the person he appeared to be was deemed desirable, the internal self he imagined as his "I" felt more starved. This was something Dodge had long known and completely took for granted, except when he forgot it.

He stretched his neck, which was beginning to hurt. He was tired of his own company. He wished Ron had come along.

Emma. How he missed Emma. He realized he was beginning to feel about Emma as he used to feel about his mother. This terrible yearning, this emptiness without her. So strange. It was so painful not watching her grow up.

It was nearly 3 A.M. It always seemed to take longer to get going out of New York than he thought. What had delayed him so much this evening? He actually could have gotten out at around eight or nine, but there was always one more call to make, some papers to put away. He couldn't bear to leave any disorder when he went out of town. Everything had to be put away, corners aligned, right angles in a calculated relationship to one another, every chair in the loft, every frame, every index card planted to square exactly with its assigned vista.

Few of his friends suspected how much time he spent straightening up. They just noticed he was late, always late. He was always late, always guilty for being late, and he suspected with dread that it might often cause anger in other people, especially women. He couldn't help it—there was always one more thing to do that just had to be done. He'd had some therapy a few years ago and they'd worked on that, whether it wasn't often sabotage. Sweet face, small compact body, but big breasts. Unthreatening and warm. He had really liked his therapist.

Well, at least he'd beat the traffic, he thought. He liked it, in a way, the loneliness of the dark wet road—he didn't even have the radio on so that he could feel it in silence—but he was almost too tired to enjoy it, unless he got into enjoying the tiredness, which at least had the advantage of dulling the sharp twinges of apprehension that arose periodically throughout the day, that had to be ignored, that called for something, anything, that he had learned not to listen to.

He thought of Susie as she had looked in bed the last time they had had sex, her eyes wide open, her expression strangely still. He had a highly developed capacity to recall such tableaux. Susie. Was that ten years ago? He was losing track of the time line of his own life. It was like looking through a Telephoto lens and seeing objects that had great distance between them squashed against one another.

He thought of the painting he was working on, a large canvas that wasn't coming yet.

He couldn't remember not being exhausted—at least during the day and early evening. As a kid he was always falling asleep in school because he could never sleep at night. He'd listen to his parents fight; later he'd listen for sounds in his mother's room, when she had men over, but also sometimes just the wordless booming of her television. Sometimes she had allowed him to go to sleep in her bed—when he was little there was his father on the other side of her and then there was no one on the other side of her—and he would lie with his face buried near her flank, eyes closed, not sleeping but not moving, so that she would think he was asleep, while she watched the *Jack Paar Show*. Later he'd listened to records in his own bed, the same record all night, often. Ray Charles: "I gambled on your love, baby, and got a losing hand."

Charlie Mingus in Amsterdam, 1964. Or to all-night radio and, with his first girlfriend, when he was an adolescent, he'd often spend all night on the phone. He didn't remember anymore what they used to talk about.

When he began to paint seriously in his late teens, it was at night that he did most of his work, and in his twenties he went through a period when he barely ever came out during the day. Drugs were made for night, anyway, and the kind of sex he liked, with all those barely postpubescent muses. Dodge liked to say he'd just about never slept in the sixties, from pure anxiety and thrill seeking, and in the seventies there were enough drugs never to sleep.

Maybe that was part of why he'd married Christine, to sleep. In a way. In more than one way. No, the truth was he didn't know why he'd married Christine. She was just the one who had been able to convince him. Or a combination: she really wanted to get married and he must have had some thought of rest. He remembered that before they were married, there were times when he'd spend the entire night in bed with her, asleep or not. Sometimes she slept and he read. But when they were married, it didn't take long for the other thing to resume. At first it was because he wanted to paint— it seemed like the only time he could paint. And then if he painted, he had to drink sometimes, so he'd go down to the White Horse, later the Odeon. And then, of course, in those days if you were in the bars, there were the girls again.

Maybe in these days too, actually. It just didn't seem all that interesting anymore. Well, there were still the girls, and they were still pretty and still often managed to wear incredibly short skirts and have those legs—where did they breed those girls to hang out in galleries and bars, those girls with those legs?—but somehow it just didn't seem tempting anymore. He kept thinking it should be tempting but it wasn't. It was funny, because it used to be. Maybe it was that everybody used to drink so much. *Was I thinking about this just a moment ago?* wondered Dodge.

Emma.

At some point being a Casanova—a label he had never interpreted as pejorative—had turned into being a sexual compulsive.
Either way, Casanova without a date was a pretty dismal spectacle.
It had once seemed a good thing, or at least an amusing thing, in
those days, to be a stud. Not that Dodge had ever thought of himself as a stud. Too feminine for that. Too aware of his own despera-
tion. His innumerable sexual conquests had been an absolute
psychological necessity. That he knew for sure. It was just galling,
now that he had given up all the screwing around, to constantly return to it in his thoughts. He wished he could forget it. What was
the point? He felt as if his mind kept insisting on grappling with a
puzzle it could never solve.

But now sexual conquest seemed only a somewhat comical
thing. Or else a gay thing. It seemed to Dodge lately as if many of
the gay painters he knew were the ones who would have been the
studs of the sixties and seventies. It was hard to tell, hard to imagine what it would have been like if so many people hadn't died or
gone elsewhere.

Well, most of the ones who were left had wives now and families. He had a wife and a family in a way, of course, even if he
wasn't living with them. Though it occurred to him that this view
of what a family was would certainly make Christine mad. She was
still mad at him. She'd been mad for a long time, and these days
whenever he saw her he felt that most of her energy was directed
at not expressing just how mad she was. She was very ostentatiously not sharing her anger with seven-year-old Emma, but that
would come too, thought Dodge, and a heaviness fell over his
heart.

Thinking about how many people, how many women were mad
at him gave him a strange kind of buzzy energy, a sort of white
noise at the center of his consciousness that made him want to
move on fast, as if he were in a cloud of white fruit flies. He pressed
his foot on the accelerator.

It was better than it used to be. The show, he thought, might be
more or less under control. The important part, anyway, since he

thought the work was all right. The work was maybe pretty good or really good. Though who knew how it would go over. With increasing frequency lately, the critics were using the adjective "major." It scared him, because he knew it was a signal for the attack to come. When would it come?

Well, he was doing the best he could, these days. And despite the ridiculous amount of time he wound up spending at this house in the country, he thought it was a good idea. That is, the idea of sparing each weekend seemed a prodigious expenditure of time— and was in fact something he hadn't done in years—but he thought it was the right thing to do now, and he felt less exhausted and pressured and insane than he usually did at this point, just about six weeks before a show.

The Taconic ended and now he coursed along country roads, very fast, the curves reviving him somewhat. Enough, he hoped. Yes, there was a pleasure in the speed, and a relief. The fatigue was beginning to become painful, and yet, he thought, this was a good moment. This, right now. He felt okay, yes, okay, just now for this moment. He liked it in this dark and rainy solitude, with only the white divider line to cheer up the glistening road, driving up to the house and thinking about the women there and that they weren't mad at him, or at least not yet, maybe wouldn't be. He saw them now in front of him as if the windshield were a television, Susie and Kay and Elise. They were delicious to look at, like cats. Or like those beautiful paper dolls he'd loved so much when he was a kid. Meanwhile, the road gleamed. The trees sped by. It was all right here in this car, for the moment.

Saturday

Dodge and Susie had dragged chaise longues to the lawn on Saturday morning after breakfast. The air was fresh with that kind of sweetness and fragrance that makes you feel your mind is clear. It was still cool and they had brought out blankets, but Susie had pushed hers away when the sun had come out. In the distance the pines looked black, the lawn a very saturated light green. Susie's body, Dodge noticed, was exactly half in the sun. He wished he had his hand on her bare belly where it would feel half cool, half warm.

"What are you thinking about?" Susie asked Dodge.

"I love the way those trees are all the same height," said Dodge, pointing to the semicircle of pines several hundred feet away.

"Yes, it is amazing," said Susie. "And they're so lush too."

"All the gold in the leaves," said Dodge.

"It's funny," said Susie, "because I didn't see the gold until you mentioned it and now that's all I see—that dappled thing."

"I dreamed about you wearing red shoes," said Dodge to Susie.

"What else was I wearing?" said Susie. Dodge had always loved the way Susie dressed. Now she was wearing a white bandeau across her chest and little short shorts. Her skin must be very smooth to the touch. Her legs were glistening a little, with suntan oil. Very faintly, under the smooth skin, he could see a few broken blood vessels, and he wished he could follow the outlines with a finger. Women's imperfections are what makes them irresistible, perhaps especially because they're so desperate to get rid of them, he felt. He loved her feet, her narrow toes, the nails painted a surprising pink. A blue vein bisecting the ankle.

"What was I wearing," asked Susie, "in your dream about the red shoes?"

"Nothing," said Dodge. "You were sitting on your dressing table in your room, in front of the mirror. I was standing at the door. You were sitting or sort of half reclining on your dresser and wearing a pair of high-heeled red shoes."

"Like a pinup sort of," said Susie.

"Yes," said Dodge. "Exactly. Because it was kind of innocent in a way. Or playful, say. For instance, you were naked but I couldn't see any pubic hair because of the position of your legs."

"Airbrushed," said Susie.

"Yes, airbrushed," said Dodge.

"I like the idea of airbrushing. I wish I could airbrush my life," said Susie.

"Your life in a way is airbrushed, at least from the outside," said Dodge.

"What do you mean?" asked Susie.

"Well, I think it's one of the things that draws people to you. Your life seems so playful, as if there isn't any pubic hair in it."

"I don't know what I think about that," said Susie.

"No," said Dodge. "I don't either. But it's a good thing. It's a kind of magic thing. Sort of like star quality, I guess."

"I mean," said Susie, "it's not true. I have a lot of muddiness and murkiness that's not at all like the magic cartoon that people imagine about my life. I have a cap on my front tooth."

"I have gum problems," said Dodge.

"Do you floss?" asked Susie.

"No, but I've been trying to use that little brush."

"Anyway," said Susie. She leaned back and closed her eyes. "Believe me there's plenty of grimness in my life."

"And pubic hair," said Dodge.

"Yes," said Susie. There was silence for a moment. Dodge thought about being in a bed with Susie. Then he thought that she was probably thinking about being in a bed with him, and that she must know he was thinking that she was thinking about being in a bed with him.

"Are you still upset about your dog?" said Dodge.

"Yes," said Susie. "Very." She kept her eyes closed. "I think about him a lot."

Does her voice sound stern? I shouldn't have brought up the dog, he thought. "Wouldn't you like to get another dog?"

"No."

Two crows waddled daintily across the lawn.

"I miss having sex with you," said Dodge.

"I do too in a way," said Susie.

"In a way?" said Dodge. "Oh, thanks."

"Well, for exactly the reason that you say to me that you miss having sex with me."

"What do you mean?" said Dodge.

"Well, you could have said 'I miss making love to you' or 'I miss being in a bed with you,' or any number of things. Missing sex leaves me out of the equation."

"That's ridiculous. It isn't really that at all," said Dodge. "You know that it's just because I can't speak."

"No, it's not just that," said Susie. "I don't think it's just that."

"But it's true for you too," said Dodge. "You wouldn't want me to say any of those other things to you. They would make you too uncomfortable."

"Why? Do you want to say them to me?" asked Susie.

"I don't know," said Dodge.

"I don't think it was good for us, that kind of sex," said Susie.

"Speak for yourself," said Dodge.

"I don't think it was good for you," said Susie.

"That's not true," said Dodge. "It's just there are things I don't say."

"I think there are things you don't feel."

"Well, but you don't feel them either," said Dodge.

"Maybe not," agreed Susie. "I don't know anymore. I feel a weird numbness. I don't even know what to do about it."

"It's too complicated," said Dodge. "Part of it is just getting through having a marriage break up. It takes a long time for the smoke to clear."

"Yes, but you know when women feel numb, it's the equivalent of a man at his most passionate."

"What do you mean?" said Dodge, defensively.

"Yeah, it's like being out in the sun. To get a tan, a man has to hang around for like ten hours on the cliff side, his face turned toward the feeble winter sun. Whereas we're always in the tropics. Even with sunblocks we get blisters."

"I don't think it's true of all men," said Dodge. "It's not true of me."

"That's what all men say," said Susie.

"Did I do something to make you mad?" said Dodge.

"I had an erotic dream about you too," said Susie.

"You did?" said Dodge.

"Yes," said Susie. "We were slow dancing." She broke off and smiled.

"Are you making this up?" he asked.

"No," she said. "Absolutely not."

"Okay," he said. "Go on."

"No," she said. "You know, I don't think I will." She opened her eyes and smiled at him. The morning sunlight was kind to her, and the whiteness of her skin made her look unnatural and milky in an attractive way. Her hair seemed bright gold.

"Come on," he said.

"No," she said. "Maybe some other time. For the moment I think I'll save it."

"What a tease," he said. "Unbelievable."

She closed her eyes and smiled and remained still for a moment to feel the sun on her face. He looked at her. *Nice*, he thought. Her eyes were crinkled shut, her mouth a little twisted, and he did find he felt like kissing her. But he wasn't absolutely sure that he really was tempted. Maybe he just every once in a while seduced out of pure habit. He realized that if he had been a more moral person, he would have called this very grim. But he was too far gone.

In the end, he was better off in his studio, working.

He touched her hair with his fingertips. He missed being really excited. That was it. This little bit of a thrill just reminded him of the rest, before authentic arousal had become so elusive. In a way, what was most exciting about this particular moment, for instance, was not so much genuine sexual desire; it was more what it felt like to see Susie without being seen, the illicit pleasure of it because it had gone on long beyond when it would have been politely predictable to look away. There was something exciting about the knowledge that she could open her eyes at any moment and catch him still looking at her.

She opened her eyes and looked into his and smiled. "Do you ever miss Christine?" she asked.

"No, not really," he said. "Or hardly. I miss being married

sometimes. I miss coming home and having someone there. But we had such a hard time toward the end that I don't miss that at all."

She closed her eyes and turned her face toward the sun again. He continued to look at her. The more he watched her, the more mysterious she seemed. She sighed. "Are you sighing in nostalgia for marriage or because you feel good in the sun?" he asked.

"I guess some of both," she said. "Very often I just have no perspective at all. Some moments of well-being in the sun here for these few minutes seem much bigger to me than those years of marriage to Larry."

"I wanted to kiss you before," said Dodge. "But I just had gum surgery."

"When?" asked Susie.

"Yesterday," said Dodge. "Three thousand five hundred."

"Oh my god," said Susie. "And does it hurt?"

"Yes," said Dodge.

"Three thousand five hundred dollars!" said Susie. "I'm going to increase the flossing."

"And you have to use those little brushes."

"I should have dental insurance," said Susie. "You know what I miss about marriage? I miss the money. I mean, at least that's what I miss about my first marriage. It's true that I'm lonely a lot, but it's a clean loneliness. But, anyway, I don't feel nostalgic for marriage at all. I feel more relieved."

"You do?"

"Yes," said Susie.

"Relieved, hmm," he said. He pulled his blanket up to his chin and closed his eyes too. "Tell me about the dream," he said.

"What dream?" she said.

"The slow-dancing dream."

She was nearly falling asleep, or sounded as if she was. "I forgot," she said, lazily.

"You can't have forgotten," he said.

"No, I did," she said.

"What were we doing?"

"Slow dancing," said Susie.

"Close?" said Dodge.

"Yes," said Susie.

"Did I have a hard-on?" said Dodge.

"Yes," said Susie.

"Were you excited?" said Dodge.

Susie said nothing. He opened his eyes and looked at her. She was still smiling, eyes closed. As if she could feel him looking at her, her smile widened a little. Then she turned her head back toward the sun more squarely and said, "Let's just have a little nap for a few moments and have another dream, okay?"

"Okay," said Dodge.

Neither of them moved for several minutes, until the sun went behind a cloud and Susie brought her blanket back up to her chin. Every other inhabitant of the house came in or out of the house during those few minutes—Billy, Kay, and Ron on their way to the pool, Elise on her way in to use the bathroom, but all of them walked softly and silently when they saw the two with their eyes closed.

On Saturday afternoon, while they were having drinks on the patio, Susie announced that she'd invited someone to dinner, an old friend of hers, Casey Rambler. Dodge raised an eyebrow: this wasn't part of the deal here. If he'd invited someone without asking the rest of the group for permission, Susie would have been furious. But the truth was that Dodge really wanted to meet Casey Rambler, a prematurely retired rock 'n' roll singer he had heard of a great deal, because they had many friends in common. Dodge had been given one of her CDs a couple of years ago and he played it pretty often, while he worked. Lot of blues in it. And he liked the lyrics, which were kind of noir and seductive, especially in combination with the photo on the cover of the longhaired woman with extraordinarily intense eyes staring straight into the camera.

"I've met her a few times," said Elise, not warmly.

"I never met her," said Kay.

"I ran into her at a party once," said Ron. "She's an incredible fox," he explained, as if this was important and surprising information for all present. There was a quick exchange of amused glances among the women. Elise groaned. "And the way she talks," added Ron as a final selling point, "is sort of a cross between Colette and your average truck driver."

"I know you'll go for her, Dodge," said Susie.

He had shrugged but he was curious. That evening, before dinner, he had lingered a moment longer than usual in front of the mirror. He resisted the impulse to lift up his lip and look at his gums. He sighed. He looked good, he thought, but he knew not to go too close to the mirror. At least he had good hair. His skin was looking leathery lately. Or was it rubbery? He squinted. He looked like a dark cowboy. Somewhat. He turned around and tried to see himself from the back. No. Not possible. He opened the closet door, which had a mirror on the inside that he slanted so that he could look into it and see the reflection of the dresser mirror. He adjusted his belt by several millimeters. Before he left the room, he made sure, again, that his jeans were over his boots. He looked around the room. The bed was made. The dresser top was bare. On his night table four books were aligned, in order of size, biggest on the bottom. There was a thread on the rug. He picked it up and flicked it into the wastebasket, gave the room one more look, turned out the light, and quietly shut the door.

He did go for Casey Rambler, though not in the way he had expected. It was her freakishness that drew him. Casey had the eerie attractiveness of a stage star, ugly-beautiful, a very powerful physical allure. Her eyes and her mouth seemed bigger than normal. Her face was marked but beautiful. She was tall and her gestures were easy and large. It was hard not to feel drawn to her, and Dodge was aware of having to resist the urge to join Ron, who had sat down next to Casey on the couch in front of the coffee table and was practically leaning over her, to the ongoing amusement of the other women and, clearly, of Casey herself. When the urge started to seem too pressing, he left the room.

He stood in front of the house. He wished he had a cigarette. He watched the sun descend a few inches on the other side of the river. He realized something about Casey Rambler had led him to immediately feel the old sense of connection, and he thought to himself, *Trouble. Stay away. Trouble.* He watched the sun some more, trying to track its journey. There was a stir behind him, and the criss-criss of gravel.

"Hi," said Elise.

"Hi," said Dodge.

"Do you feel all right?" she asked.

"Oh yeah," he said. "Fine. Just needed some air."

"Yeah," she said. "It's muggy."

"It's shmuggy, as my daughter Emma would say," said Dodge.

She stood next to him for quite a while, seeming to look at the sun too, but he worried she was waiting for something from him, which is the feeling he usually had with her. For a moment he tried to relax, but that was difficult to do without actually blanking her out, a habit that he had long ago decided it would be honorable to lose. Perhaps she wanted him to talk to her. He really didn't have much to say to her and thought it would be wrong to pretend otherwise. It wasn't that he didn't like Elise, or even that he didn't want to fuck her. But something in her came through as pleading. It was hard to say how. Like an underlying grid, some yearning thing emanated from her that had the paradoxical effect of making him want to stay silent and, above all, impenetrable. What was oddest, really, when he thought about it was that Elise didn't seem as aware of this as he was. Or was she? But when he got to that point, his mind went *tilt*. This was far enough.

Perhaps he enjoyed her pain. He knew that was possible. Sometimes Dodge felt the intensity of a woman's feelings about him and experienced a kind of pleasure that seemed to be the result of more than vanity; something about it was like a relief, and he had become aware of it enough to feel discomfort. Other times he felt the very same thing but liked it and even milked this little pang. Was it cruelty? No, he wouldn't quite use the word "cruelty." He would just think of it as a subtle twinge of surprising pleasure.

"What are you thinking about?" asked Elise.

"What a sunset, isn't it?" said Dodge. "Impossible to think about anything else."

Elise looked slightly taken aback. "Hmm," she agreed. "See you later." And she went back to the house.

He took a few deep breaths, tried to clear his mind again. He strolled out to the lawn, and when he'd walked about a hundred feet, he looked back toward the house. At the window of the drawing room, Casey was standing, looking out. She was an odd and fetching figure in the rectangle. Was she looking for him? He stood very still for a moment, but she stood equally still at the window, oddly tinted with sunset gold, framed by the embrasure like a Renaissance-ish figure in a Martha Clarke piece. He waved. She waved back.

Fra Lippi. No, a little softer. Fra Angelico.

Elise, he now saw, was still standing just inside the door.

At dinner it seemed to him as if there were already something understood between the two of them, Casey and him, though perhaps he was imagining it, he told himself. No, she was conversing with Susie, Kay, and Elise, and Ron was doing everything he could to monopolize her, but in fact Dodge could sense that it was him she was aware of.

He really liked the way she looked. Her mouth. Those boots. All that hair. He liked whatever it was that was provocative behind her gaze, even though he knew that in a different mood he would have found it banal. (She wasn't the first rock 'n' roll star he had flirted with.) But there was a great erotic energy in that sense of constant amusement. And those clothes: suede and silk, and fringes, and something that glittered around her waist. And her neck, which he could see from here, the skin was very soft. The softness of the skin of women of a certain age. It was funny that it bothered them so much, when it was so pleasurable under the lips or fingers.

They were the age his mother had been when he had loved her the most, desired her softness the most. His mother, as she looked then, often came back to him. She had gray eyes, like him, and she wore very, very deep red lipstick. Brilliant carmine lips. It was interesting that all the women he knew had been wearing lipstick lately. He liked it. He hoarded the memories of kissing a woman in the dark and knowing he had her lipstick on his mouth, or of fucking her from behind and finding smudges of her lipstick on the pillow the next morning, after she'd gone. He liked women his own age, actually. He liked the way they looked and acted and were, and the way they became in bed and around the house. He wasn't sure whether it was because it was the line of least resistance, or because they were the women with whom he had the most in common, socially and sexually, or whether it was because younger women seemed, in the end, like an awful lot of trouble, requiring more emotional vigor than he had, though they seemed to offer the opposite—the prospect of soothing and invigorating adulation always turned out to be a mirage.

But, anyway, given these women here, for instance, and that adorable little Claudine, the au pair next door, he would certainly pick one of the women at this table. Maybe, he reflected, what he liked was seeing them all together. It reminded him of something he liked from when he was young. What? He no longer knew. But the feeling caused him to almost recall something that put him in a good mood.

Maybe it was truly a more attractive generation, though. An attractive generation of women. It would be a good title for a painting, though he would have to officially call it something like *Red Study No. 18.* In his mind he watched his assistant stretch a canvas, the sound of the staple gun. It was such a satisfying moment.

Maybe he should go to a nubbier canvas. He hadn't been able to decide whether to even go as far as burlap, so that the texture would be even more prominent, the painting less a window than an object.

In the middle of the stew, Casey suddenly addressed him directly.

"How's it going, Dodge?" she asked, smiling.

"Great," he said. "How's it going with you, Casey?"

"I hear you have a show coming up."

"Yeah," he said. "I do."

"I've always wanted to own one of your paintings," she said.

"Really?" he said.

"They're not easy to live with," said Ron.

Fucking Reiser, thought Dodge.

"I'm sure that's true," said Casey. "I would consider it a challenge."

"And they're incredibly expensive," said Ron to Casey.

"But worth it," said Elise. "Worth every penny."

"What do you mean, 'They're not easy to live with'?" Dodge said to Ron. He knew it had been meant mainly as banter, but he thought it was one of Ron's most unveiled hostilities.

Ron seemed taken aback by Dodge's reaction to his remark. He wore an expression that said, *Oh no, I've done it again,* which infuriated Dodge even more.

"What do you mean," said Dodge, "'They're not easy to live with'?"

"Well, I mean, I do it, but it's not everyone who can stand the mighty torment on those canvases, you know," said Ron. As always, sinking himself deeper. He smiled at Dodge. *What a shit-eating grin,* Dodge thought.

"I don't think it's such a hardship," Susie said to Ron. There was an atmosphere of alertness at the table, suddenly, as if everyone could see that some line had been stepped over.

"Besides," said Kay, "torment is Dodge's business." The others laughed. It was so unusual for Kay to be making this sort of a joke, let alone a joke about torment, that it seemed to clear the air for a moment. Dodge felt anger rising in him with vertiginous speed, and then suddenly decided to take advantage of the moment to make the whole thing go away. He was too angry.

"What are you up to these days, Casey?" he asked.

The others looked carefully neutral. Ron speared an asparagus.

"Writing songs," she said. "Trying to decide whether or not I'm too old to go back onstage."

"That's how I feel," said Elise. "And I don't even have to go onstage."

They all leaned forward a little, as if slightly stimulated by the unusual amount of truth telling. It was surprising to hear someone as famous as Casey Rambler be so direct. It was late and the lamps had been turned on. The light was flattering, Dodge noticed. He liked having Casey there. It cheered him up. But his pleasure was impeded by Ron's remark, which had now lodged in his heart like a piece of broken glass. *Not easy to live with?* He looked at Ron and it seemed to him that Ron was avoiding meeting his glance. He couldn't believe Ron had said that. *What the fuck was that about?*

"It's tough," said Casey, "to stay dangerous."

"You'll always be dangerous," Ron said.

All the women laughed.

"Well, thank you, Ron," said Casey in an even tone. "I still take that as a compliment. But think about it. Am I as dangerous as your average rapper?"

"Well, rap doesn't count," said Susie.

"Why not?" said Casey.

"Because it's not an option for you," said Susie.

"Why not?" said Elise.

"Because I'd look ridiculous," said Casey. "But it does count. Nothing I can do onstage or in the recording studio can ever be as dangerous as the dumbest safest rap song. And a lot of them are neither dumb nor safe."

"You can never look ridiculous!" exclaimed Ron with fantastically intense mock passion. The others laughed and groaned.

Dodge spent the rest of dinner rehearsing the things that he was going to say to Ron, most of them eloquent reminders of the length of their friendship and the number of times he had helped

Ron with this and that. Sometimes he came up with a nastier sce-
nario, pointing out to Ron that he knew nothing at all about looking at art. Finding a way to say the truth, that just to get a few
seconds' favorable attention from an attractive broad, Ron had not
only talked about something he knew nothing about, making a
complete asshole of himself, but had also betrayed their friendship,
sold him down the line after all these years of . . .

"Dodge," said Susie for the second time. "Pie? Do you want
some apple pie?"

"Yeah," he said. "Thanks very much. A small piece." No, he
would say nothing to Ron. Ron didn't even understand what he was
doing. *What a fuckhead. What a lowlife.* Why was he friends with
him, anyway? Ron had been creatively freeloading off of him for
years. And now it was impossible to do anything about this without
wrecking the summer.

He would say nothing and wait until this incident got more or
less erased from Ron's memory, but he would edge away in the
meanwhile. He'd had it with Ron. He just wasn't going to get into
a thing about it. He couldn't get into anything like this just before
a show.

"Dodge," said Susie. What a nice smile she had. "Coffee?"

They all went into the drawing room after dinner. It was chilly
and somewhat damp. Casey, Elise, and Ron settled into couches
and chairs while Kay and Susie made much to-do about a fire. Billy
wandered around the room as he sometimes did. *What is the matter with that kid?* Dodge wondered for a moment.

Dodge sat down on a couch across from the others, but when
Ron kept trying to make eye contact with him, he got up and began
to meander around the edges of the room. He tried not to look at
Casey, not even to see what she was doing. Susie was wearing a very
short skirt, and it rode up on her thighs as she tried to arrange the
logs in some more efficient fashion. Behind her, Kay knelt, wearing
leggings and a big T-shirt. Shadows flickered around the room.

The fire seemed to be getting going. Susie sat down and con-
templated her handiwork. Kay still knelt behind her. Shadows

flickered around them, and for an instant Dodge made them vague glancing images on caves.

Several times Kay twisted her neck in an odd way and pulled her shoulders around as if her back was hurting her. Billy must have noticed the movement too because he walked over to Kay the third time she did it and put his hands on her shoulders and massaged them a bit. It was an interesting moment, and Dodge noted the arresting silhouette of the three figures framed by the fireplace. Very good. Very, very good. He cast his eye around various parts of the room, as if taking photographs. Of course, it was really easy in this room, with all its textures and patterns, its beams, its niches, its *boiserie,* its *chinoiserie,* its shadows, to come up with something good in the imaginary frame.

It was taking every bit of energy he had not to turn around. All he wanted to do was to zero in on Casey. As it was, though, he felt everyone had already noticed with what intense interest he had connected with her. Were the others upset? No, he was being paranoid.

How had this happened, so fast? He had made so much effort to change, and it seemed to have been worth nothing, all his effort. He saw an attractive woman and immediately became a wreck. Any second now there'd be someone accusing him of being a phallic narcissist. He saw, as in review, a portrait gallery of angry women.

What had triggered this? A glance exchanged, that contained slightly too much heat from too seductive a woman. He was like a recovering drunk who'd had a glass of scotch put in front of him. He felt she was dangerous for him, that he was starting to do what he used to do, which he'd had so much trouble not doing lately.

Ron was still nattering away. Billy drifted away from Kay and Susie, who stood up again. Dodge sensed now that there was something wrong in the body language of the entire room and suddenly realized that Kay, Susie, and Elise were all slightly turned away from him.

As always they were mad at him.

He suddenly decided he was feeling too crazy. "Well, I'll be seeing all of you," he said. "I have to hit the sack."

"Really? So early?" said Susie.

"I don't know why but I'm exhausted," said Dodge.

They called out, "Good night." Casey seemed to smile with irony. Or did he imagine it? He went up to his room and felt an attack of agonizing paranoia as he hadn't had in a very long time. He lay face down on his bed, his mind working back and forth between Casey and Ron. The abyss of Casey's attractiveness, sure to lead to no good, and Ron's snide remark. Sarcasm about a friend's work was absolutely unforgivable. It was just the sort of remark that might prevent him from working. And Ron knew very well that he was very sensitive, especially before a show. It was just incredible that he would have talked to him this way. This was why he preferred women to men. The aggressiveness. The hostility.

There was a knock at the door. *Casey,* he thought.

"Yah!" he called out.

Ron opened the door a little. "Can I come in a second?" He looked sheepish.

Dodge thought for a moment. "I was just going to sleep," he said.

"Okay," said Ron. "Listen, I'm sorry, man. I really didn't mean to upset you. But it was a stupid thing to say, anyway."

"It's all right," said Dodge.

"Your paintings save my life," said Ron. "It saves my life to be able to look at that on the outside of me. It makes me feel a million times less lonely."

"It's all right," said Dodge.

"No, I mean, really," said Ron. "I mean, I know I've never told you that, but it's true."

"Okay," said Dodge.

"It really is, man," said Ron.

"Okay! Okay!" said Dodge, beginning to laugh both at Ron's insistence and at his woebegone expression. "Okay, I'm going to sleep."

"Please forgive me," said Ron, his head still stuck in the embrasure.

"I forgive you, I forgive you," Dodge called out, laughing. "You're completely forgiven."

"Completely?" said Ron.

"Absolutely completely," said Dodge.

"Good," said Ron. "Because you're such a tormented asshole, you're capable of lying there all night stewing about it and sticking pins into a little doll of me."

"I don't have a little doll of you—I haven't had time to make one, since you won't leave me alone for a minute."

"Okay, good night," said Ron.

"Good night," said Dodge.

"I love you," said Ron.

"Thanks," said Dodge.

The door was almost closed but reopened. "Do you love me?" asked Ron.

"Yes, yes, yes," said Dodge. "Good night. Get the fuck out, please!"

He was up all night, curled up on his bed. He never got undressed. He got up once: the armoire door had creaked open. He closed it and lay down again. He curled up again. He wished he could work.

Sunday

Sunday it rained. Susie went out shopping. Elise and Ron played gin all afternoon on the patio. Billy lay on his bed and listened to music. Everyone in the house could hear: a U2 record, then Mudhoney, then an old Country Joe and the Fish album he'd found in Susie's collection of ratty LPs and made a cassette of. Kay, as everyone in the house knew since she was occasionally willing to give them hilarious synopses, was reading the chapter on art and Eros in Norman O. Brown's *Life against Death*. (She'd abandoned Edith Wharton.)

Dodge slept most of the afternoon. It was the one time he could sleep, as if his entire sleep debt were being paid off. Fully dressed,

on top of the bed, he didn't draw the shades. Maybe it had something to do with the light. Maybe it was the dark at night that kept
him from sleeping. As he slept, the door had somehow opened and
stayed slightly ajar, so that the others all peered in as they walked
by. Still wearing his very expensive black boots, black cotton
sweater, black jeans from the night before, he lay on his side on the
white chenille bedspread, his hands pressed together between his
knees, as if in a strange prayer.

Sometimes a noise would awaken him briefly. At one point he
looked up and heard footsteps and there was Claudine from next
door peeking into the room. What was she doing in the house? He
picked up one hand and waved slightly. She silently waved back
and smiled and moved on. He heard her knocking on Billy's door,
then heard the door squeaking open a crack and the two of them
talking briefly and softly and then Billy's door closing again. Dodge
closed his eyes but then reopened them and saw Claudine framed
in his doorway for a moment. He smiled at her. She smiled back.
He wondered if she was going to come in, but, no, she just stood
there.

Claudine had a very pretty mouth, heart shaped, very delicate
red lips, delicious when in repose in a very slight pout. Just the
kind of mouth he loved. She had an extremely beguiling smile,
saucy and sweet, invariably delivered with her head tilted a bit
down and to one side so that she had to look at you a little from
below. You could swear she had worked it out in a mirror, but even
that only seemed to add to the charm of the insolence you could
sense in her every mannerism. As if her seduction was arrogance
rather than submissiveness. Yes, that's what was interesting about
it. She looked at him looking at her for a moment, then smiled more
deeply, waved, and moved on. What a spicy little cookie she was.
He went to sleep again, thinking of his penis in Claudine's mouth.

Later in the afternoon it rained even harder, and when he woke
up, he'd hear the drumming on the roof and the rustling of some
animal skidding against the wet tile, or perhaps it was twigs or

leaves falling. No, too early for leaves and fall. Too early still. His mouth hurt. His stomach hurt. He had some kind of intestinal problem he didn't understand. His joints hurt. Why did he feel so awful? Maybe it was the gum surgery, some violation of his envelope. His envelope. He tried to imagine he was floating around in a perfectly closed sac, safe and pain free.

When he woke up again, the light was waning. Someone had closed the door. Dodie was making some complicated casserole, and the smells drifted up with such potency that he finally thought maybe he'd wake up. Maybe he should eat something. Maybe he could just go down and see what was cooking, though he knew from experience that it was impossible to look into the kitchen without getting cornered into a conversation with Dodie, which was more than he thought he could handle at the moment. When it rained, Dodie would say, "If we had feathers, we wouldn't mind." Still, maybe he was too hungry to stay asleep. Fat Dodie. Sometimes he had a vertiginous feeling in Dodie's presence, as if he might fall into her flesh.

And the closed door made him feel more awake too, more isolated. Who had closed his door? Dodge felt a twinge of resentment, of exclusion and abandonment. He wanted the door open, but he couldn't quite get himself to get up and open it. It wasn't so much that he didn't have the energy, though there was that, but that if someone had closed it, it was meant to be closed. It would be noticed if he opened it. It would seem weird.

He imagined Susie, Kay, and Elise, seated in a row a few feet away from the bed, questioning him. Maybe. No, maybe Kay would say nothing, but only look. Kay had an interesting way of looking, he'd noticed. Very intently, fixedly. He liked to be looked at by her, but it made him uncomfortable too. He couldn't imagine what Kay would be like in bed. She had a wonderful gravity. Very sexy. She'd look great, he thought, with that WASPy way she had of putting her hair up. Or with her face in the pillow. She had a wonderful, long, graceful neck. Not dramatic, like Casey's, less sculpted, but very inviting. He'd often wanted to put his hand on her neck as he walked past her in the dining room, just for a moment, to feel the declivities. Or maybe with her hair spread out on the pillow, very carefully. Where had he seen hair like that? In a Cartier-Bresson photograph, maybe.

Door open. Door closed. It reminded him of his mouth and his gums. "Fuck," he said out loud.

Susie and Elise, that was another matter. What the fuck was that about? Something that had to do with the two of them. He just didn't even want to think about it. The dynamics of triangles were one of the things that made his mind tilt. Maybe he was the only one who noticed, anyway, that something weird was going on there. He enjoyed it in a way, like dangerous static, but he was too scared it was going to explode.

The noises in the house had become much fainter, except for the sound of the rain. The light was falling faster now, and he imagined the sky must be that gorgeous blue smeared with gray he loved so much. His glance roved the ceiling, along the molding, then fixed on a small air bubble in the wallpaper. How was it that he hadn't noticed it before? Probably because it was under a stripe. Blue stripe. Blue stripe. He wanted to get up and pull a chair over to stand on so he could run his finger over the stripe to get rid of the air bubble. He dimly thought about being hungry but that he couldn't quite face the others. And he didn't think he could eat. His poor mouth. Poor mouth. And, anyway, he couldn't really get up, he felt; he was too heavy, falling. He lay on the bed and fell and fell, and then would stop falling so fast and just drift around for a while and then drift back to sleep, where he would fall some more.

When he woke up yet again and found that this time he really couldn't reinsinuate himself back into sleep, he lurched to the bathroom and peed, with his eyes closed, and then used his hands to rinse himself with cold water. He carefully avoided the mirror. On his way downstairs, treading very carefully on each creaky step because he thought that he might fall, he heard the rumble of

Susie's Saab recede up the road. *Oh no,* he thought. Without Susie there, it had been a mistake to get up.

"What are you doing in the dark?" Susie asked Dodge when she got home and found him sitting in a chair by himself in the drawing room.

"I don't know," said Dodge. "I just sat down for a minute and kind of drifted off."

With Susie home, the house seemed to reintegrate itself. She put on some Stravinsky and the others drifted in. They stayed in the drawing room by common consent; the rain was making the other rooms too humid, and the patio, though protected, seemed to absorb the atmosphere of the rain.

"It's a bit stuffy in the drawing room," said Billy after the moment of silence that succeeded the end of the CD.

"I'd rather be in a Jane Austen parlor than a Somerset Maugham short story," said Susie.

"Whoa," said Ron. "Well, I'd rather be in a Sharon Stone movie than in an Akira Kurosawa movie."

"Just as we suspected, Ron," said Susie.

"I'd rather be in *Robinson Crusoe* than a Samuel Beckett play," said Elise.

"What about you, Dodge?" said Susie.

"I don't know," said Dodge. "I have to think."

"Well, think," said Ron. "Even though it's not your religion. I know you'd rather be tossing farm girls into the hay and shooting cowboys."

"That's it," said Dodge. "I'd rather be in a John Ford movie."

The others waited for a moment and then laughed. "A John Ford movie?" said Ron. "What John Ford movie?"

"I don't know," said Dodge. "*The Searchers,* maybe."

"But you'd rather be in *The Searchers* than what?" said Elise. "And why?"

"You're not playing the game," said Susie.

"Yes, he is," said Kay. "Just in a more complicated way."

"It's a good game," said Billy.

"*The Searchers*," said Dodge, "because of all John Ford movies it's the cleanest. It's a clean movie: the plot is taut; the themes are precise. Every scene is clean, every frame."

"Hmm," said Ron. "The spic-and-span aesthetic of film criticism."

"I'm not completely awake yet," Dodge said. "Give me some time and I'll come up with something better. I'd rather be in an Agnes Martin painting than in a Watteau. How's that?"

"I love Watteau," said Susie.

"Me too," said Elise. "I'd love to be in an Agnes Martin *in* a Watteau."

"Actually," said Dodge, "to tell you the truth, I really love Watteau."

"Just as we suspected," said Susie.

Dodge noticed that Billy was looking at Kay. Kay was looking up at the ceiling and clearly knew that Billy was looking at her. Elise was looking at Billy and Kay. The humidity had done something weird to her hair and she looked a bit batty, Dodge thought, which somehow made her more desirable.

Despite his fogginess, Dodge now felt cheerful, as if they were a family. But feverish. Maybe he was getting a cold. Or was it just from sleeping all afternoon. He could feel the marks of the pillow disappearing from his face.

He had this sudden powerful sensation that he didn't want to really wake up—he wanted to keep it just like this, with a feeling that his friends were around him. As if he never wanted to go out again. It was dark outside and seemed to hold nothing but infinite loneliness. Maybe, he thought, in a way, this was the closest he had ever felt to being in a family.

He felt good enough so that he wished he could go into his studio now, his studio in New York. He loved his studio, more than anything, maybe. Though he hated the smell of paint, the smell that everyone loved so much when they walked in. He knew that it was in part that smell that made collectors buy when they came for studio visits. It was like an aphrodisiac for art, the smell of paint. But it made him nauseated. Often he thought he might vomit, until he really got going working. Then it went away. Then just about everything went away, and he got deeper and deeper into the language of the painting as the sole conduit for consciousness and finally just the action. Lately he'd been doing a lot of layering, and he was getting more interested in what he could do, shaping the painting with color.

He'd been using color as if it were emotion. If color could be a medium of expression, then too much color gave away too much feeling. The one he was working on now—a wonderful large canvas, an extraordinarily heavy linen weave he'd actually brought back under his arm from Holland—he'd started with cadmium red deep and added other reds to it to control the brightness and the darkness until it became exactly what it had to be, a thin veil of red with peach color with a lot of black in it. *Noir de pêche.* Manet's color. Now he was layering it, graying it, veiling it, one layer at a time. Now there was only the remembrance of red. Maybe he should call the painting that. No, too obvious. Ridiculous. The important thing was to shut out the world, the world of reference. They called him austere, but that's all it was, was the shutting out of those external references. Though all the same relationships were created inside, in the end. But that didn't have to be thought about once the painting was started. Only the door to be walked through, the membrane through which he had to pass each time, to be inside.

He got up and walked out of the room and to the dark and humid patio and poured himself a vodka and drank it, neat, and then another one that he brought back to the drawing room.

"What's that?" asked Elise.

"Absolut," he said.

"Oh, what a good idea," said Susie. "I'm going to get one. Who else wants one?"

Elise and Kay.

"All right. Me too," said Ron.

"I had such bad dreams, I've got to wash them down in a hurry," said Dodge.

"What did you dream?" said Elise.

"I don't remember," said Dodge. "I just woke up with a terrible feeling of dread."

"I hate that," said Kay. "I get that all the time."

"I used to," said Susie.

"It's from sleeping in the afternoon," said Ron. "Afternoon naps always give you weird dreams."

"I have great dreams in the afternoon," said Billy. "In New York I never remember them, but here a lot of them stick."

"Like what?" asked Kay.

Billy looked up. "I can't remember right now."

"I have terrible daydreams in the afternoon," said Elise.

"You track your daydreams?" said Ron. "That's amazing."

"No, not really," said Elise. "But, anyway, there are a lot of primitive cultures that have traditions of lucid dreaming and so forth."

"What's lucid dreaming?" asked Billy.

"It's kind of between dreaming and waking," said Elise.

"I'm in that state all the time," said Billy.

"Me too," said Dodge.

"I wish I were," said Kay.

"What's an example of a dreadful daydream?" asked Susie.

"Like I had one yesterday about a pair of red shoes," said Elise.

"A pair of red shoes?" said Dodge. How weird was this?

"Yes," said Elise.

"Who was wearing them?" asked Susie.

"No one," said Elise. "That's what was sort of dreadful about the daydream. I kept trying to make it go further, but it just stayed a pair of red shoes on the floor in the middle of an empty room."

"Was the room light or dark?" asked Susie.

"Crepuscular," said Elise.

"Were the heels high or low?" asked Dodge.

"High," said Elise. "High-heeled pumps."

"I like red shoes," said Billy.

"Who doesn't?" said Kay.

"That's a very sexy daydream," said Ron.

"No, it wasn't sexy, it was filled with dread," said Elise.

"It would be sexy if a man had had it," said Dodge.

"No," said Elise. "It would be sadistic."

"No," said Kay. "It would be an indication of fuzzy gender boundaries."

"Hey," said Ron. "Speak for yourself."

"That's funny," said Susie. "I bought a pair of red shoes today."

They laughed. "Are you kidding?" said Ron.

"No," said Susie. "I'll show you." She went to her room.

"Do you think we're becoming merged?" said Ron to the others.

"I hope not," said Dodge.

"Why not?" said Elise.

"I need another vodka," said Dodge.

Susie walked back in. "Here they are," she said. It was a pair of red sandals, with a thin strap that went between the toes.

"They're great," said Kay and Elise simultaneously.

"Wow," said Dodge.

"Let's see, let's see, put them on," said Ron.

Susie, who was wearing shorts and a white blouse, slipped on the sandals.

"At least they're not pumps," said Kay.

"Thank god," said Dodge.

"That's funny," said Kay.

"What beautiful feet you have," said Elise.

"Thanks," said Susie. "What do you think, Dodge?" she asked.

"They're great," said Dodge. "I hope you're planning to fuck somebody in those."

"Yeah, and I hope it's me," said Ron.

"Surprise, surprise," said Elise.

"Yeah," said Dodge. "Surprise, surprise."

Billy shook his head. "Jeez," he said.

"Sorry," said Dodge.

"Oh, no problem," said Billy.

Dodge was upset he'd talked about fucking Susie in front of Billy. He liked Billy.

Had he upset him? No, it seemed not. Or not that Billy would show, anyway. It was hard to tell what was really going on in Billy's mind. Always had been, even when he was a darling little boy, Dodge had felt there was something there he didn't connect with, something either hidden or so different from what he knew that he couldn't grasp its nature. He'd been surprised at how richly secretive a small boy could be.

Billy smiled at Dodge. What a smile. Dodge smiled back. It would be great—there was no doubt about it—to be under the covers with Susie and Billy.

SUSIE

WEEKEND OF JULY 25

Friday

"This room has so many windows that you feel like you're in a spider's eye," Susie said. They were having drinks on the patio, bathed in a perfect late-afternoon light. From one side of the room, you could survey the pool, and on the other, you could see the lawn leading to the rose garden. The rose garden hovered in the distance like a dim dream, nearly obscured by the growing shadows of the surrounding pines. The sun, soon to set on the other side of the river, was veiling the lawn, the trees, and the horizon in a voluptuous yellow haze. The pool shimmered in a soft blaze of last light.

"The pool looks amazing," said Dodge, looking out the window.

"How amazing?" asked Susie, too lazy to rise.

"Sort of like a setting for the Annunciation," said Dodge.

"I hope Dodie is going to announce dinner soon," said Ron.

"How can you still eat, Ron?" said Elise. "I saw you scarfing that chicken just an hour ago."

"You must be confusing me with somebody else," said Ron.

They were all here. The room smelled good, of the women's perfume (perhaps mingled with a faint scent of mowed grass). They were all clean. Several of them had just had a swim, and Billy and

Elise still had wet hair. They were drinking Bloody Marys from tall frosted glasses. Dodge was standing at the window, or rather, thought Susie, he was draped with his characteristic self-conscious elegance over the window. *What a poseur.* The others were seated or reclining on wicker furniture. They were all wearing T-shirts and jeans, except for Elise, who wore a short and sleeveless black shift from which her already very tanned limbs emerged in an attractive way. Susie found herself really liking Elise. She thought Elise added a lot to the household in her gloriously zany fashion. *What would we do without neurosis for entertainment?* she wondered.

Billy had brought a boom box in, and they were listening to French impressionist songs on some obscure label. Susie had played some Poulenc on the piano long ago. She thought of her parents' living room, the grand piano, the rug, which she'd hated. Red and black, red and black, red and black. Her mother's laughter. Her mother had a way of laughing, throwing her head back and then jolting forward and putting her hands over her face. The Poulenc, *Mouvements perpétuels.* One, two, three, four, five, six, seven. One, two, three, four, five, six, seven.

Susie took another sip of her Bloody Mary. She wore a pale gray T-shirt and blue jeans and extremely high-heeled blue sandals. The sandals made her a little sad, because she had purchased them on impulse, which reminded her of Otto. But then a good deal reminded her of Otto, and she found herself having to redirect her thoughts, again and again. It was interesting, in a way, to feel such pain over a puppy. It reminded her of what it would be like if she were still having affairs with men.

She had been so relieved when the relationship with Paul had ended this spring. No, wait, it was last year. Spring a year ago. She could never have brought him here—he would have driven her crazy. She had been so bored with him. She felt so claustrophobic in bed. The first time had been awful, and the second time not much better. The third time had been nice, but the fourth she had started to get that feeling of waiting for it to be over. And then after that it was unbearable.

He just didn't do it for her. *But then who does? Who does? Who does? Is it possible to actually lose interest altogether?* She still found herself thinking about sex almost reflexively, as if it were a sociobiological imperative she no longer had the emotional means to fulfill.

She swept the problem away from the forefront of her consciousness, as with a windshield wiper. Susie had been meditating for a couple of years now, and she was getting quite good at clearing her mind.

Though why had she purchased these very sexy shoes, if she was not interested in having an affair?

She looked at Dodge for a moment. No. Absolutely not. He always seemed just perched somewhere, like an extremely attractive thin black cat. Or a blackbird. Susie always wondered whether he had worked on the pose, and always concluded, by looking at him, that he hadn't. But then, if she closed her eyes, she knew he would have had to.

Maybe she should get a cat. Why did she suddenly want an animal so badly? Maybe she wished she could have another baby. Too late. Too late.

But there was still desire. Some time back she had understood, with a terrible start, how much desire had to do with wanting babies. But then she'd been able to set that perception aside for the most part. It was too painful. And, anyway, there was some loss that babies did not compensate for. Even Billy. Though she couldn't imagine her life without Billy as anything but desolate. But he'd taken a heavy toll on her too. You keep thinking that when you love someone, you'll have more, but the truth was that each time you love someone, what you wind up with is more loss.

Maybe it was that simple, her problems with men, and perhaps with love in general. Maybe she just didn't want any more punishment.

In a way, she still felt desire for men. No, not in a way. Definitely. She definitely still felt desire for men. But almost never for any individual man.

Was it because fantasies were more attractive than reality? No, something more complicated than that.

She looked at Ron. No. Out of the question. He saw her looking at him and met her glance. He smiled at her, and she smiled back.

It was odd: she still had desire for desire, but almost never desire itself.

But that was interesting, in a way, just like the pain over Otto. Or wishing she had more babies. She understood Kay better than Kay thought. The pain of not having more babies, it was a way of life ending. Not just not living on, but also never being young and pretty and fruitful again. She was constantly told she was beautiful, but she knew beauty didn't have to do with all that. No, it was something just under the skin, that emanated from one through the skin. Beauty radiation. It only got richer as one got older. Richer, deeper. She'd rather be her age than, say, Claudine's. Poor little Claudine.

Was she envious of Claudine? Well, yes, of course.

She had learned, finally, to let many of these feelings wash through her. It had taken quite a bit of work, but now it was a good deal easier. Often she did it now out of habit. She found that in this house, however, it was problematic because of the close proximity of the others and because of the constant promise of pleasure, both of which reawakened archaic, inchoate desire—not specific wants, but desire itself, the sort that could attach itself to anything and everything and did. Now that was a real challenge to wash away. She found herself to be almost constantly divided as to whether to relinquish herself to one direction or another. Desire seemed more immediately pleasurable, but invariably led to unsatisfiable longing that then turned into pain. Washing away desire took a great deal of willpower, but the reward was an occasional soft and pleasurable haze, sort of like the haze on the horizon now, sun and air. She yearned for that, even though she knew that very yearning would keep her from it. That soft hazy zone. She'd forget about it and then when she came upon it, she wanted to linger there. She cared less and less about all the rest. More than anything what Susie wanted now was that strange sense of abstractedness that she thought might be what many people called bliss, what was sought in meditation, maybe what was sought in many things—sex, eating, going to the beach, looking up at the sky—that soft white almost ethereal place in the mind where all is still and a little bit glowing. And all right.

Desire ruined that, its sharpness. Maybe sharp was the wrong word. Desire. Suddenly she couldn't remember. Like a burning, maybe. Yes. Someone comes along and makes you go up like kindling.

Desire was soft sometimes, burning sometimes, but then it always revealed its true sharp nature. She tried to think of the last time she had really been stabbed by desire. Paul? No. With Paul, it was merely a bee sting. She'd only had to wait until it went away. *The birds and the bees,* thought Susie. *All these birds, all these bees, always up to no good.* She'd read recently that sociobiologists were finding out that a lot of female birds were promiscuous, cheated on their bird husbands. Better than you could say for anyone here. It was amazing how much everyone in this house thought about sex and how there actually was no sex. *The birds and the bees in the nineties is the caption,* thought Susie. She looked at Billy. Billy was staring up at the ceiling, slouching in his chair, his legs straight out in front of him, ankles crossed. He was so great looking. He'd been such a sullen, odd-looking adolescent she'd despaired of him, and now he was turning into such an attractive man. If she'd been Billy's age, she certainly would have desired him. Where was the Billy of her age? There was none. There would be no Billy she hadn't created. She saw Kay looking at her looking at Billy, and they smiled at one another.

Why couldn't she have an affair with a woman? She couldn't have an affair with Kay. It would ruin their friendship. Elise? Elise was sexy, for sure. Elise was up for anything. Susie had thought of

Elise and Dodge. How would it be to be in a bed with Elise and Dodge?

Tiring. Difficult the next day.

Casey. She had found Casey attractive, so attractive it made her anxious. But then Casey was that kind of person. Everyone here had felt it. She wouldn't invite her back. *Why, I'm jealous,* she realized with surprise. That's what that extremely unpleasant pain was, she knew, jealousy. Actually, she thought she was more attractive than Casey.

But it was jealousy she felt. There had been a twinge when she thought of Claudine, but thinking of Casey, there was the twisting knife, all too familiar. Envy before desire.

Casey, of course, was bigger than the sum of her parts. There was the lure of power. Or was it the lure of talent? Talent was so magnetic.

And Dodge had been such an asshole. Whatever attraction she might have felt for him had vanished. Such game playing. But then Dodge was infantile. Always had been. Always would be. He was sexy, though, for sure. Why did she still find him sexy? Some programming flaw in herself. And it wasn't absolutely impossible that his obvious attraction for Casey had made him seem more desirable.

She'd rather be friends with Casey than have an affair with her. The fact is it was the same with women. She liked the idea in the abstract, but there was never anyone she really wanted to go to bed with.

Am I going to be a nun for the rest of my life?

She drained her glass. "I need another Bloody Mary," she said, even though she knew alcohol barred the way to the soft white place.

"I'll get you one," said Dodge. He came and got her glass and went to the mirrored trolley on which there was the pitcher of Bloody Marys and ice and lemon. He mixed her a new one and brought it to her and then went back to his spot by the window.

"What are you looking at there?" Susie called out to him. She turned the volume down on the CD player.

"The au pair girl," asked Dodge.

"Which au pair girl?" asked Ron.

"There's only one," Kay said to Ron.

"He knows which au pair," said Dodge, without turning around.

"My guess is that she comes whenever she thinks Billy might be around," said Elise.

"What?" said Billy. And they all laughed.

"And what is the au pair doing?" Elise called out to Dodge.

"Claudine," said Kay. "Her name is Claudine."

"The au pair is ostensibly sunbathing," said Dodge. "Perhaps resting."

"Well, that's my kind of au pair," said Ron, "Sunbathing at 6:30 P.M. Yes, that's what they train them for over there."

"In an extremely tiny bikini, with breasts like lovely apricots," said Dodge. "And she's being watched."

"Yeah, no kidding," said Ron.

"By whom?" said Susie.

"Well, by Dodge, of course," said Kay.

"No, not only by me," said Dodge. "Or by you via me. But also by the handsome workman."

"What handsome workman?" asked Ron. "What's going on here? I've only been gone four days and you've imported a whole chorus line of seductive peasants?"

"Apricots?" said Elise. "Apricots?!"

"Large apricots," said Dodge. "Or maybe peaches. *Pêches roses.*"

"Come again?" said Ron.

"The carpenters who have been fixing the ramp," said Kay.

"Oh, sure," said Ron. "The handsome carpenters who have been fixing what ramp?"

They all laughed. They'd each had one or two Bloody Marys by now and they were feeling quite merry. The French art songs CD ended and Susie felt relieved.

"They were hard to miss," said Kay.

"No, they were there all day," said Elise.

"They're kind of funny," said Susie. "I like those guys." Especially the tall one.

"And I suppose their last task of the day is to converse with the au pair by the pool," said Ron.

"There's just one of them," said Dodge from the window.

"The tall attractive one with the amazing eyes or the other one?" asked Susie.

"The attractive one," said Dodge. And Susie registered that Dodge had known exactly what she had meant, as if he had been following her thought, which, with the help of the Bloody Mary, carried a small but distinct erotic charge she could not resist being pleased by.

"Where is he standing?" asked Susie.

"By the fence," said Dodge. "He's leaning against the fence. The funny thing is that the girl has got to know he's there. From the angle of her body, you can tell she knows she's being watched."

"Well, yeah, but that could just be because she knows she's being watched by you," said Ron.

"No," said Dodge. "I think she knows he's there."

"Let's get a gun and shoot him," said Ron.

"Ron, you're so aggressive, even in your fantasy life," said Susie.

"Well, better in his fantasy life," said Kay.

"What do you mean?" said Ron. "I'm a pussycat."

"The perfect murder," said Elise.

"What?" said Billy. He walked over to the Bloody Mary trolley.

"Haven't you had enough of those, Billy?" Susie asked.

"We've all had enough if you ask me," said Kay when she saw Billy's expression of exasperation at Susie's remark. Always, Kay attempted to soften the edges of Susie's remarks to Billy, which amused Susie, especially since it almost always made things worse. Who knew why Billy got so exasperated? It was probably some generic need for intensity and could be ignored. Her relationship with Billy had long been an improvisation, which she performed almost like a piece of music, trusting her emotions and her common sense even when she didn't quite know where she was in the score.

She looked at her son. She loved how easily his body moved and the slight sulkiness that had stayed in his expression. She had spent all the years of his adolescence being angry at him and worried about him, and now she could at last enjoy her love for him.

She tried to imagine what he would be like in ten years, in forty years. One day both she and he would be dead, and there would be his children or his children's children. She imagined a still and sunny place in the future, a flat expanse of green. Or maybe the sea. That immortal sea.

"Wordsworth," said Susie, out loud against her will.

"What?" said Elise.

"'Intimations of Immortality,'" said Susie.

"Do you still know it by heart?" asked Kay.

"Yes," said Susie.

"Let's hear it," said Dodge.

"Do you want to hear it?" Susie asked.

"Ready!" said Ron.

"Yes," said Kay and Elise. Billy got up and turned off the CD player, which had been humming. He leaned against the wall. Dodge still lounged by the window. Ron was lying on a wicker bench. Kay and Elise sat in armchairs. They looked at Susie expectantly. *They're like characters in a Chekhov play,* thought Susie.

"We're like characters in a Chekhov play," said Billy.

"Oh no," said Ron. "Much more cheery. I mean, what's our problem?"

"Ha," said Elise.

"Let's hear the poem," said Kay.

"But you know this poem," said Susie to Kay.

"I know, but I'd like to hear you recite the poem," said Kay.

"Ready!" said Ron.

"Okay," said Susie. She got the image into her mind again, of the sea, the sand, the sky, the haze. She sat up in her chair.

> *"Hence, in a season of calm weather,*
>   *Though inland far we be,*
>   *Our souls have sight of that immortal sea*
>   *Which brought us hither;*
> *Can in a moment travel thither—*
>   *And see the children sport upon the shore,*
>   *And hear the mighty waters rolling evermore."*

Susie was silent for a moment.

"'Can in a moment travel thither,'" repeated Ron. "I wish I could travel thither."

"That was great," said Kay. "What a great poem."

"But I'm scared of traveling thither," said Ron. "I'm already having so many problems with hither."

"There he goes. He's making his move," said Dodge, who was still looking out the window.

"Well, that's annoying," said Susie.

"Why?" asked Kay.

"I prefer these tableaux when there isn't actual consummation," said Susie. She felt sad, because of the poem; she didn't know why.

"Really?" said Ron.

"Jealousy," said Elise.

"Speak for yourself," said Ron.

"Well, Ron, you're jealous of the handsome workman," said Elise.

"What? That second-rate baritone!" exclaimed Ron.

"I hope we're eating soon," said Billy, staring at the ceiling.

"We're relatively unbearable, aren't we?" Kay asked Billy.

"No, not you," said Billy to Kay.

"Oh, who then, me?" said Ron. "Or the boy's sainted mother?"

"How about putting the CD back on?" said Susie. She wanted to be filled with something other than herself.

Billy walked over to the boom box, crouched.

"Not that lugubrious Fauré, please," said Ron.

"It's not Fauré," said Susie.

"They're all Fauré to me," said Ron.

"Fauré-ver sad," said Elise.

Billy stood as the sound of Sonny Rollins's saxophone exploded the space.

"Ah," said Ron. "Now I can breathe."

"Why?" asked Susie. "You can't breathe listening to French songs?"

"Sonny Rollins changes the room," said Ron. "From a melancholy mausoleum to a sunny playroom of the soul."

"Whoa," said Elise.

Dodge said, "Now the girl has struck a pose of carefully calibrated balance between attention and insouciance."

"They're talking?" asked Susie.

"Yes," said Dodge.

"They can't be saying much," said Susie. "I tried to get that carpenter to talk to me and I couldn't get three words out of him."

"I find that a turn-on," said Elise.

"Me too," said Susie. "I must admit, I do too."

"I can't believe the extent to which all we struggle to achieve is wasted on you girls," said Ron.

"Don't call us girls," said Elise.

"What do you think they're saying, Dodge?" asked Kay.

"With their mouths or with their bodies?" said Dodge. "With their mouths they're not saying much. The guy said something and now he's looking at her. He's got his hands in his pockets. She's looking out at the pool."

"Maybe we should send Billy out there," said Ron.

"You know, you're all really sick is all I have to say," said Billy.

"He's got a point," said Kay.

"Why?" asked Susie.

"What voyeurs you are," said Billy.

"Somebody's got to do it," said Ron.

"Oh, great move," said Dodge. "What theater!"

"What happened?" asked Susie.

"He just walked away. The girl totally lost her cool and actually turned around to look at him. It really was the perfect move."

"It figures, Dodge, you'd like that scene," said Elise.

"Maybe he made the whole thing up," said Ron.

"Could you think that fast?" said Susie.

"After all," said Ron, "when you've got a pubescent girl in a bikini and a randy carpenter, it's not that hard to figure out what the subtext is going to be."

"How did you know that she's pubescent and he's randy?" said Billy.

"Postpubescent," said Dodge.

"It doesn't really matter," said Susie. "Whether he made it up or not, for practical purposes."

"And what are our practical purposes?" asked Ron.

"I don't know," said Susie. "We'll decide later. Now it's time for dinner."

That night, in bed, Susie couldn't sleep. She repeated the poem out loud in the dark to herself.

"Hence, in a season of calm weather,
Though inland far we be,
Our souls have sight of that immortal sea
Which brought us hither;
Can in a moment travel thither—
And see the children sport upon the shore,
And hear the mighty waters rolling evermore."

She thought of Ron's jokes about the fear of traveling thither. Herself, she'd like to travel thither. She wasn't scared of thither, which, in a way, was all there was left to travel to, she figured.

She thought of Billy. That kind of love makes you travel thither, actually. When Billy was small, she hadn't understood anything of what it meant, that kind of love, not anything. She wanted to go out,

she wanted to have fun, she wanted to travel, but she felt burdened
by his existence. She adored him but she felt burdened. And there
were the men too. So time consuming. So energy consuming. Then
he was an adolescent, and absolutely intolerable for several years,
as if he had a mission to prevent her from ever experiencing a
serene moment. He had made her so angry, she detested herself.
And then he got to a point where he wouldn't let her behave like a
mother. He became furious if she told him to put on a sweater. He
called her "Susie." He wouldn't tell her anything. He made everything impossible. Her therapist told her he needed to separate, and
Susie had taught herself to detach. And then...

Then it was too late. She saw how Billy looked at Kay sometimes, and it made her feel so sad that Billy should have such a
crush on Kay and not on her. So sad. And yet at the same time, it
gave her a kind of peace too. Kay had always had a real tenderness
for Billy, even when Susie herself did not have the patience to be
tender. Or something more than peace, maybe. Something complete. There was some complicated equation, as if her son and her
best friend completed her somehow, as if love could really be
shared, like some abstract energy.

Poor Kay. When Susie thought of Kay never having a child,
never giving birth, never lifting a wriggling, giggling baby out of
the bath...

Saturday

Saturday afternoon Susie swam laps, forty-five minutes' worth,
in the pool, while the others came and went. She did the crawl one
way, the breaststroke back. She tried to abstract her physical activity and get into a groove but couldn't. It was like playing scales
in a way. She thought maybe she had only been able to get to a certain point with music because she had begun to be afraid of gener-
ating the concentration you need to go into the deep trance that
enabled you to practice six or seven or eight hours a day. She'd

acquired a kind of vertigo with regard to her own psychic space. Maybe that's why she had become a costume designer. It was safer to stick to appearances.

Swimming laps was something like playing scales, something like meditation too, because you keep having to bring your mind back to your count. And then what she mostly tried to make herself think of was stroke, stroke, stroke, stroke, stroke. The radio was on, emitting MOR rock 'n' roll and inconsequential sentiment. Who had turned it on? It was so annoying. Ron slept on his chaise longue. Dodge read on his, an old guidebook to Santa Fe. Kay, looking worried, was half sitting, half reclining in an odd, impermanent pose, as if she was going to lie down and then had forgotten. Finally she went back into the house, leaving her towel and her paperback copy of *Jane Eyre* (she'd abandoned Norman O. Brown) and her glass of iced tea, so that it seemed as if she would come right back, but she didn't. Kay seemed more upset in the last few days. Susie hadn't asked anything because she'd learned to let Kay coast around until she realigned herself. Anyway, reasoned Susie, Kay knew that she could come to her anytime.

Susie imagined thirty or forty of herself, swimming. There.

"Woosh," she said as she got out of the pool.

Dodge looked up and watched her dry herself. "Was it nice?" he asked. "Do you feel good?"

"I feel virtuous, anyway," said Susie.

"Hello." It was Claudine wearing the same tremendously skimpy gold bikini and carrying a long lime-green radio.

"You look like a frame out of an *Archie* comic book," said Susie.

"Pardon?" said Claudine.

"Nothing," said Susie. "Have a seat. There's iced tea over there if you want it."

"Is it all right?" asked Claudine in her very insistent French accent. "I'm not abusing the privilege you gave me?"

"No," said Susie. "It's fine."

Susie waited until Claudine settled herself on the deck chair as

Dodge watched her over the top of his guidebook. "I'm going in," Susie said, gathering her stuff.

"Really?" said Dodge. "Are you coming back?"

"Hi," said Ron, opening his eyes but lying very still.

"Hi," said Susie. "Yes, I'll be back in a while. Maybe with some sandwiches, or else I'll call you in."

Claudine looked anxious, or looked as if she wanted to look anxious.

"See you later, Claudine," said Susie. "Hang out as long as you like."

She walked back to the house, her rubber shoes flapping. The sky was blue silk, the sun yellow lamé, the grass green organza. A very slight breeze whispered in the leaves. She felt happy. She squeezed some of the water out of her hair onto the flower bed before going in.

Inside, the house seemed fairly dark and damp. There was music coming out of Billy's room, as usual. The Byrds. Susie tilted her head a moment and listened. *Why the Byrds?* The other doors were closed and silent, all except hers, which was somewhat ajar.

She hadn't remembered leaving her door opened. She walked in and stood at the center of the room for a moment. The shade was still drawn and on either side of it two shafts of sunlight beamed into the carpet. Her bed was unmade, as she had left it, last night's clothes on a chair, the high-heeled sandals picturesque, one up, one down.

The top drawer of the old dresser was open, and Susie stared at it from the middle of the room, trying to remember whether she could have left it open. She thought not because she would only have opened the bottom drawer today, for her bathing suit.

She walked over to the dresser and looked in. Panties on one side were folded, bras on the other, handkerchiefs in the middle, socks pell-mell in the back. One of the panties was unfolded, and Susie looked at it for a while in the drawer and tried to figure out whether it could have been she who unfolded it.

Right away she thought of the carpenter, the young one, the one

Dodge said had been talking to the au pair. The carpenters had
been working on the staircase for several hours every day for the
last three days. Every day Susie exchanged a few words with both
of them on her way up or downstairs. Today she had noticed that
she had been anticipating seeing the handsome one. When she had
looked at him and he had looked back, she had realized this guy
had a particularly frank gaze. If her mind were a stage, he had
been a character on the back of the stage, watching the rest of the
action, wearing those work shoes and those jeans and the big metal
belt buckle and the T-shirt rolled up at the sleeves and that very
frank look of interest and slight amusement in those pale eyes.

Now she stood in the silent room, in her damp bathing suit,
among the patches of pale light, and thought of the carpenter's eyes
and felt this violent movement in her body—she couldn't have said
whether it was pleasurable or painful—at the thought that the guy
had gone through her underwear. And fear too, maybe. She picked
up the pair of underpants and looked at them. Pale blue underpants, polished cotton with a bit of lacework on the side. Expensive
ones, from Bendel's. It seemed to her that there was a smudge on
the side of them such as would have been made by a slightly dirty
thumb, but she couldn't tell for sure. She folded the underpants
carefully and put them back in the drawer and then stayed still for
a long moment. Then she closed the drawer and stood by the
dresser, looking at the print above the bureau, though all she noticed was how fine the engraving was, how perfect the frame.

Then she walked to the middle of the room and hugged her
arms. She put her towel on the bed and lay down. Then, just as
suddenly, she got up, stripped off the wet bathing suit, put on the
big blue terry cloth robe that Billy always said made her look like
a bunny, and lifted the sheets and got under the covers and curled
up again and covered her nose and mouth with one hand and her
eyes with the other and stayed that way, absolutely immobile except for breathing, until she fell asleep.

———

"So something happened today," said Susie at dinner. She heard herself beginning to speak, almost as if without volition. She hadn't quite meant to bring it up. Or, rather, had been trying to figure out whether she should bring it up and hadn't made up her mind. They were all in a good mood. Maybe that was it. At the moment she shivered with uneasiness. If the truth be told—luckily, she didn't have to tell it—she was in fact as uncomfortable at her own pleasure at the thought of the carpenter going through her underwear drawer as she might have been frightened by it. It wasn't very frightening after all. The only thing that made it frightening was the fact that she couldn't get herself to stop thinking about his eyes. She kept seeing his eyes, inside her mind, looking at her.

She missed Otto.

"What? What drama has occurred now to add to the saga of this eventful summer?" said Ron. "Did Claudine lose her bikini string at the pool after I left? I knew it!"

"I'm getting sick of hearing about Claudine," said Elise.

"Yes, let's put a lid on the Claudine remarks," said Kay.

"Yea, nix it on Claudine," said Elise.

"It's disgusting," Billy suddenly said, in such an earnest tone that the others burst out laughing.

"I didn't say anything," said Dodge defensively, laughing.

"Oh, no, you said nothing," said Ron. "Sure, what was that *tableau vivant* spectacle you performed for us yesterday about the sex act between Claudine and the carpenter."

"I was reporting what I saw for the sake of the group."

"I think it's something that's been happening concurrently with men generally becoming more humane and feminist," said Elise, "that they somehow have to compensate for it by being even more crude and gross whenever they get a chance."

"More humane and feminist, yes, I like that," said Ron.

"Not you, Reiser," said Elise.

"I don't see what's crude and gross about having expressed a fantasy about that girl's string bikini coming off," said Ron. "On the contrary, I think I was being a sensitive man by being in touch with my feelings and sharing with the group."

"You'd have to be blind, it's true, not to be mesmerized by the subtleties of her perpetual striptease by the pool," said Elise. "It's like Kabuki theater."

"Look who's talking about striptease by the pool," said Ron.

"But mine wasn't Kabuki theater," said Elise. "My striptease was classic vaudeville comedy."

"Musical comedy," said Billy.

"Why, thank you, Billy," said Elise.

"Well, and what happened, Susie?" asked Kay. "Did something happen to you today?"

"Yes," said Susie. "Someone has been in my underwear drawer." There was silence for a moment.

"Wow," said Ron.

"It wasn't me," said Dodge, and the others laughed.

"In your underwear?" said Kay.

"Yes," said Susie. "Someone went through my drawer."

"And how did you know?" asked Elise.

"Some stuff was out of place."

"What stuff?" asked Kay.

"Underpants," said Susie.

"Your underpants had teeth marks on it?" asked Ron.

"Fingerprints," said Dodge.

"Actually, that's not far off," said Susie.

"You're kidding," said Ron.

"Well, I think there was a mark."

"What kind of a mark?" asked Kay.

"I think it was the carpenter," said Susie.

There was a roar of laughter and discussion.

"I think you're off your rocker," said Billy. "This is like one of your things where you think something may have happened and then you talk yourself into it."

"That shows how much you know, my boy," said Ron. "Every one working in a house goes through every drawer all the time; they just usually don't get caught."

"And what makes you think it was the carpenter?" said Billy. "Why not one of us?"

"They were smudged," said Susie.

"The underpants?" asked Kay.

"Maybe you just wish it were the carpenter," said Elise.

"Well, that's true of course," said Susie. "The carpenter is rather attractive."

"Rather!" said Elise. "I'll say. Incredibly attractive. I'd fuck him in a second."

"Him and what army?" said Ron.

"Fuck you, Ron," said Elise.

"I'll have more wine," said Dodge. "This conversation is getting to be too rough for me."

"Have more wine—this conversation is good for you," said Susie. "And let's ponder the attractiveness of the carpenter."

"Excuse me," said Billy. "I'm through eating."

"Oh, I'm sorry, Billy," said Susie. "We're just being a little boisterous."

"No, it's fine, I'm finished," said Billy, and left the room.

"God," said Susie.

"That boy must have terrible Oedipal problems," said Ron.

"No worse than yours, Ron," said Elise.

"Well, that's for sure," said Kay.

"Oh, you too?" said Ron. "You're ganging up on me."

"Well, someone's got to do it," said Susie. She was upset Billy had left the room. *Do I seem drunk?* Billy could be such a prude sometimes. How could it be that she wound up having a son who could be so puritanical?

"What should be done about the underwear crime?" Dodge said. "Should we confront the culprit?"

"Certainly not," said Susie. "I'm just going to wait for further developments. Maybe he'll decide to come back at night when we're all sleeping."

"And do some woodwork or something," said Dodge.

They all laughed.

"Maybe he'll leave you a present in the underwear drawer," said Ron.

"Maybe we should booby-trap the underwear drawer," said Dodge.

"I'll have more wine," said Elise.

"Me too," said Susie.

"Me too," said Kay. "I might as well."

"Now, girls, girls, girls," said Ron.

Susie drank four or five more glasses of wine before she left the table, and when she got to her room, she dropped her clothes to the floor and slipped into bed without hunting for her nightgown.

She hadn't turned off the light yet because she had some idea she might read, though it now occurred to her that she had had much too much to drink to read, when there was a knock at the door.

She pulled the covers up, sat up. "Yes?" she called out. "Come in."

The door opened a crack and Ron stuck his head in.

"Hi," he said.

"Hi," said Susie, noncommittally. It wasn't whom she had expected.

"I have something to tell you," he said.

"Okay," she said. And pulled the covers up higher under her chin. He stepped into the room and surveyed it, trying to decide where to situate himself. Finally he walked over to the chair by the dressing table and sat down, gingerly. He looked at her. Started speaking twice before the words actually came out.

"It was me," he said.

"What?" she said.

"It was me who went into your underwear drawer," said Ron. He looked very solemn.

Susie stared at Ron, processing the information. It suddenly occurred to her that he must be joking and she smiled.

"You're kidding," she said, smiling.

He smiled too, as if her smile entitled him to be more cordial. "No," he said sheepishly.

"You went through my underwear drawer?" said Susie.

"I'm sorry," said Ron. Now he tried not to smile. He was obviously very nervous.

She said nothing. "Are you upset?" he asked.

Susie said nothing for a moment. "You're a sick motherfucker," she said.

"I'm sorry," he said.

"You know why?"

Ron still had his sheepish smile. "Why?" he said.

"Not because you went through my underwear drawer, though that would be bizarre enough, but because you let me go on and on at dinner about the carpenter."

"I know," said Ron. "I wanted to say something..."

"But you didn't."

"I'm sorry," said Ron.

"Well," said Susie. "Forget it."

He stood and hesitated. "I'm sorry."

"Okay," said Susie.

He went to the door. "Good night," he said, very awkwardly.

"Good night," said Susie. He closed the door behind him. "You sick motherfucker," she said sotto voce.

She turned off the light. She thought of the carpenter again and only now realized how delicious the image had been of the attractive carpenter going through her underwear. She had imagined him thinking about her, as he was doing it, and had felt his desire. Now if she replayed her various encounters with the carpenter, she could see he was really not nearly smart enough to be that perverse. She would probably be angrier, she decided, if she hadn't had so much to drink. She'd had much too much to drink. She missed the dog. Why had her dog gotten run over? It wasn't supposed to happen. Why had she gotten a dog in the first place? What was it about her that had made Ron behave in that way? Why did she always invite psycho behavior in one way or another? She was too spacey for her own good. She hated Ron.

She thought of the carpenter's face and the dog's face and Dodge's face and Ron's face looking sheepish and a little flushed, and then she slid into actual sleep but soon surged back to wakefulness. Ah, she didn't want to be awake anymore. She tried an old trick, of singing a song inside her mind. She picked "Mellow Yellow," by Donovan. *They call me Mellow Yellow.* She thought of Sarah Lawrence and Kay. Then she added a Scarlatti aria, *O cessate di piagarmi.* She sang both songs to herself, simultaneously, for at least forty-five seconds before she went to sleep. *O lasciatemi morir.*

Sunday

The next morning on her way to breakfast, she bumped into the carpenter. He really was appealing with his muscled arms, and those eyes of his.

"Hi," he said.

"Hi," said Susie.

"Great sandals," he said.

They both looked down at her feet. "Thanks," said Susie. "See you later."

Ron and Kay were in the dining room.

"How're you doing?" said Susie.

"Hangover," said Kay.

"Hangover," said Ron.

Elise walked in and went to the sideboard without speaking to anyone and put some eggs on her plate. Susie had only taken coffee. Elise walked back to the table, put her plate down, and sat down. She stared at her plate.

"What's the matter, Elise?" said Susie.

"The parsley on my plate is freaking me out," said Elise.

"Is there something wrong with it?"

"The green is so violent," said Elise.

Susie laughed. "I'm sorry," she said.

"No," said Elise. "I like it. It's just overstimulating in the state I'm in."

"I know what you mean," said Kay. "This morning I saw an ant on my windowsill and it upset me."

"Why?" asked Ron.

"I don't mind ants," said Susie. "I hate water bugs."

"No, it's not that," said Kay. "I just felt sorry for the ant, going on and on and on."

"It's the morning," said Elise. "Sometimes in the morning if I happen to glance in the mirror, my own breasts scare me."

"Phew," said Ron.

"Have you seen the carpenter yet?" Kay asked Susie. She lowered her voice. "I think he's in the house."

"Yes," said Susie. "I bumped into him in the hall and he was his usual cunning self."

"Any signs of anything?" asked Elise.

"Well, the thing is . . . ," said Susie. Kay and Elise were looking at her. Ron was studying his fork and plate as he ate his eggs. "I've had a confession from another party."

"Really?" said Elise. "A confession?"

"What other party?" asked Kay.

"Who shall remain nameless."

"Ron!" said Elise.

"Never mind," said Susie.

"Billy," said Kay.

"Never mind, never mind, never mind. Don't ask me. I won't tell you," she said. "But it wasn't the carpenter."

"Of course," said Ron. "You have no way of really knowing."

"What do you mean?" said Susie, with a slight edge in her voice. "What do you mean, I have no way of knowing? I just told you I had a confession."

"Well, someone could have lied," said Ron.

"A false confession," said Kay. "The plot thickens."

"Why would anybody lie about that?" Susie asked Ron.

"And when did you receive the confession?" asked Ron.

"Last night," said Susie.

"Well, that narrows the field," Elise said to Kay.

"Someone came to your room?" said Ron.

"Yes," said Susie.

"Well, someone could have come to your room with other motives and then when confronted with you said that instead because he chickened out," said Ron.

"That's stupefying," said Susie.

Ron had his sheepish smile again. "I'm just proposing it," he said, "as an alternative possibility."

"Maybe it's a possibility in the alternate reality," said Elise. "This old house must have several realities besides the one we see."

"Elise," said Kay, "I thought your parsley was freaking you out. Don't you think it's a little early in the morning?"

"I'm just getting going," said Elise.

"God," said Ron. "What energy you creative types have early in the day."

"Ron," said Susie.

"What?" he said.

"You're an asshole."

"Well, that I knew," he said. "That I knew."

"Don't mention creativity so early in the day," said Elise. "I'd like to be less creative at this hour."

"I'd be scared of your breasts too," said Ron to Elise.

"You're scared of all breasts," said Susie.

"Wow," said Kay.

"Oy, oy, oy," said Ron. He tilted back on his chair, his hands behind his neck.

"Well, you deserved that," said Susie.

"I certainly did," said Ron.

"You certainly did," said Elise.

There was a knock at the door and the carpenter stuck his head in.

"Hi," he said.

"Hi," they said.

His gaze went from one face to the other.

"How about some coffee?" asked Elise.

"Oh, no thanks," said the carpenter. "I just needed to ask Susie something."

Susie looked at her watch. "I'll be there in one minute, okay?" she said.

"Okay," he said. "I'll be by the staircase."

Susie looked at the others. "What is this?" she whispered.

The other women laughed. "Maybe he's getting ready to come in for a landing," said Elise.

Susie looked at Ron but couldn't read him. "Maybe I'll just fuck him," she whispered. "Maybe I'll just take him back to my room and fuck him."

"Have you got any condoms?" said Kay.

"Maybe he's just into the underwear," said Elise. Ron laughed.

"Well, we'll see," said Susie.

But the carpenter only wanted to tell Susie they were through and had done the best they could on the old staircase ramp. "I wanted to give you my card," he said.

"Oh, okay," said Susie.

"In case you ever need anything done in your loft in Manhattan," said the carpenter.

"Okay," said Susie, smiling. The carpenter had been very interested to hear, the other day, that she had a loft in Soho.

He took out his wallet, slid a card out, and handed it to her. She took the card. She noted the slight warmth of his fingers. "Thank you very much," she said.

"Okay," he said. "You call me if you need anything else," he said with that smile.

"Okay," she said, and she smiled back.

She stood at the door and watched him climb into the pickup. His buddy was at the wheel. She watched them drive away and then forgot herself in the morning softness, and stood there, leaning against the door. She felt bereft, as if the carpenter's departure signified the loss of an immense and wonderful possibility. The dew made the grass glimmer. The blue of the sky was glossy. Blue cream. Azure satin. Indigo pomegranate. Sapphire and ruby velvet. Powder blue licking. *Mouvements perpétuels.*

RON

Friday

Ron was irritated to hear that Billy was having a friend up for the weekend.

"There aren't enough people up there already?" he said to Dodge in the car on the way up. It was close to midnight and there were few other cars on the road. Maybe he was irritated, anyway. Dodge always drove faster than Ron found comfortable. The speedometer often hovered in the high end of the eighties, and Ron constantly anticipated being stopped by a cop cruising for just such prey as them. To say nothing of worrying that Dodge would have a momentary lapse of concentration. Ron had a very clear fantasy of a crash. Dodge's mangled head wedged between the wheel and the caved-in roof. Maybe on the horn, so the horn would blare endlessly.

"Why?" asked Dodge. "Who would you trim?"

"I don't know," said Ron. "Elise, maybe. Elise gets on my nerves. On the other hand, sometimes she entertains me."

"Like a bug, you mean," said Dodge.

"I thought you liked Elise," said Ron.

"I do," said Dodge. "I was just trying to put myself in your place. That's the feeling you give sometimes, that you think other people are bugs."

"Maybe cute little ladybugs, butterflies, interesting ants," said Ron. "Not disgusting cockroaches or earthworms."

"Earthworms aren't bugs," said Dodge.

"Daddy longlegs," said Ron.

"Sometimes women remind me of cats," said Dodge. "I love to just watch them."

"Sometimes women remind me of gorillas," said Ron. "I don't know whether to groom or to run."

Dodge laughed. "None of the women in this house are like gorillas," he said.

"Not yet," said Ron.

"Susie's like a jungle cat," said Dodge. "A leopard, maybe. And Kay is more like a bird."

"And what's Elise?"

"A little furry animal," said Dodge.

"Really?" said Ron. "I see her as something more dangerous. A hyena, maybe."

"A hyena!" Dodge laughed again. Ron laughed too.

"Or a jackal," said Ron.

"That's ridiculous," said Dodge. "Except to the extent that they're all hyenas, even the loveliest pussycat ones."

"And what about Claudine?" said Ron.

"Claudine?" said Dodge. "I don't know." The faint drizzle seemed to increase slightly. Dodge switched on the windshield wipers.

"What a little number," said Ron.

"Yeah," said Dodge.

They didn't talk for a while. Ron didn't spend too long thinking about Claudine. He felt uneasy and kept casting back to the work left undone in New York. He felt tired and anxious, as he did every Friday night. He couldn't believe he was spending every weekend of the summer in a place with no TV. No TV!!!! Incredible. Incredible. He had broached it early in the season, had even offered to

buy one for the house, but had been booed and hissed good-
naturedly by the others every time he brought it up until he gave
up. Fucking snobs.

And is this fucking rain going to continue?

"So, Ron," said Dodge. He paused while going around one of
the boulders that makes the Taconic a dangerous highway. He
hugged the curve very tight.

"Yeah," said Ron. "Aren't you going a little fast?"

"Not really," said Dodge.

Ron said nothing more since he knew Dodge was rather vain of
his driving reflexes, but he put his seat belt on with a sigh. Dodge
laughed.

"Okay, okay," he said, and let his foot off the accelerator
slightly. "So, Ron."

"Yeah," said Ron.

"What happened between you and Susie last weekend?"

Ron tensed. His mind went white. "I don't know," he said.
"What do you mean?"

"Did you have an argument or something?"

"No," said Ron. "I don't know. She was on the rag about me. I
irritate her sometimes."

Ron didn't know why he had gone through Susie's underwear
drawer. He had known he shouldn't have been doing it, but not why
he did it. He'd seen dozens of women's underwear. Hundreds. He
didn't need to see Susie's underwear. He didn't even want to fuck
Susie that much. And then he didn't know why he hadn't been
more careful, and why he had spoken up, and what the whole goddamn thing was about. He'd been as if possessed, he told himself
now. Possessed.

He hadn't thought about it too much during the week. There'd
been a lot of work. His manager was putting a tour together for the
fall. But also it was just too weird, this thing about the underwear.
It almost seemed to him he would be better off setting it aside. It
certainly was something that had never happened before, and it
would surely never happen again. The really, really weird thing,

anyway, he thought, was not that he had gone through the underwear, which, in a way, was the sort of mechanical voyeurism that anyone might do if they thought they wouldn't get caught. The door had been open; from the doorway he'd seen the open drawer. He knew they were all at the pool.

No, the really strange thing that he had done was then directing Susie to think it was him instead of that carpenter. Why? Why had he done that? Some odd sort of jealousy. Pride. Perversity. He didn't know. He couldn't analyze it now any better than if it had been someone else's act. In a way it was. *Muy complicado.*

"Are you sure?" said Dodge.

"You know I have an abrasive personality," said Ron. "Everyone's irritated with me sooner or later."

"I just think it's a miracle we've gotten through this much of the summer without arguments and fights," said Dodge.

"They don't like it that we don't take our shoes off when we come back in when it's been raining."

"Who?" asked Dodge.

"The girls," said Ron. "We track mud."

"Oh," said Dodge. "That's right." He paused. "You know who's great?" he said.

"Susie?" said Ron. He hated hearing Dodge talk about Susie. Envy morphed immediately into rage. "Dodie?"

"No," said Dodge. "Kay."

"Kay?" said Ron. "Kay makes me feel terrible."

"You're kidding," said Dodge. "Why?"

"Because she's carrying around some terrible burden of misery."

"Well," said Dodge. "But who isn't? I think she's soulful."

"Susie isn't," said Ron. "Susie seems happy."

"Well, yes," said Dodge. "But it's a form of craziness, in a way. I mean, of denial."

"That's what I need a dose of," said Ron. "Denial."

"Well, that's what summer vacation is for," said Dodge.

"I think summer vacation is just an opportunity to be anxious

in the country instead of in the city. Especially in this house," said
Ron, "I hope this weekend is more relaxed. That's what I'd like to
feel, is that I'm on vacation. I'd like everything just to be nice."

They didn't arrive until around two in the morning. They were
careful not to slam the car doors. From the front, the windows were
uniformly dark. The rain had paused for the moment. The air was
warm and moist. In the sky you could just distinguish the movement of the clouds floating away from one another revealing stars.
Ron breathed. *Yes, this is nice.*

They walked up quietly, but the floorboards creaked under
Ron's feet.

"Shhhh," hissed Dodge in front of him.

"I'm trying," said Ron.

"Shhh," said Dodge.

On the landing Dodge whispered, "Okay, good night," and
headed toward his room.

Ron was disappointed; he had hoped they'd have a nightcap.
"Okay, good night, buddy," he said.

His room smelled slightly musty but he liked it. It was neat and
old. His place in New York was very modern. That had been a mistake, but he would never in a million years have the energy to do
anything about it and, besides, it was better for the cleaning
woman.

He turned on all the lights. "Good night, buddy," he said. He
went to the bathroom and washed and brushed his teeth and flossed
carefully. Back in his room he unpacked and got into bed with *The
Sherlock Holmes Reader,* but he found himself unable to read. He
got out of bed and turned all the lights off, then got back into bed
and tried to go to sleep. He soon gave up and stared into space for
quite a while, then he pushed the covers back with a gesture of
rage and stood up and slipped on his jeans and went down barefoot
to the patio. He didn't turn on the lights. There was enough moonlight to find the bottle and the glass. He poured himself some
scotch. Drained his glass. Poured himself some more. It was amazing how much he missed watching TV. He stood by the window

with the glass, sipping, looking out toward the rose garden, though he couldn't see it, listening to the rain, until he forgot what he was doing.

Some noise in the house must have startled him. He drained his glass, put it down, walked heavily upstairs, and lay down on the bed fully clothed. This time he went to sleep.

Saturday

He slept through breakfast and when he woke up, the sun was nearly in the middle of the sky. He put on his blue bathing trunks. A plate covered with a napkin had been left by the microwave oven that, upon examination, turned out to contain some pancakes. He didn't warm them up, though, just ate them with his fingers, standing over the kitchen counter, dipping them into a pitcher he had discovered contained syrup. The coffee was still tepid when he poured himself a cup.

From the kitchen he walked straight to the pool. Now that summer was advancing, the vegetation that surrounded the path to the pool was lush and fragrant. The sky still seemed watery and pale, the pines dull and dark in the distance. Around the pool the green of the grass next to the concrete seemed deeper and richer than last week.

Susie and Elise were sunbathing, and Ron registered that Elise's body looked better than he had remembered, especially when oiled. She wore a white bathing suit bottom. The top was on the ground next to her chair. She had crossed her hands under her neck, as if to tan her armpits. Her breasts were small and high. Nice.

No, he wasn't scared of breasts. Not nice, small breasts. Well, maybe a little queasy, in a way. But who wasn't?

Susie was lying on her stomach wearing a bright red one-piece suit, her arms hanging over the chair. Then he saw the long slim boy's body next to hers and figured it must be Billy's friend. He was wearing very short blue trunks. The top of his body and his face were covered with newspaper.

"Hi," said Susie, who looked up when she heard or sensed his step on the concrete.

"Hi," said Ron. "What's cooking?"

"Have you met Alexander?"

"How're you doing," Ron said to the boy. Alexander, Ron was taken aback to note, was surprisingly beautiful. *Gay,* Ron thought.

"Hi," said Alexander.

No, Ron thought. *Maybe not.*

"Hi, Ron," said Elise.

"Mornin', Miz Elise," Ron said in a southern accent. Alexander, who had closed his eyes, again reopened them and stared straight ahead for a moment. *He thinks I'm an asshole,* Ron said to himself.

Ron's chair made a loud squeaking noise when he turned it to face the sun precisely.

Ron walked over to Susie's chaise longue, looked underneath, and got out the suntan lotion. "How you doin', Suze?" he asked.

"I like the weather," she said. "I hope it holds."

Susie was smiling at him as if everything was fine. Maybe everything was fine.

Back at his chair he lathered his arms and face and patted some extra layers of lotion onto his nose. He liked the smell of it. Coconut. He lay down. All the others lay silently with their eyes closed. He closed his eyes. Beyond his closed eyelids was the yellow flaming of the sun, the buzz of a fly. Or was it a hornet? He didn't like hornets. He liked the way the suntan lotion felt under his fingertips, on his thighs. He had a moment of well-being.

That's better, he thought sleepily. He imagined the boy, Alexander, bloody and crying for a moment, but then he cleared his mind and thought only of the yellow flame on his eyelids. Then there was Elise, Elise and the boy, bloody and mangled, as if a machine had torn their limbs from them.

Ron sat up. The others were perfectly still. He sighed. He got up and went to the side of the pool, looked up at the sky. Then he walked around to the deep end of the pool, climbed onto the diving board, hooked his toes on the board, and dived in, a big belly flop that splashed the others plentifully.

"Hey!" Susie and Elise yelled out at the same time when he came up for air. The boy said nothing, only looked for a moment at Ron, swimming the length of the pool in a mighty series of splashes.

Ron had counted thirty-five laps when it began to drizzle. He might not have noticed, but he heard Susie and Elise talking and paused for a moment.

"Shit," said Susie.

Ron swam to the side of the pool and watched the women squint up at the sky. There was still a bit of sun shining through the drizzle.

On the water, the rain made little sparkles.

"I'm going to do a few more laps," said Ron. The others were gathering their things.

"Okay," Susie called out. "We'll see you later. I'll take your stuff in."

When Ron swam his west-to-east lap again, he saw Susie, Elise, and Alexander growing smaller as they walked back to the house. Both Susie and Elise were looking at Alexander, who had the posture of someone who is accustomed to being looked at.

Ron swam fifteen more laps. Then he walked back in the rain. He felt terribly angry and sad, but didn't know why. He made himself notice the raindrops glistening on the grass.

When he walked into the house, Dodge, Susie, Elise, and Kay were in the kitchen. Elise was sitting by herself at the table doodling on a pad and looking dour. Dodge, Susie, and Kay were eating peanut butter off a knife they were passing around.

"Hi, Kay," he said.

"Hi, Ron," said Kay. "Had a swim?"

He looked at Kay and thought for a moment that Dodge was right. Dodge had always had a great eye for women. Ron hadn't noticed this softness in Kay, which he suddenly felt, like a gust of warmth, waft toward him through the prettiness and sadness that had always served as bottlenecks for his attention.

"Yes, cookie," he said to Kay.

Kay laughed. Ron looked at Dodge, who shook his head slightly, smiling.

Dodge and women. That was really something. *Fucking Moriarty.*

They decided to go for a drive, with the vague idea of finding a place to have lunch. It was raining harder and harder. Billy and Alexander had decided to stay home. As they left, the two boys were in the drawing room, slouched in armchairs, legs identically stretched ahead of them, utterly silent.

Ron wondered what the boys talked about by themselves. Did they have sex? Was Billy gay?

"Can I drive?" asked Ron.

"Yes," said Susie. "As long as you don't make any derogatory remarks about my faithful Saab."

"What, that sleek and futuristic machine?" said Ron as they approached the somewhat rusting vehicle. "Why would anyone derogate such a hot little tootsie?"

"I'm not letting you drive," said Susie.

"I take it back," said Ron. "I love this car. I love it, I love it." He leaned over the hood and kissed the car several times very loudly. "Love!" he crooned, Hollywood style.

"Okay, okay," said Susie.

The drizzle intensified. From the house came the sound of music, incredibly loud. "What?" said Ron.

"Nirvana," said Elise.

"Wow," said Kay. "So that's what they do when we're gone."

"It's just background music for taking drugs," said Dodge.

"Don't even say that," said Susie. "Please don't even think it. I hope those days are over."

"Oh, no," said Ron. "Those boys would never touch any drugs ... Not a chance ..."

"That's not funny," said Susie.

Ron got in behind the wheel of the Saab. Susie handed him the keys. Dodge sat next to Ron. Susie, Elise, and Kay sat in the back. Ron was thinking of how much he missed watching TV.

"Where to, girls?" said Ron.

"The pizza place?" said Susie.

"It's so grim there," said Dodge.

"Let's go to the pizza place and commit mass suicide," said Elise.

"I'm sick of the rain," said Susie.

"It rained all week," said Kay. "But it often clears up in the late afternoon."

"Rain and suicide go together, like a horse and carriage and love and marriage," said Elise.

"Coke and potato chips," said Dodge.

"You're in a bad mood?" Kay said to Elise.

"Horrible," said Elise.

"Oh dear, poor little darlin'," said Ron.

"And, Ron, could you please stop calling us girls?" said Elise.

"Yes, madame," said Ron. "Whatever you desire, madame."

"That's better," said Elise.

Town was a sad affair. Decades of economic depression, fake wood paneling, old plastic, an obese child on a deformed tricycle. Sitting at the counter eating grilled cheese sandwiches or spooning crackers out of pea soup, rows of curious eyes impacted in alcohol-flabby faces turned toward them.

"Let's hold off on lunch," whispered Susie.

When they were back in the car, they were silent for a moment, and then Dodge said, "America."

They laughed and groaned.

"That's not America," said Ron. "My father's country club was America." He started the motor. "All these men in the suburbs in the comfortable locker rooms. That's America. Comfort. Their wives are inside playing bridge. They're walking about the locker room with towels around their waists, about to slap one another on the back. They've got their big cars waiting for them outside. America."

"That's ridiculous," said Elise. "You think that because you're rich."

"America fifty years ago," said Susie.

"Rich!" exclaimed Ron.

"Yes, relatively speaking," said Elise.

"Or literally," said Dodge.

"What kind of portfolio do you have, Ron?" said Susie.

Ron laughed. He actually found himself embarrassed by this subject.

"What's the story on lunch?" said Dodge.

"Let's have pizza," said Elise.

"All right," said Susie. "Let's face it. We have to go back to the diner."

They got into the car in a jovial mood but fell into silence once they were on the road. At the diner they sat in a booth and played country music on the jukebox, watched the rain fall in the parking lot.

Ron wondered how much money the rest of them had. Dodge, he figured, had a bundle. His paintings were selling in the hundreds of thousands. Although half went to the galleries. But still, he must be socking it away. The girls, who knew how they survived. Kay came from a rich family. You could just sniff that around her. But she didn't behave like a wealthy woman. Susie had been married to a rich guy. She must have scored big when they broke up. Though, actually, maybe she'd refused to take any money. Susie could have money. She was the type who always had money. She looked like she did.

Though what did money mean? Half a million? Bare minimum. Could Susie have more than half a million stowed away?

Dodge must be over the million mark. Well over. Though Dodge occasionally went on shopping sprees, Ron knew. To say nothing of the fact that in the late seventies a lot of Dodge's money went up his nose. And up Ron's nose too, actually.

He thought of his checking account. His checkbook, in its leather case. The paper his checks were printed on had lines, little thin lines. He loved his checks. The paper was white; the lines were pale red. He didn't even like to think of his stock portfolio, his savings accounts, his IRA, his KEOGH, his mutual funds, his certificates of deposits, his treasury bonds. Only 5 percent. It was infuriating. What he liked to think about was his checks. The neatness, the precision of the layout. Utilitarian and handsome.

"I'm starving," said Dodge.

"Me too," said Ron.

"Be careful what you order," said Elise.

The diner must once have looked as if it had come off a train, but whatever chrome there may have been was buried underneath framed photos of fifties pop stars. They spoke no more about what America was. They ate BLTs and french fries. Ron burped out loud, and Susie and Elise said, "Yuck," and Ron said, "That made me feel better."

"Belching?" said Dodge. "God knows what'll be next."

"No, not the belching, the disgust on the ladies' faces and the 'yuck.'" He said it again. "Yuck!" he called out, louder. The waitress clearing the table in the booth next to them didn't look up. "Yuck!" Ron called out again, louder.

"You ain't nothing but a hound dog," Elise sang to Susie.

"Okay," Susie said, and dropped a quarter into the jukebox.

"Why aren't we in Tuscany or something?" Dodge said.

"We can't afford it," said Elise.

"This is perfect," said Ron. "This is exactly where I want to be."

They bantered on. Ron tuned out. He thought of his father, big belly over the band of his bathing trunks. His parents sitting in front of the cabana, in Westchester. The women parading around in their halter tops and shorts as if their thighs were not quivering. No one ever, he thought, would understand the vulgarity and the comfort of Westchester in the fifties and sixties.

He looked at the women. Sitting across the way, Kay and Elise looked slightly haggard under the fluorescent light.

He looked at Susie, sitting on his side of the booth, and thought he might jerk off tonight.

When was the last time he had jerked off? Maybe the night
Casey Rambler had come to dinner. What a piece of work she was.

"What are you thinking about?" Elise asked him.

"Westchester," he said.

"Where's Alexander from?" Dodge asked.

"What a hot kid he is," said Susie. "Isn't he?"

"Hot enough for you?" said Ron.

"No," said Susie.

"Would you ever sleep with one of Billy's friends?" Kay asked
Susie.

"I hope not," said Ron. "Billy's got enough Oedipal problems
as it is."

"Everybody's got Oedipal problems, Ron, except for you,"
Elise said.

"And me," said Dodge. "I have no Oedipal problems."

"Is he hot enough for you, Ron?" Susie asked.

"Me?" said Ron. "You bet, cookie. Would you like to see us
do it?"

"Yuck," said Elise.

"Yeah," said Ron. "You wish."

"Actually," said Susie. "I've heard that men have fantasies of
women doing it together but not vice versa."

"You mean women don't have fantasies of men doing it together?" said Dodge. "That's ridiculous."

"What's so ridiculous?" said Ron. "I have the fantasies I want
to have and not a drop more. No homo fantasies for me, no thanks."

"Then how'd you know what we were talking about?" said Elise.

"Oh, you're just projecting," said Ron.

"That would prove my point," said Susie.

"What point?" said Kay.

"That women do have fantasies about men doing it together."

"Well," said Dodge. "Maybe Ron could oblige this evening. If
it's still raining and we're bored, he could come on to Alexander."

"Is Alexander gay?" Kay asked.

"I don't know," said Susie.

"Total fruitcake," said Ron.

"I thought he was sort of ambisexual," said Susie.

"Wishful thinking," said Elise.

"Yes, he's really hot," said Dodge.

"They don't have gender the way they used to," said Susie.

"Thank god," said Elise.

"Who knows what he is," said Susie.

"Do you think Billy's gay?" Kay asked.

"No," said Susie. "But it wouldn't surprise me to hear he'd had sex with other boys. Except maybe for the AIDS thing. I don't know."

"They do it with condoms," said Elise. "They all use condoms."

"I would if I were that age," said Dodge. "I mean, with other boys."

"Really?" said Ron. "I'm going to watch out tonight."

"You wish," said Elise.

"They do have new genders," said Dodge. "Except for you, Ron, you're unreconstructed."

"Thanks," said Ron. "I'll take that as a compliment." But he felt upset. No, he felt angry. Why were they talking about his money and his sexuality? They hardly ever paid attention to him except to be hostile.

He thought of his analyst. The couch, the window, the bookshelves.

"Let's get out of here," said Susie.

"Yeah," said Ron. "Let's blow this joint."

That night, dressing for dinner, he looked at himself for a while in the mirror. Sometimes when he looked in the mirror, he could see his father, or his dead brother, or, when he was feeling really bad, his mother.

Tonight he looked for his father but didn't see him. He pulled the skin of his cheeks down with both hands, looked in the mirror at the inside of his eyelids. Awful, awful, awful. He sighed. He stopped pulling on his skin and looked at himself some more. *You ugly fuck,* he said to himself.

He lay down on his bed again. It was still raining and it was sort of dark, even though night should not have fallen yet. Suddenly Ron felt unbearably bored. Bored as if he were going to explode. Bored enough to put his fist through the windowpane. He sat up. He made a fist, but he pummeled the pillow instead. He sighed loudly, rasping as he exhaled.

He missed watching TV. It was unbelievable how much he missed it.

When he went downstairs, there was only Dodie in the kitchen, chopping celery to make sauce for the pasta.

"That smells good," said Ron.

"I hope it is good," said Dodie. She finished chopping, swept the celery from the wooden board into a quart measuring cup. She had nice hands. Nice arms, actually.

"Do you want a drink?" said Ron.

"Me?" said Dodie, and looked up at him, smiling.

"Sure," said Ron. "Have a drink. I'll get you one. What'll you have?"

"Well," said Dodie. "I wouldn't mind a beer."

He took a Rolling Rock out of the fridge and gave it to her with a glass, but she drank out of the bottle, big swigs, putting her whole mouth around the rim. He brought a scotch from the patio, then he sat at the kitchen table and watched Dodie prepare dinner.

"Rain is horrible, isn't it?" he said.

"Well," said Dodie. "If we had feathers, we wouldn't mind."

He made her talk, which wasn't hard—he'd only have to ask one question and she'd be off. She told him about her kids, her husband, her best friend, the trailer park where her mother lived. When she turned toward the sink, he watched her behind, which he felt like biting.

"So, are you happy, Dodie?"

"Happy?" said Dodie. "Happy?"

"Yeah," said Ron, taking another sip of his scotch. "You know what I mean: are you a happy person?"

"Are you torturing Dodie?" Susie asked, bustling in. She must have heard his question from just outside.

"He's shitting me," said Dodie. "He really is."

"I'm not," said Ron.

Alexander was the last one onto the patio and by then Ron was a little drunk. He thought of a number of nasty lines but wondered just how drunk he was and decided maybe he shouldn't say any of them.

Through dinner, it seemed to him, everyone kept looking at Alexander. Ron said very little. He felt himself become more and more anxious and permeated with dread. He kept refilling his glass but had the impression that he was not drinking. For some reason, this boy drove him crazy. He saw Elise and Susie looking at Alexander and actually thought he saw saliva glisten on Elise's lip.

"What's the matter, Ron?" said Kay. She was sitting next to him. She spoke softly, as if she were really interested. Kay was nice. Kay was the only nice one.

"I don't know," he said. He felt as if it was the first true thing he had said all day. She was looking at him in a friendly way. The others were talking. About what? He hadn't kept track.

"Is something wrong?" she said.

"Yes," he said. "Something's wrong and I don't know what it is."

He watched Alexander talking to Dodge, smiling. The room started to swirl. He slammed down his glass. The others stopped talking and looked at him.

"Something's wrong and I don't know what it is," he said, louder.

They were all silent for a moment.

"Something's wrong," he yelled. "Something's wrong."

"Want to go for a walk?" said Susie.

"No," said Ron. He put his elbows on the table and his face in his hands. "No, no, no, I don't want anything. I don't know what I want."

"Come on," said Dodge. The others sat, still and silent. Dodge got up, walked around the table, and pulled Ron's chair out so Ron was obliged to stand up.

Ron opened his mouth to say something to Dodge but then shut it again. Something in his belly felt terrible. Was he getting the runs?

Ron hitched his jeans up. "Well," he said to the table at large, "it's been real."

"Come on," said Dodge.

Ron looked at Alexander. "See you later, alligator," he said.

"Right," said Alexander. "In a while, crocodile."

For a long time, Ron and Dodge walked in the drizzle. They adopted a fast pace and strode down the driveway, then onto the road, squeezing to the right whenever a car passed, which wasn't often. It was totally dark out, the moon hidden behind clouds, when Ron finally said, "Okay, let's turn back." He was breathing more easily.

"Take a hot bath," said Dodge when they walked into the house.

He took a shower. He held his head in his hands and squeezed. The water pressure wasn't very good, and the bathroom was drafty when he came out. He lay down on top of the bed, but then he couldn't stand the awareness of his own naked body so he got under the sheet. He put his wet head on the pillow, a sensation he detested. He was thinking he'd go back down to the patio and have his nocturnal drink, and thought of himself looking out the dark window of the patio toward the rose garden, and then he fell asleep and did not dream any dreams that he could remember when he woke up in a state of gruesome misery the next day.

Sunday

It was sunnier, though, and he found the sun soothing. One thing about aging, weather seemed more and more important.

Must be a by-product of becoming a moron.

Music and paintings too. It was a more intense, consoling experience to look at a great painting.

He thought back to the conversation he'd had with Dodge two

days earlier about the women and which animals they were. And which animal would he be if he were an animal? A bear, maybe. He felt like a bear, slow and big and mean.

Images from his malaise of the night before kept flitting through his mind. But in a way he felt not to blame.

What was painful was to realize that the previous weekend there'd been the business about Susie's underwear. Probably, they all hated him already. Every weekend something worse happened. The summer now filled him with dread, what was left of it. Was it halfway over yet?

What came to mind now was his old analyst. Willa Richards-Ketzel. He hadn't thought of her in a while. There was a time when he could not stop thinking about her for a single second, hate for her and fear and dread of her filled his mind at all times like an infernal song. At last he had forgotten her briefly. Maybe he was getting better.

He sat up and swung his legs over the bed. His head felt heavy. No, he had to get up and go to the bathroom.

But in the bathroom he made the error of looking at himself in the mirror.

It was too frightening. He went back to bed. He lay there and listened to the birds and watched the bar of sunlight flicker on and off on the opposite wall until he succeeded in making his mind softer and felt pity for himself instead of anger and then he drifted back into sleep.

When he woke up again, Richards-Ketzel was back in his mind. Sometimes he would imagine her screaming at him. Sometimes he could hear what she was saying, sometimes not. He didn't know what this came from. Richards-Ketzel had never screamed at him. Neither had his mother, at least not as his little internal figurine did. His mother had been patient with him. Perhaps it was the screamer he'd imagined inside of her. Perhaps it was his father, reincarnated as a little old woman psychiatrist. Perhaps it was the little old lady part of him. Perhaps it was a dybbuk from several generations back.

He had never really told Richards-Ketzel about the little figurine who stood for her yelling at him in his mind. Or perhaps he had but had forgotten. Yes, he must have. Yes, of course, he did. But there had been voices other than hers. That had been one of the tasks of his analysis, to listen to these voices and tell her what they said. Her part in it had been to listen and make it seem to him as if always behind the voices he would wind up finding her again, patient and benevolent.

Patience and benevolence, he told himself. Patience and benevolence.

But now he could hear the roar of voices, roars and screams. He closed his eyes again. Patience and benevolence—he tried spelling the words out in his mind. He said them out loud: "Patience and benevolence." But at the same time there was the chorus of roars. He opened his eyes again. It was the same genteel bedroom in this godforsaken mansion in the sticks. The woodiness, the curtains, the shaft of sunlight. But he heard the roar.

"Let's play Ping-Pong," he said to Elise and Kay.

They were finishing brunch. Mounds of the *New York Times* lay among them. It had started drizzling again.

"It's grizzling," Ron said.

"What?" Dodge said.

"Nothing," Ron said.

Dodge announced he was going back to sleep for an hour. Possibly, thought Ron, Dodge just wasn't ready for another episode this early in the day. He was fleeing him. Why had he said that, two weeks ago, about Dodge's work? Dodge was about his work the way teenage girls are about their skin.

"Really? Ping-Pong?" said Elise. "What a radical idea."

"Good idea," said Kay. "I'm going crazy."

"Hey, hey, hey!" said Ron. "You're going crazy? That's the moment I've been waiting for!"

Kay laughed.

At least she can take a joke, Ron thought. *Fucking Alexander. Fucking Moriarty. Fuck all of them. Fuck them all.*

They ran to the pool house, where there was stored all the remnants of years in which leisure had been taken seriously. On the shelf, old board games. In the corner, a bouquet of badminton rackets and kayak paddles protruded from a very old golf bag.

"Okay, girls," said Ron, grabbing a paddle. "Who's on first."

"Stop calling us girls," said Elise, and took up the other paddle.

Elise played surprisingly well, though unevenly. Ron beat her quickly, slamming and spinning the ball, making her chase it into the cobwebby corners of the damp room.

"Shit," said Elise. "I'm going to have to practice."

She held out for a couple of points just before he got to twenty-one, but then he managed to keep her racing to either side of the table and finally was too fast for her.

"Shit," said Elise. "It figures."

"What figures?" said Ron as he and Kay began to volley.

"It figures that you would be such a macho Ping-Pong player," said Elise. "I can't get over how everything is an expression of personality, to say nothing of hormones. I should have known that you'd play hard and sneaky and smash the ball and need to win so badly."

Kay wasn't as good as Elise, and Ron lobbed it back to her gingerly. "What do you mean," he said, "need to win so badly. Look who's talking."

"But," said Kay, "what if you do some things in a macho aggressive way and others in a feminine way—what does that make you?"

"AC/DC?" said Ron.

Laughing made her lose her concentration and she missed an easy shot. She served again. Not much of a serve.

"What?" said Ron. Kay lobbed a ball to him with such an irresistible curve that he slammed it. It bounced off the table into the far corner of the room.

"Ron!" Kay called out.

"I'm sorry," he said. "I couldn't help it."

"I'm going to stop defending you," said Kay.

"Exactly like Ron," said Elise. "While you're busy defending him, he's getting a point."

"We're not even keeping score," protested Ron.

Kay took advantage of his talking to try to slam the ball herself, but he sent it back with little effort.

"Oh, forget it," she said. "I'm going to let Elise play again. This is hopeless."

"No, you've got to stick with it," said Ron. "How do you expect to improve?"

They played six games, the women alternating, all of which Ron won. Then the two women played together and he watched them for a while, but Kay was no match for Elise.

"Interesting, Elise," he said, as he began to volley back and forth with Kay again. "According to your theory, watching you play Ping-Pong, I have to revise everything I thought about you up to now."

"That's right," said Elise.

"No," said Kay. "Don't say that, or I'd have to revise my own opinion of myself to utter incompetence." She missed the ball. She went and dug it out of a corner where cobwebs were particularly thick.

"Yuck," she said.

Ron's teeth hurt at the thought of touching the cobwebs. Both he and Elise, he noticed, watched as Kay leaned over to pick up the ball. She was wearing shorts and when she leaned over, the line of her white underpants showed slightly.

"You're not incompetent; you're inexperienced," said Elise.

"Thanks," said Kay. She served the ball to Ron, who volleyed it back gently, but she missed again. "Okay," she said. "One more point."

She retrieved the ball from under the table, and Ron looked at her behind again. Kay came back, smiled at Ron, served. He felt slightly guilty, but only because he thought Elise might have realized he'd wanted to see Kay pick up the ball again, but a quick glance at Elise revealed she didn't seem to have noticed the stratagem.

Elise was definitely in a horrible mood this weekend. Probably had something to do with Dodge, he'd bet anything.

Ron slammed the ball neatly toward the outer edge of Kay's forehand corner, where he knew she had no chance.

"Rats!" Kay yelled.

"Sorry," he said. "I couldn't help it." He genuinely felt sorry, and yet he felt really good.

"Goddamnit," said Kay, slapping her racket down. "Shit."

"Holy smoke," said Elise. "I can't believe Kay said 'shit.'"

"Well," said Kay, "anything can happen."

"You have to get some spin on the ball," said Ron. "You play too defensively."

"That's always been my problem," said Kay.

"You don't have the competitive spirit," said Elise. "Unlike me. I have so much competitive spirit I'm paralyzed, which comes down to the same thing. That's why men like Ron always win at Ping-Pong, always. It has nothing to do with Ping-Pong."

"Sure," said Ron. "Sure, honey bunch. It has nothing to do with Ping-Pong. I know. You let me win." He spun his racket on his index finger before throwing it on the table.

They ambled back to the house, still arguing. Ron pretended he felt victimized, but the squabbling, along with the Ping-Pong, made him feel better. As if he were back in his own groove, as if last night and this morning he had been off the track and now was back on.

He probed himself for his recollections of last night's rage, but gingerly, as if to assure himself it was still in there somewhere without awakening it again.

When they emerged from the copse of trees between the pool house and the mansion, they began to be aware of the smell of fish. Dodge was barbecuing their lunch and the grill was smoking. Susie sat on a tree stump, wearing her jogging clothes, her earphones around her neck.

"I don't believe this. A fish fry?" said Ron. "Now I've seen everything."

"What?" said Dodge. He carried a spatula. He kept tugging

and touching and tapping at the fish on the grill with a very concerned expression.

"I can't believe you're barbecuing," said Ron.

"Well, there you go," said Dodge.

"The grill's too far from the flame," said Ron.

"I don't care," said Dodge.

"Well, it is!" said Ron.

"Get the fuck away, Reiser," said Dodge.

Ron went over to the grill and picked it up by the handle. He was lucky, he knew, that the handle didn't turn out to be that hot.

"Ron!" screamed Susie, incredibly loud. She still had her earphones on.

"Goddamn it, stop it! Stop it!" yelled Dodge, backing off.

Ron realized Dodge thought he was going to throw the grill or the fish at him. He laughed and put the grill back down.

"Never mind," he said, "if you don't want any help. Fuck you."

"Fuck you," said Dodge.

It stopped drizzling and a little sun came out, weak but warming. They decided to take the chance and eat out-of-doors.

"I'm not changing," said Susie.

"Thank god," said Elise. "I haven't got a thing to wear to this lunch."

Susie wiped the table. Everyone carried things out quickly.

"Billy!" yelled Susie toward Billy's window. "Billy and Alexander! Lunch!"

Alexander, as it turned out, was a Harvard student, going for an MBA. "This is my last year," he said.

Dodie came out of the kitchen carrying a very large platter on which the rather small fish lay. She had garnished the platter with a celery stalk.

"Hmm," said Susie.

"I hope it's good," said Dodge.

"It smells delicious," said Kay.

"Hmm," said Susie when she tasted the fish.

"Hmm," said Ron, histrionically.

"Ron!" said Susie.

"What?" said Ron. "What? What did I say? The fish is good, that's all. I just said, 'Hmm.'"

"And what do you want to do?" Elise asked Alexander.

"I don't know," said Alexander. "Make money."

"Me too," said Kay. "If I were going to do it all over again, I'd become a rich person."

"Weren't you rich to begin with and didn't you give that up?" said Ron.

"Rich?" said Kay.

"He means your parents had money," said Susie.

"Oh, not enough," said Kay. "And then they drank it all."

"You could have married rich," said Ron.

"I did," said Kay. "But that only lasted a year."

"You did!" exclaimed Elise. "You were married?"

"Yes," said Kay.

"I didn't know that."

"He was a nice guy," said Billy.

"Was he rich?" asked Dodge.

"Yes," said Kay. "Rich and nice."

"And good-looking," said Susie.

"Can I meet him?" said Alexander.

The others laughed.

"I've never been married," said Elise.

"You're smart," said Susie.

"I've never been married," said Billy.

"It'll come soon," said Kay.

"That's ridiculous," said Billy.

Those two are always looking at each other, thought Ron.

"I think I've got a loneliness disorder," said Elise.

"I'll have more fish," said Susie.

"Who doesn't?" said Dodge.

"More fish?" said Kay.

"No," said Dodge. "I mean, who doesn't have a loneliness disorder."

"A lot of people don't," said Susie.

"A lot of people are too busy," said Ron. "If you have kids, you don't have time for a loneliness disorder. Or maybe you're not lonely if you have kids."

"I don't know about that," said Dodge. "Everybody's lonely."

"No," said Susie.

"Some people are too crazy to be lonely," said Ron.

"This fish is fantastic," said Billy.

"Yes," said Alexander. "And these potatoes are delicious."

Can you be too crazy to be lonely? Ron wondered. Yes, of course. You could be Napoléon, if you were lucky.

"I wonder what the technical term is," said Elise, "for loneliness disorder."

"Meshuga?" said Ron.

Ron noticed Elise had small pretty teeth. He felt extremely hungry. He felt better. He liked the sun. The fish tasted good. He breathed deeply.

"I think that's a pretty good term," said Kay. "Loneliness disorder."

"And what does it consist of?" said Susie.

"It consists of, for one thing, just what it sounds like, which is to be lonely all the time. But also it means that, say, you're in a relationship with someone, a friendship or a love affair, and you feel that they are warm toward you, and in fact you think that your loneliness disorder prevents you from being closer to them, so you come closer and then they seem to emotionally dematerialize. It's like looking at certain paintings so that when you get up close, all you see are brush strokes. When you get close past a certain point to someone, instead of feeling more you feel less, as if now you can see too much, you can see the molecular basis of the emotions, so that the emotions themselves don't reach you," said Elise.

"Normal," said Ron. "That's the technical term for feeling that."

"Well, but that's an illusion," said Dodge, ignoring Ron.

"Why?" said Elise.

"That's your symptom," said Dodge. "It's not universal. Other people feel other frightening things when they get too close to someone."

"Well, they have their own versions," said Elise. "But if this is my reality, then for all practical purposes it is reality."

"You're a wonderful combination of Jean-Paul Sartre and Yogi Berra," said Ron.

"Thanks," said Elise.

"What do the molecules look like?" asked Susie.

"Indifference," said Elise.

"Well, it may be an insight into objective reality," said Kay. "Why not? I mean, the universe is indifferent."

"But Elise is not," said Susie.

"It's the Wittgenstein thing about whether the universe presents you with an enigma or whether you are only being presented with your own lack of understanding," said Alexander.

"Oh, sure," said Ron, laughing. He didn't like the way his own laugh sounded. And the others, he noticed, weren't laughing. But he couldn't stop himself from continuing. "Can you tell us anything more about Wittgenstein's position?"

"I'm getting upset," said Elise.

"Is anyone interested in a swim?" asked Susie.

"I'm interested in the Daffy Duck position," said Ron.

"What's that, Ron?" asked Billy.

"I'm not crazy—I just don't give a darn," Ron said in a Daffy Duck voice.

He looked at Elise's teeth as she laughed. He thought of her that first weekend, on the diving board. That first weekend seemed so long ago.

Dodie came in with an angel food cake.

"Ah," said Susie.

"Fantastic!" said Elise.

"That looks great," said Kay.

Ron decided to stay over Sunday night and go back in the morning. The thought of his empty apartment in the grimy hot city was harder to bear than anything else. Tomorrow afternoon he had a meeting with a television producer that he hadn't prepared for. He needed to think.

When he went back to his room to change for dinner, he lay down on the bed for a while and then made himself get up again, clear the rickety little table, and get a yellow pad out of his bag. A pen. He sat down.

He looked out the window: the foggy day was segueing into bluish gray dusk. There wouldn't be much of a sunset tonight.

He heard the screen door slam, and then Billy and Alexander, followed by Claudine, walked out in the direction of the pool house. Every once in a while Billy stooped to pick up a pinecone, which he then hurled upward toward the sky. All three would watch and listen as the pinecone knocked around the branches, and then they continued toward the pool house.

They looked like children, silhouetted faintly in the haze. Ron realized that whenever he looked at any of them, he had a painful feeling of their fragility and vulnerability. Ron felt himself filled with envy and pity for them.

That Claudine. That mouth.

He had to think. He looked at the pad, into the yellow between the blue lines.

But he couldn't think. It was like at school when you had tests coming and you couldn't study. Life had become like a series of tests he couldn't study for. He felt as if he were always flunking. He kept waiting for the point where he would figure out how to stay on top, as if it were waterskiing. He kept trying to make it into a water-skiing metaphor, and he would tell himself there were a certain number of psychomotor skills you had to have before you could stand up. Unless they all worked, you kept falling back into the water, so you just had to try and try and try again and again and again until your brain had figured out the thousand little balancing acts you had to engage in to ski on the water.

Now he suddenly realized that wasn't right at all. He'd had the wrong metaphor going there. He had assumed it was all about to happen, that it was a balancing act in the process of happening. But nothing was going to happen, he finally saw. The disequilibrium was it. This had become his life.

Billy and Alexander had brought Claudine back to dinner. Alexander had one glass of wine too many and, once he became more talkative, was considerably less charming. Billy was quiet. Kay didn't feel well. Elise and Susie had made string beans and new potatoes and had boiled corn. Dodge and Ron grilled hamburgers.

Susie still had on her red bathing suit but had put on a nice full white skirt over it. The bathing suit had halter straps, and whenever she moved a little, the place where her skin wasn't tanned showed, which began to fascinate Ron after he'd had a few beers. He'd have to force his eyes away.

"How old are you, Claudine?" Ron asked.

"I am seventeen," she said.

"And what does your father do?"

"He's an attorney," she said. (She had said, "Ee's an hattorney.") She smiled prettily. "My mother is also."

"Is your mother pretty?" Ron asked.

"Yes," said Claudine. "Much prettier than I."

"Are you fishing?" asked Ron.

"Fishing?" said Claudine.

"He's just obnoxious," said Susie. "Never mind."

"How old are *you*?" Claudine asked Ron.

"Forty-seven," said Ron. "What do you think? Too old for you?"

"Not old enough," said Claudine. She pushed back the perfect strand of hair that was always falling in her face. "You look like you are accustomed to be very infantile."

A wave of laughter greeted her remark. "You can call me in Paris in five years," said Claudine. Ron suddenly felt himself filling with hate for her.

"Do you want to get married and have children?" said Ron.

"It depends of who," said Claudine. She looked around. They were smiling at her. She enjoyed the attention. *Little twit.*

"With me," said Ron. "I'm ready."

"Look what you're doing," said Elise. "Last night it was Alexander and tonight it's Claudine."

"Claudine can take care of herself," said Ron.

"That's what we're worried about, Ron," said Dodge. "It's not Claudine—it's you."

Dodge was laughing but suddenly Ron wondered if he was serious or not. *I'm getting paranoid again,* he told himself.

"With you?" Claudine asked.

"Yes," said Ron.

"You are not married with children."

"No," said Ron. "I was married but I never had children. Maybe I could adopt you. I could adopt you and little Alexander. You could be my little pets whom I would abuse."

"Ron," said Susie. "Take it easy."

"I am," said Ron.

"Why didn't you have children?" said Claudine. "Did you hate yourself too much?" She pronounced it "ate." As in "Did you ate yourself?"

Alexander laughed but the others didn't. "Whoa," said Susie. "What happened to our nice pastoral dinner?"

"That's right, Claudine," said Ron. "I have 'ated myself always. And now my life is over, over, over. My career is in the toilet too, if you must know."

"Should we go to the movies tonight?" asked Susie.

"Yes," said Kay. "Ron, let's go to the movies."

"Your career has never been healthier," said Dodge.

"What do you think, Claudine. Do you think it would be sexy to fuck an old guy like me whose life is over?"

"No," said Claudine.

"Do you want to go for a walk?" Dodge asked Ron.

"No," said Ron. "Except with Claudine. With a little stopover in the woods."

"Ron," said Susie, with an edge in her voice.

"What?" said Ron. He hated Susie too, actually. Sanctimonious under all that charm. Charm was always, always, always, always bullshit.

"Can we lighten up here?" said Susie.

"I'm light, I'm light, I'm light," said Ron. "I'm just flipping out a little. Can't you take a joke?"

"Oy, oy, oy," said Elise.

"I think I will go home," said Claudine.

"It's all right, Claudine," said Susie.

"No, they are expecting me," said Claudine. She turned to Billy. "Do you want to walk with me to my home?"

Billy looked at Kay. "Do you want to walk over there?"

"*Me!?*" said Kay. "No. Thanks."

"Come on," Billy said to Alexander. "Wait for us," he said, addressing the space between Susie and Kay. "We'll be back soon."

What the fuck is all that about? wondered Ron.

"You don't have to walk with me if you don't want to," said Claudine to Billy. Nobody looked at Ron.

In a bubble of silent uneasiness, Claudine, Billy, and Alexander left the room. The others stayed at the table. There was a pause.

Ron thought his head would explode. "Sorry," he said. They all looked at him. "I'm under too much pressure. I'm sorry I'm acting like an asshole. I don't know what's wrong with me."

"You're not acting like an asshole," said Susie.

"No," said Elise. "You're acting like a jerk."

"Well," said Dodge. "We all have to take turns acting like jerks. That's what the summer is for."

"I'll say," said Kay.

"I just wish I could be a more dignified jerk," said Ron. He was worried about how nice they were all being. They must be frightened. Had he been that bad?

"As jerks go, you're very dignified," said Susie. "It's just not a really dignified category."

Susie can be nice. He thought of Susie's underwear drawer. The soft silken things.

"I think the time has come for an after-dinner drink," said Elise.

"Really?" said Kay.

"Or let's go dancing," said Elise.

"Or play Scrabble," said Kay.

"That's a great idea," said Susie. "There's a Scrabble set."

"I know," said Kay.

"I like Scrabble," said Dodge.

"*Scrabble!*" Elise exclaimed.

"Scrabble," said Ron. "Yes, I'd like that. Scrabble. Yes. But let's use a timer." He was good at Scrabble. He would win at Scrabble, in this group.

ELISE

Friday

Elise barely made the noon train but nevertheless found a seat on the left, the much more desirable river side, which she interpreted as yet another good omen. She was in such a great mood that she had forgotten to feel unlucky or lonely or overweight or unpleasantly neurotic, and she was, on the contrary, exhilaratingly distracted by the sumptuous sweep of the Hudson, the gorgeousness of the light, the oversize cloud formations floating above luxuriant riverbanks, summer at its most lush. She'd had a call late this morning from the owner of a gallery, one of the most desirable galleries, offering her a show this fall, and she felt better than she had in years.

For a long time Elise had thought it was possible she would never sell another piece, and though she knew better, she had experienced this as a verdict of sorts. Not that it had stopped her from working. Life would really not be interesting enough without her work, and, in any event, it's not as if there was a choice.

The train carriage was almost full. Old ladies; fat young women; a couple of babies at the other end, fortunately; salesmen with their portable computers; one man who grinned when their eyes met, revealing badly aligned front teeth.

She twisted her hair into a topknot, rested her head against the seat, and closed her eyes. Reopened them to look at the river.

Better to look at the river than to think about work. Thank god for the work, anyway, with its ample reasons to get from one end of the week to the other. So she'd gone on making her constructions, even though hardly anyone saw them except on studio visits. The direction she had taken—which bore a highly abstracted relationship to nineteenth- and early-twentieth-century sculpture—was increasingly irrelevant in the current art world context. The more others headed for representation, the more Elise felt compelled to comment on the convection of physical reality with verbal, cerebral consciousness. Once or twice a year, her pieces were exhibited in artists' cooperative shows, thought to be the kiss of death in gallery circles. Her friends steadfastly encouraged her but grew more cautious as to her commercial prospects, and she could see they were tired of the problem. She became more and more depressed, until she finally agreed to her psychiatrist's oft-repeated suggestion that she double her dose of Prozac. After a few weeks on the higher dose, she decided that talent—which she had always thought a determining factor in the universe—was really not of any more importance than life's other ephemera. (Success was much easier to grasp, as a social currency.) Talent was important, as a rule, to the holder only and maybe one or two others. And that's why—there was no mystery really—it was often outdistanced by tenacity or ambition. It was just a phenomenon of nature, but, like a beautiful undiscovered landscape, it existed whether it was appreciated or not, whether it was of any use to anyone or not. In the end, all that mattered was to work.

Her family was embarrassed by her, her living conditions, her unmatched china, her weird wardrobe, her lack of a marriage, her lack of what they understood as success.

For the last ten years, she had taught at a small college in Manhattan, a job she had gotten so soon after she had had an affair with the lubricious head of the painting department that she had never doubted the connection. He had left that same year, but she had been kept on, teaching only two courses—not enough for benefits. She knew her male colleagues were totally uninterested in her or her work.

It had seemed to Elise that maybe she should start becoming accustomed to the idea that she might soon become (already be, at thirty-eight?) one of those aging artists of not much interest to anyone, a prospect that haunted her with increasing regularity because she never seemed to get nearer to any sort of substantial recognition.

When she'd heard, within the span of a single week this spring, that the Chicago Art Institute was going to buy one of her pieces and that another had been selected for the American Pavilion at the Venice Biennale, she experienced a disbelief that she knew would never leave her, even if the actual exhibitions took place. She'd taken too much of a beating in the last fifteen years to recover, she figured. She'd never feel secure. Though she'd rather feel insecure with money and recognition than without.

For years she'd taken a little money from her father to supplement her teacher's income and wondered how long she could keep going like this. She'd bought no clothes except on sale and in thrift shops, had taken no real vacations. For a long time she couldn't even buy a television, a stereo, health insurance. Her father had given her money for health insurance, until he discovered she spent it on materials. Then he had stopped giving her the monthly check, and she had earned the extra cash for materials by leading groups of art patrons to the exhibits at the Metropolitan Museum and on gallery tours.

Briefly mirrored in the window when the train rushed through an underpass, Elise smiled at her reflection. She couldn't get over it. Chicago *and* the Venice Biennale. And now this show. *This show.* How would she get the work done in time?

Zift's gallery sold. Every piece there got noticed. There would certainly be reviews. Yes, certainly Zift had just called her, out of the blue. Well, no, it wasn't out of the blue. It should have happened years ago. If she'd been a man, it would have happened years ago. If she'd been Dodge Moriarty, it would have happened years ago.

The show. It was a tiny, tiny shift in the motion of the universe that was going to make her entire life totally different. She almost hated to let go now of the prospect of living with the humiliation of a small reputation, the shabby and skimpy way of life. She'd let go of all of the dreams of glory that had driven her to become an artist in the first place. In fact, letting go had been her one lucky break, she always thought, leading her to the realization that she wanted to work, anyway.

What now? How to reconfigure herself now? She tried to remember the last time she felt better. *Before Brian.* No. *Before Cal.*

She tried to imagine what the reactions of the others at the house would be when she told them. She imagined herself announcing the news, casually. *I'm having a show at Zift's.* She saw them smiling. *Zift called me. He wants to show my work.*

What would Susie think? Maybe she'd act as if it was nothing. No. Even Susie would have to admit it was a big deal to have a show at Zift's. Even Susie might feel at least some fraction of the envy that Elise had felt toward her for years. Envy was the real problem, in the end. The only problem.

She thought of Susie in one of her characteristic poses, a hand on one hip, her head tilted, her blond hair looking silky. How easy Susie seemed in her body. She'd felt so jealous all summer of Susie and of Kay and of Claudine and, actually, of Dodge as well. Susie and Kay for their charm and beauty and ease, and Claudine for her youth and her prettiness, and Dodge for his talent and his cool and his success. And Ron? *Ron is ridiculous.*

But maybe they would actually be glad for her. Like a long-neglected home, a feeling she hadn't had in a long time suddenly flashed back, the hope that she would be admired and nourished by other people's admiration. She felt anticipation pitch and rise in her.

Now, the thought *Maybe I could have fun* caused in her a reaction as chemical as if she'd injected an extra hit of Prozac. She felt the resignation unglue from her, as if she were stripping off an unpleasantly tight wetsuit.

I'm getting manic. The prospect of a life of pleasure. The vague, deeply, deeply soothing hope of glamour. Now was the moment. She could do it now. Who was to prevent her? She wasn't too old. Because of what it had cost her already, enduring the rejections of the last fifteen years, she had nothing left to lose.

Try to stay in the moment, she told herself. Because the thought of loss, even the very word, led her back to her most recent affair, the hideous end of that affair. At the time she had told her friends she was dying, but once they had ascertained she actually wasn't going to commit suicide, no one had taken her seriously. She had in fact died, in a way. You die each time, she had reminded herself then. One used to die but then resuscitate—as if by miracle each time—with a new man.

Elise thought of herself as an acrobat, a psychological acrobat, whose principal job was to prevent the trapeze from swinging over the chasms, in case she got the urge to jump. It was tiring work. There were many moments in between the two trapezes. There was the urge just to let herself fall. Those moments. There were so many of them. So many. Each of her ex-boyfriends to say nothing of all the guys whose names she hadn't even known. Her ex-cocaine habit. Her mother's death. Her relationship with her father. Children, anything about children. Everything she hadn't become. Everything she didn't want to wish for anymore.

Oh, her father, she couldn't bear to think about her father. Couldn't bear it.

The train wooshed back into an underpass. *I need a haircut,* she told herself, looking at her reflection.

She thought of Dodge and then let her mind slide back to the tableau she kept having of a body-to-body encounter. This image, recalled a hundred thousand times now, had become cruelly painful, even though at first it had been a form of self-soothing. It no longer soothed her at all. Elise knew that if she was not careful, she would drift into an obsession with Dodge. It was tempting because that in and of itself would act as a kind of antidepressant. That is, it would occupy so much of the mental territory that other, sadder, and more intractable problems would be pushed to the side. Soon, though, its own anguish would bloom. Was anguish really preferable to depression? She had the strong feeling that there was nothing to come from Dodge but pain. She knew his type. She knew his type extremely well.

A convoluted configuration of hydrocal and plaster flashed on her mental screen. It was the most recent piece she had started, and she didn't know why, but it seemed to hold some answer to a question posed by this problem.

Why is it that everyone was in love with Susie? What made people fall in love, anyway? The burlap and metal gave her a feeling that could almost be articulated. But perhaps that was a mirage. The piece gave no answer to anything but itself, except to one very specific problem that could not be stated in words. Everyone in the house was in love with Susie. Dodge, Kay, Billy. Even Dodie venerated Susie. Ron.

Ron's flipping out last weekend had been strangely compelling. Elise felt both apprehensive at what unpleasant scenes might develop this weekend and extremely interested to see whether he would continue disintegrating or get himself back together. Ron reminded her of her first boyfriend. She remembered that feeling, of discovering sex, and opening herself up like a flower and the crudeness and lack of discretion of the boy.

Susie was someone who opened herself up like a flower, but she didn't get punished for it.

The door to the carriage opened. "Five minutes," said the conductor, and held his hand out toward her, five fingers splayed. No wedding ring.

She had the show—the shows!—and now she needed a relationship. Maybe she needed to get married. She could see herself married to Dodge. He'd never be faithful, but she didn't care about that all that much. She didn't have to be faithful either, after all.

———

"Dodge called from a phone booth in Manhattan to say he and Ron won't arrive until after dinner," said Kay when Elise inquired. "Susie's taking a shower and she'll be down in a minute. Billy's sleeping."

"I love your shorts," said Elise.

"Oh, thanks," said Kay, looking down at her knees and frowning.

"Where did you get them?" Elise asked.

"Talbots," said Kay.

"*Talbots?*" exclaimed Elise.

"I know it's weird," said Kay, "but you really can find stuff there."

Talbots?

In the late afternoon, the three women decided to go to the gym. "I peeked in there last week," said Susie. "Testosterone Central. There are all these big beefy guys working out. It smells unbeliev-able. Muscles. Disco music. The works."

"Sounds great," said Elise, sarcastically.

"What are we going to do?" said Kay.

"Row," said Susie. "Or the machines, or anything."

It was an overcast day. Susie drove and Kay sat in the front, Elise in the back. Susie wore hot pink shorts, Kay had changed into black leggings, and Elise wore black bicycle shorts. They were tanned by now. Susie's short hair had been cropped again and she looked like a kid. Kay's ponytail looked blonder. Two lines that had furrowed Kay's brow at the beginning of the summer seemed fainter, and Elise thought maybe Kay felt better in her body. From all the swimming, maybe. Or just the tan. Or just the vacation. Whether you wanted to be on vacation or not, being away acted on you.

"Shit, shit, shit," said Elise. She had already told them about the gallery but was having problems thinking about anything else.

"What's the matter?" said Kay.

"Nothing special," said Elise. "I was just getting it out of my system."

"I know what you mean," said Susie. "That's why it's a good idea to go to the gym. I think I have cabin fever."

"I do and I don't," said Kay. "Because in a way it's great to be somewhat bored. I mean, it's a great switch."

"I can't believe," said Elise, "how positive you are, Kay."

"Me?" said Kay. "That's a joke."

Something about the way she had answered suddenly made Elise wonder if in fact she didn't have Kay completely wrong. Maybe what she thought was solicitude and thoughtfulness was depression.

"Well, being bored makes it feel like vacation, you mean," said Susie. "I don't know. Did we do the right thing in coming here and not the beach?"

"We absolutely did the right thing," said Kay.

"There you go again," said Elise.

"It's just that the beach is so glam, so festive," said Susie. "Upstate New York is so lugubrious."

"It's just economically depressed," said Kay. "Not any more lugubrious than anywhere else."

"Yes, it is," said Elise. "The colors are lugubrious. People's expressions are lugubrious. The shapes of the women's bodies are lugubrious. The kids hanging around in the streets with these Apache crew cuts are lugubrious."

"The houses are lugubrious," said Susie.

"Well, that's true," said Kay. "The pizza has lugubrious cheese on it."

"It's so much more real here," said Susie.

"Real?" said Elise.

"Not for us," said Kay. "Dodie is real. We aren't very real here."

"I'm more real than I want to be," said Susie. "I think it's being cooped up in that house."

"At our age with those men and no sex," said Elise.

"How do you know there's no sex?" said Susie.

"Well, except for Claudine," said Elise. "Claudine may be having sex with every one of those guys."

"Well, or at least every one of those guys wants to," said Susie.

"Are you having sex?" said Elise to Susie.

"No," said Susie.

"Do you think every one of those guys wants to?" asked Kay.

"Everybody wants to have sex with Susie," said Elise.

"No," said Kay. "I meant, do you think every guy in the house wants to have sex with Claudine?"

"I don't know," said Susie. "Maybe not. I think they all wanted to have sex with Casey."

"Even Billy?" asked Kay.

"Well, of course," said Elise. "They were all panting."

"I don't like Casey," said Susie.

"She's a horror," said Kay.

"I'm not inviting her back," said Susie. "That mouth!"

"Nobody is having sex. It's all talk," said Elise.

"We talk about sex much more than normal at that house," said Kay.

"But I don't think anybody really wants to have sex," said Susie. "I certainly don't want to have sex with anyone."

"Everybody wants to have sex with you," said Elise.

"It's true," said Kay. "Everybody wants to have sex with Susie."

"By now even I want to have sex with Susie," said Elise. "I'm like in a join-the-crowd configuration. Can we have a date tonight?"

Susie was laughing. "I think you're wrong," she said. "But if I were going to have sex, I'd have to do it with a stranger. I can't stand the complications anymore."

"I can't find a stranger I want to fuck," said Elise. "There isn't anyone to fuck."

"What about Dodge?" said Susie.

"Oh, I don't want your sloppy seconds," said Elise.

"Well, it's always sloppy seconds, anyway," said Susie. "Since it's always their mothers they really want."

"Oh, great," said Kay. "Great."

"What I really want," said Elise, "is an eighteen-year-old."

"Me too," said Susie.

"Not I," said Kay. "Too boring."

"Boring? That's not the point," said Susie.

"Actually, I think I've always loved eighteen-year-olds," said Elise. "When I was a little girl, I had crushes on all the guys that age, the ones who were already in college. I just never got over it. I got older, I got to be eighteen, then I got to be older than eighteen, but I never stopped loving those eighteen-year-old boys."

Kay sighed. "What would you talk about?"

"*Talk!*" said Elise.

"Well," said Susie. "It's not about talk, and it's not about sex either, in a way."

"Yes," said Kay. "But there remains the fact that you are going to be in an actual bed, having actual talk, and this kid will be close to you and will look at you and will maybe be repulsed by you."

"Are you crazy?" said Elise. "That's not what it's about in bed."

"I wouldn't know, I can't remember anymore," said Kay.

"When they're in love with you, they don't notice," said Susie.

"But what about afterward?" said Kay.

"Afterward, you can get plastic surgery," said Susie.

"Afterward, who cares?" said Elise.

"I care," said Kay. Her tone—too sincere in the context of this conversation—struck Elise, whose paranoia made her exquisitely sensitive to other people's unverbalized communications, as very slightly off. Billy's image popped up in her mind as an explanation. *No. Couldn't be.*

"How about him?" Susie said, pointing with her chin. They'd stopped at the first light in town, and a hoody-looking guy was leaning against a car reading a tabloid.

"He's waiting for his wife to come out of the Grand Union," suggested Kay.

"That's okay," said Elise. "Maybe we could do it in a hurry leaning against the car before she gets out."

"We could have him one at a time," said Susie. Elise briefly wondered if Susie was serious.

"Too raunchy for me," said Kay.

"Oh, I like them raunchy," said Susie.

"Me too," said Elise.

"If I were going to have sex, at this point I'd want it to be raunchy," said Susie.

"I'm not sure whether there's even any option," said Kay. "My guess is it's raunchy or nothing."

"How about him?" said Elise. They had turned into the gym parking lot, and someone who was clearly either a trainer or a gym freak walked by, muscular, towheaded, tanned.

"No," said Kay.

He turned just before going in, scanned the parking lot, looked at them blankly. The women laughed as the door closed behind him.

"I think they just don't notice us anymore. We're too old," said Susie.

"I'm sick of the whole problem," said Kay.

"I can't believe that guy ignored us," said Susie. "But maybe there's more where that came from. Let's check out the scene. This augurs well."

"What does it augur?" asked Kay as they got out of the car.

"AIDS. It augurs AIDS," said Elise.

At the gym they used the treadmills and the rowing machines, and an hour later they felt better. On the way out they peered into the weight room, which did indeed seem like a Testosterone Central kind of operation, nothing but weights and mirrors, the remaining walls painted black, a noisy air conditioner turned up to the max failing to disperse an aggressive odor combining sweat and metal. About eight or nine men were working out, none of whom looked up.

"They only seem cute from far away," said Elise.

"Maybe it would be okay in the dark, in bed," said Susie.

"Who cares about bed?" said Kay.

"You're kidding," said Elise.

"Well, I mean, after the first few weeks, does it really matter, anyway?"

"Yes," said Susie. "It does."

"How about after the first few months?" asked Kay.

"Yes," said Elise. "Oh, I don't know. What the fuck do I know?"

"Men are lucky," said Susie. "Because they're so superficial. It's only now that I'm too old for it to do me any good that I realize how important the superficial is."

"Do you think Dodge is superficial?" asked Elise.

"Not in his sexuality," said Susie.

Like how? wondered Elise.

"It's not that they are superficial. It's that they hope for superficial sex," said Kay. "Like Ron, for instance, who has a very complicated sexuality but is always talking about wanting superficial sex."

"Ron wants to fuck everybody," said Elise. "I don't know whether that's superficial or not. He'd fuck a rock. He's dying to fuck Claudine. I can't believe the way he was looking at her last week. Practically drooling."

"On the other hand," said Susie, "my guess is that he wanted to fuck Alexander too."

"But he didn't know it," said Kay.

"You think he didn't know it?" said Elise.

"No," said Susie. "He would kill himself if he knew it."

"That Claudine," said Elise.

"Yes," said Susie. "She's really something."

"I can't stand her," said Kay.

"Really?" said Susie. "I don't know that I'd go that far. She's too silly."

"Men love silly women," said Elise.

"It's true that she's charming," said Kay.

"She'll be interesting in ten years," said Susie.

"Do you think," Elise asked, "that Ron is going to flip out?"

"I don't know," said Susie.

"I think we should try to keep things calm," said Kay.

"What an asshole he is," said Elise.

"Well," said Susie, "he does everything he can to make everyone hate him. I was horrified at the way he talked to Claudine."

"Claudine provoked it," said Elise.

"I thought we should have helped her, but I was too stunned," said Kay.

"Claudine loves it," said Elise. "What a little tart." Susie and Kay laughed.

"Well, yeah," said Susie, "but Claudine doesn't understand that when she does that, she's allowing herself to be part of a game that's not to her advantage."

"You're very generous," said Elise. "I think Claudine understands everything."

"I think so too," said Kay. "It's a generational difference. 'Tart' isn't one of her categories."

"I don't think Ron is going to flip out," said Susie. She turned on the radio. It was tuned to an oldies station and the Kinks came on. "Doesn't it look great out?" she said.

"Yeah," said Elise, thinking that for the first time this summer, Susie and Kay had really included her. She felt good in the back of the car. She opened the window a crack. It did look great out, and it smelled wonderful because the grass had just been cut. She felt her envy for Susie was now on its flip side, changed into identification, as if Susie's beauty belonged to Elise as well.

Late that night they decided to drive to the Lickety Split, all except Billy, who had adopted an ostentatiously neutral expression that badly concealed distaste. "Oh, you're much too cool to come with us to the Lickety Split," Susie said.

"Yes, someone his age might see him with us and he'd be socially ruined in the area," said Ron.

"What are you going to do?" Susie asked Billy.

"I don't know," he said. "Hang out here."

"Maybe I'll stay too," said Kay.

Interesting, thought Elise.

"Absolutely not," said Susie. "Come on. Let's go."

Elise registered again how attractive Billy was. *Is he gay?* Why did he never bring a girl up?

Alexander. He was exactly the kind of boy she'd always had a crush on as a kid. As it turned out, they'd all been gay, those irresistible, withdrawn boys.

Kitty-corner from Ben & Jerry's, where families consumed fantastical quantities of ice cream, the Lickety Split was a decrepit bar where poor whites and blacks came to drink and dance—separately, for the most part. As the evening wore on, the songs got slower and steamier. Sure enough, by the time they walked in, Natalie Cole was singing "Unforgettable." The place was loud, dingy, and beery.

"This is great," said Susie.

Some heads turned in their direction but then turned back. The Lickety Split may have been the only place in town where the summer people, few in number this far up the Hudson, would be treated with discretion.

There were tables around a small dance floor. At the far end of the room, a pool table was mobbed. There was sawdust on the ground except on the shiny parquet of the dance floor, which was square, like a boxing ring.

"Okay," said Ron. "What will you all have?"

"Dos Equis," said Susie.

"Dos Equis," said Dodge.

"Club soda," said Kay.

"Oh, come on! Kay!" said the others.

"Okay, okay," said Kay. "Dos Equis."

"Absolut," said Elise. *One is my limit. Fucking Prozac.*

While Ron stood at the bar and waited for the drinks, they all sat down with their backs against the wall, so they could look into the room, save for Dodge, who stood and leaned as decoratively as usual.

"Why do black people dance so much better than white people?" asked Susie.

"Learned behavior," said Kay.

"What? You mean white people learn to move like spastics?" said Dodge.

"That would explain the pretension of Martha Graham's choreography," said Elise.

"I like Martha Graham," said Susie.

Elise suddenly felt terrible. *She's so cutting,* she thought as she looked at Susie and her indifferent, smiling profile.

Ron brought back their beers and Elise's Absolut.

"Here's to Elise's show at Zift's," said Dodge.

"Hear, hear!" said the others. They sipped from their bottles. Elise drained her glass and went to the bar to get another.

She came back to the table and sat down.

"Do you want to dance?" Dodge asked Susie.

They all watched. The other couples on the dance floor barely shifted their feet, so that Dodge and Susie seemed to be in motion, by comparison. They moved well together. Susie was wearing jeans and a small black sweater that suited her well. Dodge was, as always, in black.

They watched in silence for several moments.

"What charm," said Ron.

"Who?" asked Elise.

"Our Susie," said Ron.

"It's quite a scene," said Elise, very dryly, she hoped.

The theatricality of it seemed to Elise to be vulgar. Susie's jeans were too tight. *She's very narcissistic, actually,* Elise thought. *She seems very casual but everything is calculated.* She saw Susie completely differently than she had all summer, as someone absolutely ruthless. Why hadn't she seen it before?

The song finished and another began. Susie and Dodge exchanged a couple of words and then went on dancing. Elise turned her chair somewhat so that she could see other parts of the room and began to tap her foot.

"Do you want to dance?" Ron asked Elise.

"No, thanks," said Elise.

"Really?" said Kay. "Go ahead."

"No," said Elise. "I'm in a foul mood."

"How about you?" Ron asked Kay.

"Let's try to cheer up Elise," said Kay.

"No, I wish you'd dance," said Elise. "Actually I'd benefit from a few moments on my own. Please. Go ahead."

"Jeez," said Ron. Kay looked puzzled at Elise's curtness but then rose, and Ron followed her onto the dance floor. For a while Elise stared at her glass. Then she drained it. She barely felt anything though, just a great restlessness. She tried to think about her show, realized with a shock that before the toast it had been a number of hours since it had even occurred to her. But it gave her no pleasure at the moment. Maybe the pleasure was gone. It was like making a piece. It could take days or weeks, or even months of work, but the pleasure from it lasted only a few hours, if she was really lucky, a couple of days. Maybe having the museum buy a piece or a gallery like Zift's having a show of her work wasn't worth any more really, in good mood coupons, than getting enough sleep or getting a good haircut. That reminded her, she needed a haircut. *Am I getting slightly tanked?*

More and more she felt that Susie's nonchalance was a sham and that, for example, when she made the remark about Martha Graham, she knew very well that it would make Elise feel bad. There was no way anyone could spend time with Susie without submitting one way or another. She was a dominatrix of sorts, really. A very clever one.

Elise got up, circled the dance floor, which was quite crowded now, back to the bar, where she ordered a beer. Bottle in hand, she circled back toward the pool table.

A game was in progress between two rather good players. Perhaps a dozen people were watching, every once in a while calling out "All right!" at a particularly good shot. Elise watched for a while, and no one seemed to take notice of her until a man who had been sitting to her right on a window frame said, "Where's your ring?" He was dressed rather dandyishly in a tight brown shirt, tight pants, and espadrilles. Perhaps he was Caribbean. He was quite good-looking, in his thirties, maybe.

She smiled and looked down at her hands. "Very observant of you," she said.

"What's your name?" he asked, as if her sarcasm had been his cue to embolden himself.

"Elise," she said.

"Elise," he said with emphasis. "That's a beautiful name. My name is William."

Definitely Caribbean. Williaaaaaam. She looked up into his eyes. "Hi," she said.

"You want to dance?" he asked.

Once they were on the parquet together, all eyes followed them. He was wearing some sort of aftershave, which she hated and yet thought arousing. His dance style was fluid and precise. Elise glued herself to him and followed. As they turned, Elise saw on-lookers' glances slide away when she was facing them, but they didn't tarry elsewhere for long. The several dancing couples (three black, two white) who seemed inspired to open their eyes checked them out, and closed their eyes again. But in between songs, they'd look again. By then Ron was dancing with Susie.

William dropped Elise's right hand and put both arms around her. Elise saw Ron looking and then mouthing the words "Holy smoke," and then turned around so Susie could see.

Susie said something but Elise couldn't hear what it was. She turned away.

But Ron danced Susie nearer, obviously so they could hear what they were saying.

Assholes, Elise was thinking.

"You're looking very hot tonight," William said to Elise.

"I like hearing that," she said.

He sounds like an aftershave commercial, she thought, but she was excited by him. He danced closer and closer to her and began to talk softly near her ear. She couldn't quite understand what he was saying. Only felt his breath warm and moist on her ear and then felt his lips on her neck. She kept seeing them from the outside, as if she were having an out-of-body experience, and wondered if there was something shocking and somehow sinister about the small girl in her stylish curls and the smooth-talking man turning and turning on the dance floor. He kept whispering, nonstop. It was sexy and so frightening, it was repellent at the same time. It actually was too frightening to be really sexy. Was she really going to go off with this man she didn't know? It had been a long time since she had done anything like that. And, to boot, it seemed much scarier in the country. Several songs went by and she kept dancing. His hand slid below the small of her back. Ron and Susie had stopped dancing and joined Dodge and Kay back at the table. From the dance floor Elise could see them sitting silent and uneasy. Then she saw them exchange some words, arguing, maybe. *About me?*

For a long while now, Elise and William had been the only couple dancing. Now, a very large woman strode out onto the dance floor. Elise saw the others watching as the woman came and stood so close to William and Elise that the two had to stop dancing.

"Bill!" said the woman, too loud. Elise could smell her. She was wearing Ma Griffe.

"I'm busy," said William.

After that, Elise didn't listen. She stood for a moment, a storm in her head, then walked back to the table. She felt a little unsteady. She turned. The woman was standing very close to William, looking threatening, her face only inches from his, haranguing him. He looked both sheepish and angry.

She looked at the others, who seemed in suspended animation. She struggled to compose herself.

Kay stood up. "Let's go," she said, emphatically. For a moment the others just sat, surprised. "Let's go, let's just go," she repeated, and she took Elise's arm and headed for the door. Elise let herself be led. She was grateful for Kay's urgency. Kay seemed to be the only one who understood that there could be serious trouble. Once outside they stood for a moment. The air was heavy. *I'm drunk,* Elise thought. The streetlight buzzed and insects twirled in its glare. Then everything swirled a bit.

"I just thought there might be problems," said Kay.

"It's fine," said Susie.

"I don't know," said Kay. "Are you all right?" she asked Elise.

Elise said, "Yes," but she could hear it was in a strange small voice.

They were silent in the car on the way back. Elise focussed on not throwing up. When they got out of the car, Ron stretched and yawned loudly and Dodge said, "Yeah, I'm beat."

"Me too," said Susie.

"Shit," said Elise. "Shit."

"Are you okay?" said Susie.

"Yes," said Elise. "Sorry we had to leave so early."

"Yes, that was a rather precipitous egress," said Ron. "I completely forgot my parting salutations."

They all think I'm an asshole, thought Elise.

When they got into the house, they all went straight to their rooms. Soon the house was quiet and dark, except for Elise's room, for she had fallen asleep with the light on. After an hour she got up. She walked downstairs, got herself a glass of water, walked outside.

It was still muggy. But it felt good to be outside. She sat down on the grass. She ran her hand over the grass. Now there was a little bit of light in Dodge's room, just enough to see him sitting on his bed, staring out into the slightly moonlit night, but he didn't see her. She could actually look at him. She realized now what an effort it had been for weeks now not to stare at him. Then his face was, for a moment, spookily illuminated as he lit a joint. She watched him as he smoked it and then dozed off, sitting. She looked at him for a long time, still and sleeping. Maybe barely sleeping. Then she looked away for a while and forgot herself, watching the clouds drift over the moon. When she turned her gaze back to his window, she couldn't see him anymore.

She thought she heard the ocean inside her head.

Saturday

Just before Elise woke up, she had a dream that she could almost recall. Once she had a psychiatrist who told her how to recapture a dream. You lie in bed and keep your eyes closed and remember the feeling of the dream, then make up a story that goes with the feeling of the dream. Then it's possible that the dream itself will come back to you. She had tried this many times and often it worked. Once one part of the dream came back, the rest of it usually unfolded like an origami object that had held its secret only by virtue of its creases.

She pictured a streetlight, in Central Park. She thought of Charles Boyer. What was that movie?

Yes, there it was. Now a piece of the original dream came back to her. So romantic. Yes, she had seen herself on a gorgeous lawn in a beautiful light being kissed by an unsubstantial stranger until her body felt light, light, light.

She put Dodge's face on the man and tried to get back into the dream and couldn't, but fell asleep again and dreamed again. This time when she woke up, she remembered the dream precisely: There was Susie's puppy, Otto, lying on the road dead. She picked it up and brought it back to the house, believing she should hide it so no one would think she had killed it.

Even though she was still very hungover, she swung her legs over the edge of the bed and headed toward the bathroom. *Today is not the day I'm going to kill myself, so I might as well get going.* Even while she was brushing her teeth and washing, she kept seeing the cadavers of dogs and feeling this terrible dark dread.

Stop it.

Susie, Dodge, and Ron were already eating their breakfast. She heard them chatting before she reached the room, some wry remark of Dodge's, just out of earshot, Susie's laugh. "There she is," said Susie when Elise walked in.

"Hi," she said, and held up her hand by way of general salutation and walked over to the sideboard, brought a glass of grapefruit juice over to one of the place settings, and then walked back to the sideboard and busied herself getting French toast and coffee. *I just have to get through this,* she was thinking, but the others either didn't take that much notice of her or pretended not to.

"Did you sleep well?" asked Susie when Elise brought her plate to the table. Susie had an expression that Elise, with the benefit of preternatural morning clarity, saw was resolutely pleasant. *Susie does that a lot,* Elise thought. She wondered for a moment whether it was done out of habitual hypocrisy or to make other people feel more comfortable. Both perhaps.

"Yes, thank you. Did you?" Elise said.

"Very well," said Susie. "Though I kept waking up."

"There were mosquitoes," said Ron.

"I'll say," said Dodge.

"Is your screen broken?" asked Susie.

"At around three I killed four of them," said Dodge.

"Oh no," said Susie. "Didn't that wake you up completely?"

"I couldn't sleep with them in the room," said Dodge.

"It made him feel better to kill them," said Ron. "That's how Dodge can go to sleep is after he kills a few insects."

"Yeah, I got some flies too," said Dodge.

"And he ate them," said Ron.

"There are bats," said Susie. "I heard them."

"Bats?" said Ron. "You're kidding."

"No," said Susie. "I heard them outside my window—they make a weird clicking sound. Make sure you don't leave your screen open."

"Hi," said Kay, entering the room. She went to the sideboard, got some coffee, and brought it back to the table.

"Hi," said the others.

"Did you sleep well?" asked Susie.

"Not bad," said Kay. "Considering the noise. And the dreams. What is it about the country that makes you dream so much?"

"You're learning new visual information, your brain goes into overdrive, and you have to spend longer in a REM state to process it," said Ron.

"Really?" said Susie.

"I don't know," said Ron. "But it sounds good."

"Bats," said Dodge. "I like that idea."

"Maybe you'd like to kill and eat a few bats every night before you go to sleep," said Ron.

"I like bats," said Dodge.

Even in the morning Dodge was dressed in black. Elise suddenly laughed and they looked at her. "I don't know why," Elise said. She put down her fork. She couldn't eat any more of this French toast. "There's something funny about Dodge liking bats. It's just so predictable."

"Great," said Dodge. "It must be my vampire nature."

"No," said Elise to Dodge. "It goes with your aesthetic somehow."

"Actually, I know what she means," said Susie. "You should take it as a compliment."

"Yes," Elise said. And she resolved to stop speaking. "I'm just out of control this morning," she said. And then she was sorry she said that.

"I'm always mentally disturbed in the morning," said Ron consolingly.

"You think it's just in the morning?" said Dodge.

"In the morning I'm aware of it, because I remember my psychotic dreams, so I know I need to see a psychiatrist," said Ron. "By the time I see my psychiatrist, I've forgotten the dreams so I think, *What am I doing here in this woman's office?*"

"I never remember my dreams lately," said Susie.

"I remember every detail of mine," said Dodge.

"Really?" said Susie. "Maybe that's why you're so prolific."

"No," said Dodge. "I think I work despite them."

"What was the last dream you had that you can remember?" Ron asked Susie.

"There was a huge man hanging from a tree," said Susie. "And ants were eating him."

They were all silent for a moment, then laughed.

"Jesus Christ," said Dodge. "Anyone you knew?"

"I feel an itch," said Ron.

"No," said Susie. "It was a very disturbing dream."

"Formication," said Ron. "That's all I need."

"No wonder you stopped dreaming," said Elise.

"Once I dreamed of an eight hundred–pound man," said Ron. "He was lying on a bed and his flesh covered the whole bed."

"Gee," said Susie.

"Wow," said Elise. *He's much crazier than I am. Much.*

"My dreams are never that succinct," said Dodge. "Though last night I had a long fuzzy dream in which there was a black rose."

"That's funny—I dreamed about roses too," Kay said. "About the rose garden. But it was really a dream about a pride of lions, in a clearing in a forest. A pride of mangy lions. They lay there, as if too drugged by age and sun to rise."

"The sixties generation," said Ron.

"Ron," said Susie, "you're so alert early in the morning."

As if to illustrate precisely the opposite principle, Billy staggered in at that moment, looking at no one as he made his way to the food.

"Good morning," said Susie. Billy grunted. Susie looked back at the others and turned her glance upward, and they all said nothing as Billy brought his bowl back to the table and, not looking at anyone, began to eat. He had on his black jeans and a T-shirt, which he had clearly worn to bed. His hair looked extremely tousled. It was as if he was just seconds from sleep.

"What were the lions doing?" asked Susie.

There was a moment of silence, and Kay then seemed to realize that Susie was talking to her. "What?" she said.

It made Elise feel better that at least she was not the only one
out of it this morning, though now that she relaxed a little, she realized she was in a state of urgent paranoia about what happened
last night. To say nothing of the dream. *Just stay quiet,* she told herself. *Don't talk.*

"In your dream, what were the lions doing?" Susie asked Kay.

"Nothing," Kay said. "They were tired. They were just lying
there."

"In the rose garden?" said Dodge. "It's a great image."

"Not exactly the rose garden," Kay said. "The rose garden was
another part of the dream, actually."

Billy looked up. "I dreamed about the rose garden too," he
said.

Susie laughed. "He spoke!" she announced.

"Were there any black roses in either of your rose gardens?"
Dodge asked.

"Did you sleep well?" Susie asked Billy.

"Yes," he said. "Except for the mosquitoes." He put his foot on
the table and pulled up the leg of his jeans a bit. There were red
welts around his ankle.

"Goodness," said Kay.

"I think there's calamine lotion in my bathroom," said Susie.
"But please take your foot off the table."

"What black roses?" said Billy to Kay.

"They were Dodge's black roses," said Kay. "My roses were
your standard-issue roses."

"Did anyone have sex with me in their dreams?" asked Ron.

"I bet Kay's roses were not standard issue," said Susie. "Nothing about Kay is standard issue."

"Because I had sex with all of you," said Ron.

"What was Kay's dream?" Billy asked without picking up his
head.

"Never mind," Kay said.

"She's being cagey," Ron said. "She may have had a dream about lions or she may not, and it may or may not have been in the rose garden."

"I had a dream last night," said Elise.

"I read," said Dodge, "that they did some research and that most dreams solve problems the dreamer is having during the day."

"I thought dreams expressed a wish," said Susie.

"I had this dream last night...," Elise began again.

"That's the Freudian view," said Ron. "Many scientists think it's just the detritus of the day's experiences."

"Well, but that's why they did this research," said Dodge. "And they did all these interviews with people about their lives and what their problems were and then charted their dreams and, like, 90 percent of their REM sleep dreams solved problems they had during the day. For instance, people studying languages got more REM sleep."

Billy had finished his cereal and was staring at his bowl. He looked up and saw Elise, caught her eye, and smiled. Then he looked at Kay and caught her eye and smiled. Kay smiled back at him. Elise looked at Kay, expecting her to look back, but Kay kept looking at Billy, then looked at Susie, and then looked down into her empty coffee cup.

I can't believe no one wants to hear my dream, Elise thought. She probably made them all paranoid too, she reflected, though she knew that it was hard to differentiate the real effect that paranoia had on other people from the effect the paranoid person feared her paranoia was having. *I'm getting more and more freaked out,* she decided.

She looked down at her plate. There was a sprig of parsley left, which she didn't remember putting there. The parsley bothered her so much every morning that she'd gotten into the habit of removing it every day and hiding it under her plate. But there it was. It seemed incredibly green. She looked up. She had lost track of the conversation. She felt like saying something about the parsley but thought then she would surely tag herself as especially bizarre again this morning. After all, they already knew how she felt about the parsley. If she said nothing today, they might assume she had been joking the last time she had brought it up, which would be much better. She always said too much too soon in any situation, and this morning she felt particularly anxious about saying anything. Saying something about the parsley might lead to saying something about the dream, or about Dodge. The parsley did really seem too green. This green was so brutal.

"Dodge," said Susie. "What did you dream about a black rose?"

"It had something to do with death," said Dodge.

"No kidding," said Ron. "Like a regular symbol? You have floating-signifier dreams?"

"What was your dream, Kay?" said Billy.

"I forgot," Kay said.

Susie declared the topic sentence: "What a bunch of liars."

That afternoon Elise ran into Dodge in front of the house and said, "Do you want to go for a walk?"

And he said, "Okay."

They took the path through the thickest part of the woods on the other side of the road. The pines were old and very tall. The day was warm and clear, but in here it was like stepping into a dark and humid parlor.

"Deer spore," pointed out Dodge.

"Mm," said Elise.

"Well, I can see that was thrilling information for you," said Dodge smiling.

"Oh, no," said Elise. "I . . ."

"You're a city person," said Dodge.

"It's not that I'm not interested in nature," said Elise. "I just never know what to say."

"You have to just kind of grunt and emit monosyllables," said Dodge.

"Oh," said Elise, and she turned back to smile at him. Dodge seemed to her, as always, totally coherent in his environment. *What was I saying?* she wondered.

"The thing is," she said, "what's good about nature is that you look at it and you don't feel the way you do when you're in your mind that things are falling apart from one another."

Dodge said nothing. *Shit,* she thought. He picked up a stick from the ground and bent it a bit to test its elasticity.

"But maybe," said Elise, "you don't feel like things are falling apart."

"I don't know," said Dodge. "I guess it's not one of my images. I know what you mean."

"Oh god," said Elise. "I guess it's weird."

"No," said Dodge. "It's fine."

"I spend too much time," she said, "in my own mind. I'm trying to stop, actually. The other day I was reading *The Words* by Sartre. Have you read that?"

"No," said Dodge.

"Well, Sartre, it's interesting, was a Platonic idealist and substituted words and ideas for things. I mean, he used words to get to things instead of the other way around. And he said it took him thirty years to get rid of excessive idealism. He thought life was like in books. I keep thinking about that, all the time, that this is my problem too. Which is kind of odd in a way, you know, for a sculptor, but that's probably why I make constructions now."

Dodge laughed.

"Oh god," said Elise. "I feel like an asshole."

"Why?" asked Dodge.

"I don't know," she said. "I guess because you're so contained and I'm so all over the place. In fact, you know sometimes I feel like my psyche is like one of my own constructions, made of all sorts of bits and pieces, scraps of burlap, feathers, held together with safety pins, string, pebbles. But it makes me feel even weirder to say that."

"Phew," said Dodge.

She said nothing.

"Pebbles?" said Dodge.

"Well, you know what I mean," said Elise. She brushed her palm against the bark of a tree. "Oh god," said Elise. "Well, I don't know. I guess paranoia just takes up all the available space."

"Oy, oy, oy, oy," said Dodge, laughing.

"You sound like Desi talking to Lucy," said Elise.

"That's okay, isn't it?" said Dodge.

"Yes," she said, feeling much happier.

"Let's walk up this hill?" said Dodge.

Once they got to the top, there was suddenly light. The climb had been steep and Elise was somewhat out of breath. "Here"— she pointed at a grassy spot under a tree. "Let's sit down for a minute." She settled herself underneath the tree, though Dodge walked a bit farther out, to where the view was better. There were the very soft hills and hollows of the Hudson Valley. The river didn't show, the trees were too full, but it could be guessed at in the valley. After the close, cool darkness of the trees, the brightness and openness were dazzling.

"You know what's amazing," said Dodge.

"What?" said Elise.

"These eagles," he said, pointing. Elise craned her neck but could see nothing. "Their wingspan is a good five feet. How do they swoop down where the trees are so dense, to get their prey, and not catch their wings on the branches?"

Elise said nothing. *How do they, anyway?* she wondered. *If they close their wings, they fall.*

Finally Dodge walked back to the tree and settled himself against the trunk. "You're like an Indian," said Elise.

"Why?" asked Dodge.

"You make almost no noise," she said.

He smiled. "That's nice," he said. "I like the idea of being like

an Indian." He took a Swiss army knife out of his pocket, selected
a blade, and began to peel the bark off the stick he had picked up.

"What are you making?" said Elise.

"I don't know," he said.

"A switch," she said.

"What?" he said.

"A switch," she said.

"To beat a horse with?" he said.

"Yes," she said. "Or a gender switch."

"Everyone in this house is obsessed with gender problems,"
said Dodge.

"Just the women," said Elise.

"I don't know," said Dodge.

"It's like there's a third gender," said Elise.

"What do you mean?" asked Dodge.

"Well, there are women who are wives, or men's women. And
there are women who aren't. Who just are, and who work and so
forth. Who have their own identity without men." Elise looked
around. "I like the sound here, don't you?" she asked.

"Which sound?" he asked.

"All the sounds, of the birds and the little bit of creaking now
and then, and several times we've heard this weird rat-a-tat."

"A pileated woodpecker," said Dodge.

"You're kidding," said Elise. "The thing that goes tap-a-tap-a-
tap-a is a woodpecker?"

"Yes," said Dodge. "It's a nice sound, but they kill the trees."

"They do?" said Elise.

"Well, they don't kill them, but they allow the insects to kill
them."

"I can't believe I actually heard a woodpecker," said Elise. "I
love this because it's so much better than my usual situation, which
is that I'm always hearing and seeing what's not there."

"Like what?" asked Dodge.

"Oh, you know, like wolves and cello sounds."

He had finished peeling the bark. He wiped the knife on his

pants, folded it, and put it away. He sliced the air with the switch and made a whistling sound.

"That's scary," said Elise.

"You think I'm going to hit you?" said Dodge. He was smiling and looking straight out ahead of him, not at her. For a moment she wondered if he would.

"No," she said. "Why, do you want to?"

He turned his head and smiled at her. He was really great looking in this light. "No," he said. "Do you want me to?"

She laughed. "No," she said. "Why would I want you to?"

"I don't know," he said. "It's your fantasy, not mine."

She laughed. "Look," he said. "A kestrel." They watched it float down over the valley.

There was a pause. "Are you in love with Susie?" asked Elise.

"No," he said. There was another pause. "I don't need love," he said.

"Really?" she asked. "Are you kidding?"

"Yes," he said. "I'm kidding."

"About which?" she said.

"Which what?" he said.

"Which were you kidding about?"

"I no longer know what we're talking about," he said.

"Never mind," she said. She knelt and brushed the twigs off her dress. "Should we go back?" She was angry and had decided not to show it.

"Okay," he said.

They started back down the path back toward the lawn. Elise walked behind Dodge. Once they were back under the dense foliage, she felt safer. "I'm sorry," she called out after him.

"Why?" he said, without turning around.

"Never mind," she said. Maybe he really didn't need love. Or maybe he needed love terribly and would be forever unable to say it. Was she alone in this intensity? Was it love she felt for him? Was he thinking about Susie? Susie. She felt a wave of hatred rise in her for Susie, who had everything while she had nothing, absolutely nothing.

The path had widened and now they could walk abreast.

"Look," said Dodge.

"What is that?" said Elise. There was a very tidy hole.

"Groundhog," said Dodge. They looked for a while. "I love groundhogs," he said. "They're so industrious. They're always either working or eating."

"That's what I should be doing," said Elise.

"Well," said Dodge. "I don't know. There isn't cause and effect so directly when we work. It's mysterious how we work. I mean, look at that." He pointed.

"What?" said Elise. She was trying to pay attention. She was grateful he was talking to her. She was trying to pay attention, but she kept thinking of how aware of him she was. What had he said?

"Look at that," he said. "How the moss meets the tree. I wish just once I could make something that would do that."

Elise spent a few minutes looking at the spot. It was true that the color and texture of moss against the bark was almost unbearably voluptuous.

"It makes me nervous," said Elise. "To think about what I can't do. Or what I wish I could do. But then I guess everything makes me nervous, so what else is new."

"You shouldn't worry so much about being so nervous," said Dodge. "I wish I were more nervous."

"You do?" she said. She felt much better, suddenly; maybe he hadn't thought she was so ridiculous after all.

"Yeah, I think my work would profit from it," he said.

"But your work's imperturbability is one of the great things about it," she said.

He said nothing.

"I'm sorry," she said.

"No," he said.

"No," she said. "Oh, I mean, never mind."

"I'm just thinking about it," he said. "Maybe you idealize it."

"What—your work or your implacability?"

"Well, it would have to be both, wouldn't it?" said Dodge.

"You're so succinct," said Elise. "At least you're paying attention, thank god."

"I pay attention," said Dodge. "I'm only verbally paralyzed. It's always all roiling around inside, though."

"Really?" said Elise. It was interesting how much more communicative Dodge was today. Had he smoked some grass before they left?

"Yeah," said Dodge.

"But then how can you say you don't need love?" asked Elise.

"Did I say that?"

"Yes," she said.

"I can't imagine what I meant by that," he said. "Watch it."

She'd been about to slip her foot under a root. He stopped for a moment, took out a pack of Camel Lights, and removed from it a tightly rolled joint. He lit it. She watched him.

"Want some?" he asked, his breath still sucked in.

"No, thanks," she said. They had walked out quite a bit more than Elise had realized. She didn't want to talk now that he had smoked, since she didn't know quite what state he'd be in. She became aware, though, of feeling the moistness in the air more, of the very dark green of the pines and the blue of the birch.

"I'm having a contact high," she said.

"Cheap date," said Dodge.

"Yeah," she said. She didn't like the joke. "How're you doing?" she asked.

"Okay," he said. Then nothing. He held his breath. She heard the woodpecker, creaking, small peeps in the stillness, rustling.

Then: "It takes an incredible amount to get me high. I've really built up an incredible tolerance," said Dodge.

"Really?" she said.

"Yeah," he said. "I should stop, just for that reason, if no other."

"Does it help you to work?" She was surprised and elated that he was confiding in her.

"Yes and no," he said. "It makes you more verbally uninhibited but more emotionally inhibited."

"I'd give anything to be more inhibited," said Elise.

He said nothing, but she turned toward him and saw that he was smiling. She smiled back at him. She didn't want to turn and walk on. In another twenty or thirty feet, the trees would thin and the path would lead them back to the lawn. "Let's sit down and rest," she said, "for just a minute."

He took another deep toke and, breathing out, took a couple of steps toward a very wide elm, and then took another toke, leaning against the tree. Elise walked back the few steps toward him and sat down. Through the thin material of her dress, she could feel the twigs and roots.

"Get up!!" he said.

"What?" she said, looking up at him, not moving.

"I think there's poison ivy," he said.

"Shit!" she said, and lurched upward.

He squatted next to the base of the tree. "No," he said. "It's okay."

"Jesus," she said, and sat back down, very close to him. She put her hand on her chest. "You scared me so much."

He leaned against the tree and let himself slide to the ground. "Sorry," he said.

She came closer to him, not thinking, but as if pulled to him, perhaps to kiss him, but he didn't move at all, so she brushed her face past his and toward his torso and leaned her head on his shoulder. He didn't move for a moment. Her heart seemed to beat loudly, and his too, and he smelled very slightly of perspiration and paint. Her temple touched his neck and some vein throbbed there, or was it hers? Her hand was open on his back as if they were dancing, and through the thin cotton of his T-shirt, she felt his muscles and his flesh, slightly soft. He lifted his hand from the ground, wiped the twigs and earth off his jeans, and then put his arm around her. For a moment, Elise felt an immense relief. Then she wanted to sit up and look at him, but she was afraid that would make it stop. She felt him breathe deeply. She moaned a little.

He briefly touched her knee and then slid his hand up her thigh, and back down to her knee, like a caress. She put her hand on his hip and then on his crotch—she could feel he was partly hard. This filled her with tenderness for him, as if this combination of arousal and failure of desire made him seem more vulnerable and endearing than she had previously understood. She tugged at his zipper. He shifted onto his back and undid his belt and his zipper. She put her fingers into the opening of his jockey shorts and glanced at him briefly—his eyes were closed—before sliding down to take his penis in her mouth.

Then, for a long moment, she felt immersed in softness—the fragile delicacy of his penis, the yielding skin covering his testicles, the warmth of his abdomen.

But a few minutes later, he was still flaccid in her mouth. She stopped and lay with her face against his groin, his penis against her cheek. Neither of them said anything.

"Are you sleepy?" she asked. She felt his penis stir slightly.

"I guess so," he said. He pulled away from her. "I'm sorry," he said. He pulled his zipper up.

She wiped her mouth on the back of her hand. "It's not important," she said.

"Oh, sure," he said. "Right. No importance whatsoever."

She laughed and slid back up to be parallel with him. Now their faces were close to one another and they gazed into each other's eyes. He emitted a sound, "Hmm," that seemed affectionate, somehow, and conclusive, and he pushed her hair back from her face and then held her close to him and hugged her. She put her arms around him and felt that immense relief again.

"Okay," he said. "Okay?"

"Okay," she said. And everything really did seem fine while he held her.

"We'd better go," he said.

"Okay," she said.

As they emerged from the woods, he said nothing more, and with some effort, neither did she, so that she was left with a bizarre sense of her final remark, reverberating oddly. *Okay.*

When they reached the lawn, she said, "It seems too nice to go indoors. Do you want to go to the rose garden?"

"I think I'll lie down for a little while," said Dodge. "Maybe I'll come by later."

She wouldn't have gone to the rose garden without him, but since he had said he might come she went, anyway, though she knew he wouldn't. But she thought he might look out the window. She sat down on a bench, looked out. She felt desolate. Desolate.

There were gray clouds. *White clouds and gray clouds. White and gray. White and gray and blue. White and gray and blue.*

After a while she heard some voices up at the house. She didn't want to go back up. She lay down on the bench. She must have dozed off.

When she woke, the sun was only a little lower. She turned her head and saw Billy at the fountain. He didn't seem to see her. He seemed to be waiting, though.

He had changed, she suddenly realized, and was wearing blue corduroy pants. *A very nice nice blue. Very nice nice nice. Very very nice blue. Very blue.* In his blue corduroy jeans and his T-shirt, he looked incongruous and too modern to be standing by the fountain. Or like a Calvin Klein ad, thought Elise. He was too good-looking, actually. Suddenly it annoyed her.

What or who was he waiting for?

Susie? No. Elise remembered the conversation at breakfast, and it flashed on her that he was almost certainly waiting for Kay. She didn't know why, but it just seemed an absolute certainty. It went with all the glances she had seen crossing between them the last month, the strange denseness of the space between them.

Could it be true? Yes, it really could.

Well, well, well, Elise thought.

She stood and turned and walked back to the house, wondering if he saw her. She went straight up to her room and sat down on the bed. She sat still a little while, until she heard some raindrops on the pane. "Shit!" she said. She felt she couldn't stay here, that the walls would move toward one another and crush her. She got her slicker, an orange slicker she hated, out of the closet and went back outside.

The hood of the orange slicker was too big and kept falling off. The rain was gentle and she didn't mind getting her hair wet but wondered if she would soon be uncomfortable. She lifted her face to the sky, closed her eyes, and felt whatever little light there was against her eyelids and the tender drizzle on her face and for a moment felt better. She sighed audibly, almost a moan.

She walked a little farther into the trees and began to sing to herself. *All the pretty trees and flowers, trees and flowers, trees and flowers and moss.* The rain began to fall more heavily; she heard it ringing on the leaves. She selected a tree thicker than the rest and put her arms around it and put her face against the bark and began to cry.

Then she slipped down to the ground, sat at the base of the tree, and sobbed. Sometimes, when it seemed as though she was nearly finished, she would lean her face against the tree and it would start again. Sometimes she called out. "Oh, oh," she moaned. She could smell the fertile stench of the earth. She hugged the tree. Under her fingers the bark was slightly moist. She tightened her arms until the pain made the thoughts go away.

Ron found her there about an hour later. He said Susie and Kay had sent him out. Her hair and face were quite soaked.

"I'm fine," said Elise. He held out a hand, and she took it and rose. "This is ridiculous. I was just working on something."

"Working?" said Ron. "Why can't you work inside in your nice toasty room?"

"Jesus Christ," said Elise with considerable resentment.

"Temper, temper," said Ron. "Ready for a Bloody Mary?"

"Jesus Christ," said Elise.

"What were you working on?"

"I just don't feel like talking about it," she said.

A lightning bolt, as clear as a cartoon sign, flashed in the sky nearly above them.

"Jesus Christ," said Ron in turn. "Now what? Okay, Elise, let's run for it."

As the thunder growled, they bolted across the lawn to the house. By the time they reached the door, Elise was flushed and laughing.

"Ah," she said when they were back inside, pushing back her wet hair. "I feel much better."

"I think I'm going to have a nice pneumonia," said Ron. "Pour me a Bloody Mary and call an ambulance." And he headed off toward his room to change.

She didn't know whether he had been serious or not, but she did go onto the patio and got out a can of tomato juice and opened it and mixed some Bloody Marys. As an afterthought she poured more vodka. She took the pitcher and two glasses and headed upstairs. The house was completely quiet.

She knocked on Ron's door. "Are you there?" she said.

"Yeah," said Ron.

She opened the door. He was lying on his bed in his shorts, his wet head on the pillow. He looked big on the single bed. Big and nice like a teddy bear. She realized now that he was really a kind person. A good person in his complicated way.

"Hi," she said.

"Hi," he said. He didn't seem all that comfortable that she was there. "I was going to come downstairs soon."

She came over and sat down on the side of the bed. He shifted over. She put the pitcher and the two glasses on the floor. Then she picked up a glass. "Do you want some?" she said.

"Well, maybe not right now," he said.

"I'm going to have some," she said. She poured herself a glass. She downed it.

"Holy shit, Elise," said Ron.

Elise swung her legs over and lay down next to him. Then she turned and put her head in the curve of his neck. She kept thinking of Dodge. It was Dodge she was thinking about, but she was also thinking that what she wanted to do was to stop thinking.

"What's the matter?" said Ron. He rubbed her arm.

"Let's make love," said Elise.

His hand on her arm became still.

"I don't know if I can," he said.

"What do you mean?" said Elise.

"Well, I just don't know," said Ron. "I mean, I wasn't ready. I just don't know."

She slid onto him so that she was lying on top of him. She looked into his eyes, her face very close to his. He scared her up close, but she put her mouth on his. She could feel him hard. He kissed her back but weakly. He pushed her off. "I don't know," he said.

"What's the matter?" she said.

"I . . . I don't know," he said.

"Are you not attracted to me?" she asked.

"I don't know. I don't know. I don't know. I just can't talk. Please don't make me talk. Don't make me do anything." Ron's voice rose.

Elise sat up. Her face burned. "You don't have to fuck me, but you could talk to me," she said.

"I can't," he said. "I just can't."

"You can't what?" she said.

"Elise, for crying out loud," he said.

Sunday

The next morning Elise was halfway down the staircase on her way to breakfast and then suddenly thought to herself, *I just can't stand it anymore.* She sat down on the step she had been standing on, leaned her head against the banister.

Only Susie, Kay, and Ron had made it into the dining room. It was a gloomy morning and much of the breakfast was silent. When they spoke, Elise could hear them as distinctly as if she were in the room.

"I don't know why," Susie said. "I only had a couple of beers, but I feel like I have an incredible hangover."

"It's age," said Ron.

"I don't think it's age," said Kay. "In the sixties when we were kids, there were plenty of people in their forties and fifties who used to party really late and go to work early and have incredible energy."

"It's true," said Susie. "There were a lot of restaurants open late at night. You could meet someone at three in the morning for a cheeseburger."

"I read that 15 percent of all Jews have moved out of New York," said Ron. "They were the ones eating all the cheeseburgers."

Both women laughed. "Ron," said Susie.

"What?" said Ron.

"Never mind," said Susie. "I think it's people who wanted to be safe who moved out."

"Well," said Kay. "I think New York is going to get good again."

"I do too," said Susie.

"I don't know," said Ron.

"I think it's the dross that's leaving," said Kay.

"What do you mean?" asked Susie.

"Well, you know, it's those who can't take it or who value comfort above other things. Let them go. Then New York will get small again, the way it used to be before all these people came to be artists or movers and shakers. It worked better the other way."

"It's people with kids," said Ron.

"Well, but who would want to bring up a kid outside of New York?" said Susie.

"Many people, unfortunately," said Ron. "That's why they're going to have kids who thiiiiiiink sooooooo slooooooooooowly."

"They don't think slowly in the suburbs," said Kay. "They're all taking drugs when they're twelve years old."

"Oh, look," said Susie. "It's raining."

The dining room had grown quite dark. Outside, in a feeble luminosity, a light rain fell, barely visible except as an almost-glitter against the trees.

"Where's Elise?" asked Susie.

"Probably hungover," said Ron.

"Or freaked out," said Kay.

"No, everything's like water off a duck's back for Elise," said Ron.

The two women laughed. "That was something Friday night," said Susie.

"It sure was," said Kay.

"I realized afterward there probably really had been some danger," said Susie.

"There sure was," said Kay.

"Oh, that's ridiculous," said Ron.

"No, I really felt it," said Kay. "You can really feel when there's danger. I've learned to respect that."

"A rural bar," said Ron, "is statistically certainly much more dangerous than any of the jungles you've visited."

"I just felt," said Kay, "that we weren't welcome there."

"I don't know," said Susie.

"Well, we don't need to find out," said Ron.

"Oh, we certainly do," said Susie. "I mean, we're going to go back, right?"

Elise just sat on the stair, her forehead on her knee.

It rained all afternoon. At around five they all went into town, except Elise, to shop for snacks and maybe get a pizza. Elise had been reading the paper, but when she heard the car drive off, she set the paper down and went and stood at the window. Near the house the rain had so trampled the flowers that many of them lay facedown on the gravel outside the beds.

She left the room and perambulated down the hall. Ron's door was open—you could see the mess inside; Susie's and Kay's were closed. Billy's door was closed, but as Elise walked by, she started: some music was coming out of it. But she had seen him leave with the others. He must have left his CD player on. The slight sound had faded by the time she reached Dodge's door, nearly but not quite closed. Elise pushed it open with her bare toe and it swung open silently.

Dodge's room was extremely neat. The furniture seemed lined up more perpendicularly, at more precise angles in here than in the other rooms. The bed was made, a blanket perfectly folded at its foot. The pillow was slightly marred by wrinkles. Elise walked over to the bed. She lay facedown and breathed. She burrowed her face in the pillow, wishing she could be absorbed by this bed. She breathed his smell as if her life depended on it.

BILLY

Friday

Dodge and Elise went back to the city early Monday, but Susie, Billy, Kay, and Ron stayed at the house all week. Friday morning they had breakfast together. Billy almost never made it to breakfast. His theory was that the culture shock of traveling from his private universe to the weirdness of the grown-up breakfast world was absolutely not worth it, despite the fact that breakfast food was his favorite.

They were talking about the weekend. Everyone had been shifting plans around for days and it had caused endless discussions. Susie was leaving today for London, but she planned to be back by next Friday. Someone who was a friend of both Dodge's and Elise's was having a party in Easthampton Saturday, and at first everyone else was going to go along, even Billy, and Dodie was given the weekend off. But Billy had suddenly realized that the prospect of a party in Easthampton where he would be marooned whether he was having a good time or not was intolerable, and he had said he wouldn't go, whereupon Ron had said that the truth was he really didn't want to go either and couldn't take the Hamptons. Billy had considered staying in New York for the weekend but had finally decided that he just couldn't take New York in August—it would make him too aware that the summer was about to end, and he would have to face the gargantuan question mark in his future and that he was better off staying here.

After much discussion it had finally been decided that Kay and Elise were going to go along with Dodge, and they would all drive out together so that, for a few days, Billy was worried that he would have to spend the weekend at the house alone with Ron. But, yesterday afternoon, Kay had said that she had changed her mind and didn't want to go to the party and was going to stay at the house after all.

All the others planned to be back by Sunday night, late, and stay for the week. There was nothing happening now in New York, anyway.

Since then, Billy had managed to keep a lot of white noise around the knowledge that Susie would be spending the week in London and that he would be left alone with Kay and Ron for the weekend. For one thing, there might be a change of mind: with Susie, that was always to be expected. For another, Kay might suddenly develop other plans. Billy kept wanting to talk to Kay, but she didn't seem to be noticing his signals. Last night, when everyone had gone to their rooms, he had gone and stood outside her door. But he hadn't dared knock. He'd tried looking through the keyhole and it was dark. He'd gone back to his room. He wished he could smoke but, aside from a couple of slips now and then, he'd managed to maintain an abstinence that he experienced as alternately defiant and wobbly.

What if Kay decided to go after all? He didn't quite know what he would do if he had to spend a weekend alone with Ron. He might actually take off and go to New York after all if it got too bad, though the thought of a confrontation with Ron exhausted him in advance.

It was too painful to think of Kay leaving just when they would have this time together. Though come to think of it, considering how totally invasive Ron's presence always was and how impossible it was to ignore it, he knew it was ridiculous to think of this time with Kay as being alone or anything.

At least Susie would be gone. Susie took up all of Kay's attention. He shouldn't think about it, he told himself, because it would
just be too disappointing if it didn't work out, and too great if it did.
He couldn't really take thinking about either prospect.

Sometimes he felt really mad at Kay, because what he really
felt was insane joy at the prospect that he might have some time
alone with her and would suddenly become furious at the thought
that she didn't feel the same way.

On the other hand, Kay had plenty of opportunities for love affairs that weren't surreptitious. Maybe she couldn't care less.
Maybe she saw someone when she went back to the city during the
week. Billy felt sure that there were several men in love with her
and that she was having an affair with at least one of them. He had
tried to get information from Susie, but Susie had become very
closedmouthed about Kay.

Maybe that strange couple of days at the beginning of the summer in the rose garden had just been an anomaly. Or maybe she was
just teasing him and didn't know he was taking it seriously. Or
maybe it was an act, to see how he would react. Or maybe it was a
joke of Susie's and they were all waiting to see what he would do. Or
maybe it was all in his own mind.

Then he would remember how Kay looked now and then when
he had caught her eye, and it didn't seem possible. Something had
really happened. He knew something had really happened.

Last night Susie had said, "I'm assuming the three of you will
be just fine without me."

"We'll manage," said Kay.

"You can charge at Bruno's," Susie said to Billy. "Please don't
forget to eat."

"I just heard I may have to go into town," said Ron, "for a
meeting with Schultz."

"Oh, really?" Susie and Kay said simultaneously. Billy
reached in his pocket for a cigarette before he remembered there
was no pack there.

"So maybe I'll drive in with you," Ron said. "Fucking Schultz."

This morning at breakfast Susie said, "Will you be all right, the two of you?"

"We'll be great," said Kay.

"Don't touch anything in my room," said Ron.

"There's a lot of stuff in the cupboards and in the fridge," Susie said to Billy. "But Dodie won't be here. Don't make Kay clean up after you in the kitchen."

"Don't worry," said Kay.

"I'll be as neat as a pin," said Billy. "Mr. Spic-and-Span."

"No hanky-panky with that Claudine till I get back," said Ron.

"You're gross, Reiser," said Billy.

"He just had to gross us out one more time before he left," said Kay. She smiled at Billy. *Her smile.*

"Billy, will you please write down my messages?" said Susie.

"Yup," said Billy.

"You know where to reach me if there's something urgent," said Susie.

"Yeah, yeah, yeah, yeah," said Billy.

The appointed time of departure came and went. He thought they'd never leave. It was driving him crazy. Susie was late, as always, and Ron was already in the taxi, waiting. It was a rather ancient station wagon that seemed always available, as if it was used almost exclusively to ferry the few city people the forty-five minutes to and from the train. Once in a while one of the locals lost his license for a while for too many drunk-driving arrests and had to be chauffeured, but aside from that there was strictly no summer business.

Billy came out of the house and Kay was leaning against the hood, waiting to say good-bye. The driver came out of the car and was pretending to stretch his legs but was almost comically checking out the house. At one point he approached the dining-room window and actually peered in, then turned away with a blank expression. "He seems disappointed," said Ron, who, like the other two, had been watching the cabdriver. "It must be the wallpaper. They're just not into damask stripes around here."

Finally, Susie bustled out the back door looking utterly different from her usual summer self, dressed in a black almost see-
through blouse and a little black skirt and black tights and very
high-heeled black shoes. She was also carrying a black leather
backpack, incongruous but of course totally stylish. A bit too de-
liberate for Billy's taste.

Ron leaned out the window to survey her, and so did the taxi
driver. "You look either like the widow everyone dreams of fucking
or a hippie in a German movie," Ron said.

The taxi driver, looking slightly dazed, got into the car.

"I'm going straight to an interview," said Susie. "And then to
the airport."

"I'll be rooting for you," said Kay.

"Good-bye, sweetie," said Susie to Billy. "Give me a kiss."
Billy kissed Susie on the cheek.

"Have a good time," he said.

"You've got money," she said.

"Don't worry," he said.

The driver turned on the motor.

"There's some pasta salad," said Susie, at large.

"Don't worry," said Kay.

Susie hoisted her backpack into the trunk and slammed it shut.
She put her hands on Kay's shoulder. "Will you be okay?"

"Me?" said Kay, surprised.

"Yes," said Susie. Susie left her hands on Kay's shoulders and
looked into her eyes. It was one of those moments of unexpected
intimacy Susie had that was always totally endearing, Billy knew.
"Don't be sad, okay?" Susie said to Kay. "Just don't be."

"All right," said Kay, smiling. "It's a deal."

Her smile. Billy liked to see Kay smiling at someone else so he
could observe it. When she smiled at him, it was so exciting he
couldn't think, could only feel that surge of . . . what was it? Hope?

They watched the taxi drive away, then went back into the
house. Dodie was still around, cleaning up from breakfast. She was
taking off at noon, she'd announced. She'd already made plans to

take her kids to her sister's for a week. On his way upstairs, Billy heard Kay reassure her for the hundredth time that there was no problem, that it would be easy to take care of whatever there was to be done, and that, yes, she'd remember about paying the garbage guy and that there was pasta salad in the fridge.

Billy went back to his room and lay down on his bed, just to stay in contact with the tremendous luxury that he was going to be alone with Kay, that he was already practically alone with her. Against expectation, he then fell asleep.

When he woke up, it was two o'clock. For a while he lay on the bed, watching the shadows move on the ceiling. The walk in the rose garden had come to mind, vividly, painfully. What had Kay dreamed about lions? He saw a pride of lions lying down as if they were tired, and then he selected a lion and made it considerably more vigorous and savage, and then entered it. The lion went to a riverbank, lay down, and gazed at the river. Billy lost track of how long he spent as the lion gazing at the shadows and the river. The river was in the shadows. When he could make his mind really still, there was only the river.

Finally, he heard the bathroom door slam and started. He wanted to find Kay. He thought of holding Kay. *She doesn't want me*, he thought, *or she would have let me know.*

He brusquely sat up and quickly slipped out of his clothes and into his bathing suit, as if he were late. He grabbed his black towel—the one black towel in the house, which he had declared at the beginning of the summer he had dibs on. He put the strap of his boom box over his shoulder. He swung by the kitchen and put peanut butter, jelly, four slices of bread, a hard-boiled egg, a chocolate bar, two cans of Coke, and a knife in a plastic bag and strode to the pool.

At the pool he settled in with some relief and immediately picked up a magazine. He had time to calm down and soon the sun had its effect. He made and ate the two peanut-butter-and-jelly sandwiches. He cracked and peeled the egg. He said shit because he had forgotten to bring salt, but he ate the hard-boiled egg, any-

way, in two bites, drank one of the Cokes. He turned on his boom
box, pushed play on the Robert Johnson CD, and then sang along
to "Kindhearted Woman Blues." He knew all the words.

I love my baby
my baby don't love me...

Then there was a guitar solo, and Billy sang along with Robert
Johnson's guitar, lying in the sun on the deck chair with his eyes
closed. He was able, when he sang along, to clear his mind of
everything else. He could copy Robert Johnson's ironic and nasal
inflections with absolute accuracy.

An hour later Billy had sung along with every song on the
double Robert Johnson CD, eyes closed, lying in the sun, declaim-
ing the lyrics with abandon, when he opened his eyes and Kay appeared in her bathing suit, a one-piece that had thin indigo and
white stripes and made her look more tanned. Her hair was un-
combed; there was a towel over her shoulder. She leaned over and
surveyed the plate that had the edge of a peanut-butter-and-jelly
sandwich, the eggshell, and a crumpled Nestlé's wrapper.

"Mm," she said. "Great-looking lunch."

"I was starving," said Billy.

Kay put all her things down. She carefully laid out the towel so
that it was exactly in line with the sun, at more or less a forty-five-
degree angle to Billy, who had chosen to be perpendicular to the
pool. Then she walked over, took the bread corner, and put it in her
mouth. "Mm," she said. "I'm starving too." He felt suddenly very
happy. She was smiling at him and he smiled back.

That smile. Why did it move him so much?

She lay down and after a moment he reached out. He could just
reach her foot. He took her big toe between two fingers. She kept
her eyes closed and smiled. He shook her toe a little. Then he took
his hand away and lay back. He felt better. He felt incredibly nervous but he felt better. He wished he could have a beer so he could
relax, but that was okay. He didn't know what would happen, but
he thought it would be all right.

He let himself get into a white space with the sun. He turned away from Kay and let the sun come in through his closed eyelids. For a moment he thought of the riverbank, but then he pushed that away. Then he only thought of Kay lying down nearby. Or had she sat up by now? He didn't want to open his eyes and look.

"Hi!" came a voice. Billy looked up, squinting, and it was Claudine, standing a couple of feet away in an almost nonexistent bikini. She was looking up at the sky.

"Hi," said Kay, even though it was obvious to all that she was not the one who had been addressed. *Kay,* thought Billy, *is always polite no matter what.*

"Hey," said Billy to Claudine. He was wondering what he should do. He felt dread.

"Hello," said Claudine, and then said nothing else. Waited to see what he would do. He wished she would leave. *Leave!* he pleaded silently.

"How's it going?" he finally said to Claudine.

"Do you think you will want to play tennis?" asked Claudine.

He said nothing for a moment. Kay's eyelids looked as if she was keeping them closed on purpose.

What was he supposed to say. It was happening too fast. He couldn't think. "Sure," he said.

"When?" asked Claudine.

"I'll come and get you in a little while. Like an hour or something, okay?"

"All right," said Claudine. "I'll see you later." She turned to leave.

"You can stay here if you want to swim or something," said Kay to Claudine. Kay sat up.

What a jerk I am! Billy felt a haze of impacted fury that was already in the process of turning into despair.

Claudine tilted her head and seemed to consider the possibility of sticking around. Billy closed his eyes again, hoping she would see that as a hint, or maybe just to stop dealing with her. Then nothing happened, so he reopened his eyes.

Claudine twisted her mouth in a charming way, slipped a finger

under the cord of her bikini top as if to readjust it, which caused
Billy to notice again that she had exquisite breasts. Then she said,
"No, thank you very much. I am going to do some pliés, I think."

"Pliés?" said Kay.

"Yes," said Claudine. "For exercise."

She walked away and both Billy and Kay watched her leave.
The lubricity that the back of her body was intended to generate
was so embarrassing that Billy couldn't think of a joke. Kay lay
back down again and closed her eyes. Billy was sure she was
angry. *Why did I do that?* Why didn't he have the presence of mind
to just send Claudine away?

"I couldn't say no," said Billy.

"There's no reason for you not to go," said Kay, in a rather dry
voice.

"I won't take long. I was hoping you and I could hang out today."

"I think I'll go in," she said.

The tennis game with Claudine was ludicrous. For the first
time, she beat him with no problem at all. He had no concentration
whatsoever. He was just furious that he was there. He watched
Claudine's excellent form and her perfect legs in her tennis whites
and wanted to kill her. He'd actually felt a considerable amount of
desire for her in the past few weeks, which he'd managed to segre-
gate from his stronger and conflicting desire for Kay. But now that
Claudine had interfered with his day with Kay, he felt only rage.

At the end of the game, he felt no relief, just irritation.

"You didn't like to lose?" Claudine asked.

"No," he said. "I'm just in a bad mood."

"Oh," she said.

"I have a lot of work to do this week."

"Oh," she said. "What type of work?"

"Oh, you know," said Billy.

When he got back to the house, he raced upstairs, calling out,
"Kay!" but she wasn't there.

He got himself a glass, put some ice in it, and poured a Coke
into it, then went upstairs and lay down.

He went back to the river. On the river there was a barge, and on the barge there was an animal breathing fire.

Sometimes he thought of Kay, nearly naked, her flat stomach, the light on her limbs at the pool a few hours ago, the blond hair over the nape of her tanned neck, and imagined himself lying on her.

Then he went back to the river, the lion, the fire breather, the night. Soon all he saw was the night and a long, thin stream of fire.

"Hey," said Kay. She was sitting at the foot of his bed. He had fallen asleep again. He wanted to reach out to her but didn't. It was dusk.

"Hi," he said.

"Were you dreaming?"

He smiled at her. She smiled back.

What a gorgeous smile she has, he thought. It was a child's smile, in which she showed delight and all her teeth, destroying for a moment all of her melancholy charm.

He'd been dreaming about her, he now realized, and wanted to say so but didn't. He peered at his watch. "Oh my god," he said. It was eight o'clock.

"I thought you'd want to wake up," she said.

"Yeah," he said. "I'm glad you woke me up."

"How was tennis?" she asked. She pursed her lips and twisted them, as if she were upset and she was also saying to herself, *Why should I care?*

"I love your expressions," he said. "They're so complicated." He looked at her and she actually blushed. He laughed. Then he tried to both pout and twist his mouth the way hers had been. Then he smiled at her and she smiled back.

"No," he said, as if she had asked him something else. "I got back a long time ago. I've been waiting a long time." Those words spoken seemed to him to carry some heavy meaning. He couldn't help smiling at her in a way he knew was too revealing, and yet she was smiling back so it must be all right. He knew that if she was just a few inches closer, he could smell her. He knew her perfume, soft and complicated and inebriating. He wished he could put his lips on her neck. He wished he could be lost in her.

He moved his foot under the cover, until it rested near her leg. He wished she would lie down with him.

"What were you doing?" she asked. He was thinking, *I wish you would touch me.*

"I was just waiting," he said. "Are we going to have dinner?"

"Yes," she said. "Absolutely. We'll go out."

"For steak?" he said, like a kid.

She laughed. "You've been pining for steak?"

He felt oddly merry and she seemed happier than usual. *Just don't do anything, just be careful,* he said to himself, as if she were a bird or a feather or an angel. *I want her to take care of me forever.*

He got up off the bed and stood, stretched. He wished he hadn't moved. Now he was out of the bubble they had been in together when he was in the bed.

Kay's mood seemed to fall once he got off the bed. "Okay," she said. "Let me get dressed."

"All right, hurry up," he said.

"God," said Kay out loud as she left the room, in mock shock at being spoken to in such a cavalier way.

He put on the white T-shirt in which he thought he might look best.

He knew they were an incongruous couple, when they got into her car, she in the pretty summer dress, he in the T-shirt.

At the restaurant after they each had two drinks, Billy said, "I wonder what the other people here think our relationship is."

She said, "Why is it important?"

It was a large, woody place, but only three other tables were taken, two by families, one by an elderly couple who ate without speaking. At all the other tables, they were eating fried clams and fried shrimp. Both Billy and Kay had shrimp cocktails in front of them.

"You think anyone at the house knows anything?" he asked.

"No," said Kay.

"Even Susie?"

"You have an Oedipal problem to bring the house down," Kay said to him.

"Not at all," he said. "My rival was gone before there was even a fight." It was a standard line. He'd been using it for years.

"Well, precisely," she said.

"What do you mean, anyway?"

"Well, I just imagine you must have been embarrassed to be seen as Susie's date when you were a little boy."

"Oh, that stuff is ridiculous," said Billy.

"All right," she said. "What would you like to eat?"

He felt reprimanded but couldn't think of how to ask her to continue the conversation.

"Can I have the biggest steak?" he asked.

"Yes," she said. "You can have whatever you want."

Whatever I want. There had been so many questions, for years, so many things he wished he knew about Kay. He felt a great rush of love for Kay.

"Where do you get your money from?" he asked.

She laughed. "I earn it, from the sale of my books," she said.

"Really?" he said. He felt very impressed.

"Do you think you want to write, Billy?" she asked, suddenly formal.

"Maybe," he said, as if it were only up to him.

"Ah," she said.

"What do you think those people think? Do you think they think I'm your lover?"

"Billy!" she said.

"Or your nephew?" he said.

"Or my ward," she said.

"What?" he said, and smiled at her. *I may be a little drunk,* he thought. "Can I drive home?"

"No," she said.

He sulked a little on the way home. She drove back very slowly, so maybe she was a little drunk too, he thought. *Or maybe she doesn't know what's going to happen when we get home.* Her presence in the seat next to his was almost unendurably intense. He couldn't believe he was living through this without cigarettes.

"You know," he said. "I feel like I'm fourteen years old."

Kay laughed. "You do?" she said. "Why?"

"I don't know," he said. "I wish I knew."

Was it possible that Kay would let him make love to her, would let him touch her, would let him be inside of her, would let him come inside her?

Once home, she headed straight for the kitchen and he followed her. She poured herself a glass of seltzer and then poured him one.

"Shall we have a beer?" he asked.

"No, not for me," she said. "I think I've had my quota."

"You have a quota?"

"Well, I feel a little drunk," she said.

"Really?" he said. "That's fantastic. Let's have a talk."

She laughed. "You mean there are some things you'd like to talk to me about while I'm drunk."

"Sure," he said.

"No, thanks," she said.

"I think I'll have one," he said. He liked it in the kitchen with her and wanted to prolong this moment. He felt safe for a moment.

"I wonder how Susie is doing," Kay said.

She must be kidding, thought Billy. The unreality of the situation sobered him suddenly. *Nothing is going to happen. I've been dreaming.* "Susie's always doing just fine, no matter how she's doing," he said.

"What do you mean?" said Kay.

"Never mind," said Billy. "Let's not talk about Susie."

Kay walked out of the kitchen and he followed her. By unspoken accord they avoided the patio. In the drawing room, only one light was turned on and Kay didn't turn any more on. Billy waited to see where she would sit. When she chose the armchair, he went to the couch and lay down.

"Are you still a little drunk?"

"Yes," she said.

"Good," he said. "Now we can have our conversation."

"And what is it," she said, clearly amused by his bossiness. "What is it you want to talk about?"

"Let's talk about me," he said. "Do you really like me?"

She laughed. "My goodness," she said. "What a delicious child you are."

"Really," he said. "Delicious? I don't know if I like that. I wasn't a delicious child, anyway. I was a terrible brat."

"I'm sorry," she said. "I guess it's a little patronizing. You're not really a child."

"No," he said. "I do know I'm childlike in some ways. So are you."

"You're childlike in some wonderful ways," she said. "But I should be patronizing." She caught herself in the slip. "I mean," she said. "I shouldn't be patronizing. I mean, I hope you can understand that I can find you a delicious child and still take you seriously as a person."

"Perfect," he said. "That's perfect."

"I mean," said Kay, "I do think we could have an excellent friendship."

He tilted his head back, finished his beer.

"You think I have Oedipal problems?" he said. He felt emboldened by Kay's easiness.

"Yes," she said.

"Do you go to a psychiatrist?" he asked.

"Yes," she said.

"I think all that stuff is unnecessary."

"Oh, you do, do you?"

"Yes," he said. "In the end, it's much more worthwhile to understand people and yourself anecdotally."

"You're so incredibly precocious."

"Yes," he said. He yawned, despite himself. He didn't want to yawn, but he did and Kay saw him.

"Let's go to bed," she said.

Together? he wanted to ask. But he didn't have the nerve.

When they get to the top of the staircase, she said, "Wait a minute."

"Okay," he said.

She said, "Stand very still."

"Okay," he said.

"Close your eyes," she said.

He closed his eyes. She kissed him on the cheek, very softly. He felt her breath on his eyelid.

"Good night," she said, her lips next to his cheek.

When he opened his eyes again, she was headed toward her room.

In bed he waited a long time, as if waiting for her. After about an hour, he got up, went outside, and looked up at her window. It was dark.

He went back to his room, put on the Robert Johnson CD again, and smoked a joint. He still hoped she might come in. But once he was high, he saw very clearly that Kay had made her choice. He realized he had hoped that when everyone left, they would just go to bed. But that hadn't happened. Wasn't going to happen. She had made a choice. Maybe it was better that way. He could love Kay forever that way. After all, it was hopeless. What could they tell Susie? Would he tell Susie or would Kay? No, it was hopeless. He couldn't see himself running away with Kay. The odd thing is he had this combination of really explicit sexual thoughts about her where he would just see her again and again naked, would feel himself penetrating her, but then the rest of the time what he kept thinking was that he could be happy with her. He kept imagining that they were sitting in a little house together and that's where they lived and they were happy.

But it was absurd, of course it was absurd, and it would ruin their friendship to even mention it. And, anyway, she had made a choice, so probably nothing would happen.

He felt a pang of yearning for her that was so powerful he moaned. He put his arms around himself, brought his knees up under his chin, and rocked back and forth for a while.

Saturday

When he awoke he went downstairs, hoping Kay hadn't had breakfast yet so he could eat with her. When he went into the kitchen, she was stirring a huge vat of soup.

"Vegetable soup," she said.

"That's weird," he said.

"Really?" she said, and smiled at him. He felt his heart pump. He smiled at her like an idiot, and she smiled back. All of his pain of last night seemed very distant. He didn't care anymore. Felt too unbearably nervous but also happy in a groggy sort of way.

He'd have some toast. She'd already eaten, but she made the toast for him and put some jam on it.

"I feel ridiculously good," he said.

"Yes, me too," she said.

They went for a walk. She was wearing her hair in a ponytail the way he liked it and a blue cotton sweater and white shorts, and he kept looking at her knees, which were a little bony, the way he liked them. He wanted to talk to her. Maybe about something personal. Maybe talk to her about his father. He felt it was an opportunity, now that he was alone with her. But he suddenly found himself tongue-tied with pleasure just to be with her. So he only commented on the height of a tree or guessed at the temperature.

They walked out for about an hour and then back, which incomprehensibly took less than an hour, and then sat down on the lawn in front of the house.

"I can't believe summer's nearly over," said Kay, narrowing her eyes to gaze at the luminous sky.

"What will you do?"

"Go back to my place," she said. "I don't know what else."

"Do you like living alone?" he asked.

"Yes," she said. "Surprisingly so."

"I guess I'll live alone too," he said.

She was silent and he was thinking he shouldn't have said that, that he should have said he wished he could live with her. *No, that's ridiculous.* He struggled to get the words out, but then he realized he couldn't, just couldn't say anything. It would ruin their friendship forever. Kay was someone whom he would know forever, and if he said something, it would be a black mark between them forever.

Suddenly he felt so unhappy, he thought he could scream. Kay looked unhappy too and was looking down. *I've just fucked up everything,* he thought. He felt like a boor. He felt as he had when he was an adolescent and his hands and feet always seemed huge. He felt as if Kay had suddenly seen what a jerk he was.

"I guess I'll go back in for a while," he said. He got himself up into a squatting position.

"Okay," said Kay. She leaned back. Rested on her elbows. "I'll see you later," she said, wearing a neutral expression, and he realized she was probably hurt.

Oh, man, he thought. *I can't take this much tension.* He went to the kitchen and poured himself a bowl of tepid vegetable soup and ate it. *I can't take this,* he kept saying to himself. He briefly considered going back to New York.

It didn't stay light as late as it had earlier in the summer. When it got dark, Kay made them scrambled eggs and then they talked for a long time on the patio, about his school days and her travels and days from a long-gone summer at the beach when he was a kid. They could speak softly and close. The sky slowly became inky mauve.

At midnight she went to bed. He stayed downstairs.

At 1 A.M. he knocked on her door, carrying a bottle of vodka and a deck of cards. They drank and played gin rummy until at least three o'clock. Every once in a while he would say something that made Kay laugh and she would close her eyes, and he would look at her neck, her shoulders in her white nightgown.

Sunday

The next morning when Billy woke up and went downstairs, the kitchen was just as they had left it last night. He went back upstairs and knocked on Kay's door, and when she didn't answer, cracked it open and saw that she was sleeping. He looked at her for a moment. She had a bright red mark on her cheek as if she had just turned over. He stood for a long time, at the door. He thought she might wake up because he was staring at her so hard. He thought of saying her name but couldn't. He closed the door very softly. His heart was beating hard. He leaned his forehead against the door. He walked away very quietly.

He ran errands, went to Bruno's, purchased frozen vegetables. It's a lot like shopping for clothes, he told himself as he selected vegetables. He tried to select vegetables he imagined she might like. For himself, he would have just gotten Idaho potatoes for baking, but he got corn and spinach and snow peas because he thought she'd like that.

He drove back but when he reached the house, he stayed for a while in the car. He felt suffused with an emotion he didn't understand. *What is this?* He actually probed himself. He felt buoyant. He couldn't quite identify the feeling, but at some point he noticed that it occurred whenever he remembered Kay saying, "Hold still," and looking at him the way she did, a few times, when she was unguarded. It had been love in her eyes, though she didn't know it.

Or maybe she knew. *Who knows what she knows?* How could he imagine what she knew? He tried to imagine he was her. And it seemed to him that she loved him, but he knew it's what he wanted to believe. But that look, what was it? He felt this painful bliss, this painful bliss must have something to do with the feeling of being loved. Why did it hurt so?

He felt flooded and overwhelmed. It was too exciting, too poignant, too sweet to bear. He sighed. It was intolerable.

He saw Kay lying on the gravel naked and he was lying on top of her, making love to her while she held him. She held him.

He got out of the car, got the bags out of the back, and brought them into the kitchen. He was thirsty and thought he would like some coffee, but then he decided he was too speedy for coffee, so he just poured some club soda onto some ice in a glass and went to the patio. But he couldn't sit still, not even for a minute.

Then he went back to the kitchen and went to the trouble of cutting a piece of lemon to put into the glass because, he felt, he wanted something fresh and delicious in his mouth. He wished he could kiss Kay. He found himself putting his arms on the counter and leaning his head on them.

He went outside. It was still early. The morning was very fresh. The grass was tingling with dew. The dappling was vivid. The colors were intense; there was a very slight caressing wind. All was still except for the songs of several birds. Once, a pine creaked. It was the essence of summer.

Late summer seems more like summer than early summer. It was the first time he'd ever realized that.

He went upstairs. Could Kay still be sleeping? He walked very quietly to the door of her room and cracked it open again. Kay was still sleeping. She hadn't pulled her shade down and she was lying in the sunlight, diffused a little by the translucent curtains. Billy was stunned by the guilt of looking, as if he was doing something terribly forbidden. Kay looked beautiful. *It must be forbidden*, he thought, *to look at anything so beautiful and secret.*

It wasn't until midafternoon that she found him at the pool. He was in the water, doing laps.

Kay lay down in a chaise longue, picked up her book. He swam to the edge. "What's up?" he asked.

"Not much," she said, without looking up from her book.

He came out of the water and sat on the edge of the pool for a long time, watching the sunlight on the water, his legs dangling over the edge into the water. Finally, after perhaps twenty minutes, perhaps half an hour, he slipped in, as soundlessly as possible. *I'll just do ten laps,* he thought.

When he turned around to swim in the other direction, he looked at Kay each time. She was reading. Then, as he turned on lap number eight, he saw her close the book and slip it under her arm. When he opened his eyes again, she had her towel over her shoulder and was walking away toward the house.

"Hey," Billy called out. He stopped and treaded water. "Where are you going?"

She turned around. "Inside," she said. The sun was in her eyes. She brought her hand up to her forehead to shield them.

"How come?" he called out. He doggy-paddled to the side of the pool, held on, pushed his wet hair back, and looked out at her.

"I don't know," she said. "I've had enough sun."

"Where will you be?" he asked.

She smiled. "I don't know," she said. "Not far. What about you?" Then, to make up for the smile and go back to the stern thing she was doing: "Are you going to play tennis today?" she asked.

"Yeah," he said. "Probably." Though he knew very well he told Claudine he wasn't going to play today.

She turned and walked toward the house.

"Kay!" he yelled. He was leaning his chin on his arms.

"What?" she called back.

"I don't know," he said. "I wanted to yell your name." Then he tilted his head back. "KAY," he yelled. "KAAAAAAAAAAAAY!"

She couldn't help laughing.

"Did you like that?" he asked.

"I don't know," she said. "No. I'm afraid the neighbors will come running. It's like something from a weird dream."

"I love the idea that I'm a character in a weird dream of yours," said Billy.

"Oh really," said Kay. She was still standing there with her towel over her shoulder but she didn't move.

"Did you ever dream about me?" asked Billy.

"Good-bye," said Kay. "I'm going in."

And she strode away and into the house, but Billy thought she was really in a good mood again.

Kay was in the kitchen making herself some tea.

"What?" said Billy, walking in.

"Did you hear me talking to myself?" asked Kay.

"What were you saying?" asked Billy.

"You're tracking in earth," said Kay, and he examined the bottom of his feet. Then he stuck a foot in the sink. "Jesus," said Kay. "Billy."

He performed some contortions at the sink, wiggling his foot under the tap water.

"Do you want to play gin again?" he asked.

"Gin?" she said.

"Yeah," he said. "I was thinking I'd like to play."

"Okay," said Kay. "Maybe later."

He was tilted strangely to get the dirt off his foot. Kay was just standing there, looking and smiling. Then he shut off the water and contorted himself some more to wipe his foot with a paper towel. Then he switched feet and repeated the entire operation.

"Does Susie let you do this?" asked Kay.

Billy was straining a bit to reach a paper towel. "I learned it from her."

Kay laughed. "Well, then it's fine," she said.

Billy posed. "I can't believe how different you and Susie are."

"Well, that's a precise observation," said Kay.

"What's the matter?" said Billy.

"Nothing," said Kay. She tore a piece of paper towel off the roll and wiped the counter.

"No, something is the matter, I can tell," said Billy.

"I'm having a bad day," said Kay.

"Why?" asked Billy.

"I don't know. Various reasons," said Kay. She crouched and wiped the floor near the sink with a paper towel.

"What?" insisted Billy.

"Don't make me go through the trouble of making up a lie," said Kay. The kettle began to whistle. She opened the cupboard and got out a cup, then another to get a tea bag. "Should I have Earl Grey or Constant Comment?"

"What's Constant Comment?"

"It's a sort of orangy spice tea. It seems almost sweet but it isn't."

"Then that's what you should have," said Billy. "It resembles you."

"What!" said Kay, laughing.

"Right," said Billy.

"I'm sweet," said Kay. She got a bag of Constant Comment out of the tin box.

"No," said Billy. "Only when you want to be." He drummed a little with his hands on the counter. He felt the strange feeling rise in him again. It was *really* frightening having it when she was in the room with him. But far out too. It was like being stoned, really— that's what it was. Kay looked to him as if she were inside some kind of a nimbus. *This must be what love is,* he thought suddenly, all of it making sense to him at last. This incredible pleasure and pain. Does she really look that beautiful? Or is it what loving someone does to you? How could she be that beautiful? He'd always seen it but now realized he hadn't allowed it to have its full impact.

She poured the water into the mug but didn't stop in time and the water overflowed. She grabbed the cup with her other hand, then pulled it away quickly.

Billy stood up. "Did you hurt yourself?" he asked.

"No," she said. Actually, she seemed as if she wasn't sure whether she hurt herself. She seemed dazed. She seemed a little like he felt. *Maybe she feels what I feel.*

She held out her hand and her fingers were somewhat red. "No, I'm okay," she said.

He took the fingers in his own and looked at her hand, turned it over, turned it over again, lifted her hand up to his lips. He closed his eyes and kept her hand in his and his mouth on her fingers even though he knew it might be hurting her if she was really burned. He had the feeling she didn't mind. Moments went by and finally he felt her fingers flutter a little. He opened his eyes; she pulled her hand away.

For an instant they just stood, facing one another, as if anything could happen.

"Billy," she said, "we've got to talk."

He suddenly knew that if they talked, the news would be bad for him, would close off possibilities. He shouldn't have done that with her hand.

"No," he said. "No, let's not talk. Let's absolutely not talk. Please, please, Kay. Let's not talk." She looked stricken. He smiled at her. "We don't have time to talk, we have important activities," he said. "We have an important dinner. We have an important game of gin rummy to play. No, absolutely not."

It was probably his manner as much as what he said that made Kay suddenly laugh, and he laughed too.

"Here," he said. He ran the cold water and took up Kay's hand again, putting his other arm around her shoulders and bringing her over to the sink. He held her hand under the cool running water. "Better?" he said.

"Yes," she said. She was smiling. It was dubious whether the cold water was accomplishing anything, and he knew that they both knew it, but at the moment everything seemed all right. It was a relief to hold her now, as if it was legal and everything was all right. For a moment, as they stood there with both their hands under the cool running water, everything was all right. His mouth was near her temple, but he resisted the urge to put his lips there.

"Okay," he said. He grabbed a clean dish towel and dried her hand. It was a little red. "There."

"Okay," said Kay. She moved away, smoothed back her hair. "Now, where was I?" She looked at her tea mug. Put her hand next to it to feel the temperature. "Perfect," she said. She sipped a little of the tea. Sighed.

He went to the fridge, opened it, and stared inside for a while. He grabbed a yogurt and began to stride out.

"Are you going to play tennis?" she asked.

"I've decided not to," he said. He could see she was keeping her expression carefully neutral. He was pleased that she was jealous yet worried she would become so jealous she would leave. But then she smiled, and he smiled too.

"Oh," she said.

"There's not enough time left with you," he said, matter-of-factly, opening the lid of the yogurt. He turned around, opened a drawer, rattled the utensils while selecting a spoon, and then turned back, checked out her smile, tilted his head, smiled at her. Then he ate the yogurt, standing up, leaning against the counter. She watched him, smiling.

"Why are you smiling?" he asked.

"I don't know," she said. But now he knew that she knew that it was because right now at this moment they were happy to be together. "I feel better," she said.

"That's good," he said. He scraped the bottom of the yogurt container, put it down, held onto the counter behind him, and hoisted himself up, dangling his legs.

"That's slightly patronizing," she said.

He gasped, grabbed his chest as if over a mock stabbing. "Why?" he exclaimed.

"I don't know," she said.

That cottony feeling was filling him again. It was like being stoned on a light dose of LSD. Or maybe ecstasy. More like ecstasy. He almost said so but thought better of it. He had to be more careful. Obviously Kay was not so much in control, but past a certain point she realized she was doing something she thought she shouldn't do. He felt his job was to keep her just within this side of the line.

Sitting on the kitchen counter, he was quite a bit higher than she, and this new vista of her body was almost unbearably inviting. Her clavicle, he wanted to put his mouth there, and his hand on her belly. He wanted to have his mouth on her breast. He wanted to be lying down with her with his hand between her legs, just resting. He wanted her to put her head on his chest. He wanted her to put her lips on his neck, on his cheek, to have her fingers in his hair. He wanted her to come closer so he could hold her between his thighs. He wanted her to have his penis in her mouth. He wanted to change places with her and have her sit on the counter and hold him between her thighs.

He didn't say anything and she didn't either, just stood there. He thought, *Maybe she'll just stay there for a while,* so he let his mind go and allowed himself to wish for her.

She stood a couple of feet away, holding her mug in front of her, yet somehow looking open and inviting, supernaturally inviting and yet normal, standing there with her blue mug, like some eerie modern goddess.

"Are you hungry?" she asked.

"Yes," he said. "But I don't know what for."

"Is that why you had come into the kitchen?"

"No," he said. "I was just looking for you. Did you come in because you were hungry?"

"I don't know," she said. "I forget. I was hungry and I also didn't know what for. I came in and then was just standing here, not able to decide. I was standing here in the kitchen because I am an indecisive woman."

"You are?" he said.

"Yes, I am."

"What's the difference?"

"Between what and what?" she asked.

"Between standing in the kitchen not knowing what you're going to eat and standing in the kitchen because you're an indecisive woman?"

"The latter is generic," she said. She went over to where he was sitting on the counter. His heart leaped in his chest. She put one hand on either knee and shook his legs, like a little kid's. "Anyway," she said. "I guess I'm not hungry. I'll wait till later."

She turned to walk out. He slipped down off the counter and followed her.

"Are we going out again?" he asked, dogging her down the hall.

"Yes," she said. "We can do exactly everything we did last night."

He was glad she couldn't see his face because he was smiling ridiculously.

"But we've got to talk," she called out as she went into her room.

"Oh, hell," he said.

"What?" she said, sticking her head out of her room again.

"Nothing," he said. "We'll do whatever you want. If you want to talk, we'll talk."

"Thank you," she said. And closed her door.

Billy decided to change for dinner. He took a shower and stayed under the hot water a long time. When he got out, he dried himself, listening for sounds of Kay. He put on the Robert Johnson CD but then found it too intrusive and turned it off, and listened again for a moment to see if he heard Kay in the house. But he heard only the sound of the dishwasher downstairs. He threw his towel onto the bed, reached into the drawer he had left open this morning for a clean pair of shorts, put them on, and stood for a moment in front of his closet trying to figure out what to wear. He thought of Kay standing in the kitchen saying, "I am an indecisive woman," and threw himself on the bed. He curled himself up on the bed and rocked and moaned. He felt as if he was in the most intolerable pain he'd ever experienced. He felt ill with love. It was excruciating.

What would Kay say? In a way, her position was much tougher than his. She must have the feeling that she would be doing something immoral by making love with him, let alone running off with him to the house he had imagined for them. Probably to her it seemed insane, and as if she couldn't do that to Susie. But he could talk to Susie. He could do it so Kay wouldn't have to. He knew Kay was capable of framing it as a moral problem. But this kind of love couldn't be framed like a moral problem. If it was a moral problem for her, well then he felt he wanted her to love him more than she loved the idea of herself as a moral person. Was that so much love to ask for? It was very little by comparison with his love. He felt today as if all summer his yearning for Kay had prepared him for this moment in which he entered a state of perfect love. He loved her more than anything. More than any idea of himself. He might love her enough to give up having her.

He didn't think he had an Oedipal problem. He thought Kay thought he had an Oedipal problem to avoid confronting what had happened between them. Her psychological explanations were a way of packaging emotions so that they didn't have to be experienced fully. She'd been too hurt by life and now defended herself against it as if it were her enemy. But she was wrong. It could be different. There had been stranger events in the world than a relationship such as theirs. It was possible. As much as anything else was possible, it was possible.

It's true that he couldn't quite get the logistics to mesh. He thought of being together in New York and couldn't solve the problems of her friends and his friends, of how it would be possible to actually live the practical aspects of such a relationship. But in a way, Billy reflected, that only had to do with what other people thought. They could just leave. He could live anywhere, and Kay was someone who could exist outside of New York.

He could tell that what had happened wasn't going away. No matter what Kay was going to say tonight, things had gone too far to ever be taken back. He felt triumphant, in a way, to have wrested Kay's love out of her. Though she hadn't said anything explicitly, he could tell she loved him; she had let him see she loved him. No matter what happened, she couldn't take that back. Even if nothing happened between them ever, at least she loved him, at least she had let him see that she loved him. She had to love him—he just couldn't stand to be alive otherwise. He could barely stand it as it was.

He couldn't bear the thought that the others would return to the house. How would he hide what he was feeling? Did they know? No, they couldn't know. But how could they not know? No, he didn't think anyone knew.

What pain he was in. His love burned him and twisted him. His stomach was knotted and his head felt as if it were going to burst, and then every once in a while, he would get these flushes of desire that made him feel a combination of bliss and terror.

He went to the window. He felt feverish. He leaned his forehead against the glass. Yes, the days had gotten shorter. Outside, it was dusk: the hills were golden, like Kay's skin; the sky was a very gray blue, like her eyes. On the other side of the river, the Hudson Valley undulated away, woods and fields basking in the last light. It was so painfully beautiful he couldn't look anymore. He went and lay down again.

I've got to stop, he told himself. *I've got to stop tormenting myself.* He couldn't stop. Then something in him let go and he stopped trying to stop, and then Kay was not there anymore in his mind but almost as if she were there with him on the bed, stretched out alongside of him. He felt her body next to his and imagined his mouth on hers and that he will penetrate her and move inside her *and not stop moving, not stop moving, not stop moving, not stop.*

There was a knock on the door. "Just a minute," he called out. "Just one minute."

"Okay," Kay called out. "I'm ready. I'll wait for you downstairs. Hurry up so we can get out of here before they get back."

He touched himself again—he couldn't stop.

They never made it to dinner. When he came downstairs, she was on the patio, looking out toward the rose garden with a solemn expression.

"Ready," he said, standing at the doorway.

"Come here," she said, patting the faded striped cushion on the wicker chair next to hers. "Come here for a minute."

He walked over and sat down on the stool that matched her armchair.

She held out her hand and he put his hand in hers. He knew this was not good news. He still felt so filled with the last hour of loving her, of the union between nature's beauty and hers, of the moments in which the memory of her had been so vivid that it was as if she were really there, that he felt as if he were in a kind of bubble with her. He could see she was not going to tell him what he wanted to hear, but he couldn't believe she would hurt him or push him away.

He waited for her to speak. He couldn't even talk.

He sat on the stool facing her and waiting for her to speak. He kept looking at her and then he realized that what he was seeing in her eyes was love and pain, and that she was going to hurt him. His head fell into her lap, and for a while she held his head with both hands.

"Sweetie," she said. She used to call him that when he was a kid.

He moaned. It was too much to bear.

"We can't," she said.

"We can," he said.

"We can't," she said. "One day you'll see."

"Don't talk to me like that," he said, into her lap.

"What?" she said.

He raised his head. "Don't talk to me like that. You're wrong."

She looked at him silently for a long time, as if she were really wondering, he thought. She shook her head.

"Who is it hurting?" he said.

"I don't know," she said. "That's not the point."

"Do you think anyone even knows?"

"No," she said.

"Who is it hurting?" he said. "Except me, now?"

"I love you very much," she said. She put her hand on his cheek. "No matter what happens, I love you very much."

He put his head back into her lap. Dug his face between her thighs. "I love you too," he said, "Kay."

He didn't pick his head up until they heard the car in the driveway. *They're here, for god's sakes.* He looked into Kay's eyes, which seemed to cloud. She bent down to kiss him. She'd meant to kiss him lightly, and for a moment he felt her lips warm and closed on the corner of his mouth, but then he moved his face and put his mouth on hers, and it was as if the bubble that he had known the existence of earlier was reactivated and they were both inside it, their mouths the point of contact that made the bubble exist, as if they were swimming together in desire. Her mouth softened and he felt her tongue, then he heard the back door open and pulled away and Kay gasped. They looked at each other, and on Kay's face he saw only desire.

She'd made a mistake. He felt triumphant. At least, she knew she'd made a mistake.

There were several unbearable minutes with Dodge and Elise, who were both loud, talkative, and speedy from the ride up. And then he said he had to go to sleep. In his room he went to bed and waited for Kay to come. He'd left the door open a tiny bit so he could hear what was going on. Downstairs the voices continued, long into the night.

She can't tonight, he thought. *But she will.*

TUTTI

Friday

The rose garden needed watering. It needed more than that—spraying, pruning, clipping, replanting. In fact, if you were going to do it right, it would have to be reconceptualized more succinctly into compact, dense spurts of ardent color—less poetry, less ambiguous languor, more passion, more jolting attacks on the senses. Its late-nineteenth-century proportions suited those of the mansion but not at current landscaping prices. Many of the bushes were of a slightly wrong height, no longer marching in the corps de ballet. What could be done about that? She'd have to talk to Mr. Bennett about the landscape guy, Dodie thought. But at the very least, it needed more water in July and August. Dodie, looking out from the kitchen window while waiting for the water to boil for the pasta, shook her head again.

Ron held out his arm and tapped on his watch. "It's the last weekend of our youth," he said.

"Oh, give me a break," said Dodge.

Ron, Dodge, Susie, and Elise were on the patio. Dodge and Elise were having Bloody Marys, Susie a club soda, and Ron was holding a glass of milk from which he now took a measured sip. Then he licked his lips carefully. Elise watched him with a frown.

"It's truly amazing," said Susie, "that the summer is over. I have to say I think the worst thing about getting old is the speed with which time passes."

"You think that's the worst thing!" Ron said mockingly.

"Well, we have a perfect sunset," said Dodge. "You couldn't ask for a better setting for your elegiac lamentations." He leaned his head against the back of the wicker armchair and closed his eyes. While a bird warbled unheard just out-of-doors, the other three looked at him for a moment. It was hard to look away because in the glow of the setting sun, his face looked very beautiful.

"It's strange," said Susie, "how you get to love the light."

"That's because of how fast time passes," said Elise.

"And fearing the coming darkness," said Dodge, with his eyes closed.

"Right," said Elise.

"Time goes so fast for me now," said Ron, "that it practically has a Doppler effect."

"That's what life is—your entire existence is a metaphor for a Doppler effect. Time itself moves on without you, and you just create a little insubstantial wake that then disappears," said Susie.

"Hey," said Elise. "Are you trying to depress me?"

"Someone's got to do it," said Ron.

"Ah," Susie sighed.

"What?" said Elise and Dodge together.

"Nothing," said Susie. "I don't know. It's true . . . there are only a few lovely evenings left and then it's back to real life."

"Yes," said Ron. "The sand is running in the hourglass."

"Who invented hourglasses?" said Elise.

"Someone who wanted to distract himself from the idea of endless dark night," said Dodge.

"But isn't the darkest hour just before dawn?" said Susie.

"That's a line from the Shirelles," said Ron. He sang in falsetto: "Each night before you go to bed, my baby."

"Is that the Shirelles?" said Elise.

"It's like the sunset effect," said Dodge. "Just before the sun dies, it's brightest."

"But the sun doesn't die," Susie said emphatically.

"Yes, but the light dies," said Dodge.

"Are you trying to depress me?" said Ron and Elise at the same time.

Billy strode into the room and headed for the dish of pistachio nuts.

"Hi, sweetie," said Susie.

"Hi," said Billy.

"I don't know," said Ron, "if I can take this much glowing youth in the midst of this particular discussion."

"Are you talking about me?" said Billy.

"You're the only glowing youth here," said Elise. "That's for sure."

"Well, after a summer with you guys, I'm not so glowing," said Billy.

They all groaned and cried out dramatically.

"Wow," said Susie.

"Wow what?" said Kay, standing in the doorway.

"Where have you been?" asked Susie.

"Just resting," said Kay. She closed the glass door behind her. "I guess I fell asleep. I feel weird."

"Weird how?" asked Billy.

"Just tired," said Kay. She settled herself in a chaise longue. She was wearing black pedal pushers and a black tank top.

"Well, you look great," said Dodge.

"Kay always looks great," said Susie.

"She looks greater," said Ron. "In fact, I'm glad the summer's ending, because Kay's beauty would eventually have been the end of me."

"And what would the end of you consist of?" asked Elise. It was the first time she had addressed Ron directly in over a week. For a moment their glances locked and Ron gazed at her with an amused smile until she looked away, whispering, "Jesus ..." She stared at the ceiling. She had stopped noticing the ceiling in this room, but now she noted again how handsome it was, vaulted, pale green, Gothic. She squinted until she could barely see the beams through her eyelashes.

Susie sighed.

"Let's run away," said Dodge.

The door opened and Dodie stuck her head in.

"Hi," she said.

"Hi," they said.

"Don't you want to eat?" she said.

For dinner, they had leg of lamb, mashed potatoes, and corn on the cob. They drank very cold Vouvray. Ron had a beer.

"Hmm, hmm, hmm," Dodge kept saying while he ate his mashed potatoes. "Hmm."

Ron made a lot of noise eating his corn on the cob. The setting sun shed so much violent red light, they kept glancing out the window.

"There it goes," said Susie, who was sitting opposite the window.

They all paused, knife and fork in hand. There was a streak of pale yellow among the bands of orange and red.

"It looks like pus," said Elise.

There was a loud chorus of groans. "Yech!" shouted Ron.

"Oh, it's beautiful," said Susie. "Elise, it's beautiful!"

"Yeah, yeah, yeah," said Elise.

Dodge and Kay, who had their backs to the window, turned around, and they all watched and waited for the sun to pop below the horizon.

"Have you seen *The Green Ray*?" asked Elise.

"I don't go to Eric Rohmer movies," said Ron.

"Another mistake," said Dodge.

"I can't stand it," said Susie. She meant the tension of waiting for the last bit of red sun to disappear.

There. Millimeter by millimeter. There it went. Susie and

Dodge and Ron and Kay looked. Billy looked at Kay. Elise closed her eyes.

"Phew," said Ron. "I'm glad that's over with."

They laughed. They ate silently for a moment, waiting for the light to diminish.

"Maybe we could have an old-age home together," said Susie.

"What," said Ron, "and have the Beatles piped into the rooms or something?"

"Don't make fun of the Beatles," said Kay. "I'm just beginning to be able to listen to them again."

"Did you use to listen to the Beatles?" said Billy. "I don't remember that."

"Really?" said Susie.

"No," said Billy. "The Byrds. I remember the two of you were Byrds addicts."

"I don't remember anything anymore. I disremember everything," said Susie.

"I remember everything," said Dodge. "Every single little thing. All the longing."

"I remember the longing," said Susie. "I just don't remember what it was about."

"It's terrible. I wish I could forget," said Dodge.

"Take some drugs," said Ron. "I managed to wipe out a good number of memory cells."

"Have you got any?" said Elise.

"Drugs?" said Ron. "Sure. What would you like?"

"What have you got?" said Elise.

"Hmm," said Susie.

"Oh, please," said Kay. "Don't make me a witness to any lamentable spectacles."

"He doesn't have any drugs, anyway," said Dodge of Ron.

"I bet your pardon," said Ron. "I certainly could get some. What do you want?"

"Ecstasy," said Elise.

"I can get you some ecstasy," said Billy.

"I don't want to think about that," said Susie.

"As long as he's not injecting heroin, I think you should consider yourself a happy mother," said Ron.

"Billy's not a heroin type," said Elise.

Dodge sighed. "Ah," he said. "I can't believe how much mashed potatoes I ate." He patted his stomach.

Kay smiled at Billy. "I wish I could take some ecstasy," she said.

"Really?" he said.

"It's a bad idea," said Susie.

"Have you done it?" said Elise.

"Yes," said Susie. She glanced at Billy. But he only smiled and shook his head.

"And? And?" said Kay.

"It's great," said Susie. "But it's very hard afterward."

"Like everything good," said Elise.

"I know," said Dodge. "I don't know what the point is of ever feeling good when you have to go back to feeling bad."

"Yes," said Kay. "What's the point of summer?"

"Oh no," groaned Ron. "There they go again."

Dodie stuck her head in. "Are you through?" she asked.

"What are we going to do without you, Dodie?" said Susie.

"I'm going back to surviving on granola," said Elise.

"We'll be back in those dreary restaurants," said Susie.

"I'm going back to depending on my friends for meals," said Dodge.

"I'm going back to eating shoe leather over the sink," said Ron.

Dodie cleared the table. Elise and Dodge helped.

"Should I bring out more wine?" asked Dodie. They still had half-filled glasses, except for Dodge.

"I think I'll save my energy," he said.

"Okay, fine," said Dodie.

"What should we do tonight?" asked Susie.

"Go into town," said Elise, who was coming back with a big homemade apple pie.

"Wow," said Ron. "Look at that." The apple pie, he meant.

"And do what?" asked Dodge.

"The Lickety Split?" said Elise.

"Maybe we should go for a walk," said Susie.

"To the rose garden," said Billy.

"Too late," said Kay. "Mosquitoes."

"I've never hated another living thing as much as I hate those mosquitoes," said Ron.

"Oh, really?" said Elise.

They all laughed.

"When are you two getting married?" said Dodge.

"Very funny," said Elise.

"Let's play poker," said Susie.

"Wow!" said Dodge. There was quick assent.

"Do we have cards?" asked Susie.

"There are chips," said Ron. "In the drawer of the game table on the patio."

Billy knew the cards were in the drawer of his night table, but for some reason he didn't feel like speaking up. He looked at Kay. She looked back.

"I'll drive in for some cards," said Dodge.

"I'll go with you," said Elise. "Don't eat my pie," she said to Ron. She got up.

"Do you want to go on the bike?" asked Dodge.

"Sure," said Elise. She paused at the door, beaming. "Does anyone want anything else?" she asked.

In the dining room, they heard the bike roar off and then they finished their pie and drank their coffee.

Billy looked at Kay. She smiled at him and then looked away.

"How're you doing, Billy?" said Susie.

"Good," said Billy. "How are you doing?"

"Kay," said Ron. "Will you marry me?"

They laughed. "What brought that on?" said Kay.

"I don't know," said Ron. "Something seized me. Think it over, Kay," he said. "I would make you happy."

"And how would you do that, Ron?" she said, smiling and ready to get into the game.

"When are we playing poker?" said Billy.

"As soon as they come back," said Susie. "Where should we play? On the patio?"

"It's sort of buggy out there," said Kay. "The screen must be torn somewhere."

"But it's the nicest," said Billy.

"That's true," said Kay. "I'll go up and get a shirt."

"Get me one too," said Susie.

"Where is it?" said Kay, already partly out the door.

"Either on the bedpost or in the third drawer," said Susie.

"Back in a jiff," said Kay.

"A *jiff*?" said Ron to Susie and Billy. "A jiff?"

They heard the great clattering of dishes signifying that Dodie had begun post-dinner clean-up.

The three of them cleared the table and then went to the patio. It was dark and a little damp. They turned lights on, brought back to the kitchen glasses left from their predinner drinks. They set up a table and chairs.

"Does a flush beat a straight?" asked Ron.

"I'm watching out for you," said Billy. He was putting on an old Rolling Stones CD. He kept listening to a phrase or two and then skipping to the next song.

"It's like musical chairs," said Ron.

"I love musical chairs," said Susie.

"I was always great at it," said Ron.

"Didn't Elise say she was going to make a piece for her show called *Musical Chairs*?" asked Susie.

Upstairs, Kay had gone to Susie's room first, found the light. She'd stood at the doorway for a bit. The room smelled like Susie, faintly of gardenias. It was a small, rather charming amount of disorder. There was no shirt on the bedpost. Kay walked into the room, went to the closet, saw the shirt and grabbed it. In the middle of the room, she paused. She felt very tired. As if she couldn't take another step. Not physically, but as if her mind just wasn't ready to process any more of her life. She sat down on the bed, thinking it was only for a moment.

There was something inviting about the room. She thought back to the carpenter. What had that been about? She could understand, though she wasn't quite sure how, why someone had wanted to snoop around here. She sat on the bed and thought of looking in all the drawers.

Elise loved the feeling of the wind on her face and Dodge between her thighs and his leather jacket under her fingers. The moon, nearly full, had risen in the pale sky and the somewhat scraggly trees and bushes that lined the road looked deliciously sinister. She leaned into the curves in sync with Dodge. It was exhilarating and she was distinctly sorry when they reached Main Street.

They found a pack of cards at the drugstore. Dodge said, "Let's buy two."

"Are you good at poker?" asked Elise.

"No," said Dodge. "Not very. I don't have enough concentration."

"Really?" said Elise. She was genuinely astonished.

They were halfway back when Dodge suddenly turned off onto a dirt road.

She was surprised and tightened her thighs around his.

"Are you okay?" he yelled back to her.

"Yes," she called out.

"It's too beautiful to go right back," he yelled. "Let's just take a little ride, okay?"

"Great," she called out. "Great."

He stopped at the overlook. They got off and he put the bike on the kickstand. In the penumbra, they could see a huge swatch of valley, the shimmer of the water in moonlight.

"Hmm?" said Dodge.

All she could think of was him. She turned back to look at him and smiled.

He laughed just a little. *Why doesn't he kiss me?* she was thinking.

"You look great," he said. He brought his hand up and touched her cheek. She closed her eyes.

After a moment she reopened them. She felt as if her heart were dissolving in her chest. *This must be what they call heartbreak,* she was thinking, but she saw he was looking at her without rejection.

"We have to go back," he said, smiling.

"Okay," she said. But, entranced by the moonlit vista, neither of them moved.

"Are you working on your show?" Dodge asked.

"Not yet," she said.

"Zift will give you a really good show," said Dodge.

"I know," said Elise. "That's why it's crazy that I haven't been able to work."

"That always happens," said Dodge. "And then it comes."

"I keep thinking that I can't kill myself because then they'd have a retrospective of my work for sure."

Dodge smiled. "Well, I know what you mean," he said. "But you've got so much talent, it's bound to go all right in the end."

"Are you kidding?" asked Elise.

"No!" said Dodge. "Of course not. About what?"

"Have you even seen my work?"

"I saw the pieces you showed in the spring in that group show," said Dodge.

"You did?" said Elise. "I can't believe it."

"Yeah," he said. He kick started the bike and sat down. Elise climbed on behind him.

"Let's not crash on the way back," she said. But he was revving the engine and the wind tore the words away from her mouth and he didn't hear.

(However, in the course of the summer Dodge had by imperceptible degrees come to accept the fact that he would really rather not do anything to destroy himself prematurely. Now, therefore, he was a much more cautious driver than Elise would have been able to imagine. They got back safely, robbing themselves—and us—of a juicily melodramatic ending to the summer.)

"What are you doing this fall?" said Ron to Susie.

"I've got a big musical coming up," said Susie. They had gone back into the dining room. She was smoking a cigarette, the first she had lit up in Billy's presence in a number of years. The dishes cleared away, there were only crumbs and empty coffee cups on the table. At the center of the table, there was a bowl with roses in it.

"Is that fun?" asked Ron.

"I'm in a state of dread," said Susie.

"I'm going to go up and get a shirt," said Billy.

Dodie was washing the dessert dishes in the big white kitchen. The dishwasher was already full and she wanted to try to get home early tonight. Her husband had gone again, her mother was sick with her allergies, and she had left the two younger children in the care of a twelve-year-old.

When they drove up to the house, Dodge pulled up and then waited, the motor idling, for Elise to get off the bike. She lingered for a moment, and then he could feel her leaning forward a little, as if to bring her face closer to his back and neck. He almost felt her but he couldn't smell her, only the fields and the woods, which the wind seemed to have left on her skin.

She got off the bike. He brought the bike over to the side of the house, got it up on its kickstand.

He came back to where she stood. Stretched. She looked pretty in this light. What a strange girl she was.

Elise said, "That was great. Thank you."

"Oh, you're welcome," he said.

"Let's take another ride before the weekend is over, okay?" said Elise.

"Okay," said Dodge.

She didn't move. He didn't feel like going right in to see the others. He looked up at the sky.

"Shall we go in?" she said.

"Look at that," he said. "Look at Orion."

She looked up too and said, "Hmm," but clearly didn't know where to look.

"There," he said, and pointed, but he could see she wasn't looking in the right place. "There," he said again, and he stood behind her and put one arm around her and, with the other, pointed at Orion. "There."

"Oh, yeah," said Elise. "Amazing."

Now he could smell her, some floral and citrus perfume she wore, or perhaps a lotion she had put on her body. His mouth was near her forehead, and he would have liked to just put his lips on the side of her forehead, between the eye and the hairline. He'd noticed that spot many times in the course of the summer. He leaned a little closer. His lips almost touched her skin. Her hair felt soft. She felt comforting. But it was too complicated.

He moved his arm, the one that was pointing. "There," he said, "is the Big Dipper, and there is Ursa Major."

"Ah," said Elise.

The wind stirred the dark pines. The frogs loudly claimed their existence.

Billy found Kay in Susie's room, sitting on the bed. He stood in the doorway for a moment, waiting for her to notice him. She wore an almost blank expression, as if she had sat down and then forgotten herself. She looked at the floor, a few feet ahead of her. Her hands were folded on her lap. One leg was crossed over the other. She was arrested in time. There was something eerie about this vision, though her expression was unreadable, but he wasn't meant to have seen her like this—it was the expression she wore when she didn't think she would be seen. It seemed more of an invasion than when he had seen her asleep. But what was it he was seeing that he wasn't supposed to see? Why did he feel such guilt?

Did she look sad? No. Only lost. His heart lurched with pity for her. The image of Kay in her late twenties came surging into his mind. She'd been radiant and ironic all at once. Though in a way, she was at least as attractive now. Maybe more, in a way. But she didn't used to inspire compassion. He realized that it gave him a feeling of terrible discomfort.

But as soon as he felt the discomfort, all he could think of was touching her, as if the excitement of physical contact would take away all of this ambiguity.

He must have moved slightly, because her glance lifted, surprised, to him. She smiled at him. What a beautiful smile she had.

He crossed the room and came and sat down next to her on the bed.

"Hi," he said.

"Hi," she said.

"What were you thinking about?"

She smiled at him again. "I don't know," she said. "What were you thinking about?"

"You," he said. "You. I can't stop thinking about you. I think about you constantly. You live in my mind all the time."

"Well, I'm glad I live somewhere," said Kay.

"Oh no," said Billy. He felt, too much, the pain under the quip. He was beginning to feel as if there was no difference between them, no separation, as if everything she felt was something he could feel inside of himself. So then he was angry with her, because he only wanted her to feel love for him. Why was she busy with her past when he was there next to her?

He looked at her. He felt both love and rage. He wanted to lie down on top of her, that was the image in his mind, but then there was another image, that she sat still on the bed and he slapped her. He wanted to shake her. He noticed little lines around her eyes and between her nose and her mouth. But he liked those, actually. He couldn't remember having been this close to her in the light, so that he could really see her. In her eyes, he saw love for him. He knew he did. He saw her trying to stop from smiling. Her mouth was beautiful. He brought up his hand and put his fingers on her lips for a moment. Save for his hand, they sat very still. He put his fingers on her cheek.

"Not here," said Kay.

He noticed now that she had Susie's shirt on her lap.

"Where then?" he said. "Come to my room."

"No," she said. "You know we can't. They're waiting for us downstairs. Susie is waiting for her shirt. Your mother is waiting for her shirt."

"Kay, you're really simplifying things," he started.

"Don't be ridiculous," she said. "Simplifying?" She laughed.

He was stunned. Her laugh had seemed to contain real merriment. But no, when he looked at her face again, he saw how the little lines near her eyes had deepened, as if in pain again. He tried to think fast. Obviously, the frontal approach was not effective. She shifted the shirt as if about to get up.

"No," he pleaded. "Just a minute, just stay for a moment. Just let me be near you for a moment."

Elise had come upstairs to go to the bathroom and, on the way to her own room, as if compelled by some foreign will, she had opened the door to the secret book room she and Ron had discovered early in the summer and was standing in the doorway. She felt on the side of the wall but couldn't find the light switch. Finally, she just closed the door and crept quietly to the armchair, by memory.

But now, once she had settled back in the winged armchair, leaned her head against the back, closed her eyes, she heard voices in the next room.

"No," Billy was pleading. "Just a minute, just stay for a moment. Just let me be near you for a moment."

Were Billy and Susie having a fight?

"I love you," said...

Elise thought it was Susie.

"I love you with all my heart," said... Kay. It was Kay. *Kay?*

"You don't even know how much I love you," said Kay. "You can't even understand."

"I do," Billy said. "I . . ."

"No," said Kay. "You're too young to understand how I can love you."

"Kay," he said. His voice was strangled.

Then there was silence.

They must be fucking, thought Elise, staring up in the darkness. *I can't believe this.*

"All right, everyone," said Ron. He was shuffling the cards with expert speed and precision. "Dealer calls it. Dealer antes." He threw a white chip into the center of the table. "Five-card stud, the purist's game. Here we go."

"That's where you only get five cards?" said Elise.

"Oy," said Ron.

"Just deal the cards," said Susie. "We'll have a couple of trial hands."

"Trial?" said Ron. "I have good money riding on this now. Okay, here are your first cards, down and dirty."

He dealt the second card and Dodge got the ace of spades, to general cries of mock disapproval.

"A quarter," said Dodge, throwing a white chip in without looking at his down card.

They had decided the night was slightly too cool after all for the patio and had come back in to the library and there had been the usual to-do about making a fire. They had found the green felt for the card table. They had brought over some floor lamps that illuminated the table and the players, leaving the edges of the room dark. The only other light came from the fireplace. Whenever they sat quietly, they could hear the crackling flames.

Billy had said he wanted to sit out. He had dragged his chair slightly behind Kay's and was looking at her cards. She was so aware of his presence, she was having trouble concentrating. She knew she was folding good hands, but it didn't seem to matter.

Once she caught Elise's eye and it seemed to her that Elise had a strange expression.

"What?" said Kay.

"Nothing," said Elise.

"What?" said Dodge. He had been consistently winning and his pile of chips was now much higher than anyone's. He was dealing. "Okay," he said. "Seven-card stud. Here we go. A lady for Susie Q., a deuce, a tres, ten of hearts for Miss Kay, and Jake the Rake for me."

"What a surprise," said Ron.

"Sour grapes," said Elise.

Ron, who had been constantly raising the stakes with vigor, now had a smaller pile of chips than anyone else.

"Oh, Elise," he said. "We all know Dodge is your favorite."

"A quarter," said Susie, throwing a white chip into the pile.

"And you're my favorite, Ron," said Dodge.

"Do you want to get married?" said Ron to Dodge.

"Whose turn is it?" asked Susie.

"Aha, she's paying attention," said Ron. "What have you got there, a big pair?"

"It's my turn," said Kay. "I fold."

"I'm in," said Elise. "And I raise it a quarter." She threw a red chip into the pile.

"Okay, is everyone else in?" said Dodge. "Good. Here we go." He dealt a new card to everyone.

"What is this," said Susie to Ron, "with you and marriage? You've asked everyone here to marry you. Could it be that you secretly desire to be a family man?"

"It's not secret," said Ron. "How about you? You're the only one I haven't asked. We'd make a great team."

"Do you think marriage is about being a team?" asked Susie, looking at her new card.

"A quarter," said Elise.

"Fifty cents," said Dodge.

"I'm in," said Ron.

"Who is your favorite, Ron?" said Elise.

"You are, honey bunch," said Ron. "As long as Dodge is your favorite. I just can't stand requited emotions." He threw in a chip. "I'm in."

"I see your fifty and I raise it a dollar," said Susie.

"Oh ho?!" said Ron.

"What has she got?" said Elise.

"I'm out," said Dodge.

"I'll see your dollar and I'll raise it five dollars," said Ron.

"You can't raise that much until the last card," said Dodge.

"Okay," said Ron. "Then I'll just see it."

"And who is your favorite, Kay?" asked Elise.

"Me?" Kay said. She looked up startled. "My favorite is Billy," she said. She leaned back and ruffled Billy's hair. "And always has been."

"I'm out," said Elise. And she folded her cards.

"Me too," said Kay, leaving only Susie and Ron still in the game.

"Pair of queens showing," Dodge said as he gave Susie her card. "Possible straight flush over here," he said as he gave Ron the two of hearts.

"And who is your favorite?" Billy, who had flushed, said to Susie, as if to distract attention from himself.

"Me?" Susie said. "I love you all. I adore every one of you." She paused, pursed her lips. "Could he possibly have it?" she said of Ron's cards.

"He's bluffing," said Elise.

"I never bluff," said Ron.

"Oh, sure," said Dodge.

"I never bluff," said Ron.

"I raise it a quarter," said Susie.

"I'll see your quarter and I raise it another fifty cents," he said.

"I'll see your fifty cents and I raise it another dollar," said Susie.

"I'll see your dollar and . . ."

"That's it," said Dodge.

"Okay," said Ron to Susie. "What have you got?"

Susie turned over her two cards. "Three queens."

Ron turned over his cards. "I've got the flush," he said.

"Shit," said Susie.

Ron dragged the large pile of chips in toward himself.

"Look at that pile," said Elise.

"Ah," said Ron. "I'm starting to feel better. Let's go. How about strip poker."

"Seven-card high-low," said Elise, who was dealing. "When hell freezes over, I'll play strip poker with you."

"Well," said Ron. "That's the kind of weather that would make it fun."

"Only if you're more interested in pain than in sex," said Dodge. He was high, with an ace. "Check," he said.

"Check."

"Check."

"Checkaroony," said Ron.

"It's my turn," said Susie. "Twenty-five cents."

"Who isn't?" said Kay.

"What?" said Susie.

"Who isn't more interested in pain than sex?" said Kay. "Pain is so much more immediate."

"But pain *is* sex," said Dodge.

"Whoa," said Elise.

"Who bets?" said Ron. "I'm in."

"I'm in."

"And I raise it fifty cents," said Dodge.

Susie sighed audibly. The poker game had ended an hour ago. She, Dodge, and Elise were still on the patio. Ron had gone out for a swim. Susie was definitely smoking again.

"I can't even bear it," said Dodge. "I can't bear even thinking of my life in New York."

"Really?" said Elise.

"I can't bear it."

"Maybe it's better not to think about it," said Susie. "The older I get, the more I find that it's better to just order yourself about and then meekly follow your own orders, without thinking. If you really think about it, none of it is all that bearable."

"I order myself about," said Elise. "I just don't follow orders."

"I order myself about," said Dodge. "I just don't understand the orders."

"What should we do tomorrow?" said Susie. "Maybe we should plan something fun."

"Something fun?" said Dodge.

"To make us forget that it's the end of summer."

"That would take a lot," said Dodge. "But anything is fun with you, Susie."

Susie raised her eyes to the sky and then smiled at Elise as if the latter were a coconspirator. Elise smiled back.

"Everything is fun with Susie," Kay said.

"I'm going to think about it," said Susie. "I'll come up with an activity."

"I do think tomorrow night we should have a late-night swim in the river," said Dodge.

"If it's warm enough," said Elise.

"I don't know why, but that seems like a lot of trouble to me," said Susie.

"If it's warm enough, there'll be bugs," said Billy.

"Come on," said Dodge. "Who knows when we'll get the chance again?"

"I don't know," said Susie. "Okay, maybe. Let's see tomorrow."

"I want to talk to you," Billy whispered to Kay urgently as he followed her up the staircase.

"Okay," she said.

"Come to my room," he said.

"All right," she whispered. "A little later."

"All right," he said.

———

"Holy shit," said Ron. "You scared the bejeezus out of me."

It was Claudine, swimming silently in the pool. "Hi," she said. With a few strokes she glided over to him. When the moon came out from behind the clouds, he saw that she was naked.

"You come here often?" said Ron.

"Yes," said Claudine. "Every night. While you are all drinking and talking, I am here swimming."

He turned and saw that, from the pool, when the patio's lights were on, whoever was there could be seen.

"Do you watch?" he asked her.

"Yes," she said. "It's very amusing."

"I'll bet," he said.

Susie yawned. "Are we sleepy?" she asked.

"Yes and no," said Elise.

"No," said Dodge.

"Shall we do something?" said Elise.

"Sure," said Dodge.

"I'm awfully tired," said Susie. "I don't know why."

"Well, maybe we should go up," said Dodge.

"Oh, okay, I'm going," said Elise. "See you in the morning."

"Okay," said Susie. "Good night." She yawned again. "What time is it?" she asked.

"Ten past one," said Elise.

"That's all?" said Susie, yawning again. She stood and stretched.

Ron was trying to figure out whether Claudine expected him to make a pass. She certainly was tempting. She was swimming a backstroke. Her breasts glistened in the moonlight. Was this a come-on, or what? It seemed like such an incredibly obvious come-on that Ron feared a trick. Perhaps she wanted him to come on and then she would humiliate him.

Kay sat at the head of the bed, leaning against the headboard. Billy sat at the foot of the bed. One of them was in midsentence, but at the moment they had forgotten which. They only looked at each other.

Elise lay on her bed, clothes on, lights out. She felt anger clutching, drowning, sweeping, seeping through her like poison.

"So what do you think of all of us," said Ron to Claudine. "I bet you've got plenty of opinions."

"Yes," said Claudine. "I think I better had keep them to myself."

"You can trust me," said Ron.

"Oh, yes?" said Claudine, laughing. She kept swimming laps, a breaststroke now. He was in the center of the pool, where he could stand, water up to his chin, calling out to her.

"Yes," said Ron. "*Absolutement*," he added, with a bad French accent.

"*Absolument*," said Claudine.

"*Absolument*," he repeated.

"Why should I trust you?" said Claudine.

"Because I'm nice," said Ron.

"You're nice?" she said.

"I'm really nice," he said. "Under my abrasive exterior, I am just a vulnerable, nice person."

"How do I know that you are telling the truth?" said Claudine.

"I never bluff," said Ron.

"No?" said Claudine.

"No," said Ron. "Never."

Billy took Kay's hand and put it next to his cheek.

"Put out the light," he said.

"What?" said Kay. His voice had been muffled.

"Turn out the light," he whispered. He looked up at her urgently. "Just for a moment. Let me just lie down with you for a moment. We won't do anything."

Kay looked at him for a moment. He looked back, steadily. Both of them were unsmiling. She reached over and turned out the light. It was more dangerous to look into his eyes than to lie in the dark with him, for just a moment.

Elise took a sleeping pill.

Dodge masturbated, thinking of his cousin, Cynthia. Cynthia, when they were both eight years old, with her hula hoop.

Ron and Claudine had been trading quips for so long he was waterlogged.

"Okay, cutie," he said. "I'm going in."

"Me too," said Claudine. She hoisted herself out of the pool, wrapped herself in a big towel, twisted a smaller towel into a turban on her head, and said, "Okay, Ron."

"Rrrrron," said Ron, trying to imitate the *r* in the back of her throat.

"Okay," she said. She laughed again. She definitely found him entertaining. "Good night."

"Good night," said Ron. Then he stood at the pool, drying himself, watching her white towel diminish in the dark distance.

Susie, on her way up, had been stricken with a desire to go outside for a moment. But, once out-of-doors, the air seemed so bracing that she felt she had to stay out for just a little while. She went to the hammock and lay down. It was too cold out here, but it felt like she would miss this too much, back in the city. She looked up at the house. It seemed almost like a dollhouse from here. Elise's light was already out. Ron's lights were out, the window wide open. All of Billy's lights were on, as usual. Dodge's window was faintly lit. He must have a small light on. Kay's light went out.

Poor Kay, thought Susie. Poor Kay.

———

In the dark, Billy took Kay's hand. He just wanted to hold her hand. She was so happy to have him hold her hand—it was such a relief—that she could not speak. A lot was understood between them now, though neither had any idea why. Kay shivered. She had been feeling jangly and restless, but now the smoothness and warmth of his hand made her feel steady and warm; ease radiated from that touch.

Billy was torn between his pleasure in the moment and wanting to be closer, wanting to be under the covers with her, inside of her. He couldn't stand it anymore. He couldn't stand waiting anymore.

"I'm ill," she said.

"You are?" he said. "What's the matter?"

She was thinking, *I am ill with lovesickness for you,* but she didn't say it. She knew that she was crazy.

She's ill with love, he thought. *Like me.* He leaned toward her.

He smelled sweet. She smelled delicate. His hair was soft. Her skin was soft. She closed her eyes and breathed him. He put his lips on her cheek, didn't even kiss her, just wanted to have his mouth on her skin.

"This is insane," she said very softly.

"What?" he said.

"Insane," she repeated.

But it felt right. That's what was so surprising about it. The pleasure too, but also that suddenly they both felt so easy. As if whatever it is that happens with sex had happened and they were in that zone where differences like age are erased, where all that matters is smell, warmth, texture, the place where yearning ends, where yearning melts into tenderness and lust.

He buried his face in her neck. She looked up at the ceiling. Her fear returned. "We've got to stop," she whispered. "We'll get caught."

He didn't move. "Billy," she whispered.

"I can't move," he mumbled.

She put her arms around him and hugged him. He was lying full length against her, pressed against her. It felt as if the clothes between them should be ripped off. Slid off. Rolled off. Erased. She put her arms around him and hugged him hard, and it felt like a great relief to both of them. He moaned. "Billy," she whispered.

They heard footsteps in the hall. She pulled away from him and sat up. She felt really frightened. Her heart was beating hard.

He sat up.

"Okay, you've got to go now," she said.

"Kay," he said. "*This* is insane. What are you doing?"

"I don't know," she said. "I no longer know what I am doing."

"Please," he whispered.

"I'm a coward," she whispered back. "It's not for moral reasons. I'm a coward."

He tried to think of what to respond, but it was hard to concentrate on what she was saying because of his erection. He thought of taking her hand and putting it there. He thought of his ex-girlfriend, Nina, who always did whatever he wanted. Who seemed to divine what he wanted.

"I've been too damaged by life," Kay said.

He was torn between wanting to console her and thinking, *This is ridiculous.*

They heard footsteps. Kay actually gasped and started.

"You've got to go now," she whispered. She seemed frantic. She pushed him a little. "Billy. You've got to go now."

He sat up and swung his feet over the side of the bed. She suddenly was afraid that he was angry with her and would stay angry. She put her hand on his arm, but he stood up and walked to the door without turning back, went out, closed the door very quietly behind him.

Ron was coming in the kitchen putting ice in a glass of scotch when Billy came in for a glass of water.

"Night prowling?" said Ron.

"Yeah," said Billy.

"Something wrong?" said Ron.

"No," said Billy. "Just tired."

Susie came up, saw the light under Kay's door, and, recalling having seen it out before, thought Kay must be having trouble sleeping. She knocked softly. There was no answer for a moment and then Kay, softly, called out, "Come in."

Susie opened the door. Kay seemed surprised to see her.

"Hi, cookie," said Susie.

"Hi," said Kay. She was lying on her bed fully dressed. No book in sight.

"Are you okay?" said Susie.

"Oh, yes," said Kay. "Just fell asleep."

She didn't look as if she'd been asleep. She looked disheveled and flushed. Her eyes looked bright.

"Are you okay?" said Susie.

"Yeah," said Kay. "Really. I'm fine."

"Don't brood too much," said Susie.

"No," said Kay.

Saturday

Claudine was walking toward the pool looking up at the sky. *C'est douteux,* she was thinking, looking at the billowy gray clouds. She went straight to her favorite chaise longue and lay down. Every once in a while she glanced at her watch. She was timing her tan. Twenty minutes per side. It wasn't great tanning weather, though.

The sun came out. She looked at her watch. Nineteen and a half minutes. She stood up, put the towel down on the ground next to the chaise longue, and lay down on her stomach.

And so it happened that Kay and Elise, who had met on the way to the pool, didn't realize that Claudine was there. Kay lay down on a chaise longue. She closed her eyes. Elise dived in, swam two laps underwater, came out, dried herself, and lay down on a chaise longue adjacent to Kay's.

"Are you sleeping?" she asked Kay.

Kay opened her eyes. "Well, if I was, I wouldn't be now," she said, smiling. "But I wasn't. I just don't feel well today."

"In what way?"

"I guess I had too much to drink last night."

"Really?" said Elise. "I didn't notice that you were drinking so much."

"Well, I guess I didn't either," said Kay. She closed her eyes again, thinking the exchange was over. A thin cloud slid across the sun.

"I'd like you to do me a favor," Elise said to Kay.

"Sure," said Kay, opening her eyes. "What?"

"I'd like you to keep Susie out of the way tonight so that I can be alone with Dodge."

"What?" said Kay.

La vache! thought Claudine.

"Every time I'm alone with Dodge, I can tell he's attracted to me, but whenever Susie's around nothing happens."

Kay said nothing.

Elise herself was flabbergasted by her own words. She felt as if it had been something inside her that wasn't herself talking. Someone else, inside her, who knew the words.

"I know it's a strange request, but you can do it," she said.

"But Elise," said Kay, carefully, as if speaking to a very unwell child. "You know Susie and I are very close friends."

"You're much better friends with each other than with me," said Elise. "Yes, I certainly do know that. I've felt it, many times, this summer."

Kay remained silent for a moment. "I don't understand," she finally said.

"How I have the nerve?" said Elise. "Well, I have a lot of nerve, for one thing. But then, there's a lot that people around here don't understand. I heard you saying last night to Billy that he couldn't understand you. That he was too young to understand. Do you remember saying that to him while you were in bed?"

Kay didn't even flinch. There was no doubt she remembered the moment with Billy in Susie's bedroom. She looked at Elise steadily.

"Do you remember?" Elise repeated.

"Yes," said Kay. "What are you doing, blackmailing me?"

"Yes," said Elise.

"You're stupid," said Kay. "Do you think Dodge is going to go for you just because you're alone for a few hours?"

"Yes, by now he is," said Elise. "I think that's how men are."

"Maybe that's how they used to be," said Kay.

"I'm not asking for your diagnosis of the culture, just for help, just for today," said Elise.

"Dodge has been in love with Susie for years," said Kay.

"Dodge is in love with everybody," said Elise. "Or no one except himself."

"So why would you want to have a relationship with him? He's sick," said Kay.

"I have a relationship with him when Susie isn't getting in the way," said Elise.

"You don't know what you're talking about," said Kay.

"Yes, I do," said Elise.

"You need help," said Kay.

"We all need help," said Elise.

Incroyable, thought Claudine.

"So what do you say?" said Elise.

"I have nothing to say," said Kay. "Forget it."

"Well, I might have plenty to say myself to Susie," said Elise.

Incroyable, thought Claudine.

"What do you mean?" said Kay.

"Think it over," said Elise.

"Forget it," said Kay.

"Think it over," said Elise.

Ron woke up at the third burst of knocking on his door. "Who the fuck is it?" he called out. He couldn't believe someone would disturb him in his own room at this hour. He looked at the clock: 12:30. At least he hadn't missed lunch.

The door opened a crack. Claudine stuck her head in. "Hi," she said. She took one step toward the doorway. She was wearing her bikini bottom and a white T-shirt with Minnie Mouse on it. No bra, of course. "Hi, Rrrrron."

"Well, now, my little lamb chop," said Ron. "Hello there." He sat up. He slept in his shorts. He moved over and patted a spot on the bed next to himself. She came into full view. She was carrying a coffee mug.

"I don't believe this," said Ron. "Am I in heaven or what? Did I wake up in paradise instead of in the sticks?"

"I have to discuss with you," said Claudine. "I heard a conversation between Kay and Elise..."

"Would you like to come to New York?" said Susie to Dodie. They were in the kitchen. Susie was leaning against the counter. Dodie was chopping carrots. "You could work for me at least one day a week and I know I could find you other places."

"It's too late for me," said Dodie.

"Too late!?" exclaimed Susie.

"I'm forty-five," said Dodie.

"Why, that's how old I am!" said Susie.

"Do you want to go for a walk?" Dodge said to Billy.

"Okay," said Billy.

For an hour they ranged, wordlessly, down the hill, up the road, across the field of the property next door where the horses used to be kept, and then down a steep hill toward the riverbank. There they stood for quite a while.

"It's great, isn't it?" said Dodge.

"Yeah," said Billy. "It's amazing."

"What a place," said Dodge. "You can really understand those Hudson Valley guys."

"The painters, you mean?" said Billy.

"Yes," said Dodge. "What they understood about light and depth."

They looked out on the river for a long time. Dodge watched how the sun made drops of water scintillate. Billy's gaze was lost across the way among the ripe hills and trees of the other shore. The tall grasses were just beginning to yellow. The trees were as green as they can get, the very deepest emerald, lime, kelly, olive.

"It's almost too much for me," said Billy.

"Too much visual sensation, you mean?" said Dodge.

"Yeah," said Billy. "It's strange."

"Because you're not part of it?" said Dodge.

"It dissolves something that hurts," said Billy.

Dodge said nothing. The sky was of the purest blue. The sun was low, round, and tidy. There was enough wind on the bright river so that the water rippled and rushed. The trees stirred gravely. A bird cawed intermittently, but there was no discernible pattern to his cry. After a few moments Dodge turned and walked back up the hill and Billy followed him. Then they retraced their steps back to the house.

"Well," said Susie at dinner. "What shall it be tonight?"

"The Lickety Split," said Elise. "Of course."

"Groan," said Ron.

"It's true—it doesn't seem all that exciting," said Susie. "Next weekend there'll be the fireworks. That's when we should go into town."

"Are they any good?" said Dodge.

"Dodie says they're good," said Susie. "Of course we would have known for ourselves if we'd gone Fourth of July."

"Yeah," said Ron. "It's too bad we didn't have the foresight to see the Fourth of July fireworks so that we'd know whether it was worth going to the Labor Day fireworks. You know, that sounds exactly like the mistake I've been making all my life."

"All right, all right," said Susie. "Now, what about tonight?"

"I'm almost finished with *Ethan Frome,*" said Kay.

A huge groan, which the group had become exceedingly adept at, greeted Kay's remark.

"All right, then," said Kay. "Poker."

"Poker?" said Susie.

"Yes," said Kay. "It's the next best thing to *Ethan Frome.*"

"A midnight swim," said Dodge.

"That's a great idea," said Elise.

"Maybe a swim would be nice," said Susie.

"A swim!" said Ron. "Do you know what time it is?"

"Well, you swim at night, Ron," said Dodge.

"Yeah, I'm still ironing out the wrinkles in my skin," said Ron.

"Maybe we should go swimming in the river after all," said Billy.

"What a great idea," said Dodge.

"Too dangerous at night," said Susie.

"And there's yucky stuff at the bottom," said Kay.

They were finishing dinner. The men were eating second helpings of blueberry pie. The women had pushed their plates back. It was muggy. Kay had opened the second button of her shirt. Susie was fanning herself with a napkin.

"Well, I wish we hadn't started talking about it," said Dodge. "Because now I really want to go swimming."

"I know what you mean," said Ron. "Whatever I talk about, I start wanting. It's totally irrational."

"I think that's because you're really capable of wanting anything. It's just that certain parts of your brain get activated," said Susie.

"Speak for yourself," said Ron. "Certain parts of my brain have remained inactivated for decades."

"You know," said Kay, turning to Elise. "Why don't you and Dodge go swimming, since you both really want to, and we'll meet up with you later."

Elise turned to Dodge.

"Absolutely not," interjected Ron before he had a chance to answer. "It's our penultimate night. We're in this together."

"Well, but . . . ," said Elise.

"He's right," said Kay quickly. "It was a stupid suggestion." She was very flushed. Susie and Billy looked at her curiously. Elise wiped her mouth with her napkin.

They drove, in two cars in case anyone wanted to come home early, to the Lickety Split.

There the scene seemed exactly as they had left it a few weeks earlier. Luther Vandross called out his love from the jukebox. Several couples swayed, closely entangled, on the small dance floor.

They had to talk very loudly to make themselves heard.

"Now behave yourself," Ron practically yelled in Elise's ear.

"Fuck you, Ron," said Elise. "Don't talk to me like that."

"I'm just being friendly," said Ron.

"I'm going to play pool," replied Elise, who had already downed two scotches in succession.

"Elise . . . ," began Susie.

"What the fuck do you want?" said Elise. "Are you my mother?"

"What?" said Susie. "I can't hear."

Elise stood up, almost knocking her chair over, and strode purposefully to the pool table.

"Oh, shit," said Ron.

"What is her problem?" said Susie at large.

"She's really got a problem," said Kay. "I think maybe we should get her out of here."

"There's no problem here," said Billy.

They were all looking out toward the pool table. They said nothing for a while. It was too hard to talk over Sade.

Dodge stood up. "I guess I'll go over there and check it out," he said.

"I'll come with you," said Susie.

Kay put her hand on Susie's arm. "Stay here," she said.

Susie laughed. "Okay," she said. And sat down again.

It happened very fast. Those watching from the table saw it as if it were a quick shadow play. Dodge strolled up in his contained way toward Elise and the two very big guys leaning over her—two big beefy blond guys, wearing leather wristbands. "Refrigerators" is how Ron described them later. Elise didn't even acknowledge Dodge's arrival. The two refrigerators continued to jostle around the small girl. At one point one of them leaned his head back and laughed. Gold glittered violently in his front tooth, they would remember later.

For Dodge, there was a moment of perfect clarity. He was in real time in a way he never felt (except when he was painting). He heard Sade's voice and every instrument under it. He heard the bartender yell "Whoa!" He heard Susie's gasp, way across the room. He saw the gold tooth, the earring in one man's ear, the pockmarks on the other's cheek. He saw the three men swiveling on their bar stools, the beer mugs on the bar, the bartender throwing a rag down and coming around the bar, and then clear across the floor, a woman holding a hamburger, halfway to her mouth, her companion's smile of excitement, the framed sign, REST ROOMS, with the badly hand-drawn flower. He saw and heard everything as clearly as if he had hours to look and see: Elise gasp and her mouth open with fear, the man's fist coming toward his face, the gold ring. "Motherfucker," the guy said, luxuriously. The gold ring, the lips pulled back, the gold tooth, the gold earring, the fist, knuckles first.

"Holy shit," said Ron. He hurdled toward the three, but he was too late. By the time he reached the pool table, Dodge had been knocked off balance with a punch, then knocked down with another punch, and now was on the floor being kicked by both refrigerators and one smaller guy, who, apparently, just wanted to get in on the action.

It took about twelve men and four women to break it up.

Susie, Kay, and Billy crouched on the floor next to Dodge.

"Hey," said Susie. "Dodge."

Dodge opened his eyes.

"How are you doing?" said Susie. The jukebox was turned off. There was a circle of onlookers.

Dodge closed his eyes again, then opened them. "Wow," he said.

Elise was leaning against the pool table, her face in her hands. When she heard Dodge speak, she brought her hands down. Ron was looking at her. She glared back. He shook his head silently.

Dodge lay on the floor, his eyes almost closed. He could see their faces, just. He thought he should move, but he couldn't move. It wasn't that he had been beaten up; it was that he just didn't have the courage to move anymore. Was that true? He actually tried to move his leg. It moved a little.

"Just lie still, Dodge," said Susie.

No, it hadn't been a courage thing. He really had had the shit beaten out of him. Was this pain he felt? Not yet. But he was going to be in pain, weeks and months of pain, that was for sure. Would he be able to paint? While it was happening, it had hurt like crazy at first, but in a way, the psychological pain was worse. It was like this is the thing you've been fearing and now it's really happening and it's unbelievable that you can't stop it from happening. He had, in a way, stopped it from happening by walking out of his body. He felt he had stood away from the group and watched the others kicking the body that had been his. It was, he had been thinking, a lot the way he felt when he was painting. It was him outside of him. But there had been that moment beforehand, that moment of feeling completely real. No metaphors.

He was drooling. No. It was blood. Viscous on his chin. It had an awful taste. Awful.

Susie gave him a kiss. How lovely a kiss could be. He thought he could go to sleep now for just a little bit.

At the hospital, they X-rayed him, taped him, bandaged him, and put his arm in a cast. A fracture, a concussion, three cracked ribs, one broken tooth, many bruises.

"What do you mean, you won't give me any Percodan?" said Dodge. "Are you kidding?"

"Sorry," said the nurse. "But you'll be fine with..."

"Come on, sweetie," said Dodge.

"Upsy-daisy," said the nurse.

"Jesus Christ," said Dodge. "Talk about bad luck."

Three hours later Kay opened Billy's door without knocking and stole into his bed. He'd been asleep, but very superficially. He was immediately awake.

"This is dangerous," she whispered. He put his hands on her. He put his hands around her.

"I don't care," he said.

"It's just trouble," she said.

He pulled away from her a little. He was naked. She wore a nightgown. He pulled down her nightgown and put his mouth on her breast.

She caught her breath. He felt her catch her breath.

"Let me be close to you," he said, his mouth next to her breast. She breathed and relaxed. "Please," he said. He put his arms around her waist and then slid down and leaned his head on her abdomen for a moment. He heard the noises inside her. He felt her heart beating. He felt her breathing. He slid back up and put his cheek next to hers and then he kissed her. She felt as if she were falling into a deep space of darkness and pleasure. *That's odd,* she had time to tell herself. It had become so easy. It would have been so much harder to stop than it was to go on. He pulled her down so that their bodies were next to one another's. He kissed her, he pressed against her. His smell intoxicated her. He breathed against her, and she felt as if his breathing connected her at last to someplace that wasn't lonely and fragmented, as if her mind had become a sea where there was no such thing as fragmentation possible. All was smooth and roiling.

He felt in a haze, all except for his penis, which he pressed against her thigh.

Then she felt everything one at a time sharply and distinctly as if she had been feeling nothing at all for days or months or years, an ache in her breast and a white fire in her groin so that all she wanted to do was press against him. He was breathing very heavily. She was starting to see a bit in the darkness of the room and his blond head glowed a little. It would be impossible to stop now.

He reached up under her nightgown, pulled down her underpants, and touched her; he moaned and she moaned too, and then he pressed against her and she moaned again because it felt as if the fire had spread. He put his mouth against hers as if he couldn't bear not to and then she felt him fumbling and then, in a moment, he was inside her, moving inside of her, almost in all the way.

Then there were footsteps in the hall.

They lay very still. They pulled their faces apart. The footsteps faded. Kay was breathing hard.

Billy had lost his erection. He put his mouth on hers again, but she didn't respond. He pulled out of her, limp and vulnerable. He lay next to her for a moment. She was lying on her back, rather stiffly, unmoving. He was on his side. She thought she should help him, one way or another, but she felt paralyzed. She didn't know why, but she just didn't want to touch him, couldn't put her arms around him. He didn't know what to do either, felt a vast storm enter his mind. He pressed against her but she didn't move. So then he kept pressing his groin against her thigh. She didn't move. He kept moving. Finally, he came, with hardly a sound. They both lay there for a bit, feeling his semen on her thigh between them. Neither said anything. After Billy fell asleep, Kay got up very quietly and went back to her own room.

Sunday

"What about the fireworks?" asked Dodge.

"Oh, fuck the fireworks," said Ron.

"For once, I agree," said Elise.

They were on the patio; the sun was setting. They were trying to decide whether to pack up and bring all their stuff back to New York since Dodge would clearly not be coming back out here.

"I say there's no reason why you couldn't come out without me," he said.

"We won't have fun," said Susie.

"We need to bother you in New York," said Ron.

They were in their usual spots except for Dodge, who lay, in the full splendor of his cast and bandages, on a wicker daybed that had been dragged toward the center of the room. The room was bathed in dark yellow light.

"I'm going to miss this golden patio," said Susie.

"Me too," said Dodge.

"Really?" said Susie. "You're not furious at me?"

"Why?" said Dodge. The others listened with attention.

"Well, because of your mishap and for getting you into this summer," said Susie.

"Well, it's me he'd be furious at," said Elise. Somehow, Dodge's "mishap," as they were all calling it, had brought her back to earth.

"I'm not furious at anybody," said Dodge. "I love both of you."

"He's too repressed to be furious," said Ron. "You know that by now."

"Too repressed or too depressed?" said Susie.

"They fulfill the same purposes," said Ron.

"You think I'm repressed!" said Dodge. "Well, I like that, coming from you to me."

Kay and Billy came into the room.

"Where have you been?" said Susie.

"Walk in the rose garden," said Kay.

Billy was carrying a can of Budweiser. He looked like he was in a very bad mood. He settled with a cranky air into an armchair. Kay poured herself a Bloody Mary from the pitcher. "Wow," she said. "It's lovely in here."

"Our last sunset," said Ron.

"Give us a break," said Dodge.

"You have a break," said Ron.

"I miss Otto," said Susie.

"Me too," said Dodge.

"Me too," said Ron. "I've missed him all summer."

"How was the rose garden?" said Susie to Kay and Billy.

"It was lovely but sad," said Kay. "Not many roses left. The end of summer is beautiful but awful."

"As always," said Ron.

"Am I banal?" said Kay.

"No," said Ron.

"Yes," said Kay. "I am."

"The end of summer is gruesomely sad," said Susie.

"But beautiful," said Dodge.

"Oh, beauty, I'm sick of beauty," said Ron.

"Me too," said Elise. "And I'm sick of charm too."

"But charm is all there is!" said Susie.

"Speak for yourself," said Ron. "You live in an imaginary castle of charm."

"It's true," said Kay. "Susie lives in a castle of charm."

"And every once in a while, she lets us into the castle," said Dodge. "For a blissful moment."

"God," said Susie. "I don't know whether to take this as a compliment or an incredible insult."

"Take it as a compliment," said Ron. "No one's ever told me I live in a castle of charm, believe me."

"Charm is overrated," said Billy.

The others laughed. "Wow," said Susie. "What happened to you? Let me take the dagger out of my heart."

"Well," said Billy. "What I mean is, you have qualities that are more important than charm. Like, I think you're good."

There was a collective *Ahh.* Kay looked at Billy with a little smile.

"The poor boy," said Ron, "is so young he still believes in goodness."

"Just because it's beyond anything you can conceptualize doesn't mean no one else believes in it," said Elise to Ron.

"There they go again," said Dodge.

"How are you doing, Dodge?" said Kay.

"Surprisingly well," said Dodge. "Due to the excellence of these Bloody Marys."

"Are you in pain?"

"Not too bad," he said, in such a way that it was not possible to tell. "The worst pain is trying to figure out what I'm going to tell Emma tomorrow."

"You can tell her the truth," said Elise, "that you were a hero."

"Are you trying to depress me?" said Dodge.

"Can you walk?" said Kay.

"Yes," he said. "A little. But I don't think I can get back on the bike tomorrow."

"I'll drive it back," said Ron.

"You can drive a bike?" said Susie.

"I'll bet there's a lot we don't know about Ron," said Kay.

"Do you want a chance to find out in the city?" said Ron to Kay.

"God," said Dodge. "He never gives up."

"Well," said Kay, smiling. "I'm assuming we're going to get together for a reunion dinner in New York."

"Absolutely," said Susie. "Pitchers of Bloody Mary. The works. I'll do it."

"Aren't you supposed to be walking around a little so you don't stiffen up?" Elise said to Dodge.

"Yes," said Dodge. "But I'm too lazy. I'd rather revel in my last evening of golden well-being."

"You call this well-being?" said Ron.

"Well, I get to be taken care of and everyone feels sorry for me."

"You have a point," said Ron.

"It's true, you should try to walk around a little," said Kay. "So you don't stiffen up."

"I haven't been to the rose garden in weeks," said Susie. "Maybe we should all have a walk there before it gets dark."

"Count me out," said Billy.

Dodge tried to shift, and winced.

Up in her room, taking off her earrings, Kay became immobilized by pain. She put her arms down on her dresser and her head on her arms. She was in such pain she couldn't move.

That night Susie packed her suitcases. She didn't think she could sleep. They'd gone to bed too soon after dinner. Dodge was obviously in pain, though he steadfastly refused to admit it. Billy had been incredibly sullen. Kay had seemed very depressed. Elise had drunk too much. Ron's snideness had seemed a relief.

Separation anxiety, perhaps, coupled to the weirdness about Dodge. Or perhaps they'd only been getting along by miracle all summer and now it was falling apart. Or perhaps the last dinner seemed too much an anticlimax.

Susie had been bored at dinner. She kept thinking, *It's the last weekend of summer.* She felt let down. It was as if some excitement should have happened this summer and hadn't. She remembered that moment when Elise had stripped and then dived in the pool. The caption would have been "It's summertime!"

Now, back in her room, Susie couldn't read. She missed working. She looked forward to her desk, at home, the nice notebook in which she kept her ideas for future projects. The orderliness of home. Maybe she could sleep. She got undressed and put on a blue cotton nightgown, a clean one she had saved.

She padded to the bathroom and washed very carefully, brushed her teeth very meticulously. She felt like in school when you've done all your homework. She looked at herself in the mirror and then thought, *Oh, Jesus,* and turned out the bathroom light.

She padded back to her room, turned out the light, and got into bed and thought with her eyes open. Poor Dodge.

And Billy. What was his problem? She was annoyed that Billy had been so ill mannered today. What was the matter with him? What was going to happen to Billy? She wished he were more methodical. Perhaps he was too feminine. She shouldn't have brought him up herself. But men... Men.

Should she have gone to bed with Dodge? No.

She wished she had gone to bed with the carpenter.

She could hear, very distantly, very, very softly, the church bell ringing eleven. When she heard it ring midnight, she sat up again. "This is not possible," she said out loud.

She sat up and swung her legs over the bed.

She wondered if any of the others were up. She went to the door and opened it, looked down the hall. None of the doors had lights under them. She walked down the hall, went around the corner to where Dodge's and Elise's rooms were. All was dark.

She went back, put a robe on, and walked downstairs very carefully, trying to keep the stairs from creaking. Once she was on the ground floor, it seemed unnecessary to be so quiet. She knew the house well enough now to move in the dark. She knew where the creaky spots were and how to avoid them. She walked to the kitchen. She liked the feeling of the parquet under her bare feet.

In the kitchen she went to the refrigerator, got out the club soda bottle, and poured herself a glass. She drank it, standing in the middle of the kitchen, put the glass down in the sink.

She went outside, careful not to let the screen door slam. The moon was almost full. It was a very light night, but some blurry stars could be inferred. The lawn, the trees, were darkly voluptuous.

She walked a few steps across pebbles (that hurt), over the grass (that felt delicious), to the hammock, and lay down in the hammock. From here she could see the house, at an angle, so she could see the windows where they all slept. All the windows were dark. But she could imagine each of the rooms and each of the inhabitants, as if it were her dollhouse.

She breathed deep. The air was sweet and soft.

Finally, she felt herself relaxing. In her mind, she went back to the jaggedy peaks.

Susie had always used landscapes as means to visualize her psyche. Very often they were mountainous landscapes. It had taken her four decades to realize how easy the images were to decode. At her worst, she saw voids, precipices, chasms, unfathomable, terrifying abysses. When she felt better but nervous, she saw jaggedy peaks, as if Alpine, white and glistening in the sunshine.

She kept one foot on the ground so she could rock herself in the hammock, although she was a little scared that something would crawl up her leg in the dark. But she loved the feeling of the grass under her bare foot. Being in the country had made her more in touch with her senses. That was it. Every day she felt more hungry, more lonely. She felt her body in a way that she had forgotten, since these days she often didn't feel her body at all, and also years of dance classes had manipulated her awareness of her body into a more rigidly organized system. But now she registered the odd outwardness of her arms, the infinite vastness of her abdomen. Her vagina felt different than the rest of her. Her back hurt. Her feet were weird. She imagined herself floating weightless in a black space. Sometimes stars passed by, sometimes great balls of white light that would immerse her for a while so that she would feel herself weightless and incandescent. She was conscious of a vast and complex harmony in which she no longer had to look for consonances.

She felt loneliness too, gruesome loneliness, and a great sadness. She thought of Kay and thought what a distance Kay had to travel. She knew Kay's sadness. How long it took to get to this other thing, this clarity, this clear jaggedy white thing where the pain didn't go away but it meant something else, so it could be tolerated. Or so that its intolerableness meant something else. What? It had something to do with beauty, Susie thought as she drifted off to sleep, floating among the white peaks, glacial and beautiful. *Don't ask yourself questions you can't answer.* Maybe that was it. The secret caption of life. She almost eased into sleep, but just barely, barely remained awake. She wished she could open her eyes to look at the stars, but she could no longer open her eyes. Too bad, because even the night was filled with light, summer light.

Early in the summer, one beautiful evening, she had walked down from the house until she could have a good view of the lawn, the beginning of the woods, the rose garden. The light had been perfect, golden red. At the very end of the rose garden, she'd seen Kay and Billy. She could not quite make out the roses, but she had examined them earlier that day and she knew that in the spot where Kay and Billy were standing, the flowers were losing their petals. Billy was gesturing at Kay. She saw Kay tilt her head and laugh. They looked perfect, far away in that gorgeous light, her son and her friend, in that beautiful dusk, everything she loved the most, and she had felt this terrible pain, watching them. That's what the experience of beauty was, that pain. Maybe. Maybe you couldn't have one without the other. It didn't matter what the pain was about, as long as it got you to the place.

Maybe that was the purpose of pain, to enable you to experience beauty. Experiencing beauty was, in a way, a form of loss. What else mattered as much? But perhaps even that didn't matter. No. It didn't. She went back to the white peaks, to soaring in the whiteness, soaring.

In his room Dodge masturbated, visualizing Susie astride him. Maybe Susie and Claudine. In her room Elise was having a nightmare, nothing but shapes and colors, blacks and purples, nothing but pure dread. Sitting up in bed, by the light of the moon, Billy was rolling a joint. Ron had turned the light back on and was lying on his bed, eyes closed. Kay lay on her bed in the dark, eyes wide open.

Monday

In the midafternoon Dodie drove up to the house. The kids were with their father. She thought she'd get a head start.

They were gone. Funny, though, that they wouldn't want to be here for Labor Day weekend, long as they had the house. She sighed. Well, another summer gone. She looked out over the river for a moment. It looked like rain was coming.

She went through the ground floor, quickly, to assess the depth of the cleanup that would be necessary. They'd been pretty quiet last weekend after that handsome Dodge had gotten his. Pity. But why did they have to go to the Lickety Split? Dodie caught herself: she had long ago decided there was no point in trying to understand the summer people. These New York people. So restless. But this group had been one of the nicest. Extra money for everything they asked her, like ironing a shirt. Money to burn, this group. Or maybe they were just nicer. Or reckless with their money. Money. She sighed. The pickings were slim around here in winter.

She opened the door to the patio, to see if there were any glasses left there. But they had been tidy. The wicker furniture had been put back exactly the way it was when they all had arrived, the chairs facing one another, as if awaiting more conversations.

Dodie sighed.